AN IMMACULATE FIGURE

AN IMMACULATE FIGURE

ELLEKE BOEHMER

BLOOMSBURY

For their insights, interest and succour given at various stages in the process of writing this book, I want very much to thank Imogen; Craig, Diana and Roger; Carol and Vincent; Terence, Michael, Sarah, Mahesh and David.

First published 1993
Copyright © 1993 by Elleke Boehmer

The moral right of the author has been asserted

Bloomsbury Publishing Ltd, 2 Soho Square, London W1V 5DE

A CIP catalogue record for this book is available from the
British Library

ISBN 0 7475 13864

Typeset by Hewer Text Composition Services, Edinburgh
Printed in Great Britain by Clay Ltd, St Ives plc

FOR BORIS AND SATISH

'Even innocence . . . took on a dubious colour'
Graham Greene

ONE

Armed Coup

The mercenaries were recruited in South Africa with money supplied by overseas and government sources.

The Times (1982)

1

It made a picture. Rosandra White, standing in the garden, slight, straight-footed, pigtailed, banana-freckled, a soft sugaring everywhere. Rosandra staring into the sun under the bare magnolia tree. Beautiful, entirely.

So Jem remembered.

And what did Rosandra remember?

That there were guns.

They were sitting at the new café on the new esplanade overlooking a sludgy sea. Rosandra, Jem. They met by careful planning. Jem had resolved to risk his heart and called Rosandra at her hotel.

Jem asked what she remembered.

'What have you been up to since I saw you last?' he said. 'It's been a while.'

She smiled, gloriously. His heart opened.

'We need to talk for days.'

'You've travelled far.'

'Not really. In the end nothing compared to my Uncle Bass. You remember Bass?'

'Yes,' said Jem.

'To tell his stories to us children,' Rosandra said, 'Bass used to stand me between his knees, where I felt safe. The boys sat on the floor close by. My mother knew she could leave us with him. I remember feeling the rough hair of his thighs against my shoulders. I looked up straight into his mouth.'

'The African bush,' Bass said. 'From up in the sky, floating with a chute, looks like what you cough up in the morning, grey-green muck, no shape in it. And there's the river too, just like the rhyme says. You kids know the rhyme? Well, never mind. So you look down and you see all this green-grey.'

'Grey-green,' said Rosandra from between his legs.

'All this grey and green. And the only thing you know is that the river is the river and not the bush because it looks smooth, not furry. So we're dropping down, my mates and I. And we know we can't go in the bush, because there are black guys in there wanting to kill us. And we know we can't go into the river because it's full of crocs, just like any good African river. We need the edge of the river. So we aim and get our chutes just right.'

Bass pressed Rosandra's left shoulder hard, and then her right shoulder, less hard, adjusting his parachute.

'And so we make it in, very sweetly. Right on the edge of the river. Exactly as planned.'

'Sometimes we applauded and cheered when he ended his stories,' Rosandra said.

'My father once heard him boast he followed in the footsteps of General Gordon and walked up to the headwaters of the Nile,' said Jem.

'I never heard that story.'

'I didn't believe it.'

'But on the other hand many things about Bass you can believe,' said Rosandra. 'He called himself a man of Africa. He was in search of paradise. He was prepared to fight for it.'

They were drinking coffee out of brown high-glaze cups. The morning was fine, very warm for half-past nine. Steam lifted off the coffee and blew about in flags. She shaded her face from the bright light reflected off the sea. Jem looked at her hand, fingers, wrist. It was a well-manicured hand, the nails were ovals of white and pink, as in an advertisement for nail polish, for margarine. She looked after herself. She was a model now. I'm here on a shoot, she had said on the telephone. It sounded professional. It sounded like she was a stranger. At first it was her eyes alone that saved him. They were reassuring. Six years later, and her eyes were still saffron, blank. Absolved eyes, as though seeing nothing.

It's the tropical atmosphere, Rosandra thought. The heavy heat, dark syrupy sea, the chair seats scorching. Like the days spent in the sun at eighteen. But it's another kind of time. This must be growing up, seeing the past in fragments, looking back. There was the time on Eden Island, lying on the beach all day. And there was the time under the palm trees

4

at Star Palace, and the crystal cave built of rock. I wore the pink bunny suit. I didn't know what I wanted. Now it's different, having work, real work, and real plans, two weeks filming on the beach and in the elephant reserve, and free time, this chance to see Jem, drink coffee, tell news.

'Look at all this,' Rosandra said. She put on her sunglasses. 'A French-looking café in a sticky African port. It's a new thing. This place is changing.'

'It's an African phenomenon,' said Jem. 'No doubt it's happening in Abidjan too, and Dakar. And Tangier.'

She didn't respond to the names. She tapped the plastic table. The gold chain bracelets wound around her arm rattled.

'Not like this, though,' she said. 'Not this smart or newly-made.'

Some of the best things in life are because of luck, Jem thought. She was still enough of a celebrity to have her arrival at the city airport reported in the morning paper. The name must have beckoned to him, his eyes did not miss it. Before calling her hotel he had to have a small whisky but her voice put him at ease. She'd wanted to look him up, she said, but she'd left her address book back in Mbabane, which was now her home. He didn't believe her about wanting to see him – him? The geography teacher? The star-struck boy who lived next door? But he let himself be persuaded. A fashion chain-store had arranged this shoot, she said. She made it sound like nothing out of the ordinary, like a geography excursion. There would be days of concentrated filming, but the director wanted the models to relax, to look as though they were on holiday. So they must get together a few times. She planned to lie on the beach. Jem would save her from sunburn if they met instead. She had some big stories for him, one about an island, one about a casino, one about escape. So much had changed since the schooldays back in Cradock, didn't he think? Would they recognise each other? Would it feel strange?

But there was no question about recognising her. Her face was his cherished memory, and six years hadn't changed her. Her look was irregular and transfixing. There were her light-coloured opaque eyes, and the stillness of her expressions, her perfect face. And the freckles still showed clearly, delicate and unexpected and distracting just beneath her skin, her thin exquisite skin, exactly as before.

A large family settled round a table next to theirs. A flushed and solemn patriarch presided over them. He butted his chair against Rosandra's, turned to apologise, then turned his neck several more times to confirm the evidence of his eyes. For she was a marvel. Yes, it was a good word to describe her, Jem thought. Her beauty was incongruous, blonde to the roots and also blonde in the eyes. And she was a mystery. There were stories about her. Men did dangerous deeds in her company. He must hear these things from her lips. Last night he had dreamed of her. In his dream he unveiled her. There was a mass of gauze around her head which clung to his hands as he unwrapped it. The gauze seemed to knot itself. In the end his hands were tied by gauze. And she remained standing in front of him, standing still, not showing her face.

'There's so much I could say. You were mentioning Africa. I have a picture of Africa in my mind, the Africa I saw from the aeroplane. The desert and the savannah. It was pale yellow. I hadn't thought of it as so huge.'

In response to the sound of her voice the flushed patriarch turned again. She looked out to sea.

To try to give the details, Rosandra thought – watching the sea, waves, the light on the waves – is maybe not to tell everything, is to keep a bit back. But people still get the picture. It's what the agency director said yesterday. Some models are like coat-hangers, he said, I hang a costume, a mood on them. But you keep apart, Rosandra, it's your road to success. Apartness is your mood, it's resistant, almost scornful, but not ice-cold. It's an eighties look. Which was his way of saying it. What it really is, is keeping a bit back, being absorbed but at a distance. It's a good technique for being a model. For one, you don't get bored. You're there but not there. You think of something beautiful and separate and apart, like a star, a cloud.

Jem stared. There was Rosandra, in the garden under the bare magnolia tree, with sun in her pale eyes. It made a picture. Jem's head was stuck in the jasmine hedge. He was watching Rosandra. He liked to watch Rosandra. The jasmine branches left imprints on his cheeks and neck.

At that time Jem had lived in a square brick house, like Rosandra's, which stood next door. Their town was called Cradock. What especially distinguished their two yards, the Roberts' and the Whites', was the Whites' pumpkin plant, which grew along the back fence and was a generous producer. Pumpkin in many forms appeared regularly on the Whites' dinner table. The colour of its limp, untidy flowers, Jem used to think, had crept into Rosandra's eyes.

When they were still very young, just small children, Jim Roberts, Jem's earnest father, the town planner in charge of Cradock plumbing, had declared war on the pumpkin. To no avail Mrs White offered its wayward fruits as tokens of peace. Every weekend Jim Roberts made a ritual trip to the place where the pumpkin forced its way through the fence into his yard and trimmed its hairy stump. It was in part because of the pumpkin that Jem was not often allowed to play with the White boys next door. To Jim, and also to Pam Roberts, his wife, the pumpkin signified slovenliness in the mother and her children. So Jem made do with spying on the sister.

In the hedge, complicit with the pumpkin, Jem lay low and discovered the first urgent pleasures of his early puberty. Could he say this? Even now? That Rosandra standing stock still in her favourite place under the magnolia tree was the first and chief object of his desire? There she was, unknowingly giving herself to hours of his sweaty attention. In her hand dangled a skipping rope or doll. Her hair shone. That was the picture. He must have spent days spying in the hedge, else why did it look so clear?

Rosandra stood always like a figurine in his memory. The magnolia tree overhead was blighted, it never flowered. In the middle distance there was Maria, silent, very black. Maria, employed to clean and tidy the boys, occupied herself with keeping them from Rosandra. Boys represented movement and pain in Rosandra's existence and she had a taste for passivity. She moved to positions of quietness. From the garden Rosandra called to Maria to bring her milk. Rosandra's call was in a normal speaking voice. She liked to rest and to be fed. For one so finely made and supple, her step was heavy.

Stillness was still her habit. Jem watched her drink her coffee, slowly and without interest. Savouring for Rosandra would be too loud. She was not like women he had met. Heather especially, his one serious girlfriend. They parted a few months ago. He called her up one night, taking the phone out on to the stoep, to look at the view. He said, it's off. It was so easy. She just said OK, call me if you ever need me. Heather was nice that way. She used to laugh loudly, wheezing. Her handbag was bloated, full of practical things, sheaves of notes to herself, reminders. She collected recipes she found in women's magazines. She filed them in a red plastic file. She looked people in the eye when she spoke, she was not mysterious.

'So did you know all those men wanted you?' Jem said.

'Yes. That's what my friend Thony used to tell me.'

'You are so beautiful, Rosandra.'

'Yes.'

7

'You don't mind that I say it?'

He was nervous. He felt there was far too much shirt-cloth bunched up in his armpits. He had worried this would happen. This morning he had especially selected a thin cotton shirt. He lightly raised his arms to let in some air.

'No,' she said. 'You're an old friend.'

He brings back those Cradock days, Rosandra thought, when Bass came to visit. And hardly looks older. Jem the geography teacher with the same pug nose, though redder, and the fringe brushed over his forehead, as before.

'And so you do remember Uncle Bass,' she said.

Because talking about Bass was so easy. She was lucky with him, she had good chances. It felt comfortable to remember.

Jem simply nodded. He coveted her memories, he wanted to hear them – even her memories of Bass.

For Sebastiaan Sampson had been another reason Jim Roberts did not allow his young son to play with the Whites next door. That so-called Uncle Bass, said Jim at the breakfast table, that fake uncle, shifty as a snake, untrustworthy through and through. There is too much darkness in his past, too many tall stories.

'Bass was my hero,' said Rosandra. 'He was an adventurer. There was no one like him.'

There was Bass Sampson, the adventurer and teller of tales. Wherever Bass found himself before an audience, in the hotel bar in Cradock, in the spare car-parts shop on the main street, in the Whites' yard, he described his many adventures. He was excited by the suspense and tension of his own stories and projected his voice for the benefit of men who might be listening in the next room. In Jim Roberts's opinion it was all lies, pure fantasy. Bass said that he had retraced the journeys of General Gordon up the Nile in search of its headwaters, and had stood on the spot, the history-making spot, where the man met his brutal end. An African death, Bass said approvingly, ruthless, unpredicted, swift.

Jem watched soft patches of light move on the water that swung between the piers. The air was acrid. It was a day that called for lemonade, water ices, subdued conversations, for quiet intimacies. Rosandra had agreed to tell him about herself. They would clear up the mysteries between them, her mysteries. He'd done nothing but the usual things, what everyone does, training, finding a job, a girlfriend. But she was different. And in the name of old friendship – he had that small right – she would open up her life, would fill in the spaces.

Rosandra's eyelids were dropped halfway over her eyeballs. Light shone through her eyes in profile: pale yellow bulbs. He did not remember her eyes being so large, so prominent and lamp-like. But beautiful, as he had imagined, entirely beautiful.

'He could tell a good story,' said Rosandra, as though agreeing with something Jem had said.

There were many stories about Bass. These included the stories narrated to explain Bass's position in the White family. For Jim Roberts was right about Bass not being Rosandra's blood uncle. It was long familiarity that carved his name into the family lineage. Some time before Rosandra's birth her father David White had met Bass while on business near Salisbury in the Rhodesia of that time. On their first meeting he fell under the spell of Bass's story-telling.

'No one could resist Bass's stories,' Rosandra said.

Bass's friend David White died in the first year of his youngest son's life after a wiring blowout in the family living room. He had been a sewing-machine salesman. His customers had been ruddy farmers' wives from far-flung farming areas in Rhodesia and the Northern Cape, women as used to practising with rifles as to wielding a needle.

During David's early salesman days, when he was still a bachelor, he would indulge himself in a particular luxury, a night in one of the highway hotels that lay scattered along his route. Years later Bass told David's children this, stage-whispering. In David's favourite highway hotels the soft-footed waiters and stuffed eland heads suggested a faded but still respectable colonial glory. This was a nation where citizens still stood up for traditional values. To David, though he usually felt uncomfortable talking politics, those values mattered. So when one night on a drinking spree in a highway bar he met Sebastiaan Sampson, called Bass, a walking embodiment of these values, he knew he'd found a mate.

David introduced Bass to his new wife Susan as 'one of Africa's freedom fighters'. At their first meeting Bass told David confidentially, over several drinks, his voice rising for the benefit of the waiters standing in attendance, that right here in Rhodesia was the only place left in the world where people knew their place and men could find honour in battle. Every Christmas Bass was invited to the Whites' home, regardless of the hot weather or Susan's pregnancies. The first time he came he brought Susan a little iced cake in the shape of a sewing machine. He stayed into February.

Even now, knowing what I know, Rosandra thought, I miss him, I can't help it. All those stories he gave us, that's what I miss.

9

She watched a rickshaw going down the esplanade, tracing a route of small parabolas through the air. There was the thin sound of an ice-cream-cart bell. Jem moved their table to keep up with the mop-shaped shadow of the palm tree. They were nested at its centre. In the heavy light Rosandra's freckles leaped into prominence. Jem couldn't remember anything so lovely, not this close up.

It must be that she looked so right, he thought, she matched the place. She looked like she belonged on beaches. It was more than the freckles. The sunshine glossed her skin. The bare skin was beautiful. It was a shame to cover that skin in clothes.

Bass Sampson, too, when Rosandra was still quite young, recognised that she belonged on beaches. Her legs are like masts, they go up and up some more, and her hair in the sun turns as white as beach sand, Bass pointed out. Some years later Bass's briefcase became for a while a portfolio carrying photographs of Rosandra. They showed her in poses on beaches. The photographs were interleaved with maps, which prevented them from sticking together in the heat.

So it was convenient that Rosandra herself liked beaches. During the first phase of her travels her path lay along beaches. Abroad was a coastline, a sameness of sand, a marine horizon. Our Beach is your private Heaven-Haven, promised the management of Bass's favourite resort, the Eden Island Hotel.

A postcard Rosandra once sent home featured a beach in Almunecar, Andalusia, with a too-blue sky and an old fort standing on a promontory. The postcard itself was bought and written in France.

Dear Mum, boys and Jem, Rosandra wrote. I am on the beach here. I am brown and healthy. I am full of seafood. The weather is perfect. This place reminds me of home. It must be the sun and the dryness. You think of Africa.

At home Jem had a shoebox full of Rosandra mementoes. It held magazine cuttings, photographs given by Susan White, three postcards, one of them the Almunecar picture, a twig of magnolia tree he snapped off once on a visit next door. Today too he planned to gather remembrances to carry home in his inner blazer pocket like billets-doux. He wanted them. Of Heather he had nothing more than a photograph to remember her by. She had given it to him once. In the photograph she was hugging a dog, smiling, pressing the animal to her chest, protective. Now he used it as a bookmark. But of Rosandra he had to have souvenirs. Already he'd secreted the two torn sugar sachets she'd used for her coffee. He'd folded his handkerchief around them and transferred them briskly to his pocket. He put on a look of carelessness. The handkerchief he retrieved in case she might need it. She might want to press into the cloth the wetness off her lips or the pink foundation off her forehead.

'You sent us a postcard once from Europe,' Jem said.

'Yes, that must have been the time I was with Thony.'

'We had no idea what you were doing at the time,' said Jem. 'We knew though you would be doing well. We were always your supporters and fans down in Cradock. Europe, Africa – we heard the world was your stage. Everything was open to you.'

'What I'm reminded of, thinking of Thony,' Rosandra said, 'is oysters. Thony and oysters went together. He loved them. He fed them to me. I had to lie back, you know, like at a banquet, and he would drop them in my mouth. As they dropped, they moved.'

'You ate the things alive?' said Jem, feeling a small seizure of ecstasy and horror.

'That's how you eat them. And to prepare them for eating you pluck out the beards. Thony brought me whole platefuls of oysters. I enjoyed the plucking, the little rip sound the beard makes as it comes off.'

The gold chains she wore spread out from her wrist like ruches. She was settling into the conversation, Jem hoped. She liked the reminiscing, soon she'd be opening up.

'Yes, Thony loved oysters,' Rosandra said. 'He couldn't get enough of them. He had his kitchens make an oyster dish, it was one of his favourites. It was called oyster-mouth soup. He begged the recipe off a London hotel. No one was allowed to come into the kitchen while it was being made. It was a top-secret operation. I know it had a mutton base and took lots of cream. It was very rich. You know, Thony liked oysters so much he even grew his own when they were out of season. He had the method from a Victorian cook-book.'

'Yes?' said Jem.

'I can tell you what was involved,' said Rosandra.

The touch of pride with which she said it was even more fascinating than the way her lips, freckled, piebald, moved round the words.

'You fatten oysters as you do lobsters. First of all you wash them by brushing them with a hard brush, like a nail-brush. Then you lay them downwards in a pan, sprinkle flour over them, or oatmeal, add lots of salt – you are trying to persuade them they're in the sea – and after that you leave them. You repeat this every day till they are fat enough for eating. Thony liked them plump.'

11

'Oysters make pearls,' Jem offered. His seizure was under control.

'They do, if you leave them in the sea.'

'You've become a real sea-bird,' said Jem.

He had to comment but the talk felt fruitless. It was threatening to collapse before it properly began. Because the spirit of it was all wrong. They were reunited, they hadn't seen each other for six years, and she began by describing dishes favoured by this lover called Thony.

A real sea-bird, liking oysters, knowing how to eat them, Rosandra thought. It is true I've learned things. This is what I have to say – how I've been lucky, I've been able to try things out. I took chances but I didn't get involved, not really. That's my story. How I've been treated with good chances.

Jem tried to think of a new lead. What had moved her? What did she love? Rosandra sat still as a mask. It was difficult to get a clear sense of her. She was framed by a space of silentness, a bubble of quiet. The family at the table beside theirs having departed, the bubble was delicately poised, held in place by the muted loudness coming in from the distance – the waves, and the steely roar of the funfair that lay beyond the hotels, and the people on the beach. The angle of her head signalled that behind the rich hair she was staring out over the sand. She was inscrutable, a mystery heroine. Jem thought his curiosity would make him blurt and stutter.

Listening to the news this morning, shaving, thinking ahead to this conversation, Jem had in mind a consoling image, of a pale, wistful Rosandra. Imagining her he thought of Desdemona – Rosandra as Desdemona. The link was in the names, or it was her paleness. Rosandra's vulnerability, being pure and wronged?

Shaving, remembering, Jem thought of Desdemona's last words. They were short, dreamy, half dead, and a lie. Desdemona dies on a lie, she was infected by a fantasy.

He saw himself prompting Rosandra with encouraging words. Tell me about the lies. Othello, you remember, tells Desdemona about men whose heads grow beneath their shoulders. She loves to listen to his lies.

'You know, Rosandra,' Jem said, deciding to brazen it out, 'thinking of you this morning, I couldn't help imagining you as Desdemona. In Shakespeare's play. You leaving home with your big famous men and getting caught up in their adventures.'

He tried a light and playful tone but it came out uncertainly.

'Is that the story of the man who suffocates the woman when making love to her?'

She turned slowly to him for an answer. Her gaze was open, genuinely questioning. But it was all wrong. He was wronging her. He was putting her to a test, setting questions. It must be jealousy, which was a scheming emotion. He wanted her just so, nymphlike, vulnerable. He plotted questions to draw special information from her, he was setting her up.

'He is not exactly making love to her at the time,' Jem said, wanting to brush the whole thing away. 'He does suffocate her. But that's not exactly the moment I was thinking of.'

'What you say reminds me of something,' said Rosandra. 'Bass told me about a woman he had once. He met her on his travels in a place down the coast from Mombasa. She lived in a tent in the middle of the beach. She stuck shells on her skin for decoration. Her shoulders were covered with sea-shells. She was searching for the remains of the Queen of Sheba, she told Bass. She wanted to find a lost palace, or a golden skull, or the secret of life. Something like that. Bass left her when, in the middle of the night, in the middle of sleep, he found her trying to cut marks into his cheeks with a razor.'

'Bass ran away from a woman?'

'I'm not exactly sure of the facts. He told me the story once when he wanted a photograph of me with shells stuck on my body like that. I didn't want to do it at first, so he told me how pretty this woman looked.'

'And did you?' Jem had to ask.

'Did I what?'

'Stick the shells on your skin?'

Saying it made him feel uncomfortable.

'I must have,' said Rosandra. 'It was a pretty idea. A woman covered with shells.'

Strange eventualities, Jem thought, chances and single decisions unsettling lives. For though Rosandra belonged on beaches, though she wore shells next to her skin, she grew up in a town hundreds of miles from beaches. That was where he last saw her. He could picture her in that place. She could be, say, working in the local travel agency, wearing a chignon and a blue suit. She could be a wife.

In Cradock's broad main street with the high kerbs and three cafés selling newspapers and sweet coconut cakes, Rosandra's eldest brother David now owned the town's only menswear shop. Cradock was where her family still lived. Jem visited at least twice a year. People went to David White's shop to buy smart ties, and if ever there was a fancy wedding in the district and the customer was young and a bachelor Mrs Andries at the till supplied the extra service of tying the new tie with a professional Windsor knot. The last time he was in town Jem bought a 60 per cent lambswool pullover from the shop. There had been a hard frost, as was sometimes the case in late May. Frosts in May and a town where men did not usually wear ties: that was Rosandra's old world, her home. That was where she came from. Jem knew these things.

He also knew bits of her family history. He could root her in the dry lands where they grew up. He knew that, like Rosandra, her mother Susan had been a local beauty queen. From Susan Rosandra inherited her startling blondeness. With her father she shared the quality of passivity. It was a strategy of survival he developed early, growing up on the sands of the Namib Desert.

David White's childhood, he used to tell his family and his friend Bass, was marked by a fifteen-year-long battle of wills waged by his parents over the matter of their trading store. As a young boy, an only son, he had learned, when dry desert storms blew and his mother wept through the outrage of her menopause, to lie low, under the kitchen table or in the outhouse, where his father could not find him to make him work. David's mother believed they should trade in fewer goods and bigger items – furniture, coats, blankets, suitcases, tin trunks – and in a larger town. His father was sure, as sure as ten stone houses, that they would succeed just as they were and where they were, selling everything that a general store in a one-hotel hamlet three miles off the great main road north should. David's people, the Weisskopfs, were immigrants from Germany. They anglicised their name, changing it to White, some time before the Second World War. This was to keep a business going that would anyway, after fifteen years and more, be undermined by severe drought and by a declining population. And in the end, as the unsold sausage and beans tins gathered dust and the window-frames were chiselled out of their sockets, the store fell victim to the corroding desert sands themselves.

So old Mrs White was proved right. She pointed this out huskily on her deathbed, speaking again in German to a husband who would not listen and a son who had left home, taking his family's trade and his drought-cured patience to the road.

A few years later this same man, the sewing-machine salesman and friend of Bass Sampson, set up his marital home next to Jim Roberts's house in another dry place, further to the south and east. The tarred main street, clothes shops and two hotels in Cradock convinced David of its respectability and big-town potential. The house he bought he kitted out with a new pink bath, a gas stove bought from a fellow salesman, a servant called Maria and a sewing machine. His wife he discovered at the town beauty competition, held in late autumn, in June, where she won the title. Her sunflower-yellow eyes inflamed his soul, her yellow hair matched his own blondness. Susan Landman chose him because he was from out of town, a decent, upstanding English-speaking man, and when he drank beer he did not get angry or want to fight. He promised to care for her always. After his death in the wiring accident his life assurance plan provided for his family's needs.

But Rosandra, his first-born, had not depended on his cover for very long. She had discovered his friend, the African hero, and he had adopted her. Even when in Cradock Rosandra was like a foundling daughter, unmatchable. She was straw-blonde, fine-boned, perfectly formed, entrancing. It was Bass's stroke of brilliance choosing her for his plans; she was, he often said, his special find.

2

'I'll tell you what,' Rosandra said, and Jem looked up startled. 'Put on your sunglasses, I'll redo my lipstick in the reflection, and then I'll tell you some stories about Bass. That will give you another impression of him. Recent events weren't fair on Bass.'

'I already know a few Bass stories,' said Jem, sliding the arms of his glasses over his burning ears.

'But you don't see him as a hero. As much as Thony, he's the man who changed my life.'

Her lipstick was orange, orange pastel. Her breath on his top lip, as she mouthed into his Polaroids, was of lemon ice and cloves. He wanted to say something about Bass changing her life. The tone in her last comment, if he wasn't mistaken, suggested a plea. See him this way, please. But then he was struck by the soft blonde down on the tip of her nose, and the freckles there, smaller than those on her cheeks and chin, and the gummy orange threads of lipstick and saliva strung between her lips the first time she parted them. She put on her sunglasses. And then, for good measure, she flung out her hair, an ampersand of gold. There was no beauty like this.

'Everybody in my family loved Bass,' Rosandra said. 'When he came to stay life had a different rhythm. We went to bed late. Mealtimes were haphazard. My mother slowed down, she looked heavier, just like when she was pregnant with my brothers. She dropped herself into chairs, sighing. She forgot about family finances. When she went shopping the car boot was too small for what she bought, all the meat and beer, the kilo bags of peanuts and potatoes, boxes of wine. To tell his stories Bass had to eat and drink.

'Every year my mother assured us Bass would come, he wouldn't disappoint us, but still I was anxious. There were Christmas lights in

16

Main Street and arum lilies over the septic tank. It was time he came. The boys' games grew louder as the days passed, they pretended to have other things to do. But they were also looking out for him. They would run on to the road after imaginary footballs to check for his car.

'Bass would come when we least expected it. He'd be there, bellowing with opinions and greetings when we returned from the café with the milk or woke up in the morning. And already my mother would be in her chair, her eyes looking sleepy. And Bass's big man smell would be in the room. It was a smell of old khaki. Of his beery mouth and wet sand.

'I had a habit connected with that smell. When it met me at the doorway, so strong and a bit unpleasant, I would pause a moment, wanting to sneeze, but then I let myself feel the warmth of it, and I went on forwards. And there I would be, all of a sudden, pressing against Bass's huge thigh and the bristles of his sideburns and nose-hair chafing my cheeks.

'My mother sometimes told him to be careful. Don't maul the child, she'd say. And Bass would reply, Rosandra's my own girl, isn't she now? She's my pretty little pussy, prettier every year. I'd never treat her rough.

'His hand would be at the small of my back. Like a support. I'd lean against it. The feeling was the best thing I knew. I didn't know how he did it, holding me like this while with the other hand he boxed the boys' arms and knocked them about. Whenever I stood close to him he held me this way. I would put my hands on his big knees. It was our special position for the times he told his stories.

'He began, As I was telling you . . . And then he would hand his beer to me and each time I took a sip, watching Mother over the rim of the glass. The boys also helped themselves and sometimes got quite drunk. But I didn't get drunk. I held tight on to Bass's knee and looked up into his mouth that was so purple red and smelt so strong and, if I concentrated long enough, spoke of wonderful things.'

Bass's many different stories, Rosandra remembered. They were matched to the different years of her life in Cradock. The earliest tales, the ones that fitted the time when the volume of Bass's knee met the soft place just below where her ribs came together, were of his adventures up and down the East Coast of Africa. He said he could trace the curvy contours of this coastline in his dreams. He had travelled it in every conceivable way, by boat and tanker and dhow, on a bike and on foot. In old coastal towns in the north and south, he said, he met ancient wise women guarding rotting huts full of antique amulets, and proud mullahs and priests who cried up and down the streets in the name of virtue. On beaches that stretched to the Sahara and then beyond, he saw cripples with the cataracts of vision in their eyes, dispensing simples.

Across hot lands Bass had trekked, and along beautiful shores, and wherever he went he discovered that humanity was up to trickery and magic. In an ancient kingdom between the desert and the sea, he said, where books held in sandy caves enclosed truths that were yet to be discovered, and where tamarind trees grew higher and quicker than in all North Africa, Bass came upon vast bands of orphaned children in waste spaces wearing glitter spectacle frames, patent leather platform boots, fox-fur boas and shimmering stoles and sweat-yellowed camisoles and stays, cast-off finery from charities in London and New York. The children crowded round Bass. They were the first human creatures he had seen in days. He asked them what they were doing there. What are you little ones up to? he said. But they did not speak his language. The sounds they produced were half musical, half crude, each sentence ending on an abrupt clicking sound. Bass, bunching his lips, made a clicking sound in Rosandra's ear. The children in the desert laughed at his words and one of them, a sweet little girl about exactly Rosandra's age, took his hand. She wore two feather boas wrapped round her, one of mouldy old parrot feathers, the other made of nylon and metallic thread, shiny, stringier. And bouncing on her chest, her little bony chest, was an empty Yardley powder tin, hung on a thin wire loop. Fancy that.

Bass stooped down and spoke gently to the girl. He tried taking the loop from her neck. He wanted to look at that Yardley tin more closely.

'What's a little girl like you doing with a funny necklace like this?' he asked, bringing his face closer to Rosandra's. She felt she was the little girl.

But the girl still didn't grasp what he was saying. She twisted one of her feather boas in her hands.

So then Bass produced from his pockets liquorice all-sorts and coloured boiled sweets and candy pink and white mice which he conveniently had with him, just like he always had for Rosandra and the boys. At the same time he lifted the loop from her neck, just like this. And Bass slipped his hands like a noose up over Rosandra's head.

But the little girl began to cry, and in a fit of anger dashed the sweets in Bass's hand into the sand. He tried to stroke her hair, which was decorated with beads and rough with dust, but she only sobbed the louder and reached for her lost toy. Then all her friends gathered round, keening in high-pitched voices, their strange glad rags shining in the sun.

Bass wondered what to do. He raised the Yardley tin high over their heads, which made things worse. The children joined hands, and made three circles round him. They began to chant and run till he was dizzy with the movement. They were, he thought, putting magic on him, singing a spell to ground him in that earth so that he would never be able to leave.

'But I didn't stick around long enough to find whether that was so,' said Bass. 'I ran and they followed, keeping up with me for many miles, running faster than any children I ever saw. They were so thin, so light. Their strange, secondhand clothes floated behind them like wings.'

Bass spread his big arms, his hands like plates, and Rosandra saw stick children with wings like dragonflies. Balancing on air.

Like dragonflies, she almost said, as Bass shook his lips noisily and took a fresh cold beer from the cooler box beside him.

'The story about the children was my favourite,' Rosandra said. 'Sometimes I myself dream of those children.'

Jem had nothing to say. These were curtain-raisers, filling in time. They were a diversion, and not a word of them of course was true. He almost said so when she began about the glad rags, but restrained himself. He wanted to hear about the real things. The talk of children suggested something to him, a concrete memory.

'You had that friend Emmie once, around the time Bass came,' he said, wanting to prompt her.

Rosandra stripped herself of sunglasses. Her eyes were ringed with white, like cauled moons. They told him nothing. He took off his own glasses to match her.

'Yes,' she said.

'I thought of Emmie as you described those children.'

'That's a strange connection to make. Emmie doesn't come into this part of things. I see those children in Bass's story so clearly, the bony little girl, her shoulder-blades sticking out, and her feather boas and funny song.'

But Jem had a clear memory of Emmie. She was the first object of his jealousy. For in a world in which Rosandra did not have friends, Emmie had become Rosandra's friend. She sat next to Rosandra in the school playground.

Rosandra did not only avoid her brothers, Jem remembered, in general she did not come out to play. Other children gave her their new watches, spare skipping ropes and winnings at marbles for safe keeping. She liked the marbles, especially the big crystalline ones, called ghoens. She held them in her skirt and let them run through her fingers. They caught the sun, making star-shaped lights.

Then one morning, when she was about ten and Jem twelve, Rosandra and Emmie met at the public baths. It was here that the school population migrated for the summer months. They grew friendly at the shallowest end of the paddling pool where the water was warm as urine and almost as yellow. Beyond the paddling pool was a thick bed of prickly aloes, behind which the older girls hid from the boys to swop earrings and secrets. Like Rosandra, Emmie sat with her body folded and precise. Slowly they moved closer together. The third Wednesday afternoon of their acquaintance they arrived at the paddling pool at about the same time and sat shoulder to shoulder, side by side. They felt for each other's hands. Emmie gave Rosandra a smile. She had all her top front teeth missing. Without exchanging a word Emmie and Rosandra became the secret sharers of the paddling pool edge.

The friendship did not depend on to-and-fro conversation. Jem watched the two of them from where he sat kicking his legs and baking the crown of his skull on the diving board. He saw Emmie talking by the hour, but Rosandra, closely watching Emmie's lips, did not say much in reply. Jem was envious. He wanted to sit close to Rosandra, talking. Then Jem heard that Emmie did not speak English. It turned out there were lots of unusual and suspicious things said about Emmie around the swimming pool. Jenni Reid who traded swimming pool gossip told Jem this. Did Jem know the name some people called Emmie? Emmie the skollie? And there was a story going round about her parents, her mother, that just stank, that was just rotten. And she spoke Afrikaans. She was a dirty thing, a brown crunchie, worse than a rock spider, frotter than the frottest banana.

One afternoon the root of these rumours was laid bare. The Labuschagne brothers directed the unmasking. These two boys were the self-proclaimed bosses of the diving board area. They went to speak to the older girls behind the aloes. They let it be known that the problem of Emmie would be sorted out.

That day Emmie was not wearing her usual black bathing suit, which had lately grown tight on her. She had on a large item of mauve underwear, the X-tra outsize kind that portly women buy at special shops. The garment was fastened with a tight elastic band, pulled high

20

up her bony chest. The rest of her was bare. Halfway across the paving, the Labuschagne boys waylaid her.

'Ja – Emmie,' Garth Labuschagne called.

He was shaking himself dry after a stiff length. He blew water and his fringe out of his face. The dark wet hair growing down his inner thighs showed black, like oil stains.

'Show us your bikini, Emmie,' Garth said.

'Emmie, Emmie,' sang Johnnie Labuschagne, coming walking along the pool edge, balancing as though on a tightrope, to stand beside his brother. 'Where did you get that bikini?'

Emmie did not move. She stared at the two boys.

'Ja, Emmie, how come you don't cover your titties,' said Garth in a coaxing voice. 'How come your titties are so brown? Where d'you get such a good tan on your titties?'

Emmie, rigid, covered her nipples with her hands. The boys laughed.

'Emmie,' said Garth, his voice suddenly quieter and full of cunning, 'listen, Emmie. Show us your moons.'

'Moons! Moons!' called Johnnie, swivelling his body halfway round, raising a haunch and exposing an inch of white skin beneath his swimming trunks.

Garth advanced on Emmie. His expression was sober and imposing. His smile concentrated into a squint of intense interest.

'Come on, Emmie,' he said in tones of reason. 'Come on, show me those moons. The half-moon shapes in your nails.'

He held out his hands, palms downward, as if to prod her, but did not. 'This way,' he said. 'I want to see your moons.'

Emmie had dropped her eyes. She stared at Garth's feet, still covering herself.

'I don't think she wants to show me, Johnnie,' said Garth, over his shoulder, with an expression of surprised regret. 'Maybe she doesn't have any moons in her nails. No moons because she's a *kleurling*. Maybe the little Coloured wants a ducking for coming to our pool. Hey, Emmie? What do you say? Didn't your mommy tell you that Coloureds aren't allowed in the European children's swimming pool? No brown people who have no moons in their nails. Doesn't your mommy tell you where your daddy came from?'

Emmie was dumb. Johnnie stood closer. Garth folded his arms and flicked his drying fringe. Still staring at his feet, Emmie held out her hands, palms downward. Her skin was taut across her ribs. Johnnie, stepping forwards again, brought his hands down on hers, not hard, but quickly, playfully. Garth grabbed her pants elastic and flicked it.

'Her mommy can't buy her a proper bikini because on Friday nights she gets drunk and foks all the black *ous* in the field behind the bottle store,' he said.

He chucked his head in the direction of the pool and made ducking motions. Other children had gathered round. But Emmie was no fun. She didn't respond, she didn't cry. Maybe she hadn't understood. Garth jabbed Emmie in the ribs.

'Go to your own pool next time, *ou* Coloured,' he said. 'Or else ask my permission to come here.'

The other children laughed. Emmie was running.

Rosandra stared into the sun, watching the watery bubble effect that the light-rays created between her eyelashes. Emmie sat down next to her, then slid hastily into the pool, finishing the pee that began during her run. Rosandra raised her toes out of the urine-warm water. Jem watched the Labuschagne boys chase a polo ball up and down in the water under the diving board, where he still sat warming himself.

But Rosandra said she did not remember this incident. She shook her head. Did Rosandra remember beaches only?

I remember Bass like I saw him yesterday, Rosandra thought. An uncle built like a soldier. His friends had fierce dreams in their eyes.

'I can think of Bass stories that you'll find more interesting,' said Rosandra. 'As we grew older he told us livelier things. The boys demanded more exciting stories.

'That was after the time of Emmie,' she added for Jem's benefit. 'After Emmie's mother took her away from our school.'

On his travels down the African continent, Rosandra said, Bass had encountered war, and where he did he generally took part in it. Telling his stories of conflict, his language was commanding. War, Bass said, had its beauties, its true beauties. As it must, fighting in this great Africa, this vast and many-splendoured land.

This was the time when Rosandra no longer stood against his knee but sat in a chair within arms' length, Maria listening from the kitchen, Susan stretched out in her usual place and seemingly sleepier than before. Bass brought new energy to these tales. He spoke of battle, intrigue and booty, and, if he grew excited or drunk, of hidden stockpiles, glittering caches. He told of hobnobbing with heroic soldiers and warlike medicine men, who unfailingly and in every case predicted victory. Bass's stories of discovered riches were illustrated by the new props which embellished his life. In recent times he had started hauling into the Whites' house his own bootloads of meat and beer to celebrate Christmas. Money is no object between old friends, he said. His cigarettes, as he showed Rosandra, were imported direct from the USA. To match the cigarettes, his car-size lengthened. The back of the vehicle sprouted batteries of new-fangled lights. Rosandra's brothers stretched themselves beneath the display of technology and so Bass's story aids cost him the better part of his audience. Rosandra, however, remained loyal. Bass adjusted the tales of claim and conquest to suit her. He said he didn't want to give her nightmares.

'Rosandra never gets nightmares,' Susan murmured from her chair. 'She has slept like the dead since the day she was born.'

But Bass did not listen. He had hit upon a new tale. He and his friends from the old fighting days had thought up a scheme, believe it or not, to make money in Africa. They would sell African masks in Europe and America. They were thick on the ground in the continent, cheap and plentiful, ancient and newly carved masks of all imaginable woods. Bass had dreams about masks, about ebony masks, highly polished, gleaming mysteriously in the dark. He embroidered on his dreams.

'This is a continent of ancient kingdoms,' Bass said. 'If we dig and explore, we will find treasure. Fallen and buried masks mark the place where kings have fallen and hidden their magic. I would wager anyone great things will be found there. I have seen those piles of rock on the plains and in the forests, bits of wall and tower. At the time I didn't have a moment. When you're dodging bullets you don't think to excavate. But I've promised myself to return. I could feel the presence of the treasure just beneath the ground, like a water diviner. I could feel the warmth of it coming through, like sun on the ground.'

Bass ruminated long. With Rosandra as his one attentive listener he spent many moments sunk in thought. His stories were changing subtly, his ideas were turning to the future. The future spoke to Bass of glory and fortune.

One day he pounced on Rosandra where she sat. He grabbed her arms in the old way, flaring his nostrils above her, and presented a new dream.

'This is the way it goes, my lovely. In those old and forgotten times, the way your uncle sees it, so much was possible. Think of those great African kings, fierce as the devil, ears heavy with raw gold, crack fighting forces in rows behind them. On they came, scattering enemies, setting up empires. They were extraordinary, wonderful, huge. These Africans need these kind of leaders. They were mighty and wise. That's why they let the white man in. They respected his might. The white man had power, his face was beautiful and kingly. I wonder about remaking that sort of power. We need the ancient kings and their sort of power. We need to take the buried treasure, find the old symbols and masks. Put them back in place, fire a few shots. And there you are. In Rhodesia, where I met your dad, they screwed it up in the end. They began to talk.'

Rosandra lost track of the ideas. She waited patiently for new stories to emerge. But Bass spent more and more time deep in thought. There were lunches when his silences extended the length of an afternoon. Rosandra fell asleep in her chair or lying on a blanket on the grass, in the sparse shade of their one tree, the bare magnolia, and dreamed Bass's stories. Once, in a dream, Bass promised her she could go with him to dig up the beautiful masks and hold them on high. In her dream he was somewhere behind her, booming at his followers to move on and win, and she was holding a heavy mask and chanting a magic song without words. Our little princess, our magical lovely, Bass called her as she ran his errands, bringing the matches, the meat, more beer, some of it to pour on the fire and make the flames crouch and spring. He had made the outside fireplace himself, a present for Susan White, built out of concrete and brick.

'We are eaters of meat,' he said. 'We will *braai* every day over the Christmas holiday. It's on me, Susan. The boys especially must eat meat. I must have meat. It's for health. To put roses in Rosandra's cheeks.'

Sweat spilled off his reddened temples as he began the fire in noonday heat. The meat lay in its plastic packaging, browning in the sun till he converted it to charcoal. He picked the singed flesh from the fire with his bare hands, Rosandra remembered, and spread it on bricks to cool. The technique of quick, hot cooking was to preserve succulence inside the skin of ash. A bite of the meat set off an ooze of juices. Rosandra ate for this effect, discarding her chops and chicken breasts once the flow had been released. Her dress fronts were stiff with congealed blood and fat. Bass poured the benediction of his laughter upon her, watching her as she chewed, his red mouth and nostrils magnified by the heat haze that danced above the fire. He skimmed semi-chewed chops across the lawn, aiming them at the running legs of the boys.

'Faster, higher,' he shouted as they leapt to avoid his missiles.

'How will we conquer kingdoms and take a continent with those lily-soft legs?'

At the end of the day his eyes were embossed with red veins. His pupils shone black. He asked Rosandra to bring out more beer, ice-cold. He poured paraffin on the fire so that the flames flew up above her head. Her uncle was silhouetted in orange against the darkening evening sky, his face ablaze with bright sweat, like heroes on comic-book covers.

'I want a kingdom, Rosie,' he spoke out of the deep brooding that marked these evenings. 'I can see a palace in the tropical bush, and a first-class hit squad to take and defend it. A bit of Africa, all for your uncle, and for you. Where you can be queen.'

Rosandra's brothers grew impatient with these visions. They began to snicker to Bass's face. They refused his beer and went down to the river to smoke cigarettes taken from the packs in his car. Rosandra looked away when they invited her to come along and ignored their thin boys' backs disappearing out of the garden gate. She was overjoyed at having her uncle all to herself. For his part, when he was sunk in dreams, he seemed not to mind losing her brothers. Without the boys as audience he spoke more freely about his imaginary adventures, about winning kingdoms, ancient rights, old treasures. Rosandra listened. What he said came in starts, without clear endings or beginnings. But they were beautiful stories. Afternoons were dreamy and heavy, like sleep in an overheated room. Susan White retreated to the house, to eat salads and read magazines in the cool kitchen behind blinds.

'Your eyes are like bloody great lamps in the firelight, Rosie,' said Bass. 'Sticky-out eyes, but still so sexy. You'll be a match for a guy one day. Prettiness with cute freckles. And able to drink anyone under the table.'

He lifted her on to his shoulders, big as she now was, to go and look at the stars away from the firelight.

'Bright and huge as bottletops,' he said, jiggling her legs. 'Look up, you have a good perch there. You'll never see them like that anywhere else, our African stars.'

He tempted Maria out of the kitchen. She stood pressed to the sink, vigilant, fussing at Rosandra's dirty dress. He led her by her remonstrating hands.

'You have nothing to do here in this kitchen, Maria. Outside we cook, we eat,' he said, spearing steaks, 'like your grandfathers and great-grandfathers.'

Maria accepted the food he offered her in aggrieved silence. She brought out china plates for the meat, a prim, determined protest. The cans of beer she was offered, Rosandra saw, she saved in her apron pockets. In the White household Rosandra had become Bass's chief friend.

Rosandra puzzled at the shift of feeling in her family. But there was a change in Bass too. The afternoon came when for the first time Bass did not stoke the fire and did not bring out meat. After sitting for hours drinking beers he began to clear out the fireplace, late as it was. In a space to the side of the main *braai* area he burned the half-empty wine boxes. There was a Sunday evening feeling in the air, as though people had grown tired of pleasure. Rosandra went in search of her mother, who was soaking off a green mud face-pack in her bedroom. She stood quietly in front of her, waiting to be noticed. When Susan looked up, she saw her daughter as though for the first time that summer. The child was pink with sunburn and her hair was filthy. She smelt of raw meat.

'Rosandra, my darling, you look terrible. How I have neglected you,' she said.

Then Susan carefully sponged Rosandra all over. She gave the brown mark, a huge freckle something like a birthmark in the middle of Rosandra's stomach, an extra rub. In a pose uncharacteristic for evening, Bass was lying on his bed in the guest room opposite. He was blowing the smoke rings he called atom bombs. As her mother scolded, and tried to press her face into the shower stream, Rosandra was craning her neck to watch him.

'You've gone too far, Bass,' Susan said. 'She's a girl. Play with her brothers. I don't want her skin to be burned like this. We must be careful with her face.'

'Uncle's thinking about the future.' Rosandra quoted her uncle's words from the times he was looking into the fire.

In one hand Bass was tossing a bullet. It was a souvenir from his travels that he always carried with him in a purpose-built soft leather pouch. Rosandra came up to stand in the doorway, wrapped in her mother's big towel and fragrant with freesia talc. Bass rose from the bed to take down his camouflage army sack, and swept his spare change off the bedside table into his shorts pocket. He gave Rosandra a big conspiratorial wink. Rosandra decided she liked him even more than Maria, though Maria was special. Maria let her dress up on weekdays in her Sunday clothes. But with his stories and big movements Bass was the very best human being she knew.

*　　*　　*

'Your mother's suspicions ended there?' Jem asked. 'She didn't remind herself of these feelings later on, when he took you on his island journey?'

Rosandra raised her eyebrows and her shoulders. The silky polyester of her shirt followed the movement of her bones. Her eyebrows, Jem noticed, perfectly traced the line of her brow.

'Wait and see,' she said. 'You know what these things are like. There are some episodes and bits and pieces that you remember, and others, like background details, that you don't.'

But Jem had only the one memory of Bass. Jem met Bass and spent time with him on a memorable occasion when he was just fourteen, not very tall, and the Whites' uncle was so much larger and louder than life that he was cured for a while not only of snooping in the hedge but of his teenage passion for cars.

It was the afternoon that Bass decided to show off his new motor-car, a Mazda RX 7. Jem had stolen over to play. Bass allowed Jem, fidgety with excitement, to sit in the passenger seat and look out for traffic cops. He handed him binoculars for the purpose. But Jem began to have trouble concentrating on the road. He was watching the speedometer and whistling through his teeth as though manfully impressed. In fact, however, he was dead scared. He wanted to retch. He wanted to jump out of the car. He was too scared to look round and find comfort in the White children who were sitting in the back, as rigid as he was. Jem remembered their strange silence during that journey, a silence that contrasted with Bass's yelps of pleasure and, outside, the shrieking of wind and speed.

Later, when driving back, beer in hand, Bass advised him to forget about cars till he was older.

'Good motor-cars are luxury goods, Jem-boy,' Bass said. 'They are for the time when we make our million at age forty. At your age you should be thinking about guns. To be a quantity on this earth you need some good guns. You need to understand your guns. Come to me if you're interested.'

Jem smiled and sweated.

Back home he had only just enough time to slip back through the hedge, guiltily, gleefully, before his father returned from work.

'He gave us hints. We could have seen even then,' said Jem.

Rosandra shook her head.

'What I see when I look back was a man with charm. He came holding out promises like gifts. He fed us till we were too happy to move. He tore half-raw meat from chop-bones with his teeth and swallowed it like

27

toffee. One time he broke open a jar of honey and poured it over his head and then over mine and I think David's. He said he had always wanted to swim in sweetness and this was the closest thing to it.'

She would smile now at the silliness of it, Jem thought. To think of such a big man with, relatively speaking, such a small jar of honey. But he was smiling alone.

The honey made a golden mask over Bass's face, Rosandra remembered, running more smoothly when his skin warmed it. Over his eyes were golden lenses. He was laughing and licking at the honey. You look like a blind man, she said. He asked her to give him a sweet kiss, and she did, only the kiss wasn't sweet, it tasted of sweat.

'The honey,' Rosandra said, 'was intended for marinade. For the *braai.*'

Jem knew he was gawping, amazed, smitten. She made no sense. She turned stupidity into a picture of sweetness, but unthinkingly. She was baptised in honey by a brute but her thoughts were pure. It must be because she couldn't see it. She couldn't see the wrong in it, the taint, even after all this time. He wanted to kiss her, to kiss the sea-salt out of her eyes, the sweat on her cheeks and forehead.

'Remember, I was a child at the time,' Rosandra said. 'Every child loves a man like Bass.'

The orange colour had been talked off her lips.

'That Christmas of the sunburn was the end of a phase,' Rosandra said. 'I think Bass got bored with coming to see us. The yard grew too small for him, for him and his car and his big plans. He sent word the next year. It was a Christmas card that arrived in the middle of November. He said new business projects were afoot and he couldn't drag himself away from the city.'

'He must have heard about the beauty competition?'

'Yes. My mother wrote to him about that. She was proud.'

'Well then. If he knew about it, then maybe it was the beauty competition that gave him the idea of involving you in his plans.'

'Let's not talk about the beauty competition,' Rosandra said. 'It's a little thing. Compared to what happened later, it wasn't a very important event at all.'

She gazed out across the dull sea to the blue horizon. The divide of sea and air was very faint. On that far, faint horizon she tried to place, in her mind's eye, a thin blue cloud. It was absorbing to think about, the vagueness, the blue on blue. She liked to do this. She would do it when modelling. It was a way of concentrating. It was her own private apparition. A thin blue cloud. She took off her glasses. The sky sprang into brilliance. There was no blue cloud possible – it was too bright, too clear. The world was empty and as always alive, too much alive, with actions, with questions. Even as they were spoken, words became promises, promises plots, demands turned into events and adventures. She stared at the horizon. The idea of the blue cloud filtered her thoughts clean. The absolute blueness of the horizon helped, she could imagine any shape. Almost she had it, the soft-pencilled lower edge of a blue cloud. Then Jem spoke. She didn't hear what he said. But she felt battered.

'Let's order whisky,' she suddenly called out.

'I was just thinking we should order another drink,' Jem said.

The tender skin beneath her eyes quivered in the glare. It was uncontrolled, fascinating. Jem glanced twice, then she jammed the glasses back on. Something had upset her violently. A memory of Bass? She downed her drink as soon as it came. Yellow crystals budded in the corner of her lips.

There was the beauty competition. Early this morning Jem sneaked a look at the photographs, not too long, not so long as to glut himself and spoil their charm. Rosandra was in the pictures, perfectly lovely at ripe adolescence, just out of braces and teenage bras, hugging sheep.

In Cradock each year this initiation ritual for local white girls took place. It was called the Cradock Round Table Beauty Competition, it was organised as the highlight of the Cradock and District Agricultural Fair. Jem used not to attend very often because the event was for girls and for their parents, but everyone in Cradock knew about it.

The Cradock girls, bearing the hips of sixteen and faces made up to look twenty-two, inhabited a charmed circle for the duration of the show. The ramp was their passage into womanhood, blessed by their mothers, vigilant at tombola and sewing stalls and tea tables, and hailed by a watchful inner circle of community fathers. The girls walked on high, at the head level of their spectators, delicate as anorexia could make them, larded with sun-cream against the desert sun. In this way, they told the world, they were ready to step into a brand new future – overseas travel, marriage and a maid, everything that their upbringing promised. After this ceremony, certainly not before, they could be seen on Main Street with boyfriends and they could wear make-up when they went to watch the films that were shown on Friday evenings in the Sheep Farmers' Meeting Hall.

Like her mother before her, Rosandra at age sixteen won the Cradock beauty competition. She was the first girl to wear a full-length swimsuit during the final parade. The high, sheer hip-cut of the yellow suit marked an arrow down her pubis. Pointing straight down, the arrow indicated beyond the shadow of a doubt that these particular willowy legs deserved recognition. Others said it was her posture, hips, figure, her walk. Her legs bend and loop and straighten, super-slack, then tight, and see the way she places her feet, toes first, straight forward, delicate. The town – the plumber, the two dentists, teachers, fathers of friends – the men who had watched her grow, gazed up at the fresh loins of their growing daughter, saw that her bumps and hollows were all in the right places, saw that her hair shone in the sun as a 'whitehead's', a *witkop*'s, should, and gave her the prize.

Susan White alone had something further to say about the decision. She was proud, of course. She was pleased as any parent whose care during chicken-pox paid off in this way. But she worried about reasons. She argued her case about reasons at the afternoon tea table under the plane trees as a continuous golden-brown drizzle of dust and pollen darkened the cups and saucers. The tea servers on duty happened to be mothers without daughters. Behind the plane trees, camouflaged by the mottled effect of the tree trunks, maids in uniform boiled tea urns on wood fires. The maids were driven down to the fairground for the day by the tea servers. Maria was there, doling out tea bags.

'Even if I say it myself,' Susan began, 'Rosandra is good.'

'She's good,' the women agreed. 'Else she wouldn't have been chosen.'

Knowing glances passed between them. They were nibbling the lemon curd and pumpkin tartlets which Susan had brought by the boxful.

'I mean good as in character,' said Susan. '*Good*, you know. No stain on her character. The judges should point this out, I feel.'

The women exchanged glances again.

'No, don't get me wrong,' said Susan. 'I say this not because she's my daughter. Other girls win, I won once. Everyone says, yes, that girl *is* beautiful. But not good. Rosandra is good. She is like – the sweetest thing you can imagine, never angry, never sharp.'

But the tea ladies lost concentration. They looked away to the end of the ramp, to where a flesh-and-blood Rosandra moved her neck, her shoulders, her length of hair, from side to side for the cameras. Susan also fell into absorbed staring. Her own eyes mild, vague, Rosandra perfectly complied with the photographers' requests. They brought on the merino sheep whose wool and flesh helped pay for the event. Rosandra knitted her arms around the neck of a burly ewe; she laughed into the face of a gimlet-eyed ram. Because of her compliance the photographers never noticed what Susan sometimes saw as Rosandra's flaws, the occasional stiffness of her neck and back. These were as nothing to her Cradock admirers. She was a quiet charmer, nice to look at, not at all chocolate-box, a unique face in town, with an immaculate shape, a sweet ambassadress for the big agricultural fair at the end of the month.

Some people who were in the know forgave her more. They chose not to remind themselves of Rosandra's blemish. It was in no way visible, no one mentioned it, yet under her yellow lycra one-piece, in the middle of her belly, just above her navel, some people knew, Rosandra concealed a mark like a gravy stain, a freckle that had run.

'Hide it, Rosandra. Don't let the girls in the changing room see it,' Susan told her that morning, smoothing the one-piece across the offending belly.

Rosandra nodded, and immediately forgot to be aware of the spot. She didn't, at this time, think about it much. The girls in the changing room, with whom she had undressed and dressed at school for years, knew about the mark. So did Jem. Rosandra's brothers told him about it. No doubt the fathers of the community, the judges of the competition, had heard of it too. In the town, because she was an example, more spoken of than played with, the rumour of the blemish was her identity mark, a humanising thing. Marks like this were what people had to live with, even beauty queens. The village fathers honoured her in confidence. She was as complete as she appeared to them. She looked perfect. She wore a more modest costume than most. It wasn't a bad idea. Other girls picked up the trend. The next year four entrants to the competition wore one-piece swimsuits.

The spot was on her belly, not her soul, and her soul was good. Susan White spoke of Rosandra's goodness within hearing of a local journalist who was asking the runner-up in the competition about her ambitions. Miss Cradock's Princess on Look-out for Sheep Farmer, he reported alongside names of tombola winners, prices of prize sheep, the plans for next year's event, Mrs Marshall's winning apricot jam recipe, and Mother of Winner says this Beauty is also Good.

The idea stuck. The time came when in the *Sunday Times* there appeared a photograph said to be of a young woman with the distinctive and pretty name of Rosandra, but most of what could be seen was a pink spandex-clad crotch, lifted to the impertinent camera and blurred by its dancing movements. Cradock pored over the picture. The supermarket had it sellotaped up in the 'What's on' window. Rosandra's treasures were exposed in piles on the pavement outside Cradock's three cafés. She was sold out by the end of Sunday.

But the town people knew their own mind. Rosandra had won fame, she was big news, but she was also good: no one should take that from her.

'As long as she doesn't come home pregnant.'

'Or a communist.'

'Or with a communist boyfriend.'

'A black communist.'

'But she would never do that.'

'Her father was a good man.'

'Her mother is ambitious for her but means well.'

'Good luck to her.'

Some mothers felt a little jealous. Their Andrina, their Michelle, was now working at the Barclays, or married with two kids. But the *Sunday Times* cutting was kept in the fruit bowl and the kitchen drawer along with the carving knives and was shown to new maids. When you worked for your other madam, did you hear about this beautiful girl? Town fathers smacked beer-wet lips in the hotel bar. It was partly their doing, she was their choice. Bass Sampson, that big bloke, their drinking mate when he was on a visit, first made her fortune. She was a fortunate young thing: good luck to her.

In his shoebox Jem had the original photograph of Rosandra and the burly ewe stapled to the *Sunday Times* cutting. Over the years the pink of the crotch had hardly faded, and, aside from the caption, its identity, the body without the face, seemed as obscure.

But it was Mother's show, mainly, Rosandra thought, reminded by Jem. There was the ramp, tea under the trees, the conversations. And how pleased Susan had looked that day. She held her mouth in a small, tight rosebud, thinking good thoughts, about family success, about beauty running down the family line. As far as Rosandra herself was concerned she didn't much like the first walk down the ramp, the crowd stretched out in every direction, pink faces looking up. She was new to it, she wasn't at ease. She saw everyone's open, focused eyes. But then she looked up over their heads. She thought of other things. It helped. She discovered her trick. There was the blue autumn sky. There was stillness just above the noise of the crowd. She concentrated on that.

Jem saw a change in Rosandra, the effect of the whisky.

'I feel I'm spinning right round,' she called. 'It's wonderful.'

She cleaned the corners of her mouth with a bone-white knuckle.

'What was I saying,' she asked, 'a few minutes ago? Did I tell you that Bass promised to make my fortune?'

'Something like that,' said Jem. 'Go on.'

Her gold chains slapped on the table.

'It was when he came back. Six years later, as you know. He put it in a way I won't forget. He said, Glory will be your second name! Isn't that good? Glory will be your second name. I don't have a second name. My father thought Rosandra was fancy enough. Jem, my head is spinning. What are we doing here?'

'Talking,' said Jem. 'You're telling me about what you've been doing.'

He caught his own expression, quiet but wheedling.

'When he returned to Cradock,' Rosandra said, 'Bass's stories were about the future and adventure, as always. But this time he wasn't looking at the African mainland. He had his eye on a paradise spot called Eden Island. The brochures said it was a jewel, a nugget of coral, and Bass had figured out a clever way, he kept saying, of getting a part of it all for himself. A bit of tropical Africa, separate and on its own. He wanted to set up a tourist business, a shuttle service between the mainland and the island, and so make a killing and buy hotels. But for this plan he needed help. He said he needed someone who could help with promotion, who looked like a beauty queen, like the beauty of Cradock. For the first time I was really pleased I won the competition. Before it didn't matter one way or the other. My mother let me pierce my ears as my reward. Now Bass said I could come along with him as a kind of model. His tourist business would be my personal advertisement.

'Mother pointed out that I had already won honours in my own town, I'd made my name. But Bass said, Forget that. We were having breakfast. Bass ate his fried eggs sunny-side up. There was beer foam smeared all the way across his new short moustache. Is that all you want for her? he said. No, we can do better. I'll make her my star. He spoke about my beautiful name printed under pictures of my perfect figure. And on top of that, he said, he'd guard my honour. He told us he had a fool-proof plan.'

'He undertook to guard your honour? In those words?'

Jem looked into the sunglasses. She was unmoved, unflinching. She was without irony and deficient in a sense of wrong. Had she listened to

33

her own words? Bass undertook to preserve her honour, she said. She must be as bare of morality as the day she was born. Like a foetus that has not seen the sun. She sat still, upright. And it was not possible to think anything but the best of her.

'Of course,' said Rosandra, 'he was concerned about my honour. That was the way he put it. Maybe he thought it would spoil my looks, something like that, if I messed around and lost my virginity.'

3

'And so I found myself in an aeroplane, airborne, heading to the city,' Rosandra said. 'It was my first time flying. I was on an outing with Bass. I thought I'd never been so happy.

'Bass was nowhere to be seen. While the aeroplane was banking he strode off up the incline of the aisle. He said he couldn't stand not being at the controls of the machines he rode, he wanted to see how this little beast worked.

'I remember I was wearing a neon-orange stretch dress, Bass's present. It looks like you were poured into it, he told me. In the aeroplane toilet mirror I examined myself. The dress was just right. I looked streamlined. Like this, I knew, I could step into a new life. Bass said we would live in hotels with king-size beds. He was subletting the house he rented in Verwoerdburg. A city hotel was a more central, more convenient environment for business. He told me I need never again hug smelly sheep in front of rural photographers. I didn't mind the sheep, but what he said about hotels sounded promising. I'd never stayed in a hotel before.

'The orange dress irritated my armpits but it was worth bearing. Because I was changed. Bass said I was beautiful enough and old enough to go without panties in a tight dress. By avoiding a pantie-line I would look like a girl who knew my business. I squatted over the aeroplane toilet, pulled off my underwear and stowed it in my handbag.

'An air hostess brought me champagne. Her foundation was like a smooth mask, beige-pink. I thought it must be difficult to be so perfect. The bottle was a present from my uncle, she told me. He has us all charmed up there, she said. What a gas he is, what a laugh.

'The champagne bubbles nipped my cheeks. I felt I was moving into a new phase of life. I was uplifted, grown-up, beautiful. A man next to me confirmed it. He was from Britain, he said. He wanted to tell me something. He wanted to tell me that the girls in my country, the beach girls, the white girls, girls like me, were very beautiful. Never had he seen such girls, not even on his business trips to other places. Keep up the side, forget the politicians, keep the show on the road, he said.

'Politicians weren't on my mind at the time. Politicians were big men with power. But because of what he said I was pleased I'd taken off my panties. In the toilet mirror the orange dress made a perfect, smooth tube. It was sophisticated. I copied the hostess's smile, practising it.

'In this way we arrived in the city. Feeling stunned, I found myself beside Bass on the tarmac at the airport, where he was talking to the aeroplane crew. I felt the men turn to look at me. It told me something. I was in a new world, I was becoming a new person. I was also drunk. Bass breathed whisky and introduced me. He had his arm around the air hostess with the sculpted face. She waved her engagement ring under his nose and said, No takers.'

In the city hotel, Rosandra told Jem, her new life began in earnest.

'Enjoy yourself,' Bass told her. 'Take your leisure. This is your golden opportunity to find your wings, my Rosie. Discover clothes shops, find out about beauty, have a wonderful time, look at the world.'

Rosandra accepted what he offered freely and in gladness. She dipped into his pocket heavy with change. She washed her skin in gels and mousses from abroad, far abroad, names like fantasies. London, Paris, New York. In Paris, she knew, was the Eiffel Tower, New York was in the United States. Bass's island lay east. Maps of the Indian Ocean were spread on Bass's bed. They became part of the furniture, a decoration.

She bought magazines for their full-colour fashion pages, to see how she must look. She bought thrillers about travel and high-risk adventure which piled up on her bedside table. She could not find time to read. Bass sometimes brought a newspaper into breakfast with him, but the stories were not about the places they were going to. Once she glimpsed a picture of a schoolgirl running, keeling over into the eye of the camera. She was black. Rosandra turned the page because the expression was ugly.

In her room she played at fashion parades. She acted out the walk up the fairground ramp. Next door to the hotel she had found a light shop selling imported daylight lamps. She supplied herself with a light display. She created enough radiance in her hotel room to flush her skin.

Sometimes she wondered about Eden Island. Bass said it was a banana republic and she thought of banana groves crowding on to a thin strip of banana-yellow beach. She imagined eating sundaes for breakfast with mounds of ice-cream and cream, and chocolate sauce and chocolate shavings and soft banana slices. She magnified her light display with two full-length, bevelled mirrors. In the middle of her hotel room, wet from her bath, she dried and warmed herself, turning in front of the lights and mirrors, absorbed. She learned to know her body with photographic accuracy. It was an important part of her preparation. She must know how her back looked as she bent over, how her shoulders curved down. She was to be a model. She carried with her an ideal image of herself, a smooth, sheathed body, the air hostess figure, the one Bass liked.

Watching herself in shop windows Rosandra sometimes lost her way in the city. She asked Bass about the names of the streets she discovered, Claim, Banket, Nugget. Do you know about the city's gold-mining past? he said. The names come from that time, it was a long time ago, nearly one hundred years. She had no idea, but he didn't tell her a history. He had too many things on his mind these days to tell stories. There were plans to wrap up, he said, deals to clinch.

In the light of her lamps Rosandra groomed herself. Every day she covered her stomach mark with foundation cream. Bass introduced her to perfume. Like an animal, he said, find the scent that's right for you. He gave her a selection of perfume samples in a golden cardboard box. Who could resist being pampered like this? She measured her body in scent. Along her limbs, reaching gingerly, she drew waxy essences, of clove, of rose. She sported with Bass at breakfast, wrapped in scents like scarves.

'Here, what's this?' she said, extending an arm.

'Don't know. Gimme,' he grabbed, laughing.

And laughed the more as she cocked a jawbone or a hip, and pushed down his head to nose her knee.

'Careful, Rosie, careful,' he occasionally said, glancing round the room. 'Remember what I promised your mother. I don't want any of the guys around here to think I'm cradle-snatching.'

But his pleasure contradicted his words. As he spoke he nudged his nose into the bouquet of her shoulder and sneezed dramatically and laughed. His blunt-cut moustache tickled her, and then the gust of the sneeze soothed the spot.

'I have a sense of smell like no other man I know,' Bass said. 'It comes from being in the bush, training as a fighter. You learn to smell people in the bush, you learn to tell if they're near or far. You know if they're black *terrs*, or your own guys.'

*   *   *

The point is, Rosandra thought, it was good to be there, with Bass. Jem will eventually see that. Bass put on a good show, much bigger than any beauty competition. It was tempting to be part of it, but not completely involved, a participant-spectator.

She ordered more whisky.

'It's hardly noon,' Jem said.

She waved away his words. He noticed for the first time that her arms were hairless, waxed to the very top, naked to the sun.

Like a chrysalis, he thought, an unborn thing.

But he looked at her with such pleasure. She sat still as a lamp, a glowing lamp. Her hair glowed in the sun. Her back was straight, her feet pointed straight forwards. No harm came from her, she created no evil. Her voice was soft and comely. This is surely the picture of goodness, Jem thought.

Then one Saturday in the city centre, some time after the gift of perfumes, somewhere in the middle of a maze of malls, Rosandra told Jem, sipping whisky, she lost her way. Crowds pressed around her when she paused to find her bearings. She didn't have a map.

The afternoon had been building up to a thunderstorm and the heat added to the confusion. She could have asked the way back to the hotel, but then she also lost her handbag and that completely disoriented her. The bag was taken from under her arm when she was peering into a shop window, examining the shoes. She was distracted by the moving reflections of the crowd in the glass. These days she was focusing closer, objects were dimmer than before.

With those drop-dead eyes of hers, Bass once said, Rosandra would be OK in the city centre. She need only look at a man to be offered help. But at five o'clock, with the crowd running like the tide, she couldn't make any headway. She stepped in the way of a male shopper, a female shopper, and was ignored. Then after a while she came to an area of higher ground congested with residential hotels. It was cooler up here. All around neon signs were flickering on, names of discos, fast-food joints.

She approached a woman waiting on a pavement edge under a pink-purple light that said 'Thrills'.

'Ag, fok off, darlin',' said the woman. 'Can't you see I'm busy?'

Rosandra thought of Bass. Bass often said he was busy when he was doing nothing. Rugby videos played round the clock as he spoke on the telephone.

'Doll, give me a minute. I'm working,' he would call from the bed when she knocked.

The bed was Bass's work space. Around him were piled air-letters, newspapers, printed tables of calculations, plates of sandwiches showing random bite-marks, sometimes the camouflage gear that he kept from his past and wore if it grew cold. Last week electric-blue disco clothes were spread on top of the camouflage.

'Disappear into the bathroom a minute and try these on,' Bass said.

In a fast-food outlet that smelt almost pleasantly of warm offal Rosandra now asked to borrow some money. She would pay back tomorrow, she promised, she had lost her bag.

'How the hell can we believe you?' chanted a man in a collapsed chef's cap.

'Don't worry, sexy,' said his companion at the till. 'Ask any time.'

But he didn't move to lend her money.

'Have a burger,' the second man offered. 'On the house.'

'You need to get rid of just a teeny-weeny bit of that bum weight,' Bass told Rosandra as she stepped out of the bathroom in the electric-blue lurex.

He was talking on the telephone, leaning back on his elbow on the bed.

'Fifteen men, max,' he said.

As he spoke his eyes followed her body.

'Your body's almost exactly perfect, Rosie,' he said. 'With only a little work we can launch you one-two-three on Eden. It will be success like a shot. You will be our model, our star. You just need to lose that bum weight.'

'Whose model?' said Rosandra.

The lurex chafed her breasts.

'Which burger?' she asked the fast-food man in the cap.

'Our Big Man Burger, with two eggs and extra meat,' he said.

Rosandra ate one and a half burgers. The grease and slick blisters of fried egg slipped down easily. At the start of the second burger the men offered her a drink of Southern Comfort and orange juice. They poured it from a Fanta bottle stored under the till and watched her as she drank. She stared back at them. Had her make-up run or smudged that they stared so fixedly?

They asked her who she was and Rosandra wanted to say A Country Girl, because it was true. But she said nothing. She saw the man at the till turning his index finger in a little circle at his temple.

39

In between customers Rosandra told the men a story, Bass's old story about the children in the desert wearing shining clothes. But she didn't have Bass's narrative fire. The men looked at each other more often as she spoke, wrinkling their foreheads so that the neon light caught the sweat on their skin. They were a bit like her brothers, these two, nervous and giggly about listening to stories. They rinsed her glass in warm water and refilled it.

In the end it was Bass's kind of good fortune, managing to find the right sort of person at the right time, that helped her to get back to the hotel. She left the fast-food place during a rush of customers though the men called to her through the line of waiting people to stay. In the street, a little unsteady, smelling the strength of Southern Comfort on her own breath, she ran into the street-woman again.

'Got a ciggie, honey?' asked the woman, friendlier this time.

Rosandra did. She carried a supply in her blazer pocket for Bass.

'You're a sweetheart,' said the woman.

She lit up.

'Where're you off to?' she asked, exhaling gustily.

The question was unexpected. The woman must have forgotten her from their earlier meeting. The forgetting felt like a liberation. Because Bass said she was unforgettable. In Cradock all the world knew her. But here in this strange city centre she approached a person without being recognised. She was being given a freedom. Slipping into a situation yet staying on the edge of it, watching but not being identified. The woman was peering at her closely. Rosandra noticed her make-up was thick and streaky. Her eyebrows were drawn on to her face, too straight.

'You heard what I said, sweetheart?' repeated the woman.

In the city they were not used to her careful responses, the way she took time to speak.

'I have no money and must get to my uncle's hotel.'

'And the hotel is?'

The woman knew the hotel well, she said. And it wasn't far. She could walk her there. They began to stroll. The woman was on high stilettos and paused every so often to drag at her cigarette and look around. Her expression when she did this, turning her face into the street-light, was lazy and suspicious. She asked for another cigarette. Rosandra handed over the pack, saying she didn't need them, she'd given up. As the woman occupied herself with the business of her cigarettes, lighting, dragging, Rosandra stared at her; she had this new freedom. The woman pointed up to a residential hotel on the left.

'That's where I live,' she said. 'But none of these bastards know that.'

At that moment her stiletto met a pavement crack and she keeled away. Her next sentences were drowned by traffic.

'I'm here from the country,' Rosandra next heard. 'Platteland. I hated it there but I hate 't here worse.'

They approached a man walking purposefully, broad-shouldered. His moving shoes made a smooth, gleaming track, reflecting the colour of the shop windows. The woman stood still to watch him pass.

'*Sies*!' she exclaimed at his retreating back.

The hotel was in sight. The woman paused again.

'Let me tell you one thing, sweetheart,' she said, bringing her face up close again. She smelt of a sweet deodorant and her hair was smoky. 'You must drop that stare. Take it from me, an older woman.' She laughed, coughing. 'You give that stare, that beautiful, stupid stare, and all the men come running. Drop it, lose it. Take it from me.'

Rosandra dropped her eyes, thinking her staring had been rude.

In the brightly lit hotel foyer Bass was waiting up for her, worried, impatient, as she knew he would be. He caught her up in a bear-hug, roaring out his relief and ordering nightcap brandies for them both. The woman left Rosandra at the revolving doors but not before Bass caught sight of her.

The story of the night Rosandra was walked home by a whore became the new anecdote in Bass's telephone conversations. How the two of them came down the street towards the hotel, the whore stumbling and tottering. The princess led by the witch. The woman could hardly walk she was so . . . her legs were so . . . Bass's voice trailed off. He pulled Rosandra to him and hugged her.

'Read maps, girl, maps! Like the rest of us must,' Bass ended his phone conversations. 'That's what I told her. That's the moral of it. That's how you win in this crazy world.'

But he hadn't in fact told her this, or only by way of what he said on the telephone. Rosandra stood beside him, half leaning against his shoulder as though she were still a girl. She heard part of the dialogue only, but couldn't help smiling along with him, such was the power of his story-telling. He waggled his eyebrows, winked, boxed the pillow, kicked his heels. It wasn't possible to think of him silent, not moving, asleep. His room, as she could hear when she came down the passage, was always noisy. He was a man constantly in action, full of words. She remembered the woman's advice. But her eyes did it of their own accord. She liked looking at her uncle, liked listening to him. She was his loyal fan.

Rosandra's stare, Jem thought, watching her. Her eyes seen through the hedge; her eyes watching him from the photograph in the corner of his boarding room for the three years he was a student teacher. For years he lived in close relationship with that stare.

In the days when the photograph was new and dazzling Jem had it stuck on the wall of his boarding room between the sink and the grocery shelf, and he brushed his teeth and made mugs of Cup-a-Soup within its sight. The eyes to him had a speaking look. Lying on his bed he read messages into them: her eyes for his only.

The photograph was a focal point in the room. But when his friends went up to look more closely he was overtaken by wild possessiveness. The feeling was plain, he wanted to strike them back. They shouldn't touch his poster, they shouldn't gaze at it. It was his to look at: his only. He stepped between it and them. The action became habitual. He said nothing, but he guarded the picture.

Then the day came when Rosandra was *Sunday Times* news. She was a star at the Star Palace Casino, the paper said, she was a new phenomenon. But only one person, Gary, the man he was closest to, noticed the name. Jem was more relieved than he could express.

'Isn't this – ?' Gary asked, holding up the newspaper, three days old.

'For a girl next door she's got pretty far,' Jem said, as though apologising.

'Not long after the meeting with the woman,' Rosandra said, her pale eyes unseeing, at last absorbed by telling Jem her story, 'not long after that, Bass organised a going-away dinner. It was time to get on with the Eden Island plans, he said.

'Occasionally, during those last days in the city, I'd started to feel lonely. Once Bass left me for a whole weekend and came back sunburnt. He said he spent his Sunday on the balcony of a flat in Pretoria chatting to friends. They managed, would you believe it, to rig up a *braai* out there on the balcony. But then, because it was Sunday and all good Christians were indoors, they had to drive miles to some dusty old Indian store in Atteridgeville to find meat.

'But in the end, Bass said, it proved to be a very productive day. One of the guys he met had sure-fire contacts in the beauty business. He'd promised to phone up with tips before we flew out to Eden Island. There was also a photographer at the party. Bass promised to hire him to take pictures of me on the island, to fly the man out.

'As he talked Bass was pacing round the room throwing things into suitcases. At the going-away dinner, he promised, I would finally meet some of his men friends. A few of these people might be joining us on the island when business was under way. Circumstances had prevented it earlier but now, he said, as they were pressing him to lift the veil and reveal me, his beauty, it was time for a meeting. They were big guys, handsome hunks, and I was the centre around which everything was arranged to spin. I was their mascot. I was sure he meant model. I began looking forward to the party.'

On the night, Rosandra told Jem, she wore her electric-blue disco lurex. She felt her body-hair rise to the touch of the metallic thread. Her room was a concentration of heat, light, perfume, and the dance music on the radio made the mirrors ring. At first, until she became aware of Bass's voice, she did not hear the men knocking.

The friend who stood at the door with Bass, tall and serious-looking, was introduced as his lifelong mate, his second-in-command. His grey suit and sober blue school tie, Rosandra thought, did not match the deep brown tan that disappeared into his collar and cuffs. His hips were high, like her own. Bass said he played rugby, he was a mean fly half. Rosandra did not know what to say, she fingered her earrings.

'I feel good, I feel successful,' Bass spoke, filling up the silence. 'In a few days we're finally off to make our mutual fortunes, Rosie. So let's be in the party mood.'

Rosandra had dreamed about going with Bass to a dance, to a disco. She wanted to wear her new clothes and watch people do dance moves like in the films on television. But there was a hitch. Bass did not like music and never danced.

'Spare me, Rosie, cracklin' Rosie,' he said. 'I just can't think when the beat hits my brain. There's too much to think of right now. Remember, my doll, this is a business trip. Your uncle must think.'

The gift he was now offering was her consolation. In the brightly lit room the diamanté necklace flew from its wrapping in a flare of brilliance. She unclasped it, she held it up high over her head where it swung sparkling. When it came to rest on her skin it was cold against the back of her neck. Its lights were sharpened by the shine of her dress.

'It's beautiful,' she said.

She took Bass's hand, pleased.

'We need our sunglasses,' he said.

Rosandra saw the men had started a programme of serious drinking for the night. On their way to the restaurant in a taxi Bass, chuckling in his cavernous throat, brought out a hip-flask that smelt strongly of rum. The two men passed it between them, under Rosandra's nose.

'Not exactly the stuff for you, Rosie,' said Bass. 'You're the one of us who must stay beautiful. No red nose for you.'

The other man negotiated a cumbersome turn of his shoulders to look at her. Maybe, Rosandra thought, Bass intended him as her date? From closer quarters Rosandra took in his broad brow, his tan. He looked like a date.

'So we hear we can expect a lot from you,' he said.

It sounded as though he might need persuasion. He drank again from the hip-flask. He was staring at her with a solemn expression.

'Your success is of course one of our targets. But it's a two-way process, give and take, isn't it? Eden Island is a tourist paradise. We want to grab a stake in that trade. If you work with us you'll be made.'

It wasn't exactly clear, but it was more than she'd recently heard from Bass.

'I see,' she said.

She wanted to hear more, but her date, so she now saw him, adjusted his shoulders back to a forward position. The wool of his jacket felt clammy against her bare skin.

She heard more at dinner. Bass's party were the only people in the restaurant. They had the place booked for the whole evening. At the other end of the table Bass, very drunk, waved his fists in the air.

'We'll show them, we'll win them, we'll *moer* them,' he shouted, angry and overcome with laughter all at once.

This was also much more than Rosandra had heard before. She leaned closer to her date. Bass had placed him beside her. She stared into the startled gaze of a rotund king prawn on his plate. Bass's voice was lost in a din of cheering.

'Your uncle is a big man amongst us. A good leader,' said her date.

She had not thought of Bass as a leader before, but once spoken the title was obvious. The men were raising glasses to him. Their mouths exploded with his name. Bass! Eden! they called. Rosandra's date glanced over his shoulder. She followed his look. Behind them stood three waiters in a row. The men stood at ease, their eyes glazed and distant. They could have been in another room, another place. A serviette was dropped; a waiter automatically stooped and picked it up. The eyes of the waiters were on the reflection of the party in the restaurant window.

'You won't have to deal with these sort of black guys, come Eden Island,' said the date. 'They are different over there, not so sulky.'

She leaned over further in his direction so as not to miss a word. The diamante beads formed a slender column extending down to her knees, brilliant even in the dim candlelight.

'With Bass at the helm we will all have success on the island. Between evening and morning, if you like,' he said. 'And when we've set up shop everyone will want to be part of the deal. They'll do what we say. You'll see.'

She knew her expression was very still. She thought she should keep it that way so as not to interrupt what he was saying. She set her teeth, she knew it made her mouth prettier.

'I'm the best guy to tell you what a capable operator Bass is,' her date said. 'I was with him in the Congo. I saw him under fire. He's unflappable. I was called Sneezer in those days. Because when I shot, I sneezed.'

He laughed, remembering. Rosandra echoed his laughter, adding a note of appreciation. This could turn into a full-length story about the two of them, she thought, about when he and Bass were young and did soldierly things. Because he was so busy, there had not been a good story from Bass in a long time. She sat expectant. Sneezer broke his last king prawn open mightily, then prodded it at her lips.

Rosandra had to straighten up to avoid it. She took the prawn from his fork, put it in her mouth and wiped her fingers.

'You were in the Congo?' she prompted.

'It was – an assignment, a job. No reward other than cash at the end of the day. This time round it will be different. Bass says we will have more control. Within a few hours we will know if we have the upper hand. We could be in charge by morning.'

'By morning?' she said.

She did not understand.

'Yes, by morning,' he said, speaking up as though she hadn't heard him. 'It'll be a very different scene from the Congo. It was a good fight up there, we were with a good team, but I got tired of it. It was out of control. There were times when it got weird. Like the night we ran into this nun. We arrived at a convent that had been raided that day. It was chaos. The nun was one of the few survivors. Her clothes, the black uniform they wear, were ripped back and front. Maybe she was

45

raped, I don't know. But what I remember is the way she looked. She was a white bird, you know, but with this bloody black streak across her face. Just this big black streak from her left eye to the right-hand corner of her mouth.'

He tried to trace the line in the air close to Rosandra's face. She drew back. He was smiling a little.

'Out of the middle of this black streak she was screaming, just screaming like shit, running down the path towards us. And you know what, those guys with me bolted. They turned and bolted. Not far of course, but far enough to keep her at a distance. I was standing on the one side watching. And I remember thinking – I hate this shit. I hate these guys. Look at them running away from a woman, a bloody nun. I want to be my own man, I thought. Under Bass I'm sure it'll be possible. You'll know what I mean. You work directly with the guy.'

At the head of the table, around Bass, cheering and calls of Eden! broke out again. Sneezer downed his drink, and then a second. He had delivered his final line. He turned to add his voice to the merriment.

The men round the table rose and the waiters retreated. Beer and wine guttered down into open gullets. Two voices, out of key, valiant, made an attempt at singing, something like 'He's a Jolly Good Fellow', like 'We are Marching to Pretoria'. Suddenly – it felt very sudden – Rosandra's date changed the pitch of the cheering.

'But I'll tell you one thing,' he shouted loudly, downing another glass, 'if this thing's a fuck-up we are dead men.'

There followed a single pure moment. It reverberated, as though time became simple repetition, as though everything changed, there would only ever be this moment, this tinkling and falling. Downing his last mouthful the date threw his glass across the room. To the sound of its breaking on the brick floor he keeled over. As he fell and a waiter rushed up too late to catch him, he grabbed at Rosandra and caught the necklace, making a fist, dragging. The thick nylon string arched over the table, whiplashing, scattering its weight of bright beads in the laps of the guests. At the moment of its snapping Rosandra felt a sharp pull at her neck. Then the necklace hung suspended, sending shafts of light in every direction like a mass of stars. For whole seconds it seemed not to fall. The lights moved, revolving like spokes of a moving wheel. Later, when she closed her eyes, it was still there, she could see it clearly, turned from a white brilliance to a bright red shape.

Then they were on the highway, rushing along tunnels of sulphurous light. Bass was driving a friend's car, who was drunker than he. Rosandra was in the back, with the drunk man's head on her lap. She sensed a car approach at left, on the inner lane. It was the rest of the dinner guests. One of them, half hanging out of the car window, was holding a bottle and motioning for her to grab hold of it.

'Faster!' Bass egged himself on.

'They want to give us something to drink,' said Rosandra.

Bass chuckled, cutting devilishly into the path of the other car.

'Forget their drink,' he said. 'Next week you and I will have cocktails on Eden.'

Some time during the night, as Rosandra slept, they drove into a township. It must have been Soweto, but she couldn't be completely sure. She awoke staring up through a car windscreen at a fading night sky still full of stars. Motion had stopped. She had been shifted to the front passenger seat. Somewhere outside Bass was whooping. There was a familiar smell in the air of woodsmoke – it comforted. Rosandra remembered Maria smelt this way. The times Maria dressed her in the morning. The smell was also in the kitchen when Maria made breakfast. She imagined they were out in the open desert, a dry place like Cradock, till she looked up and saw low houses leading away to right and left.

'Christening the trip! Christening the trip!' someone called.

A man lay prone on the car bonnet, pouring the last of a brown glass bottle over his face. Alongside the other car, which was drawn up at an angle to theirs, stood a row of Bass's friends, their faces looking blue and dazed.

The next instant light was clotted as the man on the bonnet vomited a mess of broken prawns on to the windscreen. Rosandra rolled up her window. The street was deserted. Low-hanging mist obscured the ends of the street vista. As the sky lightened it grew very cold.

Bass gesticulated at her window. She opened the door for him. The sick man on the bonnet coughed in a mournful, querying way.

'Thank you for smiling, Rosie,' Bass said.

He was smiling, but Rosandra hadn't thought she was smiling too.

'We came to this place to see how easy it would be to take by night,' Bass said. 'Just as a *jol*, you know, a pretend thing. Seeing how it might be to shoot a couple of these black brothers and take the place in five minutes. But,' he paused for the punch-line, 'we left our guns at home.'

One of the men wandered after Bass. He lit a cigarette and inserted it between the lips of the man masked in vomit. Bass turned his face away.

'Let's get out of here,' he said. 'We've had a long night, boys.'

The men slung their friend into the back of the soiled car. He brought with him oddly sweet odours of prawn mayonnaise, of vinaigrette dressing. Rosandra lost the smell of woodsmoke. Like loud boasting, the sound of car exhausts gunned into the early dawn.

Rosandra pushed away her empty glasses. Jem saw she turned the orange lipstick marks away from her. She ordered ice-cream. She wiped her hands over the surface of the table.

'The way particular pictures stay in your mind,' she said after a silence, surprising him. 'That moment has stayed with me, when the necklace broke. That one clear flash.'

She was preoccupied with the idea. She seemed to think it significant, difficult. Her hands made a diamond shape, the index finger and thumb tips pressed together. She looked at the ice-cream in front of her as though it were entirely separate from her. As though it had arrived without her bidding. She motioned with the arrow of her hands.

'The pictures are disconnected.' She was looking for the words. 'It's like – there's this palm tree or ice-cream. *This* pink ice-cream. Or there's a cloud, that cloud, tucked in between those two high hotels. I'm talking about single things that stand out, that stick in your mind, that fix your memory somehow.'

But Jem didn't get it. He stared at the ice-cream, which was melting. People hold on to images for special reasons, he thought. There was the tourist brochure he carried in his diary for almost a year when he was at the teacher-training college. The brochure was of an island with palm trees. The place looked like paradise: it stood for his dream. He dreamed of joining Rosandra on the tropical island where, according to her mother's report, she now worked. Bass had found a job for her in the beauty business, Susan said. Soon Rosandra would be a proper beauty queen.

But his dream remained a dream. By the time he earned enough money – he packed shelves at a bottle store, he processed data for his geography professor – Rosandra was out of touch. She wasn't on Eden any more and the travel agent said the island was no longer safe for holidays. So Jem spent his money on a stereo system. The speakers were ash-grey and their fidelity was perfect. He wondered about telling her this. He saved up to come and see her on Eden; to have a holiday with her. He shifted forward in his seat, the hard plastic sticking to his skin. He should have worn long trousers today, not shorts. Shorts had no dignity, the meeting didn't look like a date.

'Isn't it what lies behind these pictures?' he said. 'Like your necklace. You remember it because of what happened that evening. It was framed by all that decadence.'

'It wasn't decadent. I remember it mainly as beautiful,' she said.

The men stood in two rows on either side of the table, cheering. She herself did not cheer, but smiled.

Her ice-cream drooled down the gutters of its fluted glass.

'Look at us sitting here,' Jem said. 'We could be a couple at a newly developed sea resort anywhere. But where are we actually? We're in the fastest growing city in the world, or so the unofficial figures say, with slums where people kill each other in full daylight. That background changes things. It puts things in a new light.'

But he had lost her, he felt wrong. She sagged in her chair. Suddenly she looked deathly tired.

4

'On my first morning on Eden Island,' Rosandra said to Jem, 'the first thing I did was to write a postcard home. Maybe you remember it. The sky that day was blue, the beach sand was sugar-white. The postcard showed a beach scene where the sky was bluer than the sea and the sand was sugar-white. I lifted what I wrote from the tourist brochure I picked up at the reception desk.'

'I remember what the card said,' said Jem.

He took a breath, bracing himself. He tried to recite. He watched her carefully but she didn't blink at his performance. She was concentrating on something else.

'I didn't know what to say,' she said. 'You see, I was disappointed, I had to admit it to myself. I sat on the new king-size bed in the new hotel room and felt shut out of something, even more than in the city. This wasn't what I'd expected. I agreed with Bass, everything we saw looked like paradise. But as soon as we arrived at the hotel he went off to his room and the telephone, just like in the other hotel. As a kind of joke he'd put me in a honeymoon suite. A carafe of chilled white wine waited in the room. I couldn't see the point of the joke.

'I read magazines. I studied the pattern of padded buttons on the padded headboard. The headboard was yellow, I remember. I was in the place where Bass said my career would begin but I didn't know what to do with myself.

'The feeling was so different from when we left the city, when we were in the aeroplane, airborne, and Bass's dream stretched out in front of us. How excited I was! My second time flying, another outing with Bass, a pleasure journey to make my fortune. It was what I wanted, it was every girl's dream. I had to press my hands into my middle because my stomach was churning.

'For that whole trip I held in my lap the Estée Lauder make-up case Bass gave me at the airport as a going-away token. I'd never owned such a thing before. I tried the make-up. In the dry aeroplane atmosphere the powder felt scratchy. Bass saw me wrinkle my nose and winked at the air hostess. She brought a wet towel. Her foundation was perfect, like an invisible mask.

'If you want something, tell Sandy, Bass told me, very confident, as though they had a long-standing relationship. Sandy didn't have an engagement ring to wave under Bass's nose. She joined us two mornings later for an early swim.

'The man on my left caught my eye. He began to chat. He was from Australia, he said. He wanted to give me a small compliment on behalf of all the beautiful girls who lived in this part of the world, around the shores of the Indian Ocean. Never had he seen such girls. He worked in the tourist line, package deals, budget tours. They had connections with the UK, Switzerland, Japan. He wanted to testify that girls from my country and also from his country were the best and most beautiful in the world, the blondes especially. Like me. It was our glowing faces, our grooming, our tans. He was on his way home now, going from one place of beauty to another. I should come over, he said, I wouldn't feel out of place – there were girls just like me on Bondi Beach. Come visit and forget about the politics, he suggested, and keep the show on the road.

'It was like the conversation with that other man, on the other plane ride. What he said made me feel warm, properly transformed, not a Country Girl any more. I was glad I had the new make-up on. His words were sweet. I practised my hostess smile on him. As before. I saw him smile into his Jack Daniels.'

Rosandra paused before she went on. The smile that had been on her face was dimming. Jem watched it go. This must be a different mood she was coming to. She folded her hands together and pressed them into her ribs. He sat back from the table, legs and arms loose, relaxed but attentive, or so he hoped it looked, an attitude of close but gentle listening, that she might like.

That first day on Eden Island, Rosandra said, Bass marked as a free day. He was a good manager and tour organiser. He left behind a standard tourist map of Port Philip, the island capital, fifteen minutes from the Eden Island Hotel by hotel shuttle. The day, Bass said, should be used for orientation. Rosandra could try to find her feet.

Bass's map looked like a treasure-hunt game. The crucial points were

51

marked with outsize pictures of buildings and monuments. There was the zoo, the island aviary, the airport tower. But the goal of the game, because it was the largest and brightest picture of all, was the hotel. The parliament buildings resembled the hotel, only they were smaller. They had the same pilasters, the grand archway, the sweeping drive. Bass slipped the map under Rosandra's door along with the hotel's daily broadsheet and a huge card showing a yellow duck shedding blue glitter tears. Miss you, it said.

The Eden Island hotel was built on the very edge of what had once been a rocky length of bay line. On the left was an artificial beach, on the right another. The sand had been flown in from the Philippines, Bass said, or Papua New Guinea. Waves splashed up against the dining-room windows.

Later that first morning, after writing her postcard, redoing her face, reading her third magazine, Rosandra decided to go out. She couldn't be with Bass but she could at least follow his suggestions, it was a way of beginning, an independence, part of the new life. She took the shuttle service from the main entrance into Port Philip. She wore her neon-orange dress because it reminded her of him.

And Eden looked exactly like a tropical island. There was robust dark green greenery; there were monkeys in the trees. From the side of the road silently singing brown children waved.

In Port Philip Rosandra walked down the narrow main street, aiming for the sea at the end, which looked green and cool. Halfway down the street she bought sunglasses, the first she saw, her first pair ever. They helped with the glare but made her vision fuzzy, more fuzzy than it already was. The street ended in a bare strip of promenade. Here she found another big tourist hotel, a sign-board boasted a French *pâtisserie*.

The *pâtisserie* was in the basement, submarine. She enclosed herself in its rosy, air-conditioned coolness and ordered three pastries. On the menu they all looked different but turned out to be the same, collapsed flaky pastry, custard studded with clots. She wondered if this was French. It tasted like her mother's custard tart, the treat she made on Sundays when she was bored. Sensible meals at home were cooked by Maria.

She lingered over the third pastry. She knew what would happen when she finished it; she would have to think what to do. She went to examine the other pastries in the display window. Some might be different from the ones she had just eaten. She found none. It was all custard and bubbles. Up in the hotel lobby she spent time at the public telephones looking through the Eden directory for names of beauty salons and exercise studios till the porter began to stare. She left without finding a good address, other than that of the salon in her own hotel, which carried a full-page advertisement. It was just past noon.

Back in the heat Rosandra imagined for a moment she saw Bass across the street, silhouetted against the green of the sea. He had come to town after all, she thought happily, to make her day. The man had Bass's broad frame and the big hands hanging. She watched him walk, looking down as though in thought, hatching plans. And there was the man walking beside him, also tall, with high hips, a shape like Sneezer's.

But it was wishful thinking. The man who looked like Bass was not wearing his kind of clothes. His shirt was dark, long-sleeved, not Bass's style. Rosandra turned back up the main street, disappointed. The shops broadcast rock music from the island's one radio station into the street.

That afternoon Rosandra tested the beach to the right of the hotel, then the one to the left. One man was swimming far out in the bay. It wasn't Bass, Rosandra checked, not this time either. The shoulders were too slight.

Their first night on the island Bass bought Rosandra dinner at a restaurant open to the four winds and roofed in thatch. They had palm leaves baked in coconut milk with chili. Rosandra ate until she thought her eyes would bleed. Bass was drinking heavily. He toasted her, their plans, the island, their arrival, many times. He remembered it would soon be her eighteenth birthday. He called the waiters round to toast 'his girl' and her brilliant future. Leaning heavily against her, he put his arm around her to escort her home. Rosandra felt a bubble of hope rise to displace her disappointment. It would be OK after all, she thought, adventure maybe had a slow start, she didn't yet know much about glamour, how success begins.

Sandy the air hostess came swimming on the third morning. After the swim she lay down to relax on Bass's second bed where his maps were as usual spread open. Her chin pointed at Sri Lanka. Her toes were working at the green candlewick pattern on the bedspread. Around her tanned right ankle she wore three gold ankle chains. The thickest, the one with the heart-shaped pendant, Bass gave to her before the swim. He bought it at the hotel shop; Rosandra advised him.

Rosandra watched her closely to see how far her foundation extended round her neck, to discover her beauty secrets. But Sandy's hair kept flopping down, cloaking her jaw.

Sandy ordered up gin and bottles of tonic water, By Appointment to HM The Queen. She wanted to get drunk, she said, because it was a dull day outside, hazy and very hot, and because soon she had to fly on again, just when she had met such nice new friends, and because what the hell it was fun to get drunk on holiday.

Rosandra found she could drink twice as fast as Sandy. Sandy sipped, Rosandra let long draughts slip down. The pale sky and pale buildings outside began to swim. Gin made Bass quiet; he lay with his eyes closed. Sandy traced the outline of Eden Island on the map with a red-purple nail.

'It's like a splodge,' she said. 'Bass, the island is like a splodge. It has lots of little coves. We should hire a scooter and go exploring. What do you think?'

'Yes,' said Bass. 'That could be a good idea.'

'We can trace the outline of the island, the whole splodge, all the way round. We can follow the map.'

'Yes, that would be nice. To follow the map. Would you like to see the edges of our island, our little paradise, Rosie?'

He turned to Rosandra lazily. Sandy was also looking at her. Rosandra wondered if there was something really wrong with her vision. Sandy suddenly had four eyes. She remembered Bass had asked a question. She forgot what it was.

'I see the island from all different angles when we fly in. We come in from different directions depending on the wind,' said Sandy, turning back to Bass.

She stretched a leg over to his bed and hooked Bass's big toe on an ankle chain.

'And how does it look?' said Bass.

'Pretty, spread in all directions, just like here on the map.'

'Then we don't need to go and ride all the way round it. You've seen it, and for myself I feel too lazy. What about you, Rosie?'

Rosandra was not saying. Her tongue, thick in her mouth, could not be trusted. She smiled and drank down her gin. The lemon slice flopped against her nose.

'You need another one of those, Rosie,' said Bass, hitching himself up on an elbow to prepare the drink.

'Spoilsport,' said Sandy, retrieving her cast-off toe. 'What do you have these maps for if you aren't going to explore the island?'

'So I can do it from this bed in comfort,' said Bass.

At this Sandy was struck down by laughter, which ended almost as soon as it started in long, regretful sighs. For these she rolled over on to her back, with her knees akimbo and her head in India. Bass refilled her glass, giving her more gin than tonic.

'Wouldn't you just love to travel?' she said. 'I look at all that space and I just want to go places. I just want to see the world.'

Her accent became slightly American when she said this. She flexed her hands in the air above her head, watching them dreamily.

'Oh, how I want to travel,' she cried, begging for a response. 'That's why I'm doing this job. So I can get out. I want to get out of this little island route. I want to go to the Mediterranean, to Florida and New York.'

New York again, thought Rosandra. The name was everywhere, on all her perfumes, on her talcum powder and make-up. She wondered what New York offered that could make Sandy put on a special kind of voice.

Bass was drinking between words. He was saying the island was good enough for him and Rosie.

'We've been planning to come over here for ages, haven't we, Rosie? To find a little paradise all for ourselves. First Eden, then the world.'

Jem saw that Rosandra was casting a new shadow. It spread from her left side. It had become afternoon. The shadows on her face too had changed shape, but the expression of tiredness, or was it wistfulness, was still there. Telling the story seemed to deepen it. She said she wanted a walk. Jem looked into her sunglasses in anxiety. She wanted to stop? To rest a moment, she said. It takes its toll, all this story-telling. She left her lipstick on the table and her lipstick-stained serviettes. They will see it's occupied, she said.

Jem realised he was hungry. The whisky carved out empty places in his stomach. They walked in silence past two odorous hot-dog kiosks. A mirage of oven-heat hung above their red roofs. Beyond the beach fell away sharply, there was open sea. They did not speak, they were caught up in the pause in her story. Jem thought about what she'd been telling him. It still didn't seem to add up. It was nothing more than a story, something like the disconnected images she described. What I did on my holiday. He couldn't see the real Rosandra in the midst of it, this woman walking here beside him.

Her shoulder occasionally grazed his own, it meant familiarity. His body was known and unthreatening to her, like a brother's. She was confirming they were close. But seen by a third person they might look like lovers, walking slowly in the heat of an early afternoon with nothing better to do but be together and all of the day remaining. He heard her feet beat time with his and the dry stir of hair on her shoulders and upper arms, covering their strange nakedness. In her throat a pulse beat, almost imperceptible, but visible in the heat beneath the outline of damp skin.

They went on walking and his world was centred in that pulse. He looked at the waves: in the heavy heat they seemed to move more slowly. They made no sound. Beside them in the street the rickshaw drew up and spun round. She turned to him: her neck was alive with pulsations, her hair was floating, the flash of the sun was in her glasses. It was a vision of truth, Jem thought, and his tongue trembled with emotion. This is what she made of him, a tongue-tied worshipper. The glare stained her freckles darker. The stains stood out, her skin looked separate from her body outline. Behind the sheath of skin he traced her own pure shape, the simple white shape as he knew it from the time of the garden, looking at her. Love, he thought, this is love. There was nothing in the world but this face and the sea. Silently he begged her not to move. She was peering at him.

'Hot-dog or another ice-cream?' she asked. 'I don't know about you but I'm starving.'

The sound would explode his eardrums. He hadn't seen the third kiosk coming up on their left. Balloons of candyfloss in clear plastic bags swung from the zebra-striped awnings. The bags pounded against one another with the sound of gongs. Flies coagulated in grease spots on the counter. He had a hot-dog; he threw half of it away. She chose another ice-cream, in a cone. When they got back to the bistro the table was stained orange. Her lipstick had melted and flooded its holder.

There had to be a photographic shoot, Rosandra told Jem. Bass promised it. It had to be planned. Rosandra telephoned round the island hotels to find a studio. She reminded Bass about his friend, the one he met at the balcony party in Pretoria, the one he said would do the job. Bass looked blank. They were in his room drinking beer with Sandy. He played with Sandy's fringe and blew in her face. He put his earlier promise down to beer talk. Sure the man could take photos, but he was an amateur, his main line was cartography. Rosandra didn't believe Bass. She thought he wanted to be with Sandy, he was putting her off.

56

It was Sandy who located the studio in a small exclusive hotel three beaches away, complete with useful props, a sand box, a wind machine. Behind a red satin curtain Rosandra pulled on her swimsuit, a new one in parrot colours, purple and green. She buried herself in the sand box. The sand was stale and moist.

Bass became a dark bulk shape standing beside the crouched photographer. Sandy was a protesting voice behind Bass. The photographer's shoulders were hulked as he lit a cigarette close to his chest. Then Sandy lurched up out of the darkness. The surfaces of her oiled face gleamed with little spots of light. She blocked Rosandra from view with her body and pointed, almost touching, where the swimsuit hip-line almost did not cover Rosandra. She was hairfree everywhere else and the contrast was obvious. Sandy scattered little handfuls of sand. The two men were still dark shapes. They had not moved or talked. Rosandra helped Sandy's repair work by sliding further into the sand.

'OK?' asked the photographer, grinding his cigarette butt into the black floor.

'Is there a problem?' said Bass.

'Nothing that five minutes won't solve,' said Sandy.

'The rash,' Rosandra whispered.

But the photographer had seen everything. He wheeled the camera closer. For today, head and shoulders only, he suggested. Sandy patted the sand in place and went back to Bass. She took him to the hotel coffee shop. The studio became very still. The photographer moved on stockinged feet. He touched his equipment with a silken touch. The lights screamed at a pitch close to silence. Rosandra thought she could not bear it. It was too fierce, too hot. Her face was red-hot. Her legs were covered in sand and invisible. This was not what she imagined back in the city, this blacked-out room with no beach, no sun, no boat on the open water. But it was a beginning. She knew Bass was relying on her. As she looked up and around, expectant, confused, the shutter clattered.

The confusion created beautiful effects: her eyes were hooded, darkened, her lips drawn out in amazement. Sandy, turning the photographs this way and that, looked impressed. She nodded at Bass. Full marks to her, she said. Bass filed the sulkiest-looking photograph in his briefcase.

After that Bass developed a taste for photography. He produced a camera with a 35–200mm. lens, bristling with electronic functions. His first pictures were all of Rosandra, always on the beach, always in her swimsuit. He was getting used to the camera so she had to concentrate hard on holding her poses. Her mouth grew stiff and dry before the shutter clacked.

The last day Sandy was on the island she sat on the beach with Rosandra and gave advice. Suck in your cheeks, she instructed, let your lips go a little bit slack and use your stare, look blank. The little facial effects matter, a telephoto gets in very close. Bass believes in you.

So Rosandra sucked in her cheeks and bit at the inner skin to keep them in place. Gradually she built up a technique to pass the time. She learned to distract herself. She made a list of things to think of – make-up and clothes, what her family was doing back home, Susan reading stretching dozing, Maria in the kitchen, the boys down at the river. Later, as she grew more practised, she thought of plainer things, of single, simple, visual things, the sky, a wave, a cloud. The blue cloud. The images worked. She concentrated so hard she forgot where she was. The bite marks she made as she focused produced row upon row of little ulcers in her mouth.

After Sandy left Rosandra again had Bass to herself. The two of them went on photographic walks down along the shore beyond the hotel beaches. The beaches here were natural formations and the sand was coarse. Bass took photographs of Rosandra buried, covered up to her knees, covered in patches, trickling sand on to her body and face. He also took other photos, of the bay, the yacht moorings, the shoreline. He was becoming experimental, he said.

One day he produced a tube of Uhu glue. During their days of walking Rosandra had collected a towel bag full of shells. 'Let's stick these on you, so you look like a mermaid,' Bass said. 'A mermaid with shell-scales, like a beautiful fish.'

Rosandra worried about the glue drying.

'The sea and the salt will wash off the glue,' said Bass. 'You have no hair for it to stick to.'

Lovingly he pressed her down on the sand. As he smeared on the glue and fitted the shells together like a jigsaw he told her about a love of his, one he met on his travels down the African coast. From her he learned about this kind of decoration. The woman liked to wear shells stuck on to every inch of her exposed flesh. Her buttocks were two smooth mosaics of shells, like rocks full of barnacles, each barnacle evenly shaped and placed. Rosandra was lulled by the words. He was telling stories again. He was very tender. Before working on a new area of skin he rubbed the spot lightly, making circular motions with his fingers. He told about the woman wanting to make cicatrices in his cheeks.

By the time Rosandra's back and legs were covered it was nearly dusk. But Bass's camera won the day. It was that time of evening when objects radiate a low light of their own. The shells showed their purples and dull pinks to advantage, the shapes were soft and ambiguous. Rosandra's half-closed eyes were full of yellow light. A drowned mermaid was washed up on shore. Her trunk and arms were limp, her forked tail was fishlike, a fleshy, marine thing.

Bass was impressed by his own successes. Photographs were spread across his room, laid out on the bed, across the maps, stuck on the walls illegally with sellotape. Everywhere were photographs of Rosandra as mermaid. Alongside Rosandra on deck chairs and surfboards, Rosandra embraced by a hotel pool lilo shaped like a pink octopus, were pictures of Rosandra's skin and limbs encrusted with shells. The photograph with the softest focus became Bass's centrepiece. A small reproduction nested in his wallet next to the picture he already had, of Rosandra as beauty queen.

And so Rosandra forgot she had been briefly miserable. After Sandy's departure, when he was not on the phone, Bass gave her more of his time and attention. Every evening they had supper together, with candlelight. She began to use the Shape-In beauty studio at the hotel to make her figure perfect.

At the studio Rosandra listened to other women talk. She picked up tips, such as the advantages to posture of sucking in your stomach sharply as you walk from your towel to the water, and how to apply a dusting of powder between layers of lipstick, to make the colour stick. Women from the studio joined Rosandra on the beach. One of them was a secretary from London, several were newly-weds, as many were air hostesses. One knew Sandy; she was on the same flight circuit. It was a small world. When the women went swimming they gave her their jewellery for safe keeping. It was like holding marbles in the school playground, seeing the sunlight flash across the shiny bead necklaces, the brass and perspex rings.

Before long Rosandra discovered that none of the women was a model.

'Models?' said Jacinta, the New Zealand masseuse from the Shape-In.

She had joined Rosandra and two newly-weds for a swim.

Yes, where are the *international* models? Rosandra asked again. She

59

pronounced the phrase the way Bass said it, always with that first, many-stressed word, *international*.

'Models usually come here on special assignments,' said Jacinta, 'with their photographers and roadies and so on. This is the wrong time of year. There are no models on the island now.'

During the sixth week on Eden Rosandra cut her toe on a mussel shell in a rock pool. It was the second toe on her left foot, the soft, pale underpad. Bass sucked it clean. His tongue felt like a rasp.

'Is that man your lover?' asked her beach companions.

'No,' said Rosandra.

'Father? Sugar-daddy?'

'My uncle.'

'Some uncle,' they said.

'Keep your wound clean,' Bass instructed. 'In the heat you'll want to scratch it, but don't. You don't want to have a scar, not even on your hidden bits.'

'He wants to fuck her blind,' said Jacinta to her friend Marinda.

'Pardon?' Rosandra said.

Because she didn't want to spoil things Rosandra didn't pass on to Bass what Jacinta told her about models on Eden. Bass was a man with a mission; he shouldn't be distracted. Rosie, he announced, have patience. Only a little while now and our cameras will be rolling.

And Bass had new plans. He wanted to fly the city business team to the island. He thought a friendly rugby tour would be a good excuse for a group jaunt; the team must be reminded of the island's fail-safe potential as a tourist resort. Rosandra caught snatches of his plans as she waited for him in his room before supper.

Secretly she hoped the men she met that last night in the city would come over for the rugby only. They seemed capable of managing the affair from afar. She remembered their blue faces in the Soweto dawn. On Eden at high tide crabs with translucent carapaces that gleamed like polished stones appeared on the beach. There wasn't a lot to do, but that was the way of paradise. She preferred to have her uncle all to herself.

One evening during their seventh week she and Bass went walking along the avenue of dark takamaka trees close to the hotel. It was humid in the shade. The sea made a white hush.

'This *is* African, isn't it?' she turned to Bass. 'It looks like Africa. Like those jungles you used to talk about.'

'The atlas says it's Africa,' said Bass.

'It's the thick trees, the fruit everywhere,' she said. 'The smells.'

It was the smell of thatch that is exuded after sunset. She knew it from somewhere. Maria? The smell of her *kaya* at the back of the house, the grass mat in it, the dried herbs in a Rose's jam jar.

'Don't forget the people,' Bass said, 'and the government. They're African through and through. They believe in things like freedom and equality but they wouldn't know how to manage freedom if they had it. You need guys from elsewhere to come in, throw their weight around and police things a bit.'

But Rosandra didn't want to think of policing. Eden smelt like Africa, it was a good place for a holiday. She drank as many Coke floats as she wanted and lay most of the day on the beach.

But maybe the most important thing, Rosandra thought – leaning back to take a break – was that technique of concentration she perfected on the beach. On Eden she learned many things, but what she took away with her, the skill she still had, was this trick, staring at the sky, focusing on one point, letting her mind drift.

How to describe it? It was centred on the image of a blue cloud. She imagined it as painted: a cloud, thin, blue, disconnected from everything, the stroke of a blue brush on a bluer space of sky. Lying on the beach, staring skywards, she imagined it forming up there, she could feel its lightness. She used the blue cloud as a charm. Thinking of it she didn't worry about a thing, not once. Royal blue Maria would call it. It was an expression they used at Maria's church to describe the colour of Mary Mother of God's dress. The colour of Mary's dress, like this cloud at night, was royal blue.

Jem watched the sea surrender movement: it was a smooth, still surface. The temperature out on the esplanade went on rising. Sweat crept down his chest and into his shorts. The story was a lengthening concertina, he thought. A concertina expanding fold after fold and filled only with air. With the heat his desire grew, to hear about the real action, when the noise began.

'Tell me about when Bass really showed his stuff,' he said.

He adored her but she exasperated him. When did Bass go wrong, and how? He wanted to hear. She seemed not to have heard him. She was sitting like a portrait, unmoving, not betraying a thing, dead quiet. She sat there more complete and lovely than he could have imagined possible in the heat. When she looked like this he was sure he could, if it was necessary, forgive her anything.

'There was a serious incident with Bass once,' Rosandra said. 'It was the time I met an islander, the only time I met a native other than the people in the hotel bar. She was a white woman, quite elderly, the last surviving member of a long-established Eden Island family. They made their fortune in sugar. The woman's poodle kicked sand in my face where I was lying on the beach, and she invited me home for tea.

'Her house was pink and large, shadowy. I remember a sense of damp and age, like things had stood in one place for many years. The jalousies were closed, the tea tasted dusty. A creole maid brought in two iced sponges. Since Cradock I hadn't had tea with cake.

'During tea the woman showed me around her living room. She said she longed for the company of young people and for conversation. She was wearing a wrap-around gown of something like silk that showed all her bones as she walked.

'She told me about the love of her youth. He was the captain of a ship in the former trading days of the island. She said she told everyone she had a chance to meet about him. It brought him back.

'Her man looked like a pirate, she said, and called her his pearl. He collected ship's figureheads from the age of sailing ships, the Homeric heads of heroes loved by the Portuguese. For him she sacrificed her virtue. When I heard this I didn't know exactly what she meant. "Sacrificed her virtue"? The woman said it meant she was with him before marriage, they had sex. From this I gathered I also had virtue. I felt proud of that.

'But the sacrifice, the woman said, was all for nothing, because the next thing she knew her captain left the island with someone else, a horse-rider in a travelling circus. The shores of the Indian Ocean was where the circus travelled. To this day she wasn't yet consoled. Her lover followed this terrible woman to Zanzibar, to Mozambique, to the Cape of Good Hope. It wasn't possible for her to follow him. She had to think of her family, her dignity. It was because of dignity she was still here.

'I didn't know how to respond. I didn't know how to talk of loving. Then the woman asked me if I was fancy-free.

'I told her yes. I was alone on the island. This was the holiday I saved up for at the end of school, I said.

'I didn't know why I was lying but it felt light and free. I will always remember how easy it was. I told the woman I was thinking about my future; I had plans to travel to London, Paris. Lying I could believe I had no past. My face could be European, American. I could be anyone I wanted, a girl with a choice of jobs and roles, an Australian beach blonde, a model from New York.

'Take extra care of yourself if you're alone, the woman said. Even a short holiday can change a young person.

'But I am changing and changing, I thought to myself. I was feeling even lighter. I sat up straighter, like a real model. I had a third slice of cake.

'In the late afternoon, when I arrived back at the hotel, Bass was nowhere to be found. The barman said he had been drinking most of the day. I walked down three beaches and found Bass sitting at an open-air restaurant, mopping up fruit-bat stew with bread.

'At first he didn't speak to me. I thought he wanted to make me feel lonely for punishment, for leaving him alone. He swallowed down two neat vodkas. For me he ordered Bombay ice-cream.

'I told Bass about visiting the woman, her big house, her lonely life. He stared at his empty plate. Then he brought his hand down on the table, silently, but as though he wanted to hit it.

'He told me I had missed an important engagement, maybe the most important engagement of the trip. That very lunch-time, in the bar, he met a hot-shot professional photographer. The man was out on a shoot for a British magazine, location was over on another island, a parrot sanctuary. He'd come over to visit Eden on a jaunt, to have lunch, to pick up talent, to look out for beautiful girls. In short this photographer was the man we needed. Bass told him he was right on target, he had just the girl.

'But at the crucial moment the girl was missing. Where was she? Bass searched everywhere. He was bent over the table, breathing bat stew and spirit. For the first time I wanted to be away from him. His breath smelt bad to me. My heart was in my stomach. I had missed a real chance. I felt sick. Couldn't we hire this man or get him to come over again? I asked carefully. Bass spat. Did I think he was made of solid gold? Did I think he could afford a man hired by *Vogue* or *Harper's* or whatever they were called when our own business project had only just begun? Whereas if the photographer could have seen me, taken a few trial snaps, done his business . . . Then Bass lost his thread. He was very drunk. His face didn't have its usual colour. His brow was creased. There was a fine sweat all over him. He drank in a hurried way, in a kind of panic.

'Then I saw it clearly. The clock in the woman's pink house had said four. I saw again her bony body and the clinging of the static as she showed me round. We were looking at some pond-green landscape pictures on the wall. I had never before seen real pictures, painted pictures as I could tell from the brushstrokes and the blobs of hardened oil. I felt respectful, like it was a church. I thought people kept paintings in strong boxes in the bank, along with their jewellery and their gold Kruger rands.

'Against the dark paintings and the dark wall the clock brought in some light. The clock face was gold, the hands were black. They stood at four. We were having the dusty tea and cake. There were the pictures, and the clock at four. Which meant that, if I was with the woman during the afternoon, I must have been in the hotel at lunch-time.

'I think I was in the hotel at lunch-time, I said to Bass.

'I paged you, Bass said, very firmly. I could see your career made before my eyes. I saw our plan shaping out – you a model, making a nice lot of money. I saw us settling on the island. I saw everyone, your mother and brothers and my mates coming over, joining in the fun. I thought we were in business, he said, but you were hiding.

'I was in the hotel, I said.

'The table was tilting from his leaning on it. Something must have gone wrong that day, something to do with his plans, because he wasn't himself.

'Then he stroked my hair roughly but gently like a father, like a real uncle. He was forgiving me. I led him away to sit on the beach. The sea was dark, the waves looked oily. Bass wandered up and down the water's edge, shouting and hitting out at the air, and gagging, and then coming back to sit down on the sand and drink from his hip-flask. He shared the flask with me. I didn't want to drink but I also wanted to keep the peace. Each time the flask touched my lips it tasted more strongly of bat stew.

'Close to dawn Bass fell asleep in the sand. I drowsed. I woke to see him staggering about at some distance down the beach. He was making machine-gun noises as though he was in a raid, acting in a war movie. The sky behind him was red, the seagulls were screaming. I looked away.

'When I awoke the second time it was bright morning. I was all alone. Then I heard Bass's voice. The darkness and anger in it had disappeared. He was singing Eight Days a Week. He circled around me and came up with the sea behind him. In one hand he held a pineapple. He told me to rise and shine. He stuck the umbrella in the sand. I could see he'd washed in the sea. There was salt in the hair on his arms and legs. Rough night, eh, Rosie? he said. He was going to leave it at that.

'But I wanted to say one thing. I screwed up my courage. I was eating pineapple and the acid was rubbing my mouth ulcers raw. I said, seeing as it was so early, it might be possible to catch that photographer. Maybe he was still on the island, we never knew. Bass stared at me. His eyes were dark because of his hangover and he was frowning. So I decided to drop it. I didn't want to see Bass frown.

'Bass lay out on the beach with me that whole day long. It was a treat. He was carefree, he was light-hearted, he told me things. He told me about the way he felt for Sandy. She did such sexy things to him, he said, such wild and sexy things. Had I seen the way her body moved, those little muscles in her inner thighs when she walked on the beach? Special women like that were rare, they could be counted on the fingers of one hand. Bass raised his left hand and began telling them off. It was like being given another story. I hadn't been spoiled like this in a while.

'There was this woman in a yellow clay house in Elisabethville, Central Africa, he said. She was fat, soft, greasy with the coco butter she smeared on herself. They would sometimes meet by night on the banks of a river where snowy lilies grew, some opening by day, others by night. And there was the woman he last embraced on a high red cliffside overlooking a huge dry plain in a rift valley. Over the crown of her small head, in the far distance, he could see a town with six minarets and a deep blue dome and a brown boundary wall. This woman often had a tearful expression, as though she were calling for consolation. It was especially so when they made love. And there was the woman in the Mombasa area, the one with the shells stuck to her flesh. Her he greatly loved, until she grew vengeful. In the state of passion she worked herself into a trance. Her eyes were rolled back, her limbs stiff like claws. She raked at her flesh with her nails, she tore at her lover's thighs. Yes, Rosie, Bass said, there's no getting round it. These are the queens of high-class love. You find very few such women around.'

'He was planning to seduce you with those stories of passion,' said Jem.

The danger of Bass was long past but his jealousy was imperious. This morning he would not have believed it, that he could be jealous

65

of her uncle. Even now. He wanted to speak like Bass and to have her follow his lips and grow dreamy at his words. He wanted to rivet her, as Bass did.

She was steadily drinking whisky.

'He didn't lay a hand on me,' she said. 'He cared for me in his own way. Almost like a father. Also like a hero, a soldier hero.'

She didn't seem to be aware of him and the heat did not trouble her. She had folded her arms and was looking out to sea. Bass's words still had the power to absorb her. She was absorbed telling a tale of addiction.

'That day was the last time I would hear Bass's stories,' Rosandra said. And sighed. 'From then on I would have to take over and tell Bass's stories myself.'

5

On Eden Island, Rosandra told Jem – moving right on, not pausing now – she was sleeping all day on beaches. It was this that explained why she wasn't sleeping at night. She picked herself up off the sand and went to bars to drink. Bass bought her cocktails made to look like rainbows. They tasted of ginger and orange and almond. Some days she ordered cocktails in bed and drank them as nightcaps. She lay in bed drinking, her face masked in Vaseline after the day's sunbathing, but she could not sleep.

She found she began to smell of her hotel room and her life in that room. No matter the perfume she might use she scented on her skin the hotel's brand of lemon toilet cleaner and old stained carpets, and something else, the stale, overcooked savour of a hungover body. This made her wonder, every so often, if she hadn't spent too long in the room. Which was another way of asking, she had to confess to herself, if life in the Eden Island Hotel wasn't growing stale. But she suppressed the thought: it was disloyal to Bass.

The mixture of insomnia and cocktails gave this unavoidable result, she found: short sleep. Most mornings, very early in the morning, sometimes just past midnight, she was waking up half drunk. She drank more cocktail to sleep again. The air-conditioning whirred, it gave an odour of petrol and aridity that along with the other smells began to cling to her skin. She settled back into the pillows. The ceiling was white. It was blank. It was fading. The last thing she would be aware of was her breathing, conspicuous, unconcerned, taking place somewhere above her sinking head. It was like lying on the beach, posing, sinking like this. But when the alcohol wore off she again slipped into wakefulness. Hours of the night had still to pass. The lights were burning. The half-empty cocktail glasses stood at eye-level, the rainbows separated out into muddy strata.

To escape her room, the smell, the view of the ceiling, she sometimes returned to the main hotel bar, the Coconut Grove, which was open all hours. She wore a pink cat-suit. Any time before four in the morning she could find Bass in the bar making friends. One night he was chatting to the island's only heart specialist, a retired British colonel from Kenya, very wrinkled in the face, another time he had just run into the chief of police. The prominent personalities of Eden formed a tight-knit drinking circle whose favourite night spot was the Coconut Grove. Bass got to know these men, as he had in Cradock, over their evening drinks, only here he did not have to go out to find them and to hear the gossip. The Coconut Grove with the credit card stickers on its gold bullet-shaped till and the exotic opening hours suited the island's élite. It offered UV light and fish-net décor. There were two mannequins dressed in hula skirts propped up against the cigarette machine.

One bad night, the end of a week of drunken naps in bed and on the beach, Bass introduced Rosandra to Port Philip's chief engineer. As she sat down Rosandra remembered she was still wearing her Vaseline mask. The Vaseline was clinging to her eyelids and she was having more trouble than usual seeing clearly. In the UV light the man made a dark purple patch heavily perfumed with Old Spice and also a woman's deodorant, sweet, cheap.

'Didn't you see us, cracklin' Rosie?' said Bass. 'We were flagging you down when you first stepped into the bar.'

'No,' said Rosandra, distracted. Because of sliding down into her chair, the cat-suit was lassoing her crotch.

'We were waving like semaphore men at an airport,' said Bass, smiling in a teasing way at the chief engineer. 'We had been talking about you, praising you of course. But you were picking up our signals. You came over.'

The engineer looked at Rosandra manoeuvring in her seat. She was trying to work herself into a more comfortable position. She turned her face to one side so that her hair flopped over her cheek, Sandy-style. She was tired, stale, it would be a chore to talk. She saw there were still several groups of drinkers around in the bar. Their shapes were doubled or skewed, the outlines watery, as though she were looking at them through wet glass. The barman had a face cleared of features.

'So,' Bass said, 'don't you want to know what a chief engineer on this island does with his time, Rosie?'

'Yes,' Rosandra politely asked. 'What does a chief engineer on Eden do with his time?'

The engineer, when her eyes met his, gave her a lingering, slightly reproachful look, as though some important matter had been resolved between them and she was slow in making a decisive move.

'Pierre was just explaining the Eden telephone system and waterworks to me,' said Bass. 'He's shown me where their water comes in, where it goes out, how far out the ships go to dump island waste. Fascinating stuff.'

Bass pointed to a diagram drawn in ballpoint on a cigarette box.

'Did you know there is only one pump system and one reservoir for the whole of Eden, that is, the main island?' he went on. 'I certainly didn't. I've learned a lot.'

'Yes, only one system,' said the engineer, drinking and looking at Rosandra the while. He weighed his words carefully. He was offering a buried meaning specially designed for her to decode. He placed his boot on her foot; she moved her foot away. She squinted at Bass's cigarette box. Bass was furrowing his pen up and down one of the main vertical lines in his diagram.

'Do you see, Rosie?' he said. 'The telephone and electrical cables and the main water pipes of the island all run down this main road. It's the artery of the island.'

With relief Rosandra saw a diluted dawn light the colour of watery tea seep under the curtains of the bar windows. It was morning. She could go to the beach, she could sleep, she could walk away.

'What do you mean by the main road?' she asked.

'The one in Port Philip,' said Bass. 'The road with the shops, where we got that pink thing you have on, where you bought your sunglasses the first day.'

He hadn't been there the day she bought the sunglasses, Rosandra remembered. She must have told him about it afterwards.

The engineer got up to go. He stood directly in front of her, his leg almost touching hers. Bass pocketed the cigarette box.

'Call me Peter,' the engineer said to Rosandra.

He picked her hand up from her lap. He kissed the side of it, the web of her thumb and forefinger, letting the heavy limb of his tongue rest for a moment in the hollow.

'I hope we'll meet again,' he said.

She slipped her hand under the table to rub the wet spot on her cat-suit and caught Bass's eye.

'That man is a good guy to be friends with, Rosie,' Bass said. 'He's clever, he's hospitable. He has offered to drive us round the island any time we like. He owns the island's only Alfa-Romeo. He likes you.'

'I need some stuff to sleep better, Uncle Bass,' said Rosandra, deciding to say it all at once, quickly, to explain being unsociable. 'You needn't worry. I'm very happy here, more than happy, but I don't sleep well.'

They were walking back to their rooms. Bass looked her up and down several times. He was standing right in front of her, closer than the engineer, their clothes in contact, first-time lovers balancing closeness and suspense.

'You shouldn't be worrying about anything, Rosie,' Bass said, dropping his voice. 'This waiting game will soon be over.'

He piloted her into his room and ordered room service. When the drowsy waiter refused to believe that sleeping tablets were on the menu, Bass paid him money. Out of a drawer he also produced some pills of his own, small and white like fluoride tablets.

'Take these for good measure, Rosie. They're great for guys who feel shaky the night before an operation. And now sleep, sleep as long as you can.'

Bass did not look like a man to take sleeping pills, but it wasn't the time for questions. It was past dawn. He kissed her on the forehead and again on the lips.

In her room Rosandra drank down four pills with the thick dregs of a chocolate cocktail. She fell asleep as the sun rose over the buildings opposite and crowded her room with light. She slept without interruption for twenty-four hours, waking with the sun at the same angle, throwing the same shadows and reflection patterns on the walls. It was as if she had been dozing for a few minutes only. There were voices in the passage, waiters bringing tea, cleaners, just as when she got into bed.

She also had the feeling of having had long dreams. She remembered little at first. There was a thin blue cloud, that was the main thing. She was lying on sand, as usual, except this sand was yellower, dryer, and the horizons all round were sand dunes, wavy lines, with wave patterns traced on them by the wind. Directly overhead was the thin stationary blue cloud. Sleeping but seeing clearly, her head on the sand, she lay still in the dream just as she lay here in bed. Details started coming back to her slowly. In the earth of the dream was a growing vibration. The air and the sand were full of sound, invisible and encircling. She heard the frenzy of planes, armoured vehicles, amplifying to a whine. It was as though she had started to dream Bass's stories. It was strange, unsettling. She felt she had slept too long.

To shake off the dream she went for a swim. But when she dived down the humming of motor launches in the water created the same effect, an encircling vibration. The horizons suddenly were alive with glitter and noise, a roaring shine.

She went for a walk to get away from the beach and came to the green avenue where she had last walked with Bass, talking about Africa. Now, at noon, the shadows under the trees were bright with moving sunspots. There was a man walking some distance ahead.

The vertical light was playing tricks with her imperfect eyes, for looking more closely she realised this was a second man who looked like Sneezer. Again he was tall and had high hips like her own. She had spoken to Sneezer that one night only but his shape was haunting her. The figure crossed the road and passed into the undergrowth. He was probably a hotel guest, she told herself. Many of the European tourists wore high-hipped slacks like this man's.

But she did not walk on. She did not want to meet the man coming out of the bushes. So she turned and then was again surprised. At the other end of the avenue were the retreating figures of Bass and the chief engineer. Both were smoking. She drew back into the shadows. Yet seeing the two men together should be as ordinary as meeting Sneezer would be uncanny. Over the last few days they must have become friends. Bass had a towel slung over his shoulders. The engineer carried rolls of paper under one arm, as engineers must. He gesticulated with his other arm. Bass followed him off the path into the trees. As they disappeared from view a truck passing down the road to the hotel carrying a load of Coca-Cola re-created the roar of the dream. The earth was shaking as though tanks were driving over it. In the dream the roar was all around, encircling, coming closer, over the horizons.

'Rosandra,' said Bass in pleased surprise. 'You're out and about already. How are you? How did you sleep?'

The engineer came up behind him out of the shrubbery beneath the trees. He stretched his lips into a smile, exuding Old Spice. Her dream was humming in her ears. She folded her arms across her ribs.

'Pierre was showing me some of the indigenous plant life on Eden,' said Bass. 'Out there under the trees. Lilies, beautiful creamy lilies, not yet in full bloom. There's a trade to be made out of them in the tourist market, Pierre thinks.'

There were no lilies in the undergrowth that Rosandra could see.

71

There was the roaring of motor-boats out on the water and a bi-plane overhead and trucks on the road. The world was uncomfortably loud, just as in her dream. She let Bass lead her by the hand towards the beach. The engineer walked on her other side.

A week after the meeting in the avenue Bass had to go back to the city on an unexpected trip. It was necessary, he said, to galvanise the rugby tour plan. He feared that his team was sitting on the job. He didn't like to leave Rosandra like this, but with that quiet watchfulness of hers he was sure she'd cope. Keep yourself to yourself, Rosie, he said, stay out of hassle by staying cool.

He waved goodbye to Rosandra from the hotel cocktail verandah. He was wearing a new sports jacket, big but not big enough for him. It lifted exuberantly at the shoulders as he flung both arms in the air. He had organised a big daily allowance for her which she left lying in a drawer up in the bedroom. To carry it round meant responsibility and she wanted to feel as easy and relaxed as before.

But to her vague surprise she found she didn't much miss Bass. The white pills dulled all loneliness and gave courage. She thought back to the morning she had sat lost and dispirited on her hotel bed. She no longer understood the witlessness of that other self, its dazed confusion. She felt older now, genuinely independent. She told a man in the Coconut Grove Bar she was an Australian fashion model visiting Eden for a fashion shoot, and he believed her. He bought her three drinks. She told him her boyfriend was a film director, that he owned an island. There was this expansive freedom in stories.

Every day Rosandra took Bass's white pills along with her regular menu of cocktails and drifted about in a half-wakefulness in which she was very languid, very carefree. Bass was kind enough to leave her with a full bottle of pills, making her promise to be cured and bright and restored when he returned. He assured her that after the tour they would try to sell her really big, maybe overseas. Rosandra's thought was that they had already come overseas to sell her. But, smiling at him, uncomplaining, indifferent, she offered no comment. She liked to listen to Bass's career plans as she did to his stories.

She wandered to fresh beaches, other hotel bars. Men approached her but she didn't like to talk too long. It was tiring. She told a corporate manager just out of London she was a beauty specialist from New Zealand. She said she lived on the beach in a house made of palm leaves. He asked to visit and take her out. She gave him a false hotel address. It was possible to wear identities like perfumes, which was a diverting game.

Some days she woke feeling a shade downcast, a little depressed, but it was nothing more she was sure than the mild side-effects of the kind white pills. On such days the skin on her face seemed slack and her eyes cloudy. In her hotel room the smell of carpet and stale alcohol grew heavier. Everything about the room had started to appear a little stale. The clothes on their hangers took on an angular, shrunken look as though they were discards, out of date. The make-up case gathered a scum of moist dust, its hinges were stiff in opening.

The pills had brought the dream of the desert and the noise, but then they also dissolved it. The dream did not come back. In fact the more pills she took the less she dreamed. Some days she woke up with a horrible roaring in her ears but that disappeared if she drowsed a little more, or had her first drink of the day.

Then one day, Rosandra told Jem, she woke with a different kind of noise in her ears, dimmer, lower, a susurration, but metallic, uneven. This time she found it did not disappear. She lay in bed listening. At first she thought the dream must have left a kind of imprint in her, or a scar, but it became clear that the noise was not in her head, not in her dream, but all around, beyond the room. There was an unpleasant taste of ripe liver sausage in her mouth, which was also odd. For supper she had had two ice-creams and two chocolate bars. The taste of the liver sausage was like blood, dried, oily blood. It could be the ulcers, but neither a drink of water nor a sip of yesterday afternoon's Mai Tai washed the taste out.

Despite the noise the corridors seemed quiet for the time of morning. The sun was high and there were flies mad with heat banging their bodies against the window-pane. She listened closely. The low noise was real and persistent, though far-off – probably heavy vehicles. She called room service. There was no reply. She went to the window but there was no one out.

Maybe she had been sleeping for more than half a day again, she thought, maybe something important and momentous had happened. Standing at the window, looking at the quiet hotel courtyard with the hibiscus in pots, she imagined an island-wide epidemic, some slow-working disaster to accompany the unvarying, insistent noise. She imagined an unstoppable tropical scourge, everyone dead or expiring in their rooms. Amidst the chaos she saw glasses of still water and bottles of something cooling, calamine lotion, standing on the bedside tables of the dying, and Bass rushing back to Eden white-faced with his maps and charts fluttering in one hand, come to rescue her. She thought of an earthquake, because of the noise, and imagined the beach and streets billowing, but if that was so the buildings would not be standing, which they were, solidly, straight up and down.

The hotel broadsheet slipped under the door explained things. It was printed on the usual canary-yellow paper. The tone was curt but upbeat in spite of the message. First it said that everyone should keep calm and go on enjoying themselves, though staying within hotel precincts. They should not forget the two hotel swimming pools, the pool tables, fruit machines, bowling alleys, Shape-In Studio and sauna, indoor putt-putt court and many facilities for kids. Then it said that since the early hours of yesterday evening a delicate security situation had developed at the airport. Government troops were dealing with the matter. The curfew – a blanket curfew, guests should note – would not last long. Telephone lines were open to Europe and America and guests were invited by management to telephone home to reassure family and friends. The limit, unfortunately, was two calls per guest.

After several attempts Rosandra got through to the hotel receptionist who began the conversation by saying she had nothing to say. Her voice was drowned out by a deafening buzzing. Rosandra went downstairs in her pink cat-suit. In the mirrors that lined the stairs she saw that Bass would have something to complain about when he returned. Her backside looked loose, not big but a bit slack, like the skin on her face.

In the foyer the only person in evidence was the receptionist who was still wearing yesterday's blue linen suit, very crumpled. The background noise was explained. Her radio was switched on, blaring out a crackle. The island's station blanked out around two in the morning but the receptionist said she wanted to catch the news the moment the radio came back on.

'I don't trust rumours,' she said gloomily. 'I want to hear the truth.'

'Does anyone know what has happened?' Rosandra asked.

The receptionist did not reply. She was new to the job, a travelling Australian, straw-blonde, with a mouth like a wince, no doubt one of the Southern Hemisphere beauties the man in the plane had praised.

Rosandra asked if she could have her two free telephone calls. She had to phone Cradock but she was thinking of Bass. She could imagine him worrying. He would be standing on a balcony in Pretoria, beer in hand, maybe listening to the radio and saying to his friends they must think about rescuing her. Rosandra marooned on Eden Island: in danger. If they didn't save her what would happen to their plans?

'The time for the free offer is over,' said the receptionist, very bad-tempered. 'It ended at noon.'

She added something about early birds and first come first served. The radio crackle deadened it.

The radio crackle also dulled the far-off hum coming from what must be the direction of the airport. Noise was pervasive in the hotel. Rosandra found a number of guests gathered in the Coconut Grove shouting opinions at each other above the sound of the barman's ghetto-blaster. In the unusual state of affairs he was taking the opportunity to test his machine.

Some of the guests had stayed in the bar since hearing the news last night. Their eyes were bleary with UV light and lack of sleep and most were drunk. The bar was littered with half-empty and untouched glasses of Mai Tai. One of the dolls decorating the jukebox had fallen down. Her skirt had flapped up over her face, showing her naked, pinched, doll's pubis.

The hotel management had announced that the entire day would count as a happy hour for Mai Tais, which had been elected Eden Drink of the Week. It was not clear who was doing the electing, but to Rosandra the choice was good. She'd developed a taste for Mai Tais. Up at the bar she found many men gathered and she was patted from various angles on her shoulders and hips. Rosandra thought for a moment she saw Peter, the chief engineer, beside her, but she was growing used to seeing illusions of familiar faces. The man was dark-haired but he was not Peter.

There were in fact no locals present in the bar today, none of Bass's friends in the island drinking group. The crowd was made up of the tanned, well-preserved, iron-haired men whom she usually saw in the covered bowling area by day. Their wives, in bed today resting, wore a fair amount of gold.

She had missed much excitement by sleeping. An old major in blue bedroom slippers who hadn't yet lost the pride of his barrel-chest described the various sound-effects he and his wife heard during the night. He stroked her hand as he did so, rubbing Mai Tai stickiness into her skin.

'It was definitely machine-gun fire,' he said. 'Da-da-da-da! Yes, it was definitely automatic fire. I wouldn't mistake that sort of sound. It came from two sources. It was very fierce at about three in the morning. You can't hear it now. They've got planes out there patrolling.'

'It must be some sort of riot,' said a younger and drunker neighbour.

He was straining to make himself heard over the sound of the barman's music.

'They must have called in the troops. They have these things all the time in banana republics. But I'll tell you something, it's a scandal to set up holiday resorts in these kind of places. Our holiday is wrecked. We're here for a week only.'

'I'll certainly be complaining when I get home,' said the major. He had repeated these words several times. 'The wife agrees with me. We'll definitely be complaining.'

He bent his head over his Mai Tai glass and concentrated on licking the gluey rim. The glass had seen several refills. His companion watched Rosandra lugubriously. The barman had turned up the volume for a favourite song, which made it impossible to go on speaking.

'*This is my Western promise, this means nothing to me,*' sobbed the song.

Rosandra was drawing a circle on an upturned cardboard beer mat. So that is what a banana republic is, she thought. A place where holidays go wrong. She dipped her finger into the patches of wetness on the bar surface and traced the outline of her Mai Tai glass. She drew a smiling face and then wavy lines, a smiling sun.

A long time passed during which songs burst over their heads with increasing loudness, and conversations infected by the volume grew angrier. Then someone announced that troops were on the march down the hotel beach and there was a rush for the doors. During the rush the old major's friend hit the barman in the face for refusing to let him use the hotel intercom to call his wife. The barman's nose leaked blood into a cocktail shaker.

At the height of the noise one of the resting wives came into the bar. She had real news. She walked round behind the bar and switched off the music. Her gold chains rose and fell on the olive-green angora swaddling her bosom. She said she had collared a cleaner who had been whispering to a waiter in the passage just outside her bedroom. They were clearly audible but were not speaking English. After payment of a few pieces of hard currency the cleaner began to translate. There had been mortar fire as well as machine-gun fire at the airport, he said. He seemed to know the terms, and made flashing signs with his hands like exploding bombs in video games. The woman made them now, imitating crudely, exaggerating the hand movements. The invading men were white; they were well-equipped; they had flash-bang grenades, shotguns. Someone died, the cleaner thought, maybe one of the government men; he wasn't sure.

The men gathered around the breathless woman and gave her something to drink for her pains. The barman, his nose blood drying, turned the music back on. He replayed a tape. '*This is my Western promise, this means nothing to me,*' the song sobbed all over again. One of the men leaning on the bar opposite opened his mouth and yelled along with the chorus. Though his throat heaved with the volume of the words his voice couldn't be heard above the music. Rosandra made her way over to the window, passing the blow-up doll on her way. With her heel she flicked the doll's hula skirt back in place, covering her nakedness. It made her look more dignified, reposeful.

Beyond the curtains' navy thickness the day looked just as it had from the bedroom: a pale sky, quiet, any sounds of distress disguised or muffled. The surface of the swimming pool a few paces from the bar windows was as smooth as cellophane.

To be involved in a coup is a kind of madness, Rosandra said, except you don't realise it at the time. People make friends who would normally avoid each other, thinking in this way to save their skins. Among the island population those who had no stake in the fighting chose either to flee or to loot. Guests at the hotels stayed put.

In the coup on Eden, Jem had read in the paper, the aggressors flew in by plane dressed as tourists and players of sport, togged up for a time in the sun. In their trouser pockets, along with their Ray-Ban sunglasses, were balaclava. As they crowded down the silver-sprayed steps pushed up against the plane five men began firing on the two security guards leaning on their rifles in the sun. Ten others, producing shotguns and M16A1 rifles out of hand luggage and bulky sports jackets, moved off in various choreographed directions, running low as though already under enemy fire. Eye-witnesses later remarked on their physical form and fitness. Some of the men wore white cotton shorts, very clean, very starched.

As if this were part of an exotic ceremony welcoming them to Eden, their fellow passengers continued for a while to fan out from the plane, walking contentedly, feeling the sun, incredulous of what they were hearing and so unsurprised. But when bullets began to ricochet off the tarmac suitcases and surfboards were dropped. There were screams, a scuffle. An air hostess kicked off her high-heels and fell flat on the ground, crying to others to follow. The doors of the plane stood open, unprotected and absurdly welcoming. The fifteen men reached the airport building. As they fired their way in, bullet-proof glass shattering, they were seen still to be wearing their tourist gear, psychedelic pink headbands, dayglo nose cream, rubber sandals.

Within hours the island population divided itself off from the outsider in its midst, who was the tourist, and the tourist was uncomplaining. The big international hotels were turned into enclaves of foreigners huddled together, which they had been before but no one then had stopped to notice. Picturesque bus trips into Port Philip were for the time being cancelled. The rustic eating houses along the beaches were declared temporarily out of bounds. Some local staff slept in the empty rooms at the hotels but the majority stayed away. Food stores stockpiled for emergencies such as these were opened and the carefully preserved delicacies of the Western world laid out each evening on vast buffet tables. Drinks went at cut-prices. At the Eden Island Hotel a competition was held to compose the most cosmopolitan cocktail possible. A rainbow drink, redolent of Parfait Amour and named the Internationale, won the prize. The Coconut Grove made record profits. From the point of view of the guests the hotel could have been anywhere – New York, the Algarve, the Bahamas. People drank together, and if they remembered occasionally panicked together. But concentrated companionably round the pool they were in general having a more sociable time than before. Surrounded by security guards fat with secreted arms, the hotel was a fort with an overcrowded disco at its heart, a circle of safety embracing as much fun as any guest might desire. Most people, anyway, didn't miss the local bat curry, and everyone agreed that Port Philip was a dump.

The emergency lasted four days. The management was prepared to turn the place if need be into a first-aid centre, if need be into a hospital. But things did not come to this pass. Only once, on the second day, the Eden Island Hotel gave direct assistance in the crisis. For a few hours it served as a morgue. The island had refused to house its single crisis casualty.

On the second day, Rosandra told Jem, a tropical storm emerged out of nowhere and turned the late morning into evening. Bass's bottle of pills was nudged off its glass ledge by the vibration of thunder and emptied itself into the washbasin. She was aware of an unusual vitality. It was the freshness of the air, the moisture, the rain in grey waves striking the windows. She tidied the room, spreading out her clothes, as if preparing for packing. Movement seemed right, the activity of getting things ready, the feeling of moving on. Beneath the noise of the rain the radio sounded dimly, its crackle hoarsened after the thirty-six-hour muttering. She was following the receptionist's example by keeping it on.

As the storm indicated the weather was turning damp. Almost overnight a rash of mildew had spread across her clothes, purple-blue like varicose veins, crusty, lichen-shaped. At a distance the clothes looked like maps, showing archipelagos, jagged coastline, inlets, islands. There had been many maps on this trip, Rosandra thought, Bass's maps, spread on beds.

Rain smashed against the window. The hotel could be a ship at sea, battered by waves. A gust of wind tore past, for a moment clearing the glass of running wetness. A wind-tossed shape flew by, a kick-board or a sun umbrella, the cardboard roof of a shanty. For all the guests in the hotel knew they could be in the middle of a storm at sea, entirely alone, miles of vicious empty water around them. Suddenly the radio's mutter slid into a fragrant and rousing melody. Mozart's Thirty-ninth, the announcer said, quietly, by-the-by, as though nothing could be more normal.

An hour later the radio was still playing. The bed was covered with small piles of clothes, high as suitcases are wide, arranged in like colours, as though this were a clothes shop. Rosandra felt she was getting more organised, really moving on. She thought about tidying Bass's room. She would have to collect his things if she left, if they had to evacuate.

But when she unlocked the door with the key borrowed from the housekeeper Rosandra found that Bass's room – it was surely Bass's room? – was completely empty. It felt unfriendly. The rain had made the air inside chilly and the bed looked impossibly flat and forbidding. She had been remiss in her duty to Bass, she thought. She had not made sure the management were keeping his room for him. He had said to leave things just as they were, the jackets on the hook, the aftershave on the bedside table, so that he could move straight back in on returning. But stepping inside she found the room thoroughly cleared. There was no sign of him anywhere, not even the husks of his presence, a cash slip under the side table, a toothpaste tube top. The room was simply empty. It felt cool and anonymous as though it had been like this for days, waiting for the next guest.

She went downstairs. If someone other than yesterday's receptionist were on duty she might be able to find out what had happened and set things right. She was glad she met no one on the way. She was feeling stupid and confused, as though some important change had happened, some loss or challenge which had passed her by. Bass would not be pleased when he returned. She was trying to be more sophisticated but she was not yet very quick. And he hated being disobeyed. His brow would darken, crease and seem to shrink, like the night at the restaurant out on the beach. Imagine him finding his things packed away somewhere, his orders ignored, his presence dislodged. The ghostly deserted room made her feel nervous, or more than nervous – cheated. It wasn't Bass's fault but the look of the room signified she was alone. That was the final point: Bass had left her.

The reception area was deserted and in near darkness because of the rain. There were no guests arriving, there were no departures, and the weather was keeping everyone else indoors. The island publicity brochures lay on the desk in two neat, high piles. Rosandra heard sounds in the direction of the bar and down the far passage where the fruit machines were. A curving blade of rain struck against the front entrance glass, and again. The hotel was being stormed from all sides. It was truly a ship in a stormy sea, a battered island. An island, Rosandra thought, is a tight space, especially in a crisis. Even in a crisis as invisible and controlled as the one now taking place. The crisis was somewhere at the airport, low-key and mysterious; a scrap maybe between rival parties, or the unrest Bass had described and predicted?

'I don't think you want to be waiting here,' said the Australian receptionist.

She came through the swinging doors which led to the bar. The doors went on beating and swishing behind her like paddles. Rosandra saw her hair was unbrushed. Her face looked moist, wrinkled by moisture, bare of make-up, as though she was just out of a bath.

'You don't want to be waiting here,' she said again, in the same neutral tone.

She pushed at Rosandra's upper arm. Her touching was close, intense. There was urgency in it. Her expression was different from yesterday, not indolent, not annoyed. The lip skin was filmy across her teeth. She was up very close, pushing. The crisis was near yet invisible; invisible yet affecting the way people behaved.

Rosandra heard thunder. If there was news of an invasion from the airport on the radio, or noise of gunfire or mortar attack, it would not be audible from this room. She thought of encroaching tanks, a circle of tanks just beyond the hotel grounds, mushing up the soft-sanded artificial beach. There would be men with sharp masked faces peering out of visor slits in the machines. There would be violent vibrations in the sand, as in her dream, and men in tanks looking out like rats.

The receptionist had Rosandra pushed almost to the door leading to the fruit machine area. They were far from the main desk. The desk gleamed darkly, newly polished. From here Rosandra could see the whole room, a long view down to the windows curtained on the outside with rain. Then she saw she had been mistaken earlier when she thought the place was deserted. There was something behind the main desk, a shape lying on a stretcher. The receptionist saw her stare and let go of her arm. There was no point in protecting her any longer. Her tone was off-hand, as though it was a bore to speak the obvious.

'It's one of them. The rebels,' she said. 'He just arrived. The government doesn't want him – they've had their business with him. He's on his way home now. His home is where a lot of our guests come from. Management said they would take him, discreetly, at least until order is restored.

'You shouldn't have seen this,' she added.

It did not look right. It was not the presence of the stretcher, despite the body on it. It was the solidity of the form, Rosandra thought, visible and real in the midst of a crisis that was invisible, that no one knew anything about. The man looked squat under the sheet covering him, quite ordinary. Two short feet in rugby boots and khaki socks stuck out from under the sheet. His head was visible at the other end. He must be wounded.

The receptionist was watching Rosandra stare.

'Don't worry,' she said, still off-hand, matter-of-fact. 'He's dead. He won't do any harm.'

She gave Rosandra a last ceremonial push and left. The swinging doors swished. A cleaner came softly down the stairs, her feet in large sneakers. The sneakers had American flag badges on the lace flaps. She wore a head-cloth patterned with bright yellow and orange speckled bananas. She seemed to know about the body. Her eyes passed smoothly over it, and over Rosandra. Looking out at the rain she clicked her tongue against her cheek. She began dusting the picture frames.

Because of the dim light, because of staring too long, Rosandra was no longer seeing the stretcher very clearly. The piles of pamphlets stood straight as before, but looked on the point of toppling. She peered around her. The cleaner was on her second picture. Despite the soft dusting sounds she was making the room felt cavernous, darker. Rosandra was awkward. She was in the presence of death. Though it was still the body seemed alive, lying there behind the desk. She went up closer. A person should do something, some little thing. It must be the bare face of the man that was making her feel especially ill at ease. A dead man should have the privacy of a cover so no one could ogle at him. She was ogling, even if myopically. How does a dead man look? He would have, maybe, milky blue eyes, a fresh wound, darkening, his mouth open with a final cry, a word.

'I'll cover him,' she said to the cleaner in explanation of her movements, but at the same time she turned away from the body.

What she said was a kind of request. The cleaner's hands were capable, brown and capable. She belonged to the island; she knew what to do. But the cleaner cast a tongue click over her shoulder.

Rosandra thought about lifting the sheet. She could let it fall over the face. The features would come through the sheet. Too close. She felt the edge of the reception desk butt her ribs. She looked into the dark trough behind the desk. There was the face of the man. It was not too bad. The eyes were closed, the mouth squashed but intact. He looked a little ill, greenish but not ghastly. He was simply an ordinary face, not dead-white, corpse-like, not monstrous. His face looked too commonplace and familiar to look ghastly. On Eden men's faces kept looking familiar.

Looking at him she remembered sitting in a car in a Soweto dawn and Bass laughing and the smell of prawn cocktail and vinaigrette. Across the bonnet and windscreen in front of her lay one of Bass's friends: this friend. The same face. Bass and his friends were playing a game, a mock-up game, she couldn't remember what.

The cleaner came up from behind Rosandra. The feather duster brushed her bare arm. The feathers felt sleek, cool, surprisingly cool. The cleaner briskly took a crumpled corner of the covering sheet and let it drop over the face of Bass's friend. She was staring at Rosandra, strangely defiant. The features of the man did not show through the blue cloth yet Rosandra seemed still to see his face. The eyes were smudges, dark holes staring up at her. The face was a mass of dark blue shadows, its features were stains.

Three days later the crisis was over, but as the beaches on either side of the hotel had been washed away in the storm swimming in the bay was still forbidden. The airport was open again, two international flights arrived that morning, both almost empty. The government continued to confiscate foreign newspapers. Opinion was that the invasion was embarrassing in some way. The government were caught off-guard; they had been complacently hauling in tourist riches and giving no thought to island defence.

In the Coconut Grove a waiter offered more detailed news of what had happened. He sat surrounded by a row of untouched Internationale cocktails bought for him by curious guests. He'd heard, believe it or not, that the rebels hijacked a plane. Once they saw things were going badly they caught a ride back home on a plane that arrived at the airport about the same time as their own flight. They were crooks, but they had courage, courage and cheek. They left the one man behind, the one who died. A disgrace, said the old major, a bloody disgrace, but his reproof had lost its edge. It was not clear whom he was chiding.

Paralysed by much alcohol and regretful that all the excitement as well as their excuse for drinking had now evaporated, the bar inmates had taken to telling and retelling each other the same stories of the coup disgrace. Rosandra sat apart with her glasses of Mai Tai not knowing what to think. Should she feel abandoned? Or else delivered and saved from this small disaster of Bass's making? And, more, after this event, did she miss him or not? At no point had she been in direct danger, and yet he'd left her alone, without a word, without help.

She remained the only woman in the bar, the wives of the drinkers still seemed to be resting. Men sometimes bought her drinks but mostly they left her to her silence, the new quietness of things, these empty hours flavoured with cocktails and cigarette smoke. She tried not to think about the coup. She no longer had dreams. She was waiting to decide, something, what to do, when, but choices were hard where opportunities had shut down. Because now there'd be no Europe, no success on Eden, no London Paris New York, or glamour, and Bass looking proud.

She decided to visit the old woman in the pink house, to see how she had weathered the four days. But she was not at home. She had left for a family retreat in the hills as soon as the crisis broke, the maid said, looking glum and hostile at having been left behind. She made tea and brought out an uncut cake. It was smooth, round, white; it could be the same cake as the time before.

The maid did not ask her to sit down so Rosandra walked round a little, killing time. She looked at the pond-green pictures. They were even muddier than before. The gold-faced clock on the wall again said four o'clock, which it was, or just about. But the clock did not tick, the hands were stuck at four. She wondered. Maybe Bass didn't lie that day. Maybe she wasn't in the hotel that day when he needed her, as he'd said, perhaps he had looked for her after all to announce the career break he'd discovered, the wonderful photo opportunity.

Under the silent clock an old dark brown telephone stood on a three-legged table. She lightly touched the frail bakelite. There was only one person she thought of calling but he would be busy trying to get rid of a hijacked plane. The waiter was right. Bass had a sort of courage and style; he liked to look like a hero. It had been a big gamble, two gambles, the coup and the hijack, and both took guts and strategy. Bass tried to secure his bets and made sure of things; however, luck was not on his side. He had found friends on the island, he had paid waiters handsomely. He spoke to cocktail crowds of people on the telephone. Maybe he expected less government resistance. He also knew the hotel management: they said they would keep his room for him. Did they tidy it when they realised he would not be coming back?

The maid opened a door and let in warm sunlight. She was being asked to leave. But the simple gesture was also telling her something else. As Rosandra stepped outside she saw it clearly. That she must make a clean break, must leave the island too. There was nothing more for her to do here; no one to see; no chance of a career. She wondered if Bass would try to get in touch. She thought not; she hoped not. It would endanger her chances of slipping away: he would think of that. He thought of strategy. If she left quickly no one would notice her passing. On the beach in the big enveloping sarong she looked like everyone else. She blended. People didn't remember her as Bass's friend. They wouldn't miss her at all. She no longer had companions, no one to keep watch on her, and she had plenty of pocket money for travel.

But there was one thing she couldn't forgive Bass. That he hadn't called from the airport. He had courage and style. Couldn't he have smashed into a call-box with his flash-bang grenades? She imagined the litter of broken glass and toppled luggage trolleys scattered around him. His voice would have been loud amidst the surrounding noise. He would have been banging the machine to make the coins scuttle through. He would have held his rifle aloft in readiness. Thank you, Rosie, for being my cover: that's the first thing he would have said.

'Most stories are made to be told again,' Rosandra said, 'but some, don't you think, can be spoiled by being repeated?'

She looked into their various cups and glasses. All were empty. Neither she nor Jem made a move to order anything more.

'A story can feel wrong,' Rosandra said. 'There might be a bad teller.

Or the person listening is in a bad mood. Maybe he expects too much from the story. It's not exciting enough. You don't have to tell a story many times to have it go flat. Look at what I've just been telling you. We spent all these hours and I didn't even manage to give you Bass's kind of story. Bass's stories have real first-hand excitement. You listen to every word. You know who's going to win, who the hero is. There's a proper conflict, with real danger, explosions. I could listen to one of Bass's stories today.'

The palm tree beside the table was a uniform brown, a dull evening colour that blended with the muddy haze gathering in the sky along the horizon. Seagulls were coming into shore. Jem wanted to hold Rosandra's body against his chest. He imagined his arms encircling her. She was a woman like no other. She brought the flavour of adventure, but remained outside it, untainted. He breathed deeply, yearning and relieved. She had just apologised for her story. She was embarrassed about the time with Bass: that was her sense of being compromised. She wanted to forget about it; she was aware she had been used. His worries did her no justice. Maintaining her posture, her grace, she unburdened herself of the past with Bass. Thony's tale would follow, tomorrow, next week, whenever they could meet again. But for now she was clean, and he was in her trust. He wanted to invite her home. He thought about extending his arms. Then she moved.

'I want to leave,' Rosandra said, rubbing the goose-pimples on her smooth, hairless arms. 'It's been a long day. Going over things like this in the heat can be quite tiring.'

Jem stood up as she did, watching her.

'I want to go to my hotel and have a bath,' she said. 'I have a long week ahead. We're in the studio for a few days, then out on the beach. For today I've had too much sun.'

From appearances that was difficult to tell. Her shoulders were white as alabaster.

TWO

Arms Trade

. . . illegal shipments to South Africa included equipment which could be used to develop a missile capable of carrying nuclear warheads. The technology shipped to South Africa included photo imaging equipment used to determine the performance of missile tests, telemetry tracking equipment which receives signals from missiles and gyroscopes used for the inertial navigation (or guidance) systems of missiles.

Financial Times (1990)

1

Jem looked down over the deodar trees at the end of his yard. With the last of the day's heat draining from the air the evening sky was still and clear. The change brought out the dark sweetness of the flowering bushes which lined the short drive leading down to the road. The white and mauve flowers on the bushes shone out against the dark, waxy leaves. Moths, white flowers moving, danced among them.

At unexpected moments during the past week the memories of their day together, of what she said, of her face, her shape, had come to him like flashes of vision: Rosandra, her neck quivering with pulsations, her hair floating, the light of the sun in her glasses. Gazing, he had no words. It was a vision of truth. Even now he trembled with emotion. The glare, he saw again, stained her freckles darker. Beneath the sheath of skin he traced her own pure shape, the simple white shape as he knew it from the time of the garden, staring at her.

She was imprinted on his memory. The thought satisfied him. He imagined her hair spread out by the breeze. He wanted to look into her eyes, look deeply like a lover – see her eyes not as they were last week, though they were beautiful then, but clearer, brilliant, transfixing, as he was used to seeing them in the photograph on his wall. Tonight, he hoped, her eyes would be uncovered. At night she would not be wearing sunglasses. Tonight they had a date to meet and talk again.

His bungalow stood on the edge of a high ridge overlooking the city centre and there was no better place on a summer's evening than his stoep to catch the first coolness blowing in off the sea. Most evenings after supper he sat here, thinking a little, gazing out. He could see ships lined up along the horizon, waiting to be docked. Hidden behind the trees, to the left, disguised, were the tall buildings on the esplanade, among them Rosandra's hotel.

Jem fetched a beer from the kitchen. His shoes crushed the little bee carcasses littered across the stoep, the yellow pollen sacs protruding. A day's heavy surfeit of frangipani had killed them.

This time last year there would have been two of them, him and Gary his college friend, sitting out here like old boers on the stoep. They were at the time the recent co-owners of this snug bungalow. Then they were joined for a while by Heather: Heather cutting out recipes, painting murals for the kindergarten where she worked. The three of them spent long evenings outside, drinking beer, saying thank God for the peaceful view. People on the other side of the ridge, who looked inland, entertained themselves these days with the spectacle of township brigands and warlords sweeping across the valleys and wiping each other out. People said things looked depressing that side of the ridge. This sea-facing side was different, easier on the eye.

Not that anyone wanted to pretend harsh realities didn't exist, least of all Jem. He saw himself as a realist and worried about the state of the nation, the violence. But the smooth dark flood of the night coming over the Indian Ocean washed against this ridge and it was a quiet special sight. He tried to enjoy it and not to worry, at least for a few hours of the day. These days however he watched alone. Heather had gone; Gary married a few months ago. He'd needed to set up his own home so Jem bought him out of the joint ownership. Nowadays Jem drank an extra beer on Gary's behalf and watched the sky in silence.

Some days, trying not to worry about politics, he wondered about marriage. The short, unsatisfactory thing with Heather wasn't what got him thinking. Rather it was a question of timing, the fact that the present moment seemed about right. It made sense that a man who had a house should find a wife. His job was stable: teaching geography he could bet on the fact that the earth changes but endures and people do not lose interest in it even when a country is falling apart. The problem was that, apart from Heather, he didn't have much experience of girlfriends, or more generally of knowing women. When he thought of women he thought of Rosandra. During his time in the army there was a photo of her stuck to the iron *kas* beside his bed. She could be his chick his flame his wife. He let the other guys believe their own speculations.

In England a year later, Jem remembered, half ashamed, in the squat in London where he lived for a time, he came out and said it. Yes, that's my girlfriend. Yes, she is great cool horny. He lived with other travellers; he was travelling, or made believe he was travelling. He hoped his lie wouldn't reach the ears of people at home. But he grew worried as she became more famous. That was the time she was with Thony, learning about oysters and taking business-class flights to Europe, the same time that he was poor and guilty in London, subsisting in a squat. He'd come to Europe to think about things and take in some urban geography after training college but he travelled no further than London and thought about things hardly at all. On his first day in the city he went down to see the Thames, which was a mud-flat, greasy and littered with discard.

He came back home to start teaching, Rosandra on his mind. Heather once asked him if he knew that local celebrity, someone called Rosandra White, well she grew up in Cradock just like him. Jem couldn't help blushing. Now, especially after seeing her, it seemed impossible, preposterous, that he once showed the picture, said, my girlfriend, Rosandra.

Rosandra said, 'So it's already time for the second story. The week has flown by, hasn't it? The hours pass quickly in my kind of work. I lose myself in the situation, I forget where I am. I like the feeling. But I haven't forgotten my promise. This is the story you probably haven't heard much about, aside what the papers said.'

He tried not to look too eager but he felt vulpine. He wanted to believe well of her and he wanted to love her. He would hear anything she had to say.

She added, 'Fair's fair, Jem. Some time soon you'll also have to tell me bits about what you've been doing these last few years.'

The restaurant had oyster-pink trim, and bamboo growing in Zulu-look earthenware pots. The windows to the street were dark glass, the ventilation was bad. There was a smell of burnt oil. Outside in the narrow street there were delivery entrances and dustbins in rows, the back ends of the beach hotels.

'This is the city's latest Chinese restaurant,' said Jem. 'They say the food is authentic.'

Gary had reported this on the telephone last week. Gary also told Jem to book ahead to avoid disappointment. Jem did. Tonight had to be perfect, a proper date. He changed his shirt three times before going out. He did not put on aftershave because he possessed only Old Spice, the brand used by Rosandra's chief engineer. He used mouthwash. The mint cleared his throat.

He watched the way Rosandra sat down. He caught a glimpse of it last time: he made sure of it now. The slow bend of her hips. With her left hand she lifted and loosened her oyster-pink napkin from its tight fan fold. She flowed down into the chair seat.

'When we were in Europe the last time Thony told me they were opening Japanese restaurants all over the continent,' Rosandra said.

And this is only a Chinese restaurant, Jem thought.

'In France there were also African restaurants. Imagine an African restaurant in this city. In Africa. It would feel out of place somehow. I'd feel out of place, I think.'

She was making small talk, she wasn't criticising his choice of restaurant, he told himself.

They ordered the menu for two but Rosandra ate only the pork. Jem watched her sucking the sweet and sour sauce off the separate chunks, swallowing tenderly, exquisitely. Even the few days away from her had blurred the beauty of her throat. He watched the bulge of the swallowing sliding under the constant pulse in her skin.

Jem likes me, Rosandra thought. All these years and he still wants to be my friend. Back in Cradock we didn't even know each other that well. We were children, we didn't play together. He stared a lot, still does. But his interest is kind, so I don't mind. There are good people in the world.

She stopped eating after her second vodka martini. There were sounds of wetting and crushing. Jem was making them. He was systematically cleaning up the food and scraping the stainless steel dishes. Because he was nervous. He thought it would be better, after last week. He'd heard some of her news. She'd told him about a bad time and none of it was too hurtful or shocking. So what was frightening? That the worst lay ahead? She might have been more closely involved in the dark things that were said of Thony. She might after all be a consenting party, an active agent, self-willed. And Thony was an unknown quantity. When she said his name there was the hint of a sibilant in it, showing familiarity, a whisper, like the way it was spelt in the papers. The name was short for Anthony, of course, a stupid pseud spelling.

Jem's swallowing was loud. It was this nervousness, this need to hear: he must hear. The more she said the more he wanted to know. He had to know the depths, the very depths. Else how could he love her? Without full knowledge, could he adore her? She sat at ease, her chopsticks were untouched. Last night he trained himself to use chopsticks. He practised for hours with a soup bowl in case his clumsiness would offend her, who had been dined in Europe. But her eyes were noncommittal about the restaurant, the food. She was looking thoughtfully over his right shoulder.

It's all about taking things as they come, Rosandra thought, this unexpected discovery of Jem's friendship. It shows it works, moving with experience. Good things can happen. It doesn't always work out of course, taking things as they come, you can't bet on it, I know. But there's always the chance of a positive turn, like now. It gives a boost. Especially after a hard week's filming. It shows how to be open to luck.

'You mustn't expect too much from these things I tell you, Jem,' said Rosandra. 'It's just things I've done. Most of it's over and finished with.'

'I find it interesting,' said Jem.

The first night with Thony, she thought, I'll tell him about that. The car was going too quickly to think of consequences or destinations. Artificial stars wheeled in a purple sky.

The second vodka martini struck like a scalpel through the pork packed under her ribs. It cleaned her. She straightened up. She felt she was rising, elongated, a thin vertical fountain, a rising spirit. In his gardens Thony had fountains. Peacocks with tails like fountains wailed in his walled city.

'Back in the city, back from Eden,' Rosandra said, 'I found a furnished bachelor flat. It was my first time living alone, standing on my own feet. I was proud of myself. The last weeks on Eden had been a good preparation, learning independence.

'The building was in the city's flatland, close to where I once met the woman, the one who showed me the way home. There was a butcher shop below. In the back yard of the shop they used axes to hack up carcasses. In the front the meat was displayed on tables in piles. The blue tinge of the cellophane packing turned the meat a bright red colour. The butcher supplied me with mini-steaks and also bacon for breakfast.'

'Your mother and other people in Cradock worried when the news about Bass broke,' said Jem. 'Everybody was talking about it. It was a scandal. It sounded dangerous. We wondered what had happened to you. We thought you might be caught up in it in some way.'

He wanted to say, none more than I. Foolish Susan White was willing to believe that Bass was innocent. He wasn't a mastermind, she said, even though the papers named him. His fun-loving made him guiltless. Bass would have saved Rosandra in time, Susan was sure. He was a hero and a soldier, he kept his promises, and he knew Rosandra was a good girl.

'The first week in my new flat my mother came to spend time with me,' said Rosandra. 'It was Ascension weekend, a long weekend. My brother David paid her train fare. He was earning his own money in the menswear shop in Cradock by then.'

As if he didn't know, Jem thought. During all these years he'd visited the Whites, he chatted. His father never changed his mind about Susan White, but Jem was loyal. The family valued his advice – he had been overseas, he was a teacher.

When the town heard about the rumpus on Eden, Jem told Susan that to safeguard her immunity they should not ask around for Rosandra, not call the news service in the city. They judged from the reports in the papers she wasn't involved or in direct trouble. Then, a few days after Bass and the others were taken into custody, Rosandra called her family from the city airport. She was home and dry, free of any danger. Susan told her not to come home to Cradock. It was important not to break the momentum of her career. The scandal was an inconvenience but Rosandra could still make it as a model. Susan wanted her to know that her own belief held firm.

During the Ascension weekend Rosandra gave Susan her pink cat-suit and the orange sheath dress.

'Mutton dressed as lamb?' Susan asked.

She was standing in front of the mirror in Rosandra's flat, wearing the orange dress.

Rosandra was manicuring at the window-sill. At the butcher shop below a dog licked a bloody puddle.

'You look lovely,' she said. 'Orange suits you. From behind you look eighteen.'

Together they went shopping. Susan liked the indulgence, the city thrill. She gazed at her daughter in amazement and mild envy. The danger Rosandra survived so nonchalantly, so fortunately, was glamorous. Trust Bass to come up with a spectacle, glamour, danger, dare and hard play rolled into the same experience. It was a scandal but it was flashy. As Susan gazed fascinated Rosandra said over and over again that she'd had a fantastic time.

'I told my mother I had a ball on Eden because she liked to hear it,' said Rosandra. 'But the fact of the matter is that I had nothing to say sorry for. Bass spoiled me silly, as he promised. At the same time, unfortunately for some, he also concocted a mad plan. He wanted to play rugby or soldiers, it wasn't clear. Luckily I wasn't part of it. Staying behind on Eden as a tourist, cluelessly, I could slip into safety. Bass protected me with my own innocence. He left me a fat portfolio of passable photographs, and an allowance too.'

'Each week Bass gave me pocket money even though all expenses at the hotel were paid,' Rosandra told Susan.

Susan smiled, and continued to smile and to listen to the stories of Rosandra's good fortune. The girl deserved it: her personality was sweet, she did no harm. But the news had come of Bass's trial and conviction along with the rest of his rugby team. Susan wondered if the lawyers would find things out, about his friendship with a beautiful model for example. If Rosandra was named her career would be severely damaged. Was she safe?

'Bass has been all over the papers,' said Susan. 'They talk about him in Cradock. Maybe someone some time will mention that you knew him.'

'Don't read the papers,' said Rosandra. 'Don't worry about what people say.'

Rosandra generally acted as though Cradock was a place where she no longer belonged.

'I used to buy the Sunday papers when you were first on Eden,' said Susan on another occasion, 'to see when they'd feature you.'

After the coup scandal broke Susan and Jem scanned the newspaper pictures, half loath, half eager to find mention of Rosandra. The paper was spread on the jasmine hedge between their gardens with the sharp twigs pricking through the pages. There were images of aeroplanes on runways and airport buildings and a picture of Bass, always more or less the same one. He looked washed out and medium grey and was squinting confidently at the camera in bright sunlight as though assessing a tricky try. There was a picture of the dead man, spread-eagled, lying on the tiled floor of the air terminal, looking as though he had dived for a ball and missed. Jem cut out the photographs.

'I think Bass tried to call us once in Cradock, a few days after the thing happened,' said Susan. Her voice was sly. 'I put down the phone.'

It sounded like she regretted it.

'I won't be getting a phone,' said Rosandra.

'And if Bass calls us again? After gaol? What then?' asked Susan. 'You never know, he might want to start things up again. He still might want to do something for you. Maybe he owes us something after this mess.'

'If he calls you,' said Rosandra, 'put down the phone. Or tell him I'm filming in New York.'

Being on Eden taught her something, she thought. She could mention New York as though she knew the place.

'Don't you need a phone to get jobs?' said Susan. 'Especially in modelling?'

'I phone them from the butchery,' Rosandra said. 'I've made friends with them down there.'

Susan left for Cradock wearing the orange dress. The colour brought out her liver spots. Rosandra gave her some high chisel-toed mules to improve her leg-line, especially at the back. To her brothers Rosandra sent love, and a Lacoste shirt each. She promised to write to Jem. Susan said he had become a serious, dependable young man. He was a college student now. He was always asking for news. Susan, kissing her daughter, also promised to write. Neither meant what they said, it was a way of saying goodbye. Susan ran her hands over Rosandra's cheeks, fingered her hair and told her she could still go far. This was only a little hitch. Nothing could hold her back if she didn't let it. Rosandra nodded, wanting to believe her. She sent the portfolio of Bass's pictures to various well-known model agencies in the city.

'On Eden after Bass left I thought hardly anyone recognised me,' Rosandra said. 'But in the city I really blended into the crowd. There are a lot of blondes in the city. Even the model agencies didn't single me out.

'I found a job helping in a fast-food place, not of course the one where I drank Southern Comfort. I learned to find my way around flatland, which turned out to be quite easy. I also worked as a baby-sitter. I put up notices in the hotels in that area to get in touch with tourists and guests who wanted to go out at night. I was put on the books of three hotels as a service. I had money left over at the end of the month. I had clothes, courtesy of Bass, and make-up. I was very free and independent. Sometimes I went out alone. I took taxis because ordering them made me feel even freer and more independent. I found a disco venue attended by a lot of women, where the men, the few that there were, generally stuck to the bar. I wasn't much at the bar myself. I think it was after the coup that I stopped drinking. Because of that I lost weight.

'The disco was held in an old residential hotel. It had a mirror ball and huge old speakers like black fridges. The clientele was mostly the mothers and daughters of Portuguese and Greek immigrants in that area. The floor was polished like a mirror. The mothers told their daughters not to dance wide-legged, in case their panties showed. Especially if they wore stilettos the daughters often slipped on the polish, screaming, and were saved by the men standing round. The men had loud ties and hot eyes. Then the mothers would come hurrying to guide the girls back to their seats.

'Sometimes after the music ended at eleven I made conversation with the women. I told them things I thought they'd find interesting. I said that I travelled with a circus troupe around the Indian Ocean. I'd also been a beauty queen in an island kingdom. They half believed me and I liked that. They brought me baklava. One of the girls and I made dates to go window-shopping on Sunday afternoons. Her name was Netta. We made a few of these dates. She said she had a man she was seeing on the sly but I never met him. She asked me if I had a boyfriend. I said yes, he was on business in Zaire. She carried cheap chewy toffee bars and five different kinds of mascara in her handbag. No one else bothered me with questions. I was so free. For a while no one bothered me at all. No agency phoned the butcher to invite me for a test. They must have looked at the strange photographs of my skin covered with shells and brushed them to one side.'

'You mean to say that men suddenly stopped noticing you?' said Jem.

'I don't know,' said Rosandra. 'By and large I didn't notice them. I felt anonymous.'

'But then one day you gave way,' said Jem, straight out, hard. 'When Thony came along.'

'I gave way?' said Rosandra slowly, as though thinking about the meaning of the words. 'No, not really.'

She bent her cheek delicately towards the table surface, feeling for her bag on the floor. Jem stared at the pattern of greasy scrapings in the stainless steel plates. A calculus of curves. The main meal was over, he thought. They could leave at this point. He needn't hear the rest of it. He could spare himself the torture. He could, but he was also unable.

She surfaced holding a large coffin-shaped powder compact.

'Not "gave way",' she repeated.

Her tone was purified of emphasis.

She looked at herself in the compact mirror. She bared her teeth, checking for blemishes, food rind. Under the low strip-lighting she saw she was ugly. Her face was a rash of freckles. She turned the mirror from Jem's view.

97

'OK,' said Jem. 'You didn't give way.'

But she had grown decisive. The compact snapped. She hit the table with it several times, like a hammer. At a neighbouring table a man muttered viciously in a woman's ear. A pile of stainless steel plates was dropped in the kitchen. The clattering went on and on.

'No,' she said, 'I didn't give way. I felt in charge of things. Thony represented a chance, a new opportunity. He asked me to be part of his show. And I still wanted to model. Bass gave me a taste for that kind of thing. So I chose Thony. I stepped into his show by choice.'

She sat in her characteristic still pose, her eyes unflinching in their expressionlessness. She drank a mouthful of her vodka martini slowly and without interest.

She does not savour, does not declare herself, Jem thought. My daughter doesn't strip, said Susan White when the pictures of the pink crotch hit the streets of Cradock. She hasn't told me anything about such goings-on, Susan averred.

He ordered coffee for himself, a big coffee. Now that the moment was on them nervousness came in sharp bursts and closed his throat. He wanted to know everything but there would be consequences. For him, jealousy, regret; for her, maybe, shame. She had given herself, say, on the very first night of the meeting, in the car, in a swimming pool, or, no, somewhere more sophisticated, more pseud, on an open roof, or a balcony, under the stars, exotic plants in pots standing round, a place much more exotic than Bass could have imagined possible as a background for love. Jem's chair felt hard and uncomfortable. It was suddenly cold. The piped Hong Kong pop music was monotonous, oppressive. Thony ate oysters raw, ripping the beards off them. He tipped them into Rosandra's mouth, letting them slip quivering, alive, from their shells. Oysters were an obvious symbol of desire. It said nothing for Thony's approach.

The first night with Thony, Rosandra remembered, she slept mainly alone in a strange bed, slept till noon in a place where everything was unfamiliar and looked man-made and stars revolved in a purple sky. They drove for three hours. The place had a name with a ring to it, like Las Vegas or LA. This was one better than Bass, she thought. This was a new kind of freedom, a rush into the future. Being in Eden gave this confidence. She put herself in the way of luck.

It was a Tuesday, she explained to Jem, late at night after baby-sitting. It was in a pizza joint. In front of her were two hamburgers. It was one of those pizza places that cater to ordinary tastes. The neon light overhead had a pinkish tinge, it seemed to strip things. The eyes of the anorexic woman wiping tables looked aghast. The burgers, especially the pickle, had a plastic sheen.

She was thinking about lights, about buying standard lamps for her flat, about putting in a shower fitting. Bass once said there was nothing like a shower. A shower gets the skin tingling like a man in need of love. But this was not the right time to be thinking about showers. Drought warnings were being distributed to each flat in her block. It had not rained in the city since her return from Eden.

She finished the first hamburger. She lifted the second so that the woman could wipe the table. The music in the place was distracted. The loudspeaker above her head was playing a different radio station from a transistor tucked somewhere behind the till.

The man said, 'Can I join you?'

He had been watching her from outside, she had spotted him, his face a smudge behind the glass. He came towards her purposefully, as though she had beckoned. He pulled at the chair opposite, forgetting that it was one of those chairs that come with fast-food joints, screwed to the ground. On his left hand he wore three gold rings. She put her second hamburger four-square on the table. The bulk of the first hamburger felt reassuring inside her.

'Looking at you from out there,' the man said, 'I wanted to tell you how beautiful you are. You have the most beautiful hair I have ever seen.'

'I use a camomile rinse,' said Rosandra, after a pause.

It was the first thing she thought of to say.

He ignored her. He stood behind the chair opposite, holding on to its back. His hair and nose shone under the neon. He spoke as though from a podium, full of the confidence of his feelings.

'I want to take you away with me,' the man said. 'Please let me tell you this. I have been looking for a woman like you for years. I want you to come with me and share everything I own. I want you to be part of my life. This is my approach and I mean no harm. Please let me speak. I must tell you this. You are beautiful, a perfect beauty.'

'Sorry?' Rosandra said.

She took a bite of her second hamburger. It was cold. Inert moist bread, very floppy. Would Bass come up to a woman like this? If he did he would bring champagne.

The man pulled a gold chain from under his cuff. His tie was pale gold. The tie pin was marked with a 'T'. He dragged the chain off his arm and put it on the table where it made a dull rattle against the formica. She looked at the chain. The central link, no bigger than the rest, was formed differently, in the shape of a 'T'. She felt the edge of her seat against her thighs.

'Please take this,' he said. 'It is a gift.'

His stare was unblinking, his nose spade-shaped, sweating.

'It's a token.' He pushed the chain further towards her. 'It will mean everything to me if you take it. I want you to share my life.'

At that point, Rosandra saw clearly, something in the world changed. The conversation became a drama, it was the opening of a new phase, a new story. The choice was simple: either she took the dare or she did not. She picked up the chain and wound it round her arm. He bent over to click the clasp. He exuded heat, just like Bass did when she was a girl begging for stories.

'Let me take you for a drive,' he said. 'Give me that pleasure.'

She had seen the car being parked, just beyond the greasy window. It was red, long, low. He must have seen her from the road. He guided her towards the car, very lightly touching her elbow. She left her bitten hamburger. She was fascinated, she had taken the dare. Her life was about to change: changes held dangers but also unforeseen opportunities, a thousand fairy-tale promises.

But after his opening lines the man had exhausted himself. He drove in silence. Speed roared past the windows. They were far out of the city, in the dark veld. Once, suddenly, he drew up and stepped outside, cracking his bones. Dust blew around the car, fiery red in the headlights. Rosandra tried to get out too but was locked in. He released her, coming over to her side with the key.

'There must be a control for the door,' she said.

'But you deserve to be treated this way,' he said, 'like a lady, a princess.'

He walked away from her, along the white kerb-line. Dogs howled indistinctly in a far settlement. The sky was white with stars. Rosandra walked in the opposite direction, thinking he needed to take a pee.

'Please do not walk away.'

He came after her.

She stopped. Now it might happen – the overpowering on a deserted country road, the nightmarish adventure. She tensed, but no hand touched her.

'Are you familiar with Maseratis?' he asked, standing a little distance behind her.

'I'm not.'

'You smoke,' he said.

It could be an order or a question.

'No,' she said. 'Do you want a cigarette?'

She still had the habit of carrying cigarettes with her.

'I do not smoke. I despise people who smoke,' he said. 'I knew you were not a smoker.'

She was glad she had not produced the box. There was tension in him. His neck snapped irritably as he moved it. He touched her elbow, lightly.

'We must continue with our journey.'

She followed him. This was not a mere drive, it had a purpose. There would be an extravagant end, a revelation. As the car moved on speed dispersed her anxiety. He is too intent on pleasing me to hurt me, she thought. The thought was obvious, almost an anticlimax. He wants me so much he won't do harm, he keeps his distance. She relaxed and slept.

'I love you, I love you,' she woke once to hear him say.

The night was still dark, the constellations in their former order. He was murmuring the words to himself, thoughtfully, without urgency. She slept again, more deeply.

Then suddenly the stars flamed into closer proximity. The man opened the door on her side of the car and helped her out. She was clumsy with sleep. Overhead, at the top of a tall, floodlit pyramid, fluorescent wheels of pink and green spun. They flashed, disappeared, emerged again. On five sides avenues of tall palm trees glimmered with golden lights. Beyond lay water, reflections of the lights. Between the two widest avenues was an immense dome, brilliantly lit. She could see its full extent because of the waves of light, now pink, now gold, now green, that flooded over it. Rosandra had not seen so much brilliance since the light displays in her first hotel room. She could feel her eyeballs turn as she watched. This was a palace, a place of light, an empire. The man was guiding her to a small bungalow where a single white light shone over the door. His touch was at her elbow and as they walked he spoke. He mentioned Venetian glass: it was frangible, it looked like it was made of air, of bubbles of light. He mentioned antique porcelain, white and blue and speckled with gold, the speckles in the shape of flowers, tiny narcissus, its beauty so pure, its skin polished to perfection, wet like a membrane. As the door opened to let her in she realised slowly that he was comparing these things to her.

2

The next morning, Rosandra told Jem – drinking her vodka martini – the place was still full of light, this time sunlight. The sun striking the swimming pool directly outside made a conflagration in the room next door. He had opened the curtains and was sitting against the light. Rosandra could barely make out his features. She held her hands before her eyes. She remembered her diamanté necklace, suspended in the air, sending shafts of light in all directions like a mass of stars. He was a voice.

'I thought you would never wake up,' Thony said.

But she had awoken once before that night, or that morning. It was as dark around her as the inside of a heart or spleen, a deep, inner place. The complete darkness seemed wrong and alien after the display of light. She had forgotten the drive, the guest-house, her host pointing decorously to the bed. She had forgotten how she came to be enclosed and flattened by the hot night.

She knew only touch. It was warm, a pressure. She was aware of surfaces, above, below, touching. She was rooted, pressed into a narrow space, into a split, rubbed inside the split. She was lying on her stomach and a great weight was lying on her. She thought of spirit possession, of a force of fate or guilt bearing down. The heaviness covered her everywhere, wherever she felt no bedding, no sheet. The covering was human. She could feel bone held tight by muscle and she tried to move.

Her movement had been expected. The weight on her was holding breath, waiting. Then it too began to move. The darkness was dense. He was rubbing up and down, very directed. The pressure increased. It became concentrated at her lower back, her tail, and down further, darker. She felt her flesh open to the force. Then the movement

103

stopped. The weight pressed tight against her, tense, determined, and he spoke into her hair. She tried to move her head but it was clenched. His elbows clamped her shoulders, his hands held her head in place. Her eyeballs were pressed into the pillows. She saw constellations of coloured lights.

He said she was a goddess, Artemis, Persephone. This place was waiting for someone like her since he first planned it. It needed someone like her to grace it. He wanted to hold her and keep her, he wanted to enthrone her in the midst of all he possessed. Stay, he whispered, please stay with me.

So that was it, Jem thought. That was when she lost her virginity? That night. It was brutal, she had been taken, he came into her like a beast. There could be no worse than this, no deeper degradation. However, her face seemed as pale as it did this morning, as blank, and pure.

In the white light shining through the louvre windows of the guest bungalow, Rosandra went on – absorbed, as though Jem had not interrupted her – in the white light coming through the hot louvres, sat a fortyish man, smooth-shaven, dressed in black and well-covered round the middle. Was it he, the man of the night before, in the restaurant, in the bed? The pastel furniture under bright light looked familiar and reassuring. The man's hands were soft, and he had small soft dewlaps. He was waiting to welcome her.

In bed she had checked for bruises, buried pains, then she checked the sheets. After the long night and its strange happenings she felt surprisingly fit and light. There was no evidence of what she remembered, nothing like blood, no traces. She was untouched. Feeling between her legs was the last test. But there was no ache, no give, no sensitivity in skin or bone. Maybe it was a dream, a result of the long journey, arriving in an unknown place. Which meant there was no reason for shyness now. If it was a dream she was free to meet his eyes. There was a strange fixed smile on his face which made his cheeks smooth as peaches. He nodded as if approving of her, rating her highly. This man had not come into her bed. She felt very light and freed, also hungry. Outside, laid out on a white plastic table next to a small round swimming pool, she saw fruit and big puffy rolls. A large brick of butter had dew on it.

'It's all for you,' he said. 'Sit down. You must be hungry after last night.'

He watched her eat. He urged her to take more food, he pressed fruit upon her. An Indian waiter in a gold and red turban brought in passion-fruit juice.

'You have no black men here?' she asked.

'Our black men have other jobs, in the kitchens, behind the scenes. Our guests have got used to particular standards of appearance. We have a lot of foreign guests, that is, from overseas, Europe and so on. We like to keep up a good show.'

From over the brick wall around the swimming pool came sounds of splashing and laughter.

'Where are we?' said Rosandra. 'I thought these were dry lands.'

She had finished her meal, and the man kept his eyes on her, searching her face, in quest for responses.

'I still have everything to show you,' he said.

He leaned over and took her hands. He was clasping them prayerfully. The individual hairs of his indigo stubble were showing just beneath his skin.

His speech burst from him as though he could not hold it back, but what he said was slower and more connected than in the pizza place. As he spoke the voice in the night came back to her, and the breathing and the feeling of suffocation. However, it couldn't be the same voice. This voice was smooth, not choked, and it was considerate. The memory of the night grew fantastic. The daylight made it impossible. She tried to hold his gaze.

'You are the most miraculous thing that has happened to me,' he said. 'Can I tell you that again? I want to tell you again. How can I express how happy I am? I have had good fortune. I have been lucky in love, in my career. But you must be the high point of my luck. Once I used to do no more than dream of creating this place. I dreamed of making a pleasure extravaganza in the dry veld where everyone, old and young, white and black, could amuse themselves and have fun. I will show it all to you – my eighteen-hole golf course, game park, botanical gardens. In those days, when I was deep into my daydreams, I used to imagine having this woman, this beautiful woman beside me, someone who would stand for everything the place would mean to me.

'I will be honest with you. I have searched for her – my ideal woman. The rich and famous come here, a lot of beautiful people. They come in spite of the politics. When I built this place I knew this. Moral clout is like a mosquito bite when a man has power and fulfils dreams. The lovelies of the world enthusiastically come to this place and I spend time with them and promise them the world, but even the special ones have seemed not quite right – too loud, too wooden, too well-known. In the end I decided I was on the wrong track. I didn't want a famous, well-known face. I wanted someone – how can I say? – fresher, someone who could grow into this place, someone who would really *feel* how important it is.

'I began searching around our country. The story of that search would take many days. I started humble, in small places. I thought, that's where you find the unspoilt beauties. Two were nearly but not quite right. I travelled to a town called De-Nyl-Zyn-Oog, the Eye of the Nile. I stayed in the single hotel in town. It faced a dry park where there were only cactuses and a monument to Boer War dead. I met a beautiful young thing in that town who dressed like Olivia Newton-John in *Grease*, four years behind the time. She had her baby sister with her. Then that baby sister turned out to be her child. The woman I wanted could not have that kind of responsibility.

'I went on with my travels. I used to make the outings on odd weekends. I drove thousands of miles. In a coastal resort I found a long, tall woman who couldn't speak a word of English. She was straight out of a Free State cherry town. She was fresh as a cherry, a daisy, she looked like Bo Derek, only more perfect, and she had her hair done in beaded plaits. She was the proper article, a woman of the future, an Afrikaner with her hair done like these African women wear. But there was nothing in her, no drive or fire.

'This place needs a woman with a kind of spirit. You have guts, I saw that last night. You came with me without a backward glance. I have plans for this place, to make it even more fantastic. I need a woman who can share my vision. I'd almost given up my search. And then I saw you. I don't want to embarrass you but occasionally you must hear these things. You are the One. I want to make you part of this place. I want to know all about you, about that beautiful inner secret that makes you shine. Leave whatever it is you do behind you. Stay with me.'

Rosandra tried to keep her reply simple.

'My name is Rosandra,' she said. 'Rosandra White.'

He had put down her hands as he spoke. Now he took them again, his touch light, crisp. They couldn't be the same hands as held her last night.

'I am Thony,' he said. 'You can call me that.'

She noticed the sibilant in the way he made the first sound.

'This must be Star Palace,' she said. 'The casino.'

'You've heard of it?'

'Yes. I've heard of you too.'

'I hope only good things.'

'I can't remember exactly,' she said.

This was true. She had read about the building of Star Palace in magazines on Eden Island, about the incredible and completely successful plans of a businessman called Thony Brandt. It made an endlessly adaptable magazine story, the miraculous creation in the drought-stricken veld. The man wanted to create a pleasure place, it was said, a fun factory, symbol of a new nation at play, well-to-do, money-spinning and without prejudice. Rosandra remembered photographs of gaming tables, imported palm trees, girls dancing in feather costumes. It was a place built on a fantasy, it was everybody's dream. The fiancées and ex-fiancées of Wimbledon stars jetted in for the weekend, international singers gave concerts. The place raised national morale because it was international in its clientele, and 'international' – that was the word – in its race laws, and not a little foreign because it was not built on national land.

'It's a casino isn't it?' asked Rosandra.

'A triple casino, in fact, and also much more. I will take the pleasure of showing you round. What we have here is a complex of three hotels, cinema, show bars, gaming salons, and the Dome Concert Hall. I built it all. This is not the land of apartheid any more. This place is a world apart from all that. Everything is of an international standard. Each hotel has a different style. There is the Spanish American hotel, the Southern Californian, the Australasian. Visiting Star Palace is like going overseas.'

When he talked he did not use his hands or move in his seat or change his tone. Only his mouth moved from the bottom lip. But the speed of his words made what he said sound like a saga, a discovery, with the final shape of things hanging in suspense but sure to be spectacular. That was the joy of stories, Rosandra knew, that suspense.

'What about the water?' she asked. 'How do you manage that?'

'It's a superb question,' said Thony. 'Water is the secret of this place. At a distance of about twenty-five *kays* from where we are sitting my engineers have constructed a massive battery of boreholes and storage tanks. So although the drought here is severe we have unlimited water. While you're here you can have your baths full and take long showers and you can swim in ten different swimming pools. Do whatever your heart desires and forget there ever was a drought.'

That afternoon Thony drove her out past the golf course to a dry river valley.

From the look of the place a disembodied mining force had been at work, delving with a vengeance, casting out the rocks and boulders which volcanoes had buried. The bed of the river and its once rocky banks had been graded flat and the valley sides were chiselled. After the pearly waters of the hotel complex, the dull red earth and scorched grass were nude and unsightly. Rosandra squinted at the scrub at the end of the valley to try and make out how it once looked, but she saw only brown fuzz, the beginning of savannah land. Beyond that was a featureless blue sky, without a cloud.

'I want this to be an aquapark with a massive water course, the biggest in the Southern Hemisphere,' said Thony, pointing haphazardly in all directions and looking at her the while. 'There will be slides, fountains, whirlpools, spinning baths, and water chutes. There will be a wave-pool for surfers. It will be so great and so exciting and crazy that kids will persuade parents to drive them maybe three, four hours, it doesn't matter how long, to get here.'

Rosandra looked at the shaved, dead earth, cracking in the heat. She tried to see blue pools and naked people at sport. Giving up, she scanned the sky for traces of moisture. She had not faced this much open blue sky since Eden. The sky was an unwanted memory. Burning, without relief, it was stark and daunting. She could see no blue cloud, no point of focus. She squinted again, making the effort and trying to imagine it, the blue cloud, but it eluded her.

'It takes imagination to see it, doesn't it?' said Thony. 'It is a mammoth conception, a world-scale project.'

He was focused on the underside of her chin and moved his head a little as though to see it from two angles.

'Sometimes my brain burns with all the ideas and I want to get out here and work night and day to get it done. The burning is the same kind of feeling as I had when I saw you last night. It's something unstoppable. Total.'

The sky was too bright to gaze at any longer and the valley was of no interest. She looked down into his eyes.

'What fascinates and thrills me about you, Rosandra,' he went on, saying her name slowly, with feeling, 'is that you don't flinch or blink at any of this. I've been watching you today. I've shown you some amazing things. Star Palace is a blend of the world's best star-studded resorts. And your response is – how can I put it? – deadpan. In the best and most beautiful sense. You calmly take it in. No surprise registered. Just super cool. It's the kind of spirit I like, this coolness. It's what I need for this enterprise. It's a prime antidote to funk. I could feel it when I came up to you yesterday. You just looked at me with those eyes of yours. Another woman would have run but you just turned your eyes on me. You don't run away.'

She was only half listening. He led her out across the forced and crumpled clods of earth in the river bed, which collapsed into dust underfoot. She wondered about her stare, what it was that attracted him. When he spotted her last night she was keeping to herself, having her supper. He too stared, he did it almost without blinking. There was a kind of pull in it. His eyes offered unspoken questions. She thought about the dark heavy beard beneath his skin and his daring and the dry touch of his hands. These things somehow matched, yet somehow did not, the energetic words, the quiet touch. Last night in the pizza place she wanted to give him her whole arm, so that he could touch the length of it lightly and then again, so that she could properly get the sense of his touch. But then she also wanted to watch, to listen, to wait and see, take things in slowly, and she kept her arm to herself.

They were heading towards a group of low boulders scraped to a shine but not dislodged by the graders. The edges of upreared shavings and scabs of parched mud scratched against Rosandra's ankles and the feeling made her hair stand on end. There was nothing here to look at, it was very dry and scraped, the earth looked in pain.

Then she saw the aloe plant, a small one, grey-green, behind one of the boulders. The last aloe plant she had seen was in Cradock. A bed of them grew behind the paddling pool, the place where she sat with Emmie when they were friends. This one was by itself. It fiercely clenched its leaves together, making a pod shape. It was hiding something in there. It must be the bloom, though the drought could have starved it. She could see it from one angle only, looking from above. It was a brilliant vermilion, a proud colour, it was unashamed.

'If ever I need inspiration,' said Thony, leading the way back to the car, 'I think of early pioneers, people in America building in the desert, and the settlers and trekkers here. And if I really need to think up energising ideas I think of the ancient Greeks. They had those first brilliant concepts of how to go about things. They had logic and they also had vision. Do you know what they said about love?'

Rosandra didn't know. She wondered if an aloe could be transplanted.

'They said something, I can't remember exactly, but something to the effect that each person selects their adored One according to character. It goes something like, the adored one is the god whom the lover follows. His adoration turns the loved one into a god.'

He sighed richly.

It was more than high time to say something in return.

'That was good,' Rosandra said. 'It sounded very true.'

At the car she asked if they could dig up the aloe and take it home.

The next morning three hot-house aloes were waiting on her doorstep. They had glossy leaves, shining spikes. The aloe in the valley had broken off at the roots. When Rosandra pressed her foot against it, under the leaves, to lever it out, the stem had snapped. Filled with remorse, she covered the stump with sand.

Insult upon injury, Jem thought. Cheated in body and in spirit. First he entered her bed on the first night. Then he said the kind of words that he, Jem, had saved and cherished over the years. That he had hoped to whisper to her one day. You are my adored one, my very goddess. Or he wanted to go to a far place, never to see her again, and write the words on a card, slip the card in an envelope, send it to her.

He was trying to concentrate. Her lips were moving, sliding over her teeth, under her make-up, saying things about Thony. The strings of lipstick-coloured saliva and alcohol stretched and broke as she spoke. What was she telling him? He must listen again, he'd asked her to say it all, to tell the lot, Bass, Thony and more, and she was obliging.

'I felt stunned,' she was saying, 'to be included in all this! The second night at Star Palace Thony took me to a dance fantasia from Rio. But all of it was like a fantasia. A carnival show. It was so much bigger than Bass's scheme. I was face to face with a man who ran a twenty-four-hour show, who controlled the whole thing. Even the strange dreams were part of the magic. At night the air at Star Palace was full of the sound of three discos and the whispers of people playing hide-and-seek in the dark.

'On the morning of my third day there I made my decision. That afternoon Thony sent a driver to the city to hand in my notice at the fast-food place and to pick up the clothes from my flat.

'That evening Thony took me for a drink at the lake-side. He brought his face up close. He had his fingers wound through the gold chain on my arm. I hadn't seen a man's face this close before. I thought, this is the man who built Star Palace. I stared. He let me stare. He said he wanted to tell me where he began, so that he could demand the same privilege from me. He said he wanted to know what made me tick.

'I remember exactly what I replied. I come from Cradock, I said, very straightforward.

'I told him I went to school in Cradock. I came to the city to work. I wanted to be a fashion model, I said.

'But he said, not so fast. He had questions to ask of me, in his own good time. He offered his own story instead. He said he imagined it wouldn't be half as interesting as mine.

'At school, he told me, he worked and played at everything, rugby, water polo, chess, the school-wide stock-exchange competition. If real money had been involved he'd have made a packet. At university he won scholarships. He went to Oxford, in England. And at Oxford he played the stock exchange and won some money, and won awards and cups and medals, and then hearing grim news from home his goals became clearer. He said he saw what this country needed. What was needed was guts, guts and brains. He felt he had it in him. So he left Oxford and forgot about his degree and bought a piece of Bantustan. He said, the rest is what you see.

'And it was true. He was the magician in charge of it all. That was clear to anyone. Staring at him I saw the liquid swimming across his corneas. He had an ordinary body, I thought, made of skin and water, but he did extraordinary things. He pushed my hair back away from my eyes. His fingers felt light like the touch of a seed-pod. He seemed caring. He made everything look very simple. He said what he felt. From the first, nothing at Star Palace was as interesting as listening to him speak.

'Then, on that same third night, my strange dream was repeated. It began as before. Inside it felt airless, too warm. In bed I couldn't find a cool place. I stripped down to find coolness but when I woke up again it was even hotter. I ached, I was being forced down into the mattress. It was that sensation of the other body again. It had returned.

'The body made a total cover. I wanted to move but it wasn't possible. There was sweat everywhere. The sweat became warm liquid trickling down my waist. My cheeks were wet, my mouth was squeezed. Any movement was a mistake. If I moved the pressure seemed to go deeper. My head was pressed from the base of my skull.

'It ended when I bit my lip. I'd been telling myself to keep still. Whatever the thing was would go away, like a dream. Then I felt my lip give to my teeth. I couldn't help it. I hit the side of the bed and the body unbalanced and rolled over. The bed was wet with sweat. A person left the room. He walked with Thony's step.

'I should of course have guessed. Like at the pizza place, his approaches were sudden and unexpected.

'He was waiting for me in the living room the next morning, in the same chair as before. It was definitely him and no dream. He looked untidy, he must have slept in the chair. I felt embarrassed. My lip ached. What I thought was a dream was too hot, hot as a real body is hot, filled with force. It should have been obvious. I'd thought it must be a dream because everything at Star Palace seemed dreamlike. But Thony had told me about his passion, what his feelings were. I should have known.

'But the daylight helped. His body was different. It didn't look dense and strong as the body in the night had been. And he was considerate, very considerate if you take into account the force of his feelings. The first thing he said was that it wouldn't happen again. I saw his lips tighten as he watched me. I believed him, I realised the situation had to be accepted. There was nothing to be done. I'd fooled myself and had to live it down. He said I must use ice for my mouth, that he would try to make reparation. I believed that he would.

'Later at supper he explained that he'd lost his head. It was what I did to him. He couldn't forgive himself but he lost control. After the last time I'd said nothing. He'd wanted to lie with me again.

'He picked up my hand as he said this, his touch as gentle as it had been the day before. He put my hand against his cheek and sniffed my skin. I was happy that he did that. He was a different person from last night. He was making things right.

'He said he hoped I still wanted to talk business, that I would stay at Star Palace. And he had a surprise for me, a real treat. He held out a set of car keys. It's round the back, he said, a Ford Escort RX 3, all yours. He told me it was white as my name. It was for being so fierce and beautiful. Those were his words. I love you, he said.

'Then I was embarrassed all over again. I had to tell him I couldn't drive.'

3

Thony kept his promise, Rosandra told Jem. After that awkward night she wasn't again interrupted, though during the day he touched her often and spoke passionately as he showed her round, watching closely for responses. When she was alone Rosandra stayed in the bungalow. Thony reserved the pleasure of accompanying her in discovering his kingdom. He said she mustn't wander to places he had not yet shown her. He was jealous of his pleasures: he wanted to watch her eyes.

As his companion, Thony said, Rosandra must learn a few basic things, in addition to driving. She was in the public gaze, predatory cameras in Star Palace were a menace. She must learn to keep low, not to go out too often. Then there was her skin. She might be a rural Cradock girl but she was white. A tan could look robust and a little common. She was perfect in every way. The effect of pale freckles on white must not be spoiled.

Rosandra did not object. She liked to sit and watch and to be quiet. With a gentle finger Thony touched the individual marks on her face as he spoke. He touched the scab on her mouth. Once, kissing her goodbye, he licked it lightly.

Every evening Thony took her out in the car to drive around the Star Palace boundary road. Giving her instructions he folded his hands over her own on the controls, and smiled with the pleasure of watching her. When her aloes rotted because she watered them too often he ordered three more, and then again when these also died. He presented her with oysters flown in from the coast and imported French champagne, one day a whole bath of it. He asked to watch her step into it, wearing her swimsuit, then turned, his face in his hands, his lips working and tears in his eyes. He told her to accept his gifts without thanks and without protest. But there were so many gifts, so much to say thank you for, that she had long given up on comment. She took what he gave. She felt honoured, overwhelmed but honoured. It was her show; it was her decision to come here; it was working out all right. The early shame faded. It was her choice to receive.

'I want to spoil you silly, my Rosandra,' Thony said. 'You must let me. I want to captivate and please you.'

She asked for spectacles.

'Contact lenses, any colour,' he offered.

'Glasses,' she said. 'To see.'

With her new glasses she could focus on the land beyond the Star Palace lake and the individual fountains and each fairy light. And she discovered scratches and stains on things, cracks where there had been smooth, uninterrupted spaces. On the tubular sculptures in the garden, the legs of the dancers beneath their tights, the velvet of the blackjack tables, the blazer pockets and turbans of the waiters, the marble tiles of the hotel vestibules, nowhere were there perfect surfaces. It was a discovery to see clearly again; she hadn't seen this way since Cradock. But the discovery was a shock. The world was more exposed than it had been, it was uglier, there was more detail in it, few plain surfaces. And she could see Thony's eyes at a distance, always watching her, holding no expression.

Yet Thony was a marvel to have happen to a girl – to this day Rosandra thought so. Whatever else had happened she had to be grateful to him. For a time after her lip healed it seemed nothing could interfere with her luck. The night visits they put far behind them. Thony offered opportunity, true promise beckoned in everything he said. The waterways, buildings and big dance shows were symbols of his kind of intention. Thony could deliver, so he said, and she knew how to wait. He called her every morning from his office, to speak his moving words, to muse about the future, travel, promotional tours. He called from Rio and Paris, places where he flew for a day, three days, on business. Things had changed: the important phone calls now came to her. He showed a lover's tenderness and thoughtfulness. He was important and he embraced her with his importance, his visions and praise.

But most of all, Thony told Rosandra, he was interested in her poise. He said he loved her golden hair, her endless legs, the turn of her neck, its irresistible, birdlike pulsation, her honey-coloured, unbelievable eyes, her flowing carriage, immaculate figure, but most of all he adored that added touch, that gloss of perfection. It was the reason she got away with freckles and avoided looking like the girl next door. He called it the secret something of her beauty and examined it from behind sunglasses with an unblinking gaze. By and by his gaze turned into questions.

'You drive me wild, Rosandra,' Thony said. 'Where did you learn these tricks? How did you discover that charm?'

Rosandra told him about the Cradock Round Table Beauty Competition. She'd walked the ramp, people applauded. To be beautiful in Cradock a girl smiled and tried not to be loud or unmannerly and she imitated the make-up style of the woman who ran the boutique on Main Street. And after that she had left for the city and there she put together a portfolio. What more was there to say?

'You are too modest but you are also the picture of discretion,' Thony said. 'What you mean is that it all came naturally. Not by design but to the manner born. And so it may be. But discretion works with indirection. You make me wonder.'

He watched her at table, over drinks on the lake, at the extravaganza shows in the Dome as she sat squinting at the stage. At public events he did not allow her to wear her glasses. He took the pleasure of slipping them off her nose himself.

One day, a fortnight or so into her Star Palace stay, he invited her for a swim at his private cove on the lake. He himself did not swim. He watched her walk down to the water. Then he asked her to do the walk again. Pretend you are performing on that Cradock ramp, he called, laughing with delight as he watched. She was so lovely, so unbelievably lovely!

He asked her to come closer. He reached for her hand.

'You're not embarrassed that I ask you this?' he said.

'I'm not embarrassed,' said Rosandra.

She meant it, she liked seeing his pleasure. He was getting something in return.

Then Thony asked her for the liberty of sucking her toes – they were so small, so neat. As he brought her left foot to his lips he noticed the mussel scar on its second toe.

'That looks like it was an evil wound,' he said.

'No,' said Rosandra, 'it was nothing. Things like that happen when you grow up in the desert. It was an aloe plant in the school grounds. It cut me one day when I was playing.'

'You mean you trod it underfoot?'

'That's what happened,' Rosandra said.

115

Almost every night, if he did not have business engagements, Thony plied Rosandra with fragrant wines in his three restaurants. She matched him glass for glass. This was Bass's training.

'Weeks go by and you are still unknown to me,' Thony said. 'You are a blank slate. I feel you have a secret you can tell me, Rosandra. Trust me so that we can work together. Where did you learn to hold yourself like a professional? Tell me about yourself.'

She was proud of her answer. 'People say I am beautiful,' she said.

That was good, very general and no lie.

She told him more about Cradock. She searched her memory for new facts. The Great Fish River flows along the edge of Cradock, she said, and there are dams and pools in and around town where children can play. The town has many churches but David her father wasn't religious so they weren't in the habit of going to church. He lost his faith on the road, her mother said. When her mother told her this she imagined a tissue dropped and flying from a car window, shredding with the force of the wind. Describing it, Rosandra smiled but Thony did not.

She told him her father sold sewing machines, but fancy this, Susan her mother couldn't sew. She told him Susan at sixteen was also a winner of the Cradock Round Table Beauty Competition. Susan was ambitious for her, Rosandra, and gave her a pretty name, a name to stand in lights.

But Rosandra would not speak about Bass. The reason was simple, it was clear in her mind. She had left Bass, she had left Eden Island. That time had passed and it wasn't right to bring it back. Also it was clear as daylight that knowing Bass was a dangerous thing. He could bring her trouble, though she couldn't put any name or picture to it. She was thinking of her new independence. This freedom. It would be a pity if by mentioning Bass Thony would see her in a different way.

She wrote to tell Susan she had been discovered, she was in training at Star Palace. The name said everything. Susan would know it from magazines. In all the country no address was more prestigious for a girl who had a figure and who dreamed of success.

One morning, to mark their one month anniversary, Thony showed Rosandra the private grotto at the heart of his Star Palace kingdom. He said this grotto represented his plans and his dreams.

The hill that enclosed the grotto, Thony explained as they walked, was man-made. Its shell was built of Namaqualand stone. He paused at the dim opening to the cave passage to create a dramatic entrance. As they moved into the dimness he began to speak, very slowly at first, pausing at the end of sentences, about something called total strategy. It was a notion in the air when he came back from England to start making his fortune, he said. It influenced his life, his complete opposition to it, the government's total strategy to deal with the invasion coming from the north.

As she listened Rosandra thought of hugging sheep. That was about the time he was talking about. Before Bass, before going to Eden and learning things. She was trailing her hand along the passage wall, feeling the way, the roughness of the stone, the surface dark but dry. He went on talking as they walked. What he was saying meant a lot to him, his voice was deep. He spoke about total strategy being wrongheaded, it meant everyone being on their guard, it meant allowing only a small proportion of blacks to make wealth. He warned her about sharp stones overhead, poking out of the grotto walls. Then he raised his arm and stepped into a chamber at the end of the passage. He switched on the lights. She was right behind him and his arm came up against her ribs, blocking her path.

The sound of surprise she made sounded thin and damp in the enclosed space. It was the brilliance that struck her, like being plunged into a universe of stars. Everywhere she looked were clusters of bright stones encrusting the roof and walls. Coloured lights hidden in corners illuminated them. Thony, pointing, named pyrite, amethyst, porphyry, jasper, quartz. He waited for her to absorb it. Her stunned silence made him look pleased.

He said he had had the grotto made to his own specifications. Jewellers from the city and stonemasons flown in from Germany worked for three years to complete it. There were national stones here and stones from foreign lands. It was a symbol of ambition, of all he wanted to achieve.

As they moved around the grotto, antennae of white crystal overhead glowed into focus, reached out, retreated again. Thony went on speaking, his voice smooth, flowing with the lights.

'For the creation of national wealth and security you must get as many people as possible to believe in a nation,' he said. 'You must encourage lots of people to make money, no matter their colour. People must glory in their own potential. This country of ours is a place of risks and chances. It's a place of futures. There's room here for real heroes of fortune who will gamble cleverly with their futures and come out tops. With luck you have success. And out of success you build security. You deal with enemies and convert them into business

117

friends. Cleverness is the operative word. And vision. Amazing ideas like this cave.'

'Yes, it's very pretty,' Rosandra had to say, though she wasn't sure she was understanding everything he said.

He turned to her. The brilliance of coloured stone encircled him. He looked other-worldly, inspired, like a magician, and Rosandra felt cold. He took her arms above the elbow and rubbed them. The friction made the hair stand on end.

'Rosandra, I've created miracles of integration on this barren earth. One day I stood on a piece of godforsaken ground and I said, here I am going to make things happen. One day this cave was a piece of dry open veld. Now you see the change.'

As she nodded she felt the hair on her arms still standing erect and she saw the lights move in his eyes.

When he fell silent the cave seemed very quiet, very earthen, deep. Rosandra turned round, looking up, watching the lights glance over the stones. So Thony must have heard the sounds of the third person in the cave before she did. Because suddenly there was complete darkness. He had turned off the light switch. Then she heard it too. Somewhere there was a low rubbing sound. Thony brought out a torch and shone it round, but there was no one else in the main chamber. They stood very still, watching the torch flicker round, the crystals lighting like distant fireworks. Thony's face showed up elongated, disembodied. His loud breathing almost masked the other sound, the persistent rubbing.

He motioned with the torch that she leave first. The passage was lighter than the cave, not difficult to navigate now that her eyes were used to darkness. They must have missed the third person on entering, because of moving in from the daylight. But now she was clearly visible inside the mouth of the passage, a cleaning woman crouched close to the wall, working in a shallow alcove, mopping dirt off the stone. Rosandra stepped carefully around her and they murmured at each other, a kind of greeting. Then she waited at the entrance. The woman was a dim shape, close against the wall, very dark in the general blackness, working from a bowl she held in her hands. Thony must not have seen her, he could not have heard Rosandra's greeting. He was backing down the passage, his torch still trained on the chamber. It was in this way, no doubt, that he stumbled against her. Her bowl clattered on stone. The woman sighed, a long, regretful sound. Then the rocky passage amplified sharp sounds, like striking, two strikes, like body hitting body, or hand on flesh.

When Thony emerged from the passage his hands were marked with gluey red clay. He tried to rub them off on the dry rocks around the grotto mouth. That woman shouldn't have been there, he said, there is a special cleaner for the grotto, the place is private. He looked agitated. Rosandra stood a little way behind him. His hands were soiled, excessively soiled. It unsettled her to see them. She tried peering back into the darkness. She thought she saw a shape crouched there. But she turned quickly when Thony spoke her name. He did not touch her, his hands were still muddy, but he came up to study her face, he made her meet his eyes. He said nothing. On the walk back he began to talk again. Yes, it was a mistake on both sides, Thony said, that woman shouldn't have been there and he didn't see her. It was a bit of a shock, they both agreed, stumbling upon her like that. It was also a shame, Rosandra thought, the sight of that crouched, cowering body, spoiling the vision of the starry beauty, all the lights.

Later in her bungalow she removed the hair on her arms from wrist to shoulder for the first time. She used her leg-waxing kit. In the still, crystalline beauty of the grotto the hair had looked desperately untidy. She felt humbled by the wonder of Thony's creation. Also the distress she had felt stayed with her, and the memory of the scuffle in the grotto, Thony's eyes. She wanted to do something, something painful and dramatic like this waxing, to match that splendour she had seen, to offer Thony a clear sign, a sign of effort. He believed she was perfect. She must show her good intentions. She'd seen the anger in his eyes. She didn't want him to grow disappointed in her. He mustn't have reason to doubt her and grow agitated, to come up and check on her expression, her support.

There was one last special place Thony showed Rosandra, a private room just off his office, at the centre of Star Palace, just over the casino rooms. Thony said the room was his final showpiece. It was here, perhaps even more than in the grotto, that his heart lay. To this place he and his chief agent alone had keys.

The colour scheme in the office was pale green. Three framed pictures hung on the wall behind the desk, white squares of slightly different tones. White Reflections they were called.

'I like that semi-pun,' Thony said.

Rosandra didn't get his meaning. She was distracted by the desk, which was black and did not match the room.

The ante-room was different. It was windowless and felt subterranean. Thony turned the lights low. As her eyes adjusted Rosandra saw the paintings on the walls. There were dense leaf designs, foliage, darkly coloured and superimposed, murky blues and greens. There was no story in them. They reminded her of something she had seen elsewhere, on the island, yes, in the home of the old woman. In the time that had passed she had grown no more used to paintings. She squinted and stood this way and that, trying to see something she could recognise.

'Confused?' Thony said, watching her.

It sounded like he was pleased about it, like he had caught her out. He knew something about her, that she knew nothing about paintings.

'Well, you won't be confused for long,' he said. 'Paintings are part of what I want you to do for me.'

He led her up to the largest canvas. It had an ornate gilt frame clustered with roses, which Rosandra liked. Close up the canvas became a jungle scene. There was a moon, a big rubber plant.

'A tiger,' said Rosandra.

'Well done,' said Thony. 'But this isn't Henri Rousseau himself. It's the school of – an imitator.'

'Are these yours?' said Rosandra.

'Yes,' said Thony, 'hand-picked by me or by my assistants. As you will find out, Rosandra, this is one of the great advantages of dealing in this line of business. Sometimes you get to pick what you like.'

In all there were five paintings in the room, the green shadowy scenes they were peering at, a large canvas on the wall opposite, its subject more or less the same, and facing the door, under very low light, something that looked like a photograph, a cityscape. Rosandra looked forward to it. It looked more plain.

'I think you might like this,' said Thony, leading her up to the painting. 'It's my most expensive piece.'

They stood looking for some time before he spoke again. Rosandra's legs were beginning to ache at the knee.

'This was painted by an interesting man,' said Thony. 'A Dutchman – van der Heyden. In the late seventeenth century he developed a plan for the street-lighting of Amsterdam. The lighting plan worked for that city for hundreds of years.'

The talk of numbered centuries unsettled Rosandra. She thought of the main road north that cut through Cradock, the line of pylons running along it, extending way into the brown distance. It was strange that there should be that sort of distance in time. It was as strange that the differences were worth mentioning: the seventeenth century, the hundreds of years. The first permanent building in Cradock dated from 1813, a long time ago.

'You can see this man's engineering skills reflected in the detail and construction of this painting. It's all very exact, as in a photograph.'

'Yes, as in a photograph,' said Rosandra.

But she felt nothing for the picture, the spires and gables and bare trees. A moment ago she liked the contrast with the others, the clear outlines. As in a photograph. But it wasn't a picture of anything familiar.

The grotto experience had been display, a show; the visit to the picture room became the first moment of real preparation. Back in the cream office Thony ran a finger lightly up and down the hand he had been holding since he led Rosandra in. Her fingers had grown cold, her bared arms developed gooseflesh. She didn't know what she dreaded.

'That was your introduction,' he said, moving over to the other side of the black desk. 'And if you're in agreement, Rosandra, in the next few weeks I'm going to be asking you to look into buying a few art pieces on my behalf. You'll be going to Europe for me. This is nothing too ambitious, just a trial run. You'll have a helper who knows his stuff. At first he'll make the important decisions. It's a task that suits you – you absolutely look the part, picture of beauty that you are. But I don't want you to worry about it. I assume you've done nothing like it before but it really isn't as grand or difficult as it sounds, just very useful to me.'

'I truly know nothing about paintings,' said Rosandra.

'I know, I know,' said Thony. 'What do you think I knew at first? We all learn through practice, as you did on the Cradock competition ramp. As I said, you will have a helper. He'll be there to sort out the tricky stuff, money exchange, money changing hands, value, and so on. Watch, learn, don't let out any trade secrets. Europe will be all around you. See where it all stems from, where old beauty lives.'

Rosandra had been in Star Palace no more than two months but Thony moved fast. He came to see her one morning at eight. It was as hot as noon.

He stood out in the glare at the bungalow door.

'The time has now come to involve you, my beautiful love,' he said.

He looked at her with concentration, as though deep in thought. His face was pale and fresh, his cheeks soft.

'This afternoon I'll be meeting with the representative of a European golfing association to see if we can organise a championship on our course. We expect liberal groups here and abroad may organise boycotts. There will be some logistical problems to discuss. Then I will serve drinks in my office. I've invited some other business associates. Especially for you I've invited my overseas agent, Michaelis Herder, who is just back from Brazil. I want you to meet him. You two are the ones I want to send to Europe together to buy me some art.'

The air-conditioner had run all day and Thony's creamy green office and green ante-room were icy cool. There were no more than thirteen people present at the party. Other than Rosandra they were all men. Against the background of the paintings their positions seemed patterned. They stood apart, arranged against the walls in groups of two and three. They were men who had the look of sincerity, who knew exactly how to master it. Though she was the only woman and was wearing white, no one paused or looked up when Rosandra came in.

'I want you to wear something very expensive, very light and summery but stylish,' Thony had said in the living room of the guest bungalow.

He came to sort through her clothes. He picked out the white immediately. It was soft and long, of clinging crêpe-de-chine.

'Sylvan, timeless, sylphlike,' he said. 'This is it.'

He retreated chastely so that she could change.

'Please don't mind that I ask you this,' he said as she came down the passage to meet him.

Then he rose to take her hands.

'Perfect,' he said. 'Just what I imagined. You know your stuff, Rosandra. God knows how you do it, you lovely Cradock enigma.'

He lightly let his finger run down the length of her hair. He kissed the air just over her eyes.

'Come,' he had said. 'You look immaculate. Now to meet the world traveller and my loyal agent, Michaelis Herder.'

The agent came in soon after them, still buttoning his suit. He was taller than anyone else in the room. Rosandra knew this must be Michaelis Herder because of the way his eyes met Thony's, immediately, directly, and without expression on either side. The look was a greeting.

'But he is black,' Rosandra said, surprised.

'That's Star Palace for you,' said Thony. 'I told you about my ambitions.'

'And his name,' she said. 'Michaelis Herder?'

Thony was looking past her.

'To be exact, Michaelis is brown. To be exact, Cape Coloured, as they say. His name is his own business. Perhaps he invented it. What does it matter?'

His voice was raised for the other man's benefit, hailing him. Before Michaelis quite reached them Thony leaned forward and grabbed his hand.

'It works every time, you Star Palace rep, you brown man,' said Thony. 'People are surprised. You're a true representative.'

As they released hands Michaelis looked at Rosandra in a way that made her drop her eyes. It was direct and knowing.

'The goddess,' he said. 'The one the boss tells me about on international phone calls to Rio. Pleased to meet you.'

He did not shake Rosandra's hand. He towered above her. His elocution, which was melodious, very English, spilled over her. She felt her body sway back a little to accommodate his height. Thony lightly touched Michaelis's shoulder again.

'I'll leave you to get to know each other,' he said.

Almost at once Michaelis began to talk. He did not take his eyes off Rosandra's face. His intensity was like Thony's. There were silver glints in his hair, though he looked no older than thirty. The Waterman in his pocket was gold. His face and nose and cheeks were broad, perfectly proportioned. Photogenic, Rosandra thought. As he talked he seemed to tower closer, so close that Rosandra had to move back, inching first along the wall, then stepping away from it.

Michaelis said he was feeling hyper-excited, charged, there was no word for it – manic maybe. Latin America, Brazil, Rio, did this to him. It was the energy and rave, the good life. It was a place to score deals. They tried you there, they knew their stuff and their equals. It might as well have been carnival time, every night they took him out but the next morning at eight-thirty they would all be sitting round the discussion table again. No wonder that at the end of it all he had a sense of achievement.

'Let's drink to it,' he said, knocking his glass against Rosandra's before she had time to raise it.

'Sexy is a good descriptive word, don't you think?' Michaelis went on. 'You think of a man with a perfect physique, or a woman, a beautiful woman with a bit of *je ne sais quoi*. Like you, of course. Thony has brilliant taste.'

As he talked Michaelis looked over Rosandra's crown at where Thony stood at a little distance from them. He was with two other men; they were all keeping a silence. Rosandra's mouth felt dry, it was hanging open. She closed it.

'Yes, sexy, like you,' said Michaelis. 'Though that white dress makes you look very pure, very unprotected. Like a bride, a pale bride.'

He smiled at what he was saying and inclined his torso slightly. He seemed to honour her with a bow, but even as he did so his eyes continued to range across the room. He had worked himself into a position close to the wall with Rosandra facing it.

'Sexy is a word I use to describe clever things,' he said. 'Things like technology, things that work well and do it intelligently, efficiently. I think of a precision bomber, an absolute signature of genius. It is that sort of sexiness I managed to get our hands on in Rio, that kind of intelligent, beautiful stuff.'

He threw back the last of his drink in a quick motion. He began to move along the wall.

'No doubt we will see a lot of each other,' he said. 'I have this strong _déjà vu_ feeling meeting you, like we've met before. I'm sure it bodes well for the future.'

She had been on the point of interrupting him. She was lost again, as with the pictures. There were things she didn't understand, like the sexiness he said he'd bought. What was it, in what way was it clever? It was art maybe, but how could landscape pictures be called sexy? He must think she knew these things. At Star Palace one had to be in the know; those in charge asked the questions. They organised the displays, they decided what was marvellous, who was sexy, what should be on show, what should be admired. She didn't feel she was one of them yet.

A few days later the three of them met privately, Thony, Michaelis, Rosandra. Thony announced it as a casual business lunch, but he and Michaelis discussed the viability of investment in Rio nightclubs for most of the meal. He told them he would be in a hurry but he stayed for liqueurs. Over coffee he also informed them it was his forty-fifth birthday, but then he forced down Michaelis's arm when he raised it for a toast.

'I celebrate when there is something to celebrate,' he said. 'We will celebrate when the two of you return from Europe.'

'Europe,' said Rosandra, trying to join in the conversation.

Thony frowned at her, his first frown.

'Michaelis will fill you in,' said Thony, 'I don't deal with that side of the trip. The main thing is you'll need a fresh passport. One of our managers got the forms for you today. He was on a scheduled trip into the city and he was passing the Department of Justice anyway. It's not necessary for you to go in yourself.'

'Why do I need a fresh passport?' said Rosandra.

'He doesn't want other stamps in it,' said Michaelis.

Thony thanked him with a nod.

'I'm not sure I brought my passport to Star Palace,' she said.

'Your old passport is in your bungalow,' said Thony. 'I saw it there. You will have to say it was stolen in order to get another.'

The conversation had taken on a tone Rosandra did not recognise. Thony was speaking rapidly, he was extremely curt. This must be business, she thought, informed discussion. Flattery changed into cool politeness.

'In addition, you will not be wearing glasses,' said Thony.

Michaelis murmured agreement. It was a foregone conclusion.

'It doesn't look good. It's obvious and so hardly bears saying, but you mustn't forget you are our representative because of your look, unconventional yet perfect. It should be appreciated in its entirety.'

The conversation was unfolding as though it was written down, they knew exactly what was coming next. Rosandra took off her glasses and squinted at the blur around her.

'How will I see the art?' she asked. 'Without the glasses?'

'There are contact lenses waiting in a case in your bungalow,' said Thony. 'On the dressing table where your old passport lies.'

That evening he came to see her at the bungalow. He was once again tender. He gave her a gift, a leather passport holder tooled with the Star Palace logo, two concentric circlets of stars. His touch was soft, and lingered. She hoped he would let his hands rest longer. The certainty of touch – it smoothed over the confusion of the last few days. She did not fear his body. When she thought of him she thought not of the dark early pressure or his hands stained with mud, but of lightness, his dry touch, his skin too delicate for his beard.

He had a special meal brought in, smooth, delicate foods, oysters and peeled grapes and lychees and raw fish, served on white bone china plates. He fed her the oysters, letting them slip off his fingers into her mouth. She wasn't sure of this at first but he held her throat with his hand till she swallowed. He said it was a good trick to make novices eat.

She had taken a swim that evening, just before he came in. Twice he asked if the droplets on her face were not tears. Then he gave her an air ticket. The flight was scheduled for the next week, the destination was Nice.

'One more thing, you beautiful, inscrutable enigma,' he said at the end, getting up to leave.

He was quiet, as if thinking carefully. He took Rosandra's hands but kept her at arm's length.

'I want to prepare you for something. Michaelis will be carrying a pistol. We deal in some very pricy objects, so it's obviously for protection. That I don't need to explain. But I do want to put your mind at rest. We have cleared the weapon with airport security and they'll personally be escorting you on to the plane. In time, as you get better known and more practised in this business, you may want to carry arms too. We can arrange that. I would in fact encourage it. Guns are useful things, very sexy, and divine to hold.'

He used Michaelis's word, or had Michaelis copied it from Thony? She wanted to say, I cannot shoot, as the other day she said, I cannot drive, but it didn't seem right. She knew a man who was a soldier, who carried guns. It felt like she should know about these things. Bass must have smuggled his guns past airport security, on this end of his journey anyway. But Thony was above-board and better organised. Airport security supervised his arms.

4

And so – as Rosandra told Jem – she found herself in the business class section of an aeroplane, airborne, and still marvelling at her good fortune, the plushness of things, the luxury. How buoyant she felt! Most of the passengers around her were businessmen in the peak of well-being and success. Michaelis pointed out that many of them had done business with the city offices of Star Palace Ltd. They visited Star Palace on weekends to play sport. Most of the women, he said, were the mistresses of these men. On all sides champagne corks were snapping and the mistresses yelling at the foam spuming on to their stockings. Michaelis was in another row. When she looked back at him he raised his brows in greeting. Rosandra felt like she had been flying all her life. To Europe from Africa, she thought. The Eden trip now seemed like a picnic outing, a morning excursion. This was magnificent. She looked down at Africa and the setting sun.

But Africa wasn't much to look at, grubby yellow mainly, whereas she imagined stark contrasts, jungle green, sapphire lakes, a bright Sahara, conical mountains, Bass's images. That is where we live, she told herself, that is our Africa. But it was too far away to feel anything much. Michaelis ordered her champagne.

And then the two of them were sliding from lane to lane of traffic along a sea-front, past tree-ferns, pedestrians, a sudden whiff of fresh bread interrupting dense car fumes, black-clad old women, maybe fish-wives, cleaners, young women in short flared pastel-coloured skirts, looking almost familiar and disappointingly commonplace when she expected their beauty to be more polished, well-established, mature, either middle-aged or ageless. Grubby pink and white ice-cream kiosks passed, pink flowering bushes, pennants fluttering round a second-hand book mart, bits of wasteground, lushly overgrown, the grey-white sea-haze, the sea-board again; yet all of these impressions not as she expected, not suited to what she imagined, not as glamorous, not European, nothing like the images she carried with her, of gilded Swiss chocolate, or French-named skin products in ground glass bottles, or of cathedrals resembling carvings in stone. A billboard flashed by, a young white-blonde woman in pale lipstick and a sixties bouffant advertising cigarettes, which, because of the bouffant, looked more like it, like European style.

Michaelis's driving was leisurely. He swung the wheel with wide loops of his left arm, and she watched him, thinking to imitate this casualness and take corners with this kind of ease when next she was driving at Star Palace. But his holiday attitude did not lead to conversation or introducing new sights to her. Maybe Europe wasn't enough like Rio. She pressed her eyes with her fingers to relax them. It was the new lenses; her eyeballs felt congested. Images were swirled together, concentrated like in the convex surface of a spoon. The concentration made her head buzz. There was too much to see.

Michaelis drove into a roadside hamburger joint, complaining of hunger. The cars in the car park shone in the heat, blue, red, white, usual colours. In vain Rosandra looked for a sign, a label, a marker to say France, Europe. She scanned the formica tables, plastic tile floor, illumined standard menu list over the tills, the squeezable ketchup and mustard bottles, reading the labels, 'ketchup', 'moutarde americaine'. On Eden there was a real French *pâtisserie*, on the French coast she was eating her first meal in a place stripped of character. This couldn't be France, she thought. Michaelis consumed his hamburger without comment, hers was tough and tasteless. He was not interested in going outside, to look around at the sky, boulevard vista, passing cars. He was drinking German beer out of a can. Whereas they should, shouldn't they, be uncorking a dusty dark green bottle of the oldest wine, and the light should be amber and syrupy, strained through thick panes of blistered glass, as it was in television advertisements back home selling the civilised pleasures of Star Palace? And there should be cigar smoke, and marble-topped tables, with the half-moon marks of slow cleaning showing on them in the half-light, and jasmine sprigs in old wine bottles, and beautiful young men standing round in graceful poses, Grecian, bejewelled, gay. In Thony's wine bar at Star Palace gay men who made the long trip from the city came to drink Chardonnay wine and to meet each other on Saturday nights.

But the hotel room, finally, was different from Eden, also from the Star Palace bungalow. Instead of pastels and neutral designs it was custom-made, richly robed in bold colours. A laminated notice hanging on a painted hook by the door described the room in four languages. It was possible to take the card off the hook and walk round the room with it.

Rosandra followed the description round the room. Along all four walls ran a gold-yellow wallpaper panel with a cornice relief motif, the notice said. Beside the marble vase of Italian silk roses the visitor could examine for himself the Louis XIV ormolu remake mantelshelf clock. The effect was grand, Rosandra thought, though maybe not perfect, not perfectly sexy. The carpet showed tracks of brushing. There was a yellow scale in the bath, a net of long dark hairs blocked the plug-hole.

In her experience international hotel bedrooms were beginning to look like airport lounges. Even this one. It was the used atmosphere, she thought, the tiredness, the lingering strain. These rooms were full of the shadows of sick-headaches, lagging moods, guilty swallowing of pick-me-up pills, douches of eye-drops. Behind the imitation wainscot doors, here in this kind of bedroom, under this naked neon in the bathroom, international sports stars, business magnates, fashion models, statesmen, also perhaps Thony, paused between appearances. They stretched, eased heavy earrings, rubbing the earlobe, checked for dandruff, ladders in stockings, food stains. They sat down heavily on the bed, like this, and stared dumbly ahead of them, yawning, thinking of freshening up at the washbasin. They combed out the loose hair that would collect in the plug-hole.

In a private gathering on the top floor of an old beach hotel Michaelis took Rosandra to an exhibition of icons. Thony was extremely interested in icons, Michaelis said, they were attending on his behalf.

'It will be a chance to get your hand in. See how people look at art.'

'What are icons?' Rosandra asked as they parked.

'Icons are objects of worship associated with Russian Orthodoxy,' Michaelis said. 'They are made of beaten gold.'

In the hotel penthouse she could not miss the gold. The icons were very bright and alarming. In the controlled dimness of the big room they blazed, breaking the spotlight beams across the corrugations of their age.

It was an image that would stick, these old bright faces, Church Fathers, saints and mentors, keeping their own counsel. She peered into face after face but the images had no meaning that she could discover. Their lips were stiff. The flat gold spaces left marks on her retina like bruises. Her eyes ached. She pressed her eyelids open with her fingers to ease the strain of the lenses.

'I don't think I understand these,' she said. 'My parents never took me to church.'

Michaelis hushed her.

'Watch, listen,' he mouthed.

He was looking over at a small group of men in a motley of outfits, dark suits and colourful beach shirts, as if he recognised them, as if he was trying to attract their attention.

'These things are very expensive,' he said.

Rosandra found a face named John Chrysostom which had the features of John Lennon. Multiple crosses intersected on his breast and in his blinding gold robe were cyclones of jewels. It made her dizzy to look at them. She moved on. Michaelis kept watching the men. He might be wanting to make a purchase. Next to the John Lennon picture there was a Mary figure done in flat black contours whose face, kind and watchful, was oddly reminiscent of Maria's back in Cradock. Her gown was plain blue and she had a halo like an armband of bronze. In the grey womb floating in the middle of her flat breast a child was imprisoned in an attitude of dazzlement.

'Jesus Pantocrator,' said Michaelis, staring into the eyes of the womb-child. 'He started out small.'

Rosandra looked all round the room for a memorable image, one that she could later describe to Thony. To say she liked a picture that looked like Maria, her mother's maid, wouldn't be the correct thing to do. The last icon close to the exit was very small and dark. A man was smoking in front of it. He wore dark glasses against the icon blaze. Rosandra stood behind him. A brown Jesus was unhappily suspended above a river that was a sheet of silver. Rosandra saw her white crêpe-de-chine reflection in it, and that of the man in front, the patch of his glasses. She saw that Michaelis was talking to the group of men. In the picture people were watching Jesus from the shore, except that in fact they were all looking out of the frame. The river, flat and metallic, did not look ready to receive the Christ child.

Later Michaelis came round and stood next to Rosandra. The man in the suit had moved on. She felt she had seen as much as she could absorb.

'The value of this stuff is its age,' said Michaelis, scrutinising her expression. 'In the next few days you'll see things you may like more.'

Her stomach groaned.

'Let's go and find the wine and the snacks,' said Michaelis.

But most of the food was already eaten. On a platter lay a few cold chicken breasts. A thick deposit of paprika and yellow grease had coagulated in their folds.

After the icon exhibition Rosandra was given three days of time to kill. Michaelis left town on business, art hunting. He'd heard of exhibitions in coastal resorts further west, he said. Rosandra must be ready for an excursion any time. Ready, he added on an undertone as though someone might be listening, meant not wearing her white too-virginal dress.

Because of Thony's instructions Rosandra carefully rationed her outings. Once she went to a maritime museum filled like a junk room full of mouldy old rope and rusty anchors. Another time she had a coffee at a pavement café which she enjoyed because it seemed the right European thing to do but was spoiled by the coffee being too strong and, as she saw in her pocket mirror, staining her teeth dark yellow, and she worried about paying for the complimentary chocolate.

On a third outing she bought a sky-blue sun dress and a postcard of what looked like a Mediterranean scene. In the picture there were white buildings clustered round a pebble beach. It might have been the place where she was, though she hadn't yet seen anything that looked like the ruined old fort on the knoll in the background. It was then she wrote the postcard home that Jem remembered, the postcard about being brown and happy and remembering Africa.

'But you said you were tanned,' Jem suddenly interrupted her. 'You'd only been there a few days.'

'That's right,' said Rosandra.

'So you couldn't have been tanned when you wrote it.'

'Yes, that's right,' she said. 'And I did not get tanned. As I already said, Thony didn't want me to.'

'I have kept that card all these years,' Jem confessed unhappily. 'I could show it to you. I think the place in the photograph is in Spain. It's not French at all.'

'Better just to throw it away,' Rosandra said.

The second exhibition Michaelis and Rosandra visited was held in a fin-de-siècle orangery in a town on an estuary several resorts west. The work was contemporary and foreign, a collection of West African paintings.

'It could be interesting,' said Michaelis, coming round to open the car door for her. 'A touch of old Africa. Thony might like that sort of stuff for his reception rooms.'

'I like your dress,' he said out on the road, scanning her sky-blue lap. 'It's more suitable, more Mediterranean.'

Rosandra thought he was being pleasant and so smiled. But Michaelis did not smile.

The orangery was loaded with white-hot light and the paintings streamed colour, red, bright blue, clear ochre-brown. Guiltily, because of the notices and the barrier cords, Rosandra put up a hand to touch the surface of a painting. It felt molten, almost soft, as though the oils were turning back to liquid in the heat. The touch gave a sensation of reality. The picture was a thing made, it had ingredients, was real, though its subject, multi-coloured lines, was as difficult as ever to work out. It was a feeling she would remember, this realness. A painting to describe to Thony.

The work on display was by two Togolese brothers. Michaelis waved aside a guide who offered to tell them about African art traditions. He headed straight for a set of orange and brown panels and set about examining them from various points in the room. Each panel showed a tall, slightly elongated figure, a hawker, a baobab, a gnarled-looking Eiffel Tower, a man on a bicycle with a large head-load.

Against a neighbouring wall Rosandra found a mural of a market, real life, done like a cartoon.

'Thony told me you were canny and perceptive,' Michaelis said, close beside her, 'but I've been breathing down your neck for a full five minutes without your noticing.'

'I like this picture,' said Rosandra.

'Forget this one,' said Michaelis. 'It's run-of-the-mill street art. It's the ones in the corner, there, I was looking at that you should be interested in. They're good, carefully achieved, very intriguing.'

Rosandra looked again at the elongated figures.

'Maybe I can't make out quality,' she said.

'I'm having the set reserved for a possible purchase,' said Michaelis. 'I'll call Thony tonight.'

'Can we get this one too?' Rosandra pointed at the painting she had touched.

There was no harm in asking; Michaelis carried Star Palace cheques.

'Now that, if you're interested in knowing, is solid rubbish,' said

Michaelis. 'It's an African painting with pretensions. If you're black, and I can talk, you either imitate well or not at all. You don't produce half-baked work and bad imitations.'

But Michaelis told her as they left that she had done well. He noticed her looking more closely and thinking about the art. The blue dress opened a new chapter. She was starting to get things right and that was good. Rosandra was the one who in the future might be finalising the deals. Michaelis's expression was friendly, but he could be mocking, she knew so little. He turned to nod at her. The nod was decisive, it seemed convinced.

Later he took her out for an ice-cream as a treat. The café was in a side street where the few chairs and tables standing out on the pavement looked lost, scattered in amongst half-empty newspaper stands. They sat in companionable silence. Rosandra's sun-bloc melted and collected on her top lip and her ice-cream tasted of bubble gum. She wondered if she liked Michaelis. It was easier to be with him than with Thony. He stared less, he wasn't so concerned to hear what she had to say. Occasionally he looked at her suddenly, quizzically, as though surprised he had a companion on his travels, but mostly he seemed preoccupied with his own thoughts.

Two days later Michaelis took her for another ice-cream and told her he had confirmed their flight home.

'What about the panel paintings?' asked Rosandra.

'What about them? I decided not to get them,' said Michaelis.

He was wearing dark glasses. His hair gleamed in the sun. Rosandra's eyelids rasped over her contact lenses.

'Did Thony say no?'

'No, I decided against purchase a few hours after we saw them and so I didn't need to call him. They were OK as far as ethnic pictures go, but I decided they weren't valuable enough. No point in shipping them at high cost. I decided to get an icon instead. You see how it works, Rosandra, things happen quickly and suddenly in this business.'

'Which icon?' said Rosandra, thinking that if Thony asked she must be able to say.

'Maybe you won't remember it,' said Michaelis. 'There was a saint in it, wearing a large gold collar. It was valued very highly because it came from an unusual place, some remote town in Georgia, from behind the Iron Curtain.'

On the way home Michaelis and Rosandra had seats side by side in the plane. Michaelis was studiously drinking whisky and responded to

133

Rosandra's comments in monosyllables. He said he was suffering from post-purchase tension. She tried to entertain him. She told him about circus troupes that travel the Indian Ocean circuit, about a woman she once met who decorated herself by plastering shells on to her skin, about the way her father, David, used to race their family car on the main road outside Cradock, her home town. And when they landed in St Helena for refuelling she asked him, by the bye, how he would set about capturing an island such as this one, if he wanted to, say, in a coup?

She expected surprise, but not that he would turn on her with an expression of intense interest, his preoccupied look suddenly focused.

'What do you ask that for?' he said.

'I was looking at the island lights as we were coming down,' said Rosandra. 'I thought it looked easy to take by air.'

'Thony has a point about you being sharp and not letting on what you know,' said Michaelis. 'But take it from me, if you want to control an island, you buy it.'

He repeated the instruction later that night, but only after amusing himself by plotting out on his dinner napkin an elaborate coup attack plan involving rockets and maps and flash-bang grenades. The coup plan became a game and grew more involved the more whisky Michaelis consumed. Rosandra traced the island outline, trying to make it exactly unlike Eden, bottle-shaped, without branches and tentacles, and Michaelis drew inky pictures delicate as spider webs to illustrate equipment.

'Here are your RPG-2 rocket launchers,' he said. 'And your fragmentation grenades, foreign-made, some RKG-3s, some RPG-6s. Shall we assume these people have external or international contacts?'

'Yes, we can assume that.' Rosandra nodded.

She proposed moves, and plotted them on the map. He countered them with crosses and pictures of explosions. Tiny diagrams of machine-guns pointed like arrows across the paper. His Waterman flashed from side to side. The ink came off on his hands.

Before they both fell asleep he made sure to tear up the paper, very small. In the morning he stowed the remains in his half-eaten Danish.

'As far as I could see we didn't have amazing success on that art excursion,' said Rosandra to Jem, standing up now for the first time, stretching. 'But still, there was something about that trip, like a charm, a hidden spark. It was then that things began to happen. Things became busier and much more intense.'

Following her lead Jem changed his position. He watched her back arch as she stretched. It was so fine, so very fine. He stared for a minute, looked away at the oyster-pink trim, the Zulu pots, then stared again.

'Thony threw a party to celebrate our return,' Rosandra said. 'He was incredibly happy at what we had to report. He first heard from Michaelis in his office. Michaelis had to give his opinion of my performance, so the talk was confidential. Then I told Thony my side of things over dinner, about finding Europe no different from home and liking the African art. I was sure he'd praise me. But he just beamed from a distance. During the whole interview he didn't touch me. I couldn't remember seeing him smile like that before.

'It was at the celebration party a few weeks later that the photo was taken which appeared in the *Sunday Times*. And so I got a name, I became a Star Palace personality. Thony gave me an official invitation to all the extravaganza shows. The only restriction was, I had to promise not to gamble. I was naïve, you see. He didn't want me to get into trouble.'

'I saw that *Sunday Times* photograph,' said Jem. 'Cradock was buzzing about that picture.'

'There was hardly anything to see,' said Rosandra.

'There was enough,' said Jem, trying to smile.

'Do you remember it?' said Rosandra. 'Remind me.'

'Mainly there was you wearing a pink leotard.'

'It was a bunny suit,' said Rosandra. 'Thony wanted the party to be fancy dress. For each person to come as their favourite fantasy. Thony himself didn't dress up. He said it was the host's privilege. I thought it was a pity because he would be so good in fancy dress. But he concentrated on getting me to look right. There were plenty of second-hand bunny girl costumes backstage at the Dome. I found one that was almost the right fit, only a bit long around the waist. My tail came off during the dancing.'

'The picture shows you were enjoying the dancing,' said Jem.

'You mean my fanny was sticking into the lens of the camera?'

'Well, in a way. You were bending over backwards, I think. The shot is from below.'

'And what else do you remember?' said Rosandra.

It took no effort of memory, Jem thought. The *Sunday Times* picture was not his favourite but it was safe in the box. He could draw it for her, though she might not like that. It would mean telling her about his stash of souvenirs.

'There's a crowd of people in the background, very colourful. The faces are distorted, they're wearing masks and make-up and things. No one's looking at you. I suppose the photographer took a chance shot?'

'I don't remember,' said Rosandra. 'So I couldn't tell you.'

'It's difficult to make out much because of the lights coming from all directions.'

He was betraying how well he knew the picture. In a minute he would have to confess: Rosandra, the clipping is part of my archive, my memory-kit, the way I've kept in touch. Like the Spanish postcard, all three postcards, all the messages you ever sent.

'The light display in that disco was fantastic,' said Rosandra. 'Thony laid out the works. International disco designers came to take notes from what his men had set up. Thony said there were more sophisticated light effects concentrated in that space than in any other pleasure centre outside America.'

This is saturation point, Jem thought. This is the point beyond which I cannot listen further. It was the whole scene, the accumulation, one episode after another, all of them painful, and the name Thony repeated and repeated. He was feeling hungry all over again, jittery with an excess of coffee. He wanted to yawn, but at the same time his face muscles wouldn't relax. The need to hear about Thony had lifted. He had his surfeit. The man was a corrupt ego, he collected beauty only to damage it. It was a miracle Rosandra had survived as she did, still lovely, with her still, mask-like face. And yet she was in full flight. Thony gripped and fascinated her. Jem watched her eyes grow far-seeing as though she was living that time all over again. It was uncanny. Thony enchanted her, he captured her will. She was saying things that, in another place, another time, she couldn't possibly believe.

'The best thing of all about that affair of the photograph,' said Rosandra, 'is that it wasn't me at all.'

'The newspaper said it was. Thony "Star Palace" Brandt's new flame Rosandra bares all, it said.'

'Your memory's fantastic,' said Rosandra. 'But, really, even though the photograph showed the dancer in a good light, I think it wasn't me.'

'Why?' said Jem.

'The bunny girl costume wasn't unique. There were two other girls at the party in bunny suits. The photographer took the picture from

136

below, but no one was filming that low down. One of the other bunny girls danced on a table that night. The photographer said it was me because everyone wanted pictures of me. And then the bunny suit in the photograph had a tail. Mine didn't. It came off.'

'But the photograph was taken from the front,' said Jem. 'A tail wouldn't have been visible.'

He didn't know why he was arguing the point. Any talk at this stage was futile. Another day, after a break, in better humour, he could show her the picture. And she would back down. She would see herself in it, her hips, carriage, the line of her stomach and legs, her own perfect figure.

'Of course it's nothing to me if it *was* me,' said Rosandra. 'What I'm saying is, it's funny that it *wasn't*. Especially after the fuss.'

'You should tell your friends in Cradock that,' said Jem. 'Some people keep the clipping to remember you by.'

5

The photograph acted as a kind of magic screen through which she moved into a differently charged existence, Rosandra said – sitting down again, now leaving her glass untouched, rearranging the forks and spoons on the table, lining them in a row. The photograph took her name, it claimed her identity, it made her into something: a figure that people remembered, hot-pink, a tease. For a few weeks, when she opened the weekend papers, she was surprised by images of herself. She never knew what pictures might confront her, with what sort of expression her face would look back.

The photograph brought strange recognitions from strangers, day trippers to the casino, weekend guests. She began to wear her tinted glasses constantly, even indoors, and she kept the thick blinds in the bungalow down. Parents pointed at her for the benefit of their children. She wore longer skirts, she wanted to cover up. People were seeing in their mind's eye, she thought to herself, the photograph's hot-pink cleft. Pictures appeared in a magazine gossip column. Rosandra walking beside Thony; Rosandra sitting at a table by the lake's edge; Rosandra wearing longer skirts. In all the pictures she looked pale, starved, blankly staring. The gossip column called her the White Queen. The beauty page in a Sunday paper pull-out section suggested girls avoid sunbathing to obtain her white look. The article went on to advise girls already tanned to use pale foundation, pastel powders. Girls with brown complexions were not advised at all.

In the new hubbub of attention Rosandra worried about doing her job for Thony. There was no time to see him privately, or talk about Europe and art. But he did not complain about what had happened. He offered an opinion only when a women's magazine called up for a beauty interview. He mentioned the intrusive publicity such an article would bring, he said Rosandra must think of the implications of the new image. It tired her, it might make her look trivial. She was a Star Palace representative and that role carried responsibilities.

Rosandra refused the interview. She began to leave the telephone ringing and to stay inside the bungalow during the day. Beauty, especially beauty under spotlights, needs conservation, a little rest. She massaged herself, she rubbed nail cream into her nail beds, she slept most afternoons. But the efforts were unproductive. She must have been more taxed than she realised. Her skin stayed dry, her nails broke more vengefully than before, her legs seemed to sag when she walked.

In truth, she began to think, she might not be worthy of a beauty article. The publicity experience exposed weaknesses, flaws, underlying blemishes. Feeling vulnerable, she rubbed foundation cream of a lighter colour into the mark on her stomach and began to reapply it two, three times a day. One evening she spent five hours waxing and plucking her arms and armpits, to eradicate every hair.

She thought of the embarrassment – people saying she was not as beautiful as she was made out to be, putting their fingers on her freckles and her odd-coloured eyes looking out at them from a glossy page. They would explain her retreat in this way: she wasn't as beautiful as the rumours said. Her hair these days looked lack-lustre and tired. Her posture was bad. Sitting, she leaned too far back; standing, she bent back at the knees. She had no beauty tips to pass on. More than that, she wasn't feeling beautiful. She was eating too much. Her body was looking more soggy. People would think she was bigger than they imagined, too much hip-fat, too much looseness on the upper arms.

Bass would explode with the irony of it. All this just when she had the chance to grab the limelight and organise serious shoots with important photographers and become professional. In fact there were two ironies, the first had another folded into it. Because the time hiding indoors out of the light, eating, did nothing for looks. Maybe Thony wasn't exactly right about the effects of the sun. The freckles were more than prominent in her pale face, they were loud, and her fat was rising like dough. For the first time in her life she was growing larger in the stomach. She noticed it soon after the celebration. It began with her flesh puffing out from the dents made by her hipbones, then the soft bulge extended up to her ribs. She pressed it and it gave, a bloating. Day after day, she could feel, she was swelling a little more.

At first, to disguise this new largeness, she wore long pullovers like miniskirts. She turned up the air-conditioning to endure the warmth. At night she went out, wearing her pullovers. Thony took her to his air-conditioned Star Palace night spots for drinks.

'Yes, it was definitely not you,' a male croupier said to her in the Marina bar at the Southern Californian hotel one day.

The Marina was another of the wonders of Star Palace, a chrome cube cantilevered over a gaming salon. Below, at Rosandra's feet, row upon row of fruit machines roared. Back at the entrance to the bar, in one of the telephone alcoves, Thony was having a word with the Marina manager.

'In the paper, I mean,' the croupier said in response to her blank look. 'I think that photograph was of one of the other girls, not you.'

He was speaking in a spirit of camaraderie. He seemed to want to reassure her.

'I definitely think it was one of the other girls,' he said.

She knew he was staring. He was looking at her hips and thighs where the pullover lay spread.

She kept watch over her changing shape in the full-length mirror in the bungalow bathroom. One night she stripped naked and probed her swelling from every direction with surgical precision, prodding deep and pressing gently. She examined herself from the front and in profile. She had to admit it: the stomach was definitely bigger than last week. The pores around her navel looked pressed open from within, like reversed teats. The skin was under strain. Her mark was growing. It was no longer a blotch, it was the Antarctic continent. The stretching turned the brown colour to aubergine and elongated its tentacle edges. The morning's skin of foundation cream showed cracks, deep ones, as in dried mud.

She worried about carrying a malignancy inside her, a thickening, gnarled growth, suddenly conceived. It was oval-shaped, she imagined, a knotted seed. Growing, it would become pumpkin-like, rotting, sprouting polyps.

But on the other hand, she thought, looking on the practical side, the bulge could have something to do with abnormal swelling, something premenstrual. She hadn't bled since Europe, which was very late. It was an after-effect most likely of the air trip. These things happened, extraordinary retentions of fluid, all surfaces convex. Her bulge was taut, hard, and held no pain. Even her eyes looked as though they were bulging. The signs weren't normal, but then it was an unusual cycle. Loaded, waterlogged, she felt that she would burst with fullness. She forced her stomach into her jeans, wore her pullovers, and waited.

Thony noticed changes.

'Your eyes seem to be extra shiny since Europe, Rosandra. The trip must have agreed with you. You're looking very well, very robust.'

One day she ordered fresh flowers for the bungalow from the housekeeper, Mrs Lawrence. Mrs Lawrence was a slight woman with a mild baby-face. She came from Preston, in England. She told Rosandra she loved Africa. It was the clear air, the valleys and hills lovely beyond description, she said, and of course the joviality of the black people, especially at Star Palace. She'd moved to Africa as a child, and all this time she'd enjoyed only the best service.

'The press attention is doing you good,' she told Rosandra. 'You're looking radiant.'

'Thank you,' Rosandra said.

Mrs Lawrence bent closer and looked furtively from side to side. Her clothes were steeped in a soft-pink odour, a fabric softener.

'I studied that picture in the papers,' she said. 'I'm sure it wasn't you. They wouldn't let something like that go through, I'm sure. Mr Brandt would have stopped it.'

'I was wearing a pink outfit, like the girl in the picture,' said Rosandra, knowing that as housekeeper Mrs Lawrence would have supervised its washing. 'But it needn't have been me. There were other people in the same costume at the party.'

'I'm sure there were,' said the housekeeper soothingly.

That evening capers and tomatoes were served as side-salad in the Uluru restaurant, Thony's favourite. Thony sat to Rosandra's left, where he could look at her profile and also survey the rest of the room. Rosandra speared a long kebab of capers on her fork and slid them off down the middle of her tongue. The taste was like something she'd been waiting for, green, salty, tangy and not quite there, as though her taste buds were still expecting the bulk of the flavour when the swallow was already complete. She ordered two more salads. Meanwhile Thony was talking about her new public image. Generally, he concluded, the results were positive. She'd made the choice to take things calmly; he was pleased.

'It could have gone badly wrong,' he said, eating his kiwi-cream dessert. Rosandra speared up her third helping of capers and tomatoes. 'Though of course I should have trusted that anything involving you would be charmed.'

People in the city office phoned him about the photograph, to congratulate him for finding such a dazzling chick. To this day his managers were accusing him of keeping her in the dark. Where d'you find this kind of material? they asked. Not through want of searching, he said. If he was honest he might almost say he felt envious, like he wanted to be in their place. He was thinking of them ogling her, of their desire, of what they wanted to do with her.

Rosandra looked up, surprised. Thony was a man in power: it didn't suit him to feel envy.

'It's the fact that the picture looks scandalous, naturally, that gets them fired up,' he said. 'That's the beauty of it. And everybody knows you're my special interest. The photo shouts out, We're having a ball and doing it beautifully. It's a very lucky picture.'

Rosandra was glad he felt that way. It was good he was pleased, she said. She ordered a fourth salad.

'You're not on a diet, I hope,' Thony said, looking her up and down. 'You don't need to lose weight, my beautiful one. Your mirror will tell you that. *Au naturel* you are just right, just perfect.'

'The funny thing is, I don't think the picture is of me,' said Rosandra.

Caper vinegar was carving a hole in the wall of her stomach.

'On the night of the party I lost my bunny tail. The photographer came to the party late. The person in the picture couldn't have been me.'

'You sly thing,' Thony said lightly, as though what she said was meant as a joke. 'I should trust you to come up with a clever story like that. It's not quite clever enough though. If I remember, the photograph was taken from the front. There's no tail visible. But that's immaterial in the long run. The world thinks it's you and that's what's important to us. Whether it's you or not the thing has done us no harm. It's a small social world out there in the city and they need these big single images. They think of that picture and then they think of the excitement of Star Palace. And meanwhile we continue with the original plan of getting you more involved in the serious side of business. What I say at the end of the day, Rosandra, is bravo. Bravo for putting Star Palace even more securely on the map.'

He left the table while she was still eating salad. There was an evening meeting with his casino managers, paperwork to do with the aquapark, but he'd see her before bedtime, he promised, he'd walk by the bungalow to say good night.

Rosandra stayed in the dining room for some time, digesting the capers. The lights were turned down but the waiters had not yet come in to clear. Green messes of kiwi-cream lay clotted on small white plates across the length of the room. The Vivaldi had been switched off and the DJ at the Rama disco next door was practising chatting to an empty room. He was a little nervous. His teasing comments ended on a warbling note. Rosandra felt desperately nauseous but too heavy and slow to make it over to the Ladies. When she gagged into Thony's kiwi-cream plate, there was no issue.

Rosandra waited up that night for Thony. She put on her glasses. They were dusty from disuse. The Star Palace late-night chemist sent round pills, yellow and bitter, which they promised were good for nausea. She was swallowing the pills and still in her clothes when Thony walked through the front door, or didn't walk, she observed, watching from the kitchen, but slid in his smooth, precise way, holding the door ajar, gripping the handle.

'I think I must be pregnant,' she said, straight out, not coming forward to meet him.

It was easy saying it. She'd wanted to be matter-of-fact. If she got the tone right he might take it well, as a slight hitch, a brief interruption of their plans, which, by and large, was how she saw it. She heard her voice sound ordinary, as she wanted it. She had planned to add his name. Thony, I think I am pregnant. But she had guessed she might not manage it.

He sat down slowly, raising his trouser legs neatly, one at a time. He chose the most comfortable chair, the large old Lazi-Boy armchair that had loose hinges. He usually referred to it as the kitsch chair. Now he sat heavily and with relief on its edge and the smell of fresh eau-de-cologne flooded the air. Rosandra felt her nausea sink but wanted to cradle her stomach in her arms. The capers had tautened it. The stomach went before her past the sink and the sideboard and the landscape paintings on the walls by Betty Cilliers Barnard, John Kotze, other unfamiliar names, flat desert landscapes, as she walked up to him.

'What makes you say that?' said Thony, looking at her lower torso.

Rosandra raised her pullover and shirt. The bulge was unmistakable.

'How is it possible?' he asked.

She paused, gathered breath.

'The stuff creeping round and in,' she said.

*   *   *

143

So they were making their way through the darkened back stage of the big Dome dancing theatre. Rows of costumes hung in the shadows on silver-painted rails. In a corner stood a wooden crate stamped Chris de Burgh. There was the back-stage smell of old sweat, rubber soles, dusty lights.

Rosandra went first, groping in the semi-light; Thony bumped into her from behind, chuckling as though it were a game of catch. They were walking quickly, excited. They had hit on the bunny girl idea over drinks in the bar. Rosandra said she wanted to be Dolly, as in *Hello Dolly!*, like Barbra Streisand. Thony said Annie Hall, Fanny Hill, Norma Jean. Then they decided a bunny girl was an easier bet.

'I know there's a suit here to fit you exactly,' Thony said, his voice at her ear. 'There were lots here when last I looked. Feel for the silkiness, Rosandra, the nylon. That'll be the bunny suits.'

But she identified them by the fluffy tails. They brushed against her arms. She changed in the half-light on the other side of the row of clothes. She thought the bunny suits made a safe continuous barrier. The last she knew Thony was squinting up at the light system overhead.

Then he had grabbed her round the waist from behind and was pressing himself hard against her. She was holding on to the bunny suit; it was half on her body and she clutched it crumpled in a coil around her waist. Her arms were moving in the air, jerking, like interrupted breaststroke. It was hot again, very hot on her lower back, like the first night. It was like wetting herself twice over, the sudden heat, and the shame.

Her bunny tail was askew, soaked, its fastenings loosened. Thony waited for her in the foyer of the building. Seeing him standing there in the blaze of Tivoli lighting was a shock. It gave her a metallic taste in the mouth, the taste of capers, iron, blood. His face was familiar to her and yet, she realised, unwelcome, like a strange meeting in a mirror, seeing the reflected face of someone who has watched a long time unnoticed. It was the face she remembered from that first night under neon, exposed, gleaming, before he began to speak. Her skin felt sensitive and dirty. Back-stage she had pushed toilet paper down into the bunny suit to soak up the wet. Body hollows and crevasses, arses, make good warm dams and storing places, she thought. The sperm lay there that evening and then started travelling. When the photo was taken.

*   *   *

Thony was staring at her middle.

'I'm sure it's possible for that kind of thing to happen,' she added. 'The stuff travelling round and in, moving through the nylon fabric.'

He looked up at her, a quick throw of the chin; his eyes seemed to have shrunk into his skull. His beard stood out black. The dank smell of his skin was not disguised by the eau-de-cologne.

'Utter rubbish,' he said. 'An absolutely rotten theory. I expected better of you. The real question is different, Rosandra. The real question is, what have you been up to on your travels, or indeed here, under my very nose?'

He was like a father, reprimanding, suspicious. Bass on the beach that night, eating fruit-bat curry, reliving his soldiering days.

Thony pulled at her hands. She wanted to stay apart, keep the distance, but her weight unbalanced her and she slipped down on the Lazi-Boy beside him, all elbows and knees.

'It was Michaelis?' he said. 'Tell me. Or some guy in the hotel in Nice when Michaelis wasn't looking? I'll hear the truth from you, Rosandra. We'll purge you of that secrecy. Was it that croupier I saw you talking to the other night?'

His breath was hot and his hands left patches like red burns as he felt up and down her arms, checking for something. Yet there remained a control in his passion, a controlled watchfulness, and she felt, as she watched his hands move, a slight, resigned relief.

'Oh you little bitch, you beautiful dangerous little whore,' he said. 'Give an inch and see what happens. Send her to Europe on a responsible venture and she comes back pregnant. If I find someone has been messing in my space, Rosandra, I will blast the man off the face of this earth, and I will kill Michaelis too. He should have done his job, he should have been watching out. It was part of the deal. As for you. You I will punish in ways you haven't even imagined in your nightmares.'

'I don't often have nightmares, I don't think.' She spoke quickly, interrupting his flow.

But he ignored what she said. He pulled up her pullover, then her shirt, and her stomach was fully exposed. It seemed to lift up proudly of itself. She felt she was hiding behind it. The mark stood out in purple. A magnetic storm, a mortal wound.

Thony fell dead quiet: he had not seen the mark before. Her bunny suit covered it, the night masked it. When he lay on her in the dark she was belly-down, her face in the pillows. It was as though he was witness to a humiliation. His gaze shifted over to one side; his lips puckered, repelled, offended. She dragged the pullover from his hands and drew it over the mark.

'Rosandra, that can't be a pregnancy,' he said.

He leant heavily into the chair and it flipped back. They were lying back together, side by side, the stomach protruding. Thony sighed. His hand was placed protectively at his side. Rosandra saw he was carrying a small pistol. The hand covering it was lightly braced, but tired.

'For self-defence,' he said, seeing her look. 'As I explained when you went off to Europe. Carrying guns makes sure of things.'

He was saying something for the sake of it. His anger was gone, and his heat. The sight of her stomach had quelled him. She looked away. The bulb in the big glass dome overhead made a yellow saucer of light. She thought of the dance floor at the party, the gold-tinted mirrors covering the walls, sandblasted with stars, the converging rows of lights in the airfield pattern. The cameras as they started flashing merged with the light display. She thought of dancing between the nameless figures, wearing the fancy dress. She was spinning round and round, legs meeting, slightly parting, meeting. She was moving unseeing to the music, forgetting, forgetting about her wet bunny costume, Thony's desire, people staring. There was freedom in it, the blinding lights underfoot and overhead, freedom in losing balance, spinning through the illumination, carelessly, trying to think of nothing at all.

They were lying close, she and Thony, side by side in the lavender-blue early dawn light – like man and wife, she thought – as she fell asleep.

Then, more than half asleep but too drowsy to move, Rosandra felt Thony slipping his hands over her body. His hands were very light. Not like at night in the bed, not hot at all. She tried to lie very still, to breathe like a sleeper, but there was no need for pretence, he was concentrating on something else. Her stomach was covered. The skin of her mark was warm. She felt the buttons of the Lazi-Boy and the metal joins in it cold under her back. He had taken off her clothes and also her glasses but he draped her shirt over the stomach to cover it. Through her eyelashes she could see the dawn sky paling, white lavender. His fingers were pressing at her, insisting and checking. She felt warm, moist. She tried to stop the moisture coming. She was meant to be asleep. But it continued, the fingers and then the moisture coming out of her body.

She woke again with Thony making coffee.

'Rosandra, you're not pregnant,' he said from the kitchen. 'You've eaten something bad. You're tense and tired. That stomach may be a result of all the hullabaloo with the photograph. Women's bodies do crazy things. One or more of the dancers here is always off sick.'

She was glad he was calm. She could speak.

'I feel sure I'm pregnant,' she said.

It was a relief to share the load, even if it repelled him. The stomach had become a kind of guilt, also a discomfort. The coffee was making her want to retch.

'I have the symptoms,' she said. 'I'm nauseous. I'm craving things. Right now I could walk blocks to get some toast, something light and dry.'

It struck her she was being more honest than she'd been with him before. Always she dutifully took the food he offered. These days she held her hand to her own throat to swallow down his oysters. She ate his delicacies, the salty black mess of caviare, the slippery *crêmes brûlées*. But in this early light – the perfect blue sky at the window, quite cloudless, like on the first morning here – honesty about something as simple as food made things more plain. Honesty was a firm defence, it proved innocence. It proved she was a person to trust. He would see that. If she was in the wrong, if she'd touched someone else, wouldn't she hide the evidence? Wouldn't she go away somewhere and get rid of the pregnancy alone?

Thony ordered toast for her from the Uluru kitchens. Stroking her thigh down its inner length, he said he would call a city gynaecologist he knew, a man he trusted who came up to Star Palace to play golf. He avoided looking at her stomach, she noticed. She followed his eyes. He patted her hair as he said goodbye.

In the bathroom, as soon as he was gone, Rosandra put in her lenses and checked her body, low down, inside herself. She'd done this once before, she remembered, that first time, much more anxious than she was now, and more ham-handed. Yes, she checked, it was all right, she was still closed there, quite tight, even after Thony's touching.

However, sperm could get through tightness, as any schoolgirl knew. The virginal skin is not an impermeable membrane. The older girls learned the term in biology classes: 'impermeable' was a difficult word used to describe cell walls and human skin. The young girls did not know the word and heard in it a sound of mystery. There was probably some truth in the theory. Rosandra

147

imagined the hymen like a sieve, perforated with tiny holes, each tiny as a sperm.

Most of that morning she sat in the living room and drank tea, waiting. From her chair she stared at the blue sky, saw that the early bright heat was creating clouds, masses of white. But there was no blue cloud, it still eluded her here, the blue stroke on a bluer space of sky. She looked away from the window. She noticed that in the bright sunlight her shadow looked maternal.

At lunch-time she ate several packs of prawn-flavoured chips and a jar of cheese spread. Most of the afternoon she watched cartoons for children on television. She had the feeling of waiting for something important. It would be Thony, because he would have a solution. There were advertisements on television for baby food, a pine kitchen and bright orange and green vegetables jumping merrily in a pot, a mother beaming at purée in a jar. There was also a baby. He had chubby cheeks, a high colour. The baby was a strange pink apparition, but it occurred to her that being pregnant – if this stomach was a pregnancy – meant becoming a mother, having children, being someone quite different, losing shape. Rosandra got up, feeling ill. On the white carpet of Thony's bungalow she brought up a yellow fudge of prawn chips and cheese spread. The bulge under her shirt was an outrage, a fright. Bending over the toilet, retching, it was unmistakably there.

At five that afternoon storm clouds clotted out the sun. In the purple light the birthmark showed up more livid than before. It looked like the outer stain of a hidden infection, Rosandra thought, an internal bleed. She felt her way around the bulge again, looking for nodules of disease, little toadstools deep under the skin. But the bulge was simply smooth, simply convex. It was a pregnancy. She decided she needed immediate help. She must call someone herself.

Regina was on the switchboard that day. Rosandra had met her a few times in Star Palace bars. She came over to chat when Thony talked business with men at other tables, in corners of vestibules, in telephone booths. Regina was from Sebokeng, old Sharpeville; she was friendly. She liked Nina Simone and high shoes with peep toes and missed her family. But she said no job in the Republic paid like this one at Star Palace. Here she could afford to wear different shoes each day of the week and on top of that send her sisters shoes as presents. On the night of the celebration party

Regina too had worn a bunny suit. She had dyed the fluffy cotton tail black. It's for solidarity, she explained laughing with a table of white friends. It's black like my skin, the skin of my people. She laughed so loudly the table fell silent and her friends did not know where to look.

'Long-distance, please,' Rosandra said.

'About time,' said Regina. 'You haven't called anyone outside of this place since you arrived.'

Rosandra heard a whistle of air. Regina would be dragging on a Lucky Strike. She always had a cigarette on hand.

'You're too quiet over there by yourself,' said Regina. 'It's good you're phoning. Why not use the boss's direct line?'

'He's busy,' said Rosandra, lying.

Regina was able to see whether Thony was on the telephone. She had the illuminated telephone controls of the hotel complex in front of her. But she said nothing. Her voice disappeared. Electric crackles hurt Rosandra's ear. The storm had covered the western sky.

'You're through,' Regina said after a while.

There was an empty ringing space, then the small sound of a telephone.

But Susan White was not at home. No one was home, not David, not Maria. And Maria always used to be there. Rosandra was disappointed. She wanted to hear their voices: Susan, slow, amazed, cheerful, and Maria.

'You want to try someone else?' said Regina, butting into the sound of the distant phone.

'Yes,' said Rosandra.

She gave Jem's Cradock number.

'You were there, I think, but it was a bad line,' Rosandra said.

She called me, Jem thought, suddenly alert. He did not remember the time. Was it true? There were any number of bad lines, attempted calls. When could it have been? What was he doing at the time? Looking round in Port Elizabeth, East London, for a teaching job, thinking about joining the army? Maybe his father answered, angry at the interruption, grumbling down the dead line. What misfortune, what bad luck, what mischance. It made him want to grab her wrists: I wish I was there for you – destiny split us apart.

149

But what could he have said to her then? I saw your picture in the papers. You must be Rich and Famous now. No, not that, the same thing that her mother would have said. He would have wanted to give good advice. If she had got through, if he had heard her. A case of the lines that did not cross. He saw the threads of missed possibilities fraying out from that moment. She would have loved him, he would have protected her. Instead she continued with Thony. Ludicrous: she relied on Thony for help.

'Hello. Can you hear me? Hello? Guess who this is,' is what she said on the line to Jem, speaking the words loudly into the static, thinking, could Regina hear?

'I think I need help,' she whispered, but only once.

While manicuring, Regina sometimes lifted an odd receiver. She knew many things. She had the latest information on the night manager's affairs with three different women around Star Palace, a waitress, a tour guide and his fiancée, a cosmetics rep. His Black Ladies, she called them, and co-ordinated the various clandestine calls across the hotel complex. In return, after the day's work, the night manager ordered up whisky sodas for her, and double-decker bacon burgers from the late kitchen.

'I wouldn't mind him myself for a bit,' Regina was known to say, 'seeing as he likes black ladies like us.'

The static noise had dwindled to a lonely bleating, like a fading radio signal.

'Hello,' said Regina, uncomfortably close. 'Don't worry, it's me. You got trouble there?'

'It was a bad line.'

Rosandra put a hand under her enlarged stomach, where it was comfortable, and comfortingly smooth.

'They're all bad today,' said Regina. 'Especially to the south. It's the storm. You trying to call home?'

'Yes.'

'About time, eh? Maybe better luck tomorrow. You should be like me. Ask the boss to have your family come to work at Star Palace too. My brother works here in the gardens. My sister's coming next month. She'll be in the El Mar casino.'

So Thony's idea of integration was working out.

Rosandra ended the conversation. The storm passed without breaking and the sun came out. There were light outlines to the clouds and silver linings to the hills. Bright light struck her mirror. Looking at herself she confronted a blankness: her own eyes, pale, seeing-nothing eyes. So that was how it was. What had Bass said? Drop-dead eyes. Drop that stare, said the woman who walked her home the night her bag was stolen in the city. She came up closer, scrutinising the stare with interest. The pale eyes, staring but unseeing, light and empty, a bit like Thony's, a kind of protection, as though she had no thoughts.

A waiter knocked at the flat door.

'Whisky and soda,' he said. 'Like the madam ordered.'

A torn piece of cash slip on the tray said 'Love, Regina' written in blue eyeliner.

Rosandra took the drink though she knew she should send it back. It was clear Regina had some idea in mind, a sharp signal of refusal was needed. But once Rosandra drank down the whisky her nervousness was dulled and she felt stronger. She thought about going somewhere, by herself, finding help in the city. People would know about pregnancies there. She could take the car, she had been round Star Palace many times in it, Thony said she drove well. But there was the problem of the security gates. They might not let her through. The guards would lean into the car and so see the stomach. Thony would be angry, his rich dark beard would stand out. She thought again of Regina, because Regina knew many things. But she was also feeling drowsy. She remembered her mother's drowsiness when she was pregnant. Susan sat in her armchair with her head on one side and sometimes listened to Uncle Bass's stories and sometimes slept.

Eventually Rosandra decided to find Thony herself. It was after sunset and he had not yet called. Under cover of darkness she made her way to his office. She put on a wide raincoat for good measure.

When Thony opened his office door the reason for his delay was explained. In a bed of bubble plastic on the black desk lay the icon Michaelis bought in France. The spotlight over the desk was the one source of illumination. The icon gleamed. Beside it on the black desk surface was a thickly folded computer print-out.

'You did yourselves proud,' said Thony, leaning on his elbows, absorbed.

Rosandra could not remember this particular image at all: the severe, tawny face, thin nose, much gold. She was wearing her glasses today. Maybe that made the difference; there was none of the irritation of the contact lenses. But even so the icon was very bright. It burned. She looked up for relief, at the White Reflections, shadowy in the half-light, at their bent shadows, hers and Thony's, in the reflecting glass. Her bulge didn't show. She looked at the print-out, a list, names alongside numbers, MX, RPK, 301, 30L, detailing perhaps the other items in the exhibition. Thony caught her focus and straightened up. He made a wry mouth at her whisky breath.

'That's not for you to see at this stage, Rosandra,' he said, fatherly again, turning the print-out over. 'Later, though maybe sooner than you think, you can see these things. But not right now, while you're distracted by this stomach business. To put your mind at rest, what this details, in a phrase, is new security equipment for Star Palace.'

'There must be a lot of security needed,' said Rosandra, thinking of the difficulty of getting beyond the entrance barrier, driving to the city.

'Yes, it pays to be security-conscious. If anything should go wrong out there in the Republic it's not inconceivable that we will have to defend ourselves. It pays to be prepared. We must guarantee the uninterrupted pleasure of our guests, especially those from overseas.'

He was speaking quickly, as if he didn't want to dwell on the subject.

'I don't understand,' said Rosandra, wanting to.

'Oh, you lovely thing,' said Thony, a shade of his early warmth in his voice. 'Don't worry about it now. You will find out, you will be hearing about it, as I said maybe sooner than expected. There have been strange things happening in some places in the Republic even this past month. Violent protests, rent boycotts. These are signs of race war – exactly the kind of things that we at Star Palace don't want. I was watching the latest reports on TV today but they tell you nothing. I informally asked Regina to find out about the situation for me, seeing it's her part of the world. So far I've heard nothing.

'But come,' he said, bringing his face intimately close, 'let's not talk about these serious matters when we have this beautiful thing in front of us.'

He took her by the elbow and led her over to the next room. There he switched on the spotlight over an empty space on the wall.

'Yes,' he said, 'that's exactly it. I've had that bit of wall in mind for something special for over a year. I thought the icon might look right elsewhere, in my own suite, but no, this is the place. Now Rosandra, if you could perfectly complete my pleasure. Go over and get it and hang it for me.'

Things took a long time from that point. Speech was slower, thoughts slower still. Rosandra stood and looked into the darkness of the room, at the gables and spiny trees of the large painting, and the darker paintings, the foliage, the undergrowth. She knew before he started speaking that he would ask her to hang the icon, and at the same moment she knew she would not do it. It wasn't right. She didn't feel able, especially today. The icon wasn't for her to hang. It represented a demand but she couldn't obey it. Her thoughts moved hesitantly, from reason to reason. It had to do with not having the right. The icon was a beautiful thing, to be admired by experts, and she wasn't in the know, not yet learned. She hadn't chosen it; it didn't belong to her; it wasn't right for her to hang it. Thony would understand.

He was holding her by the shoulders.

'Rosandra!' His voice lilted. Calling coo-ee as in hide-and-seek. 'It's all set up for you, my love. There's wire attached to the picture, and here's the space on the wall. Now come.'

'I don't think I want to,' said Rosandra.

She thought it so strongly she felt she'd already said it: no. She repeated herself. I don't want to, she could hear herself say.

'Michaelis was here a minute ago,' said Thony. 'I told him I was giving you the privilege. It depends on you to hang it, Rosandra.'

'I can't.'

She backed away. She discovered her hands were folded under her stomach. She had guarded them there.

'You're not relying on your condition to excuse this kind of irrationality, are you?' said Thony, suddenly concentrated. 'I really do hope not. That would be unforgivable. At such an important moment for me.'

He switched off the second spotlight and walked back to his desk. In her embarrassment she could have exaggerated it – she felt she had been embarrassed for hours now, for days, the Star Palace experience becoming a discomfort, her training all a *faux-pas* – yet she caught, as he passed her, a look of sharp anger, also disgust.

'I won't force things,' Thony said, after a silence, patiently, as if resuming a meeting after an unwelcome hitch. 'For the time being let's leave the situation as it stands.'

He smoothed bubble plastic over the icon's face.

'But let me make this clear, Rosandra. I will not hang this thing myself. I'm depending on you to do it. It's what I want.'

She stood on the other side of the desk, hanging her head, feeling sinful, abject, and pregnant on top of it. She had made a mistake, more than one mistake. She felt shamed. But there was no choice in the matter. She couldn't hang the icon, not even to please him. It did not belong to her.

'Incidentally,' said Thony, standing by the door, waiting to show her out, 'I've just been reminded of something. Tomorrow you and I will be flying to Europe. At one stage I wanted to send Michaelis, but you and I together will be a better team. We can kill several birds with one stone. I have an old Oxford friend in London, a physician on Harley Street. He can give you an examination. That way we preserve utter discretion on this matter. It will be even better this way than seeing my contact in the city. I also have some phone calls to make in London, better made from there than here. Then I'll take you out to a place you may enjoy. All you should do for now is pack your bags like a good girl.'

As Rosandra passed he gave her a small pat on the buttocks. The touch was new, brusque, not as delicate as before.

'You beautiful thing,' he said, very matter-of-fact.

So it was Europe again, seemingly larger, more shadowy and water-logged: London this time. Over Northern Europe Rosandra wanted to look out for the neat canal and street patterns that she imagined from Thony's painting, but he had given her pills for her nausea, which made her sleep. She had no memory of the air trip, only of the ride in a London taxi cab, Thony far off at the other end of a wide seat, exhaust fumes in the car, diffused pearly light outside, and brick houses in rows going past the window, grey trees, rusty guttering. Then the houses grew to look more like hotels, white-painted, grand, and the signs on shop fronts spelling out familiar names in bold lettering at last resembled the writing on Swiss chocolate and read like well-known proverbs: Harrods, Fortnum and Mason, Lloyds Bank.

'You've been in London, haven't you, Jem?' Rosandra said. 'I remember my mother telling me that. You were living there? Working?'

She waited for him to reply. But he heard her question as though from a distance. His thoughts were circling around one point, fixed on it, testing it from this side and that. The fact she hadn't hung the icon. It meant something very important. It was a sign of shame. In the Dome with Thony she felt shamed, and in Thony's office she felt guilty. She said so. She was wronged but she sensed her own part in it. It was difficult to concentrate on this idea. It was late. Yet this much was straight. She'd confessed. That was why she couldn't touch the icon. She didn't want to involve herself further. Instinctively, yes, instinctively, she knew it wouldn't be right.

154

Rosandra ordered a whisky and soda and did not ask Jem if he wanted one.

How it began to go sour, she thought. From that time in the office. I stood hanging my head, I spoiled Thony's treat. The icon burned, like a star, like fire. It was impossible to touch, so perfect. I couldn't hang it. It wasn't right.

But then the situation was cleared up a little, Rosandra said, by the visit to Thony's friend. The taxi ride took them straight from Heathrow to Harley Street. During the examination the physician's hands felt warm and wet. When he gave her the diagnosis, 'hysterical pregnancy', he could not keep her gaze. She saw his forehead up close as he looked down, the clean, pale wrinkles, the chin crumpling as though in suppressed strain, like cramped-up laughter. Thony, sitting beside her holding her hand, merely nodded.

There was no cure, the physician said, coughing a little, the problem would deflate and disappear of itself. There was no clear cause, these things happened to women, especially the young, impressionable ones. It could mean they secretly wanted a baby; it could mean they were frustrated and bored. Thony slid Rosandra's captive hand on to his knee and told the doctor there was no fear of boredom in her life. The physician didn't look up.

But his look of discomfort must be because of the strain of keeping her secret, Rosandra thought. Because an hour ago she had shared a special secret moment with him. To the doctor, as he laid one hand tenderly on her birthmark and put three wet fingers inside her, she gave up her hidden virginity. Her hymen broke at the touch of his skin, the intrusion made a low, muffled pop. And she didn't regret it. It would be a secret. This man would keep things private, these small questions of honour. His lips were cramped with the secrets he kept in.

Coming to terms with a bogus pregnancy probably needs a few hours, Rosandra guessed, but in London there was no time. Thony flew to the Isle of Man for the afternoon, a trip which, he said, would save him in phone calls. He had a small company on the island, and though it usually ran itself, on account of the new security needs at Star Palace it was demanding attention. He sent Rosandra on an excursion to three art galleries with a list of paintings to see and to tick off, but she fell asleep on a bench in the first gallery, the National Gallery, in front of the first painting on her list, something pinkish, and when Thony met her that night he was so excited about things in general, the negative diagnosis and the afternoon's successful business arrangements, that he forgot to check her list.

He took her to a wine bar, in part a coffee shop. Day-old newspapers lay scattered across copper-topped tables, more papers than she'd seen in one place before, and the walls and ceiling were resinous, the colour concentrated in bands, like tide marks of cigarette smoke and conversation gathered over years.

'The coffee here is very good,' said Thony, prompting Rosandra to take a seat in a corner.

'You know this place well?'

'If my trips take me to this city I come here. Michaelis likes it too. He discovered it.'

An Alsatian came up to scrutinise them and Thony buried his hand in the pelt of its neck.

'I know this fellow,' said Thony. 'He comes to check out everybody who drinks here. You can't blame him. Everybody could be anybody – drug barons, newspaper editors, owners of Star Palace. Anyone.'

He looked at her archly as though he was teasing her, playing on double meanings. But she was too bewildered to work it out. She watched him drink two brandies with dedication, carefully. She put a hand to her own glass, she thought of proposing a toast, but it looked like there were other things on his mind. Something in his manner was different, the slight lift of the head, the short statements. She saw an international businessman, no longer her admirer, but a big man with deals up his sleeve, more art works in the offing, a sports competition, equipment for the aquapark. He leaned back to look at her, usually he leaned forward. This gave him a look of distance, it could be of disdain.

But she couldn't blame him. The pregnancy scare was off-putting, there were no two ways about it. He chose her for her perfect beauty, and now look at her. Fat, squishy, weighed down, she was an eyesore, no object for a lover. The dimness in the place was a mercy. She wished she had a corset, whatever large women wore, a kind of firm brace to bind the extra weight.

A cheeseboard arrived with the coffee. She ate Brie, Thony insisted on it. He fed her small pieces and she savoured for the first time·the smooth-toffee, cool-mould butteriness of the cheese against her palate. She let it lie there, feeling it sink back slowly against her uvula.

'Nice cheese,' she said thickly.

'The coffee's good too,' said Thony. 'I should get something like this joint rigged up at the Palace.'

He sipped and sniffed his coffee for a long while. But because his voice was always smooth, whatever his mood, it seemed that there was no break between this comment and the next.

'Tell me, Rosandra,' he said, 'how you came to know Sebastiaan Sampson, the coup-man and hijack specialist?'

A roaring began deep in her ears, dull and deafening. She remembered it from somewhere, but there was no time to place the memory. She felt blindly that this was a crux, a break in everything that had been. It was the matter of the icon; a punishment. It hadn't taken long to come.

'Do you know Bass?' she said.

It felt usual saying the name, easy as a greeting, as though – were it not for his expression, the new critical note – they were simply swopping memories.

'It's interesting that you counter with a question, Rosandra,' he said, 'for being generous with information is not, if I may say so, something that has distinguished your behaviour of late. I do not know Bass Sampson, no. I have not had that pleasure. I'm told he is great fun, a good mate.'

'Oh yes,' said Rosandra, 'he's my uncle. That is, a friend of my father's.'

But she could barely hear Thony's response for the roaring in her ears. The noise distorted perception. The ceiling patterns blurred even inside the contact lenses. Two women sitting at the window were swallowed up by night. Giddiness would tumble her out of the chair if she did not uncross her legs, sit steady, breathe calmly, slowly. Thony knew. And yet, now that he knew, it seemed puzzling that it took so long. Thony was an important man, he had ways and means of detection. But he had picked his moment. Now, after the doctor's. And he was using what he knew to blame.

'An uncle?' said Thony. 'I didn't know that. Maybe, when we have a moment later on, you'll be able to tell me more about the details of the relationship. But to answer your question, it's Michaelis who knows your uncle. It's Michaelis who identified you. The first time he met you he felt he'd seen you before. It was at the time of the European trip, when he had a chance to get to know you, that he worked it out. One of the features that betrayed you, ironically perhaps, was the way you play to a public eye, my beautiful Rosandra. Along with the Eden Island stamps in your old passport, it was that disarming stare of yours and your unmistakable poise that gave you away. As you know, those little ways also teased my brain. Someone trained you, it was obvious to us.'

'I trained myself,' said Rosandra stubbornly. He had to believe it, it was true. 'Bass made it possible by helping me to leave Cradock, but I did the work myself. I read the magazines.'

'These sidesteps, too, are disarming, but if I were you, Rosandra, I would finally leave the Cradock episodes out of this discussion. You don't give your friend Bass his due. Things became very clear to us the day of the party, especially from the way you played to the camera, raising your tits and swinging your tail, lifting it right up in the air like an invitation. Very impressive stuff, very practised. Many people noticed.'

'That *Sunday Times* picture wasn't of me,' said Rosandra. 'The picture was taken from below.'

'That story, as you know, does not make sense,' said Thony with patience. 'Let's have more coffee.'

He knotted another moist string of Brie on top of a biscuit and beckoned her closer. Then he ran his finger along her eyelashes and down her cheeks and breathed on her mouth till she opened it.

'In we go,' he said, a little teasing, putting the biscuit on her tongue.

'It's time to stop being coy,' he said. 'Look, we don't blame you for this Bass connection, or for hiding it. In fact it works in your favour, in a way. It means you can keep a secret. That could be useful if you continue running errands and so on for me. But you will understand I am hurt at the lack of trust. That feigned ignorance is a sort of ingratitude, isn't it? I made things very comfortable for you, I invited you to stay at Star Palace free of charge. Then I asked you a few questions and you gave nothing in return. And after that you faked a pregnancy. What am I to respond to that?'

'I'm sorry,' said Rosandra.

'You don't have to say that. I like reasons, not excuses or apologies. As I said, your secrecy may work out better for you in the long run. I'm simply trying to get to the bottom of the situation. I'm expressing my own feelings as well as wider corporate interests. Michaelis, who's a clever man, very astute, a black devil, thinks your silence says a lot for you. In case you were wondering, he recognised you not from direct memory but from a picture your friend – your uncle – was showing off once at a social gathering. He and your uncle have an acquaintance in common, a man who lives in Pretoria. This friend is one of the small handful of Sebastiaan Sampson's friends who managed not to be seduced by his silly coup plans. At the party Bass was boasting about his beautiful young helper. He had a photograph showing you as a beauty queen. Maybe it was a picture taken at the famous Cradock beauty show. Michaelis remembered your face from that photograph.'

'That was before the coup,' said Rosandra.

'Of course,' said Thony.' 'After that disaster no one would be interested in knowing the man. About the coup, by the way, Michaelis reports that you showed a certain significant chink in your armour. On the way home from Nice, when both of you were drunk, you asked him about coup strategies and the business of conquering an island. Now that was a boob on your part. It assumed stupidity in your companion, a wrong move. At first, naturally, giving you *your* due, Michaelis thought that you were trying to probe some of his secrets and find out his connection with Bass. But then he remembered the friends of Bass Sampson tended to show a certain naivety. They are sharp of course but finally not that clever. And then all the connections began to fall in place.'

'I was not drinking that night,' said Rosandra.

'Rosandra, don't worry about the excuses,' said Thony. 'Let's be businesslike. In our eyes, I repeat, you are not in the wrong. Why I'm going on about things at this length is for a purpose. Or two. First, when you have the time, I want you to tell me, or Michaelis, what sorts of things you learned from Bass Sampson. How did he go about his business? Who did he know? What did he show you? These details are what we're interested in. They could be useful if we're going to include you in some of our own deals.'

'I wasn't involved,' said Rosandra.

She felt dull-witted. Thony ignored her. He merely prolonged a blink as she spoke.

'The second item is more simple. I've told you a bit about carrying guns. Now tomorrow when you go to the airport I want you to do me the favour of carrying part of a gun. Not a whole one. You'll have learned some of these tricks from your time with Bass. The gun part will be on its own in a very small case. I would take it if I were going with you, but I will be making one more trip to the Isle of Man tomorrow, and then I will fly straight into Heathrow. I'll join you there. Tomorrow morning I will personally put the equipment in your bag and at the airport someone will take the bag for a minute and remove the case.

That is all. You take a taxi, then you get on to the plane. And in case you feel worried about what you will be carrying, it won't be travelling on board with us in any form. Air-freight people will be taking it from you, they'll deal with it. There is nothing to worry about at all. Several governments know about this exchange. I have authorities on my side. In that I am different from Bass Sampson.'

That night there was a high wind. A toppled dustbin clattered its corrugations on the pavement. Rosandra stood at the window of the hotel bedroom. She saw how the wet street perfectly reflected the orange circles of the street-lights. Once the poker faces of icons had made dark patches on brilliant gold backgrounds.

Thony lay sleeping, very quiet, facing the ceiling, his arms by his side. It was the first time they had shared a bedroom but he behaved as though he were alone. He stripped to his underwear, scrubbed his teeth with a dry brush, climbed into bed. At no point did he look at her. She was sure of this, she stared at him throughout. He slept immediately.

The day had been very long, very wasting, Rosandra thought. It had torn at things, battered them, reduced them, like this wind. The wind gusted through vacant spaces. Spent, reduced, alone, emptied: so she felt. The wind tore at the tarpaulin covering a flower stand opposite. There were people somewhere – voices coming and going in a room across the passage. There was no one in the street, which was strange, it being London, a capital. London, Paris, New York, the cosmetics said.

She lay in bed with the starched sheets crisp against her chin. The furniture looked threadbare, the light was weak and off-white, not flattering. Thony's breathing was hardly audible. He would wake before her, slip the thing he had spoken of, a part of a gun, into her handbag and leave. He was unflappable, he made aquaparks out of drought lands. Michaelis Herder his assistant swung the steering wheel with ease. There would be little to it, she would carry the part; she was more experienced now, and able. To look cool, unconcerned: she could do it. It was very little to offer and she owed him so much. Especially after today.

Imagine the day if they had the one errand only: Harley Street. If Thony had no other business in London. Only the morning appointment with the physician. Whereas she was meant to be beautiful, a representative, an advertisement for Star Palace, a wonder, all Thony's words. Michaelis did his job; he was able. He carried guns, spoke French, selected art works. He was a black man from a Cape slum but he put all that behind him. He had things to say about icons, he offered explanations of Russian Orthodoxy. Before the French trip she would have said Russian Orthodoxy was communism, which is what they were taught at school.

The wind stirred up a restlessness. She was back at the window, her face against the glass. It vibrated against her cheeks. Especially after today she owed Thony something, to try like Michaelis to be practised, professional, to hang a picture just so with poised and confident hands, to hold in her stomach, to suppress that folly. It was a sorry disgrace, a hysterical bulge, the most shameful thing: to come to London with a bogus pregnancy, nothing but a gross flatulence. She was a pretence to herself. She pretended to Thony and abused his trust. The way he picked her out in the restaurant after a search of months and chose her out of hundreds of others. The way he put ideas and money and his will behind his promises. Rosandra: Star Palace icon.

Her stomach ached, which wasn't nervousness, or shouldn't be, and wasn't emptiness, after Brie and biscuits. There had been nothing in there ever but the doctor's warm fingers pointing to her shame. The window-pane was cool and her stomach touched the sill. Thony sighed, stirred, but still faced the ceiling. She would carry the thing tomorrow and hand it over. Her posture would be good, her look indifferent, as he liked, as seemed to impress him. He would meet her in the airport lounge wearing his medium grey suit and his travelling perfume, a tight undershirt of chypre fragrance. She would meet his eyes straight on and then half drop her eyelids, saying yes, it's OK, I managed.

On the pavement below Rosandra saw a puddle, caught by the wind, half lift into the air, making a twisted membrane, a figure-of-eight, and then fragment. That was something. A radio was switched on in the room next door. It chose outer-space sounds, then difficult jazz. The uncertain tune filled the empty spaces, the high ceiling over the silent sleeper's head. The sounds crept around her body, around her empty stomach. The wind would not let her sleep.

A week after Thony and Rosandra returned from London another big party was held in Star Palace, in the cavernous Marina Functions Room just off the Dome. The bar was festooned with green raffia and for two hours cocktails all over Star Palace were free.

The party was to mark the first wedding anniversary of the nation's Minister of Finance. Republic newspapers reported it and local newspapers applauded. Extra fruit machines were rolled into the Functions

Room in honour of the occasion. There was a great deal to celebrate: it was not only love, it was also mutual benefit in business, reciprocal success.

Before the coming of Star Palace, as everyone knew, its small and unrecognised host nation boasted a capital city the size of a village. With the building of Star Palace, in a magic flash, the nation won an unofficial new capital, and the largest golf course in Africa, the continent's only man-made grotto, and the second largest aquapark in the Southern Hemisphere. In return Star Palace received from its small hosts lakefuls of free water, kitchenfuls of cheap labour and almost unlimited autonomy. All this the anniversary party toasted.

More recently further reason for celebration had been added to the account. Star Palace had offered to team up with its unprotected host in matters of mutual security, should this become necessary. So Thony Brandt was clapped on the back by the Minister, and Thony himself had the privilege of kissing the Minister's wife. There was gay laughter and loud, lively gossip, the mark of any good party, and there was an endless supply of sparkling wine, courtesy of the Republic beyond the borders, who grew it, bottled, bought and sent it, for they too were overjoyed at the success of the Minister and that of Star Palace too.

Of the many people present as many had their hair done in the three five-star boutiques at Star Palace, or bought their fine jewels in its showrooms, or bought their jewels elsewhere, but with money that Star Palace made. The battalions of kitchen staff were happy, being paid overtime in food and cheap Republic wine, and behind potted palms ministers and Star Palace men carried on energetic conversations, for their business and their schemes for mutual benefit were never quite complete. Everyone looked their best, even Rosandra, who had eaten nothing for a week and appeared very late and then only briefly, like the star she was, though everyone noticed her anyway and looked her up and down.

'You look gorgeous, Rosie,' a woman expectorated in Rosandra's ear.

Rosandra smelt the whisky. It was Regina, resplendent in inch-long false red nails and a platinum-blonde Supremes-style wig. She saw Rosandra stare, and laughed.

'You like this blonde black girl image, eh, Rose? It makes people look. Man, do they look. Especially all the men from the city cruising here tonight. But what I say is, if you can't beat them join them. You should try it next time. A colour change. Like I said to Tina at the bar a minute ago. Colour yourself black, Tina, I said. Paint yourself black. Go chocolate. Be in the majority.'

Regina was bent over laughing, rocking on her high heels. Rosandra gave her arm for support. She pressed it into Regina's side.

'What do you say, eh, Rose? It will be better than wearing the bunny suit, don't you think?'

Sucking in the saliva of her copious laughter, Regina fingered the cloth of Rosandra's dress. It was gold crushed silk, and wrapped her bosom in ruches.

'Where'd you get this stuff? Europe?' Regina asked.

Regina knew almost everything.

'Thony bought it in London for me.'

'Some have it all,' said Regina, taking a generous swig of her drink.

'But it's not very comfortable,' Rosandra said.

Earlier in the bungalow she had to press herself into the dress. Despite her diet it gripped her stomach cruelly. It made her breathless, holding it in.

'But doll, it's beautiful. You're beautiful,' said Regina.

She kissed Rosandra fulsomely on the neck, and as she did so teetered forward again, a little drunk. Rosandra felt Regina's weight against her arm, then Regina's hand, suddenly, surprisingly, on her stomach.

'You OK there, Rosie?' she said. 'London was OK for you?'

For a minute Rosandra was confused. Regina's voice was coaxing and tender. What had she betrayed? Regina suspected a scandal, she was looking for information. It was difficult to evade the consequences of actions. One day she phoned home and now Regina was asking questions. If Thony found out Regina knew things there would be more trouble. He would again be disappointed in her.

'Don't mind me,' said Regina, watching her closely. 'Tell me to shut up if you want. I just pick up info there on the switchboard but I don't pass it on. I heard nothing special, promise. It's just when a girl starts phoning home when she's never done that before. And when she starts looking a bit fat and blown up. Then a girl like me starts wondering.'

'It was nothing, Regina,' said Rosandra.

It was no pregnancy at all, a phantom, a shame, but no cause to fear.

'I was going to say I could help you. Girls, black girls I mean, have a lot of babies taken out of them right here at Star Palace. There is an Indian doctor in the El Mar Hotel. He stays as permanent guest and I think Mr Brandt knows what his job is. There must be some service, don't you think? There is so much fucking here. All these men from the city, and all these bunny girls.'

Regina kissed Rosandra, painting whisky and soda across her cheek.

'But I'm so happy for you it was OK,' she said. 'Don't tell anyone what I just said to you. You never know, one day a friend maybe needs the service. In Star Palace a girl must keep secrets. Now, can you spot a white boy for me who will buy me a drink?'

Rosandra felt the zip of her dress cutting her waist flesh. She wanted Regina to stay. She held on to her arm longer than necessary but Regina drew away. A white woman in a pants suit intercepted her delicate progress across the room.

'That diet, Reg,' said the woman. 'The meat diet.'

Then Regina was hugging the woman and kissing her on the cheek. Rosandra could still feel the warm patch on her stomach, a protected place, where Regina's hand had been. She felt jealous of the other woman. The feeling surprised her. It was nagging and hungry and came very suddenly. She moved nearer.

'Rare as a good man,' Regina laughed.

'It's exactly that,' said the woman. 'Just lean and raw and then, wow, look at me now.'

They were turned away from her, absorbed in their conversation. Rosandra wandered outside on to the patio beyond the bar. Coloured light reflections blinked in the pool. Her dress reflected the lights. She stood for a long time, trying to breathe some stretch into the fabric. But she felt stronger, stronger than at any point since London, since France. For Regina was a potential ally, she had touched her, she had offered support.

A man was at her elbow offering a cigarette. He was well-dressed, imposing, as were most of the men at Star Palace. She might have met him before. He was smiling at her knowingly.

'The evening lights are in your dress,' he said, his voice soft.

'Yes, I noticed,' said Rosandra, and walked away, back to the bungalow.

The next day Rosandra booked a ride for herself in the Star Palace minibus to Nieuw Israel, the town in the Republic closest to Star Palace. The bus was full of kitchen staff with the day off and a few long-term hotel guests who came along for the outing. It was not the correct way for Rosandra to travel, but taking the car or ordering Thony's chauffeur would mean telling him about this little shopping trip, and she wanted

164

to slip out quietly and be back by early afternoon, getting on quickly with her plan and then springing her surprise.

The plan was a diet, Regina's idea. The surprise would be her new streamlined stomach. She wanted to buy twenty-eight steaks, a two-week diet. Thony occasionally gave her money to buy clothes and jewellery at the Star Palace boutiques: she would draw on some of this allowance. Since overhearing Regina's friend at the party she couldn't help thinking of steak. She imagined the taste of rare steak against her palate. She felt the saltiness. She could have ordered the meat at Star Palace but that would spoil the surprise. This past week, though still dismissive, cool, Thony had been more pleased with her. She'd hung the icon for him, just as he wanted it, with poised hands. She felt she must do it, to consolidate the airport exchange. The gun part – a long black cylinder – had been safely handed over. She did that task for him; she managed. The icon too she must lift, suspend, balance, and then stand back, nodding: this is what I can also do.

She knew what sort of meat she wanted, thick wide pieces, tender, full of blood. Exactly like these steaks piling up in columns of four on the marbelite counter in the butchery in Nieuw Israel.

The butcher's body was ruddy and well-larded, as a butcher's should be. His hands lay flat on the counter now that he had served her, the skin veined in dried blood. The woman who stood close beside him was as sturdy, probably his wife. Her expression was wary. Biltong hung in bunches in the doorway, catching the dust blowing off the main street outside. Sunlight browned the carcasses hanging in the windows.

'Big party?' said the butcher.

'Ja,' said Rosandra.

She remembered how to speak, how to behave, friendly, not too winning. There was a butcher's like this in Cradock. She stood close against her mother's leg and the butcher bent down to stroke her hair with a bloody hand and gave her a vienna sausage, dangling a floppy end. Bass shopped at the same butchery. He went alone and came back with a bootload of rump steaks and chops.

'You want some home-made biltong?' the butcher said. 'We give biltong to all the pretty girls who come here.'

With the sound of the word biltong, said with a nasal flavour, so familiar, Rosandra imagined the salty meat on her tongue, that tang of blood. It was very pleasant. The taste went with the memory of the butchery in Cradock. After each visit she saved a piece of biltong for Maria, who saved it in turn to eat in her own room after work.

'Thanks,' said Rosandra, 'but no thanks.'

The woman stared unblinking, breathing noisily.

'Then have this piece of our own home-made *sosatie*,' said the butcher, holding out the stick of wrinkled meat.

She slid the first piece off the stick with two fingers. He watched her chew with pleasure.

'I'm Piet, this is Anna, my wife,' he said.

'I'm Rosandra. Rose,' said Rosandra.

'You know how to cook these guys?' he said, patting the packs of steak.

'No,' said Rosandra.

'Here, Anna will tell you.'

He pressed Anna's side where the tightness of her bra made a cushion of flesh.

Anna stared on. Piet reached over for greaseproof paper and the steaks. When Anna's silence did not end Piet sighed and looked apologetically at Rosandra.

'Don't worry,' he said. 'Her English is not very good. I learned my English many years ago in the mines. My boss was English.'

It was Anna's turn to jab Piet in the ribs. Two more customers had arrived, one white, one black, the one standing at the white counter, the other at the black. Twenty-five miles away from Star Palace the divisions were firmly in place. Piet went over to the black counter.

'*Sy kom van daai plek af,*' Anna whispered in scandalised tones as he passed.

Rosandra caught the remark and understood it – she comes from that place, Star Palace. But it was of Cradock Rosandra was thinking. Hearing the Afrikaans and being in the butcher's was so like Cradock. It was like listening to Emmie – Emmie speaking Afrikaans. Emmie's face now came back clearly. Her voice. Their feet, hers and Emmie's, in the water, their feet pressed against one another. She and Emmie ignored the other children in the pool. While she watched her lips Emmie taught by example her own guttural language. The sounds that were so strange in the classroom seemed easy in Emmie's mouth. Rosandra heard certain phrases repeated over and over again. About Emmie's mother's boyfriends – there were many boyfriends – and the terrible shame Emmie could not describe and that made her cry, a dark shame in a one-room house without curtains at the windows. And the way Emmie cried without making a sound. It was sad, that memory, but it felt good to remember. She hadn't thought of Emmie in years.

166

Out in the street the town presented more familiar scenes. Rosandra walked the dusty concrete pavement along Main Street, built up high to avoid storm water and spraying mud. So it also was in Cradock. There was the bar with half swing-doors and a fashion shop with home-made chutneys on display alongside fading dresses. Under dry sticks of acacia trees close to the council buildings sat black women with dusty faces, making a rough queue.

She walked over to a park area, beyond the acacia trees. In the drought there was not much of a park to speak of, not much grass, a few old benches, a swing frame, a see-saw stump. Along one side ran a dry stream bed. The stream was lined on both sides by small bent willows that had given up on bending down to the absent water by shedding their branches. The one brave feature in the lifelessness was the broad bed of cactus and aloe growing luxuriantly in thick parallel rows down at the far end of the park, at right angles to the stream. Rosandra walked over, feeling the dust on her toes, the sun burning her crown. It was good. She had brought no sun-cream but for a while she could take the risk. It would not show. If Thony asked any questions she had the steaks as proof of goodwill. She found a place between two luxuriant rows of aloes where, but for the stream side, she was perfectly hidden. The earth here was smooth and dry. She put the steaks in the shade of a cactus.

She had an hour before the bus departed. She stretched herself on the ground, raised her skirt to bare her legs and folded back her shirt so that her stomach too could feel the sun. Last she covered her face with tissues to keep it from burning. Her skin warmed quickly. The sun was very strong, very good. With her arms she made a tent over her eyes. This was a perfectly safe place. There was no danger that anyone would spot her. She could not see her own stomach mark and that was itself a pleasure. The park was perfectly still in the heat. It was noon, almost lunch-time. She spread-eagled her legs, raised her shirt higher and doubled the covering of tissues, men's tissues, Thony's. Whoever might see would recognise nothing, a dark stomach mark without a face.

Till she heard voices there was no sound but the whine of green flies gathering around the meat. Sweat ran over her chest and down her neck and quickly evaporated. There was no wind, no disturbance, until the voices, two men's voices. Their footsteps must have been muffled by dust because by the time they were audible they were close, on the park side of the aloe and cactus bed. The voices broke the rule of quietness

167

in the park. Though low, they were urgent, clipped. Rosandra drew her shirt down over her stomach, automatically, quickly, and lay still.

In the stillness the voices were diffusing widely, not clear but surprisingly loud. One speaker dominated. It must be an effect of the diffusion and the blurring of the sound that her ears began to play tricks on her. She could make believe a familiarity to the voices, one voice, the louder one. It must be part of seeing Cradock reflected everywhere in this small town – *déjà vu*, Michaelis called it, a phrase he liked.

She knew this voice, she was sure. She had recently heard it, though she could not place it. It was like – yet not like. She turned her head in the direction of the park, gingerly, so as not to upset the tissue covering. The sounds were clearer now. No doubt the conversation was private, but there was a tease in the familiarity and she had to listen. Yes, she knew that expression, not the inflections, not the manner of putting words together but the pattern of tones, defined by the stillness.

But no, she decided, it could be no one she knew. The voice she thought she recognised was speaking Afrikaans. It spoke a sentence very emphatically. *Jy sal dit kry voordat jy die land moet verlaat* – you will get it before you must leave the country. Again she thought of Emmie. She hadn't heard this much Afrikaans in one day since the time with Emmie at the pool. When she heard conversations in Afrikaans, in the bar, at the airport, the words made vague shapes only, giving an impression of meaning, nothing solid or spelled out. To make sense she had to listen carefully, to string the words together as they came, one by one. However, this time she was too slow and the men began to move off in the direction of the stream. Rosandra edged carefully into the meagre shade of the cactus, keeping her head covered. It was time for the bus to leave, but she couldn't show herself. The men would gather that she might have heard what their privacy had revealed. They might recognise her: these days strangers knew her face.

She kept her body rigid and the voices again grew louder. The men were moving up between the first two rows of plants; they too were seeking cover. There was a crunch of sand, dead grass, but that faded as they came to the smooth, harder earth between the aloes, just across from where she lay. Again she knew the louder man's voice like that of a friend. It was unsettling, not knowing who it could be. It was like seeing Bass with the engineer in the avenue on Eden Island without expecting him to be there. The men lit cigarettes and the smoke spread slowly and wide, as did their voices. She could smell it. The flies were wild at the meat, interfering with the voices. Then someone cleared his throat to speak again in Michaelis's manner, preparing for a difficult, perhaps sensitive, sentence. And so it must be Michaelis – of course Michaelis – but without the perfect English. It was Michaelis meeting strangers under cover of aloes, confidently speaking Afrikaans.

Rosandra felt her way across her stomach to check that her shirt was pulled well down. The tissues were still covering her face. Michaelis must not see her. This was for certain. She had caught him out. She thought of the restlessness in his eyes, the pent-up energy in the way he stood. If he saw her here he would not be kind.

Identified and placed, the voice began to make more meaning. Michaelis was putting a point across, but seemed hesitant, cagey, was picking his words carefully. The other man wasn't helping him; he listened silently. Michaelis said the thing would be in order, the important delivery, before the weekend. He'd checked it with the boss. The two men were so close she could hear their exhalations of smoke. Michaelis was pausing in the middle of sentences. Or he was using gestures, as he sometimes did, as he did in the aeroplane describing coup strategies, making his points with pauses, a finger tap, counting items off on his knuckles. We're getting in a consignment of three hundred and thirty PPSH sub-machine-guns. The apartheid state is expecting delivery of two hundred and fifty. Eighty we can divert to you. That is in addition to the ten SAM-7 ground-to-air missiles, the one hundred AK-47 assault rifles, thirty of the lighter AKM rifles, and the ten RPG-7 rocket launchers we've managed to get on the East European market. Michaelis counted these items twice over. In addition there'll be the usual consignment of hand grenades, mainly RDG-33s, RPG-6s. If you want them. Right, yes, said the other man. And the shipment of RPK machine-guns expected some months back, it's on its way. When it arrives some of the guns can be diverted.

Smoke drifted. Then the other man spoke out suddenly, more loudly, breaking the whispered level of the conversation. It was a way of speaking Rosandra knew from Cradock, from the Cape, a black man's Afrikaans.

'We trust you to keep absolute secrecy.'

'But of course. For the sake of the struggle.'

'Our fighters will thank you, comrade.'

Michaelis did not reply. Rosandra imagined a hand-shake, a touching of shoulders. They began to move off.

She thought they would be heading back across the park together, but they must have parted ways at the end of the row of plants, close to the stream and the willows. One of them, it must be the unknown man, was standing at the end of Rosandra's row. She heard him give a low, fluting whistle. He called out to her, White chick. He must be able to see the soles of her feet. He whistled again, higher this time, more questioning, tempting. The sound must be meant for her. She tried not to stir. She must not move. Through the tissues she saw a fly settle above her eye. From this moment, she thought, the world will change. This man will hail Michaelis and he will come over and recognise me, striding up, angry, knowing what I know, *that* I know. Thony will be told. She was snooping in the park at Nieuw Israel, she is cleverer than we imagined; she is spying on us, she knows more than she lets on.

But the other man freed her. When she did not move he gave up whistling. He said something indistinct to himself, about sunbathing, drunk whores in small towns sleeping it off in the park, these white 'women people' had nothing better to do.

Despite the dryness Rosandra was soaked with sweat. Her stomach mark ached, it must be sunburn. From now on, she said to herself, she must move very slowly and steadily, with steady thoughts, one thing at a time.

She stayed in amongst the aloes and cactuses several hours, till the sun was lower and, she imagined, Michaelis well out of town. The meat was beginning to smell. The flies were everywhere, on her legs, settled on the wet patches in the greaseproof paper. She watched them cluster, did not brush them off. Though her thoughts were not clear, not connected, she had to try to make sense. The situation looked uncanny but there must be logic in it somewhere, a reason behind it. If Thony was the boss and had the cash it was he who must make the connections, his presence explained things. Alongside his talk of the security situation and the secret gun part in London, there was Michaelis in this park, under the disguise of another language, mastering two styles of speech, two kinds of friends, the state and its enemy. As well as aquapark parts and art, Star Palace was dealing in a great number of arms, and with different groups of people, dealing in secret pistols and black tubing and computer print-outs the size of icons bearing lists of numbers – numbers and letters that were names of arms.

This calmness she was feeling, this acceptance – so this is how it has been, this is the situation, in this way it's explained – this calmness, she thought, was her best defence. She could keep control. It wasn't distinctly heard, but what she'd learned, the shaded meanings, garbled lists, strange implications, these demanded action and that action was plain and simple. Today she must leave Star Palace. Even today. The certainty was soothing. At the beginning she bathed in Thony's attention. She thought it was all for her, that he wanted her for her face and figure: this was her career, her break. But he had other designs. He had questions. There were other plots that lay behind his interest, other demands in his searching look. He sold arms here, gathered them there. What was the struggle Michaelis referred to? What was the role cut out for her? But she couldn't find this out now. She had to leave. She had to take the questions with her, to think about in some other place.

And so in the end the false pregnancy worked in her favour. It distanced her. She could trust that Thony no longer needed her. Since the London trip he'd visited only once, to give the gold dress for the party. And there was his look of disgust that time when the expanded stomach mark was exposed. The effects of that, she was sure, unlike the bulge, wouldn't disappear. It was necessary to leave Star Palace, even today.

In the late afternoon, when the shadows in the main street of Nieuw Israel were blue and warm, she went back to the butchery and asked Piet for a ride to Star Palace. Anna squinted at her over a tray of sheeps' brains leaking a whitish liquid. Rosandra became aware of her red face, her crumpled clothes. Anna saw them too and turned her eyes to heaven.

Rosandra waited until five, when Piet closed his shop. The café next door had a big battered refrigerator standing out on the pavement. She sat outside and ate chocolate-flavoured water ices on wooden sticks. A young girl in a green gingham school uniform doled out the ices and collected the money in her chest pocket.

On the drive to Star Palace Piet's friendliness grew more formal. Anna's disapproval had dampened his interest. Or otherwise it was the lurid glow of Star Palace that affected him. The glow was visible across the flat veld from miles away. The pink and green lights, already wheeling and flashing, did not blend with the sunset. As they drew closer Piet's body clenched, he began to address Rosandra as miss. Then the Dome came into view and he gave up attempts at conversation. Politely but firmly, he said he wouldn't be driving on to Star Palace grounds. He dropped Rosandra some way from the gate and she did not hear his goodbye.

She met the guards at the security gate carrying her leaking pack of steaks before her like an offering. Getting past them wasn't difficult. She lifted a finger to her mouth, pointed at the pack resting on her forearm, the blood very visible now, and announced in a stage whisper it was a surprise for the boss, special delivery from Nieuw Israel, this week she wanted to play the wife. She was smiling because of the tension in her cheeks. It pulled her lips taut and apart. The guards smiled back.

But it wasn't necessary to explain so much, to be so wordy. To Mrs Lawrence on her bungalow check Rosandra said only that the meat was a surprise. Regina demanded no explanation at all. Rosandra brought her steak as a gift, the few pieces that still looked fresh after being exposed to the day's heat. Regina's nail file was balanced between two switches on the board in front of her. She was teasing her hair.

'How can I help you?' she said, looking at Rosandra through her comb.

Again Rosandra marvelled at her perception. Maybe Regina knew it all already, more than Rosandra herself knew: how Star Palace worked, the double dealings – were they double dealings? – the underhand exchanges. The night manager and his three lovers, wasn't that a kind of double dealing? Regina connected up voices, she controlled the telephone lines. She laughed at men; she had solutions to their love threats. She also kept her information to herself.

But what she said next was revealing. She asked if Thony was behaving himself. She didn't expect Rosandra to come by to visit so soon.

'I think Thony's fine,' said Rosandra, not wanting to lie to Regina. 'He was fine when last I saw him.'

'Can I make you tea?' Regina asked. 'I've got my very own kettle here, and some ginger biscuits.'

Rosandra almost sat down. Regina might not be in the know but she would have answers, or a cousin somewhere, a safe house, advice. For this was very like a problem with a man. The result was exactly the same. That she was leaving him.

Then she put down the meat, and next to it another parcel, the gold dress and a new waxing kit, an expensive one, only recently bought, and with that there was little more to say. Regina simply nodded when Rosandra said she needed a short break. From behind the switchboard she produced a bottle of whisky and made motions of pouring. Rosandra refused. Thony was in meetings all day, and though for the present they were safe from detection everyone recognised Rosandra, and knew Regina. People would say they'd been together, Regina might be blamed in some way. There was no time for conversation and a drink, no time to find out if Regina knew anything. She would have to leave in uncertainty – it was how she came.

'You must take the car I'm using,' Regina said. 'You can't go in yours. Everyone knows the boss's madam's Escort. It will get you into trouble.'

She did not bother to describe the trouble.

'People will also recognise your car.'

'Not this one,' said Regina, giving her keys. 'I usually like to give girls I know a bit of help. But this is where I really have something to contribute.'

She made great play of looking furtively around her.

'I'm using the night manager's Peugeot at the moment,' she explained. 'I bribed him into it, in exchange for not telling the fiancée about his other girlfriends.'

'I can't take his car.'

'Of course you can,' said Regina. 'I'll tell him some little story. Maybe he won't even notice. He's just started his night shift. You drive to the city and leave the car at the main Peugeot Centre. They know him there. Leave a note. I can write it for you. Then hire a car and go on your way or do whatever you've planned. You need a holiday, I think.'

Rosandra wanted to put her arms around Regina. There was no proper way to thank her. She wanted three, or five, or seven cocktail dresses to give her, golden, silken, with multiple ruches. And she wanted to drink tea, eat ginger biscuits, hold hands, go driving, but Regina turned away to write a note to the car dealer. The switchboard had started to flash. People were finishing their meals, beginning with evening tasks, remembering to make phone calls. And that meant it was time to leave.

It felt brave driving out of Star Palace, Rosandra said to Jem, passing under the illuminated gateway, through Thony's security and in defiance of his instructions, out on to the dusty road. It felt brave because of the look of the thing. But in fact she hoped just to control the unfamiliar car and not to betray her inexperience. It was the manager's car, big and new, that did the trick. The guards recognised it, and the car fitted in with the story of the surprise dinner and the elaborate plan to please the boss. Again she hinted at secrecy. Holding a finger, again, to her lips, she said the night manager had given support, and now the guards, too, were accomplices. By their silence they would help the success of the plan. The guards, the same three, simply nodded. It was about time

173

for their shift to end. Before she had finished her excuses they were waving her through.

And then once again the road opened to her and again it felt like an adventure and an escape story. Life was working itself out through these kind of patterns, she thought, repeat patterns, feelings like *déjà vu*, spinning round and on. There was the get-away vehicle, and the road, straight and dry, and this time the alibi and the accomplice, or four accomplices. Once again it was a journey with no imaginable end, going with the movement, taking the chance. In uncertainty she came here; she was leaving no more certain of events. Uncertainty held danger; however, danger was part of an escape story. Without it there was no suspense, no gripping end. But it was also true that the danger part in adventure stories didn't take account of small distractions and preoccupations and smooth continuities – like keeping her eyes on the road and the car wheels away from the kerb and small night animals. And feeling hungry. And as the hours went by and the dark grey veld slightly rose and slightly fell to the left and right there was also the increasing distraction of the pain in her middle, where the dark stretched skin of her stomach mark was badly sunburned and felt mangled and fried, and seemed to radiate heat. For a while the discomfort distracted her from thinking about Star Palace, about Thony, about leaving him for good.

But it wasn't possible to listen any longer. Jem was now, at last, yawning loudly and uncontrollably. He was hearing her story in snatches, in between the sound of his own breath. Things were too far gone to apologise. His yawns were gross and obvious. The restaurant staff too were being obvious. The music had been switched off and for more than an hour no waiters were present. The dustbins outside were piled high. The proprietor was standing in a tactful and decisive position at the door.

'Rosandra, can we continue with this another time?' Jem said.

She spoke of uncertainty and was transfixed by her own fascinations, sure of the charm of her descriptions. But this was unfair. Didn't he ask her to tell her story? Didn't he want this? His thoughts weren't connected. Things would be better when they met again. He could confess his own feelings. He could speak the certainties of all his years of desire.

She did not apologise for the length of her tale. She rose gracefully and turned on her heel and nodded at the proprietor as though in simple greeting as she passed.

'Maybe you can go on with what you were telling me tomorrow?' Jem said at the entrance to her hotel. 'You said you were staying in town another week.'

'No, tomorrow isn't convenient.' She spoke brusquely, as though the matter had been discussed and decided and this was just a reminder. 'The next few days aren't convenient at all. This week we go to an elephant reserve somewhere inland for a short veld shoot, to model leopardskin beach wear, crocodile accessories, African things like that. After that, during my last few days here, I've two important things to do. They're errands, no, visits.'

'But I'd like to see you somehow, one more time, maybe after all that,' said Jem.

His voice was out of control with tiredness. What he said was a plea.

'Of course we must meet again,' said Rosandra, touching him lightly on the shoulder. 'Maybe on my last day here, when I've done everything else and I'm free. Then I can hear your part of the story. I'm sure I've talked for far too long.'

THREE

Armed Response

Africa is a hard country and to survive in this country you must act hard, because only the strongest survive in Africa.

Karen Strydom, wife of mass murderer Barend Strydom,
Guardian (1990)

1

Today Rosandra was in white: she was pale, she looked strained, but her hair, bound in a gold banana-clip, sprang from the constriction like an emanation, an iridescence, despite the humidity, and her freckles made intricate archipelagos over her face. Over the telephone last night Rosandra told Jem she would be at the same café as the first time, two weeks ago. Make it early, she said, before the mid-morning heat. There she sat; he came up from behind. She sat in the same chair, the same position as the first morning, but limp, tired, her shoulders sagging, her legs stretched out and looping, sagging, her white shirt loose, and the whole effect duller, not as radiant as before. Jem's heart went out to her. She was down here on a job, and he made it no easier, taking up her time. Or her friend was right, whatever his name was, Michaelis Herder, white was not a colour she should wear. It brought out the pallor of her face.

But again he was not being fair. The minute she saw him she sat up, she seemed to lift, her eyes shimmered; she was not wearing her glasses. He took her arms in greeting, feeling the young bristles of the upper flesh on his hands. He wanted to cup her chin like a lover, or not like a lover, not like Thony, adoring and aggressive, but like a friend. Jem longed to look into her eyes, gently, to love the right way, with care. He wanted to kiss her, two kisses, one on each cheek, but she had released herself before he could purse his lips.

'Coffee again?' she said. 'Or would you dare to try ice-cream this early? It's hot enough.'

He chose coffee; Rosandra ordered strawberry ice-cream.

'I'm tired of coffee,' said Rosandra, 'I was here hours ago. I wanted to get out of the hotel and breathe the air. I ordered at least ten coffees. You can see the bill. Then I took a rickshaw ride. We went all the way to the end of the esplanade and back. I managed to capture one of those picture moments, the ones I told you about. It was the ostrich feathers of the rickshaw foaming up in front of my face. They came up each time as the driver leapt, lifting in the air. They were dyed green. They were like a green fountain. I haven't found one of those moments in a long time. Today's blue sky must have reminded me.'

She smiled at him and began on her ice-cream.

'Did you know that strawberry ice-creams will be more difficult to get hold of in this country,' Jem said, 'now that sanctions are being enforced? We get strawberry concentrate from overseas.'

He wanted to begin the conversation with something interesting but Rosandra gave a slight shrug. Her movements today had the look of resisting a heavy weight. It was part of her tiredness, Jem thought. When she spoke her voice sounded wrong, her sentences collapsed at the end. Yes, her tiredness must be his fault; he blamed himself. He tired her out. First he interrogated her, and then at the restaurant he failed to listen closely to her whole story. He was wasteful of her speech and her time, no better than Thony Brandt, demanding information.

But today he did have something of importance to say. He had not forgotten she asked him for episodes of his own experience. She wouldn't have to remind him. He would offer a part of his life, as a gesture of gratitude, confirming their contact.

Most of last night he spent on his stoep preparing what to say, finding the best incident, something true, something of himself, but also a plain story, to tell without digression. Her mind was straightforward, plain-thinking: it was one of her attractions. She saw things in clear colours, without fussy edges. It was like the images she carried with her like charms. What she liked was a far cry from Thony's bombast, those speeches about grottos and ambition, long descriptions of dreams that, if you looked at them more closely, were in fact only boasts.

However, sitting on the stoep in the evening's quiet with beer and the view, what he had to say seemed less difficult than it was now. At home he could anticipate her expressions; he imagined her quiet, listening face. He forgot that face was mainly expressionless, and that her stare was vague and blank; her eyes did not meet his own. He needed to see her always, he thought, every day, so as not to lose these impressions. He watched her throat swell as she swallowed the ice-cream. No memory could re-create that thickening, that fullness. He watched the pulse beneath the skin.

Jem said, 'I will tell you about my time in the army.'

180

'Yes. I've been waiting for this,' said Rosandra.

'It was a hard time,' said Jem.

'Yes?' said Rosandra.

Rosandra thought: So, Jem's turn to carry a gun. He must be nervous about telling me this, he's sweating. I won't look at him directly, to avoid embarrassing him. The palm tree above his head with the sunlight shining behind it makes a star-shape. In the rickshaw the feathers thrown up into the air over the driver's head made a green fountain, a peacock's tail, a star shape. One thing merges into another. If you take a step back, take a little distance, objects begin to flow and merge. It's a good trick. Staring half awake, staring at the sky, you see this shape grow more like that one, a star or a cloud, a cloud the shape of a comet, a blue cloud in a blue sky.

'You want to make the right decision,' Jem said. 'Going into the Defence Force represents a big decision, a moral decision. You know the issues. You've heard them around. Now you need to make up your own mind.'

'Tell me about the issues,' said Rosandra. 'I must have missed hearing them at the time.'

'The arguments go on and on,' Jem said. 'There were a few people talking about the issues at training college. People were saying they didn't want to fight on the side of racism. They didn't want to carry a gun to keep the white man as boss, even though these people were white themselves. But that's how we were feeling. We weren't feeling right about the government. That time I was in London. It was to get out of it all. But I came back no more decided than when I left. What we faced was the six-year gaol sentence for conscientious objectors. It wasn't a bright prospect.'

'Why didn't you go to fight on the other side?' Rosandra asked.

'What do you mean?'

'Like I said.'

'But what do you mean?'

It's the same as last week, two weeks ago, Jem thought, the conversation already changing direction, the meaning getting lost.

'If you don't want to carry a gun for the white man,' Rosandra said, 'carry a gun for someone else. The opposite side.'

'That wasn't the point at the time,' Jem spoke more rapidly. 'It was this particular army we were worried about. I didn't want to leave the country or go to gaol. My problem was wanting to stay and so having to fight for the state.'

181

Arms create divisions, Rosandra thought. Thony tried to broker arms. One day he bought arms to sell to the state, another day Michaelis sold arms to the state's enemy. She tried walking away from these knotted connections. She walked out to the night manager's car, neon-green and pink lights burning in the sky, washing over her skin, Star Palace ablaze as usual, and the keys of the car bony and real in her hand.

Behind her, she imagined as she drove, the room she'd just left was already changing its shape. If she turned back the cupboards in the bungalow would smell chilly, though still half full of her clothes, and the drawer from which she'd just taken her make-up, the waxing kit for Regina, the last of her dress allowance, would open with difficulty as though long unused. Fragments of her time there, an earring, a price-tag, would remain scattered, unseen, like dust, like dead leaves blown into corners.

She drove down Thony's spruce tar driveways and date palm avenues, so new and transplanted and alien they seemed as she looked at them with fresh eyes, leaving. She drove slowly, with concentration, easing the car carefully round the corners, wary of its unfamiliar power. And she saw Jem was speaking, looking down as if ashamed.

'What happened then?' she said.

'I went home to Cradock to try and sort myself out. I spoke to my parents. My father said it was important for people to do their duty for their country. He'd done his national service so I should too. But he didn't answer my questions. I'd hoped there might be answers buried somewhere in Cradock.'

'I miss Cradock sometimes,' said Rosandra. 'The dustiness. Also the desert light. You can see in it. It shows you all the cracks.'

'Then when I finally found an answer it seemed so obvious, so ordinary even,' said Jem. 'It happened the day I climbed the little *koppie* behind the industrial area on the east end of town. You remember it?'

'No,' said Rosandra. 'Maybe my brothers knew it.'

'From the *koppie* I had a view of most of the town. Cradock had become an important place on the political map by then. Did you know that? It was the home of a black leader who was mobilising his people. I read about him in the newspaper but of course there were no signs of his presence in the white town.'

'Maybe I wasn't in the country at that time,' Rosandra said.

A view of a town, a political map, she thought. She wasn't much more used to maps than when she spent time with Bass on Eden Island; a little more practised, yes, but not much. She drove down the dry road leading away from Star Palace without a map. There was only the one main road and she knew the way. She tried to find music on the car radio, music good to listen to, an accompaniment to leave-taking, a rousing escape tune, something to take her mind off her sunburn. There was a noise of static, and then an advertisement for Texan cigarettes, and when she was far out on the main road a station had Madonna singing.

It was one of the ambitions Thony told her about once – to tempt Madonna in spite of sanctions to come and sing in the Dome at Star Palace. He would lay waste to his golf course for that, he said. To get her he would give even his paintings, his landscapes, his White Reflections, his cityscape. Rosandra wondered that anyone could care so much. It was the puzzle of value, the value set by Thony's dreams. How many paintings were worth how many guns, she wondered. How many guns would Thony buy and sell for Madonna? The road lay straight, grey and corrugated in the car headlights. What was the scale, she thought, guns against singers, singers against paintings? She had no idea, and yet, she slowly began to realise, it was no longer her concern. With every hour she drove these things were further and further behind her, left in the distance – guns for singers for icons, a rhythm to which to drive.

'I know everyone has this experience at one time or another in our country,' Jem said. 'Sitting on that *koppie*, I turned away from the town and looked at the land. You know, I felt the land. I felt it in my bones. The size, the breadth of it, so much sky to breathe in. It excited me. I didn't want to protect it. But I wanted to stay a part of it, I wanted to be in it. So I went to the army.

'But then, soon after I'd joined, they assassinated that Cradock community leader. It's odd, I forget his name. His car was forced off the highway. Thousands of people came to his funeral. They came with banners and freedom songs. He was a highly respected figure. You know, our home town became a place of pilgrimage for a weekend. When I heard the news I wondered if my decision was the right one. About being in the army. But by then it was too late.'

'Who is they?' Rosandra said. 'Who killed him?'

'Is that a question?' said Jem. 'Do you need to ask?'

'It's a question,' said Rosandra.

There were creatures in the headlights as she drove, she remembered. They were grey as the drought. She felt dust and grit on her tongue, not unpleasant, a taste of earth, of mud face-pack if she got some of it in her mouth by mistake. She wore scarlet lipstick, fine gold foundation, and Tampax: after the pregnancy she was bleeding again, Star Palace sloughing off, draining away. She felt prepared for anything, a long drive, the city, danger, the world. A few hours ago she was surrounded by intrigue and nervous; now she was delivered, moving, going with this motion, uplifted by this success, for the time being free.

'The state got him,' Jem explained, persevering despite her blank expression. 'I was meant to be fighting for the same state. But there was nothing romantic about fighting. It was nothing like Bass's stories. Being in the bush pretending to defend the border. There was no action or adventure at all. We were so bored. We just sat around. Day after day. Because of my geography training I got jobs helping with surveying. One week I tracked some elephants along a river and took photographs of them. In the end I didn't have to worry about shooting for the government. I didn't have to shoot. Two years after joining up I was sent home.'

And so she drove to the city without stopping, Rosandra remembered. Had she stopped she would have had to decide what to do next, whereas moving with this present minute there was release from choice, and excitement. She had money, she had clothes. Thony said she was not a woman to run away, but in running away what new openness she discovered, what interest, this freedom of movement, alone and without plans.

'So that was my time in the army,' said Jem, very uncomfortable because she still wasn't listening. 'That was what I had to say about the Defence Force.'

'Yes,' said Rosandra, 'I'm glad you told me that. While you were speaking I was thinking of when I left Star Palace. What you said about important life-decisions took me back.'

She was lying with every word she said, Jem thought. She made up things to say. She showed no interest, hadn't listened at all. And why should she? Her life was much more intriguing than his, it was full of fascinations, embroidered with fantasies. There was no telling what was false, what true. She could have dreamed up parts of it, those strange, unlikely bits trying to explain and excuse things, like when she said over and over again it wasn't her in the *Sunday Times* photograph. Even the part about Thony knowing Bass and threatening her with the information. Even that could be an excuse.

It came down to the one plain fact of her stories and embroidered memories being more interesting than anything he could tell her. Her stories were real stories, inventions, with suspense in them. It wasn't difficult to listen to them. He liked to listen and it made him love her more. Love works that way. He loved her and love purifies, it forgives. It forgets consequences, it justifies bad actions. He loved her more than he did last week, two weeks ago, more than before she began to tell him her past. He wanted to believe the best of her, but knowing the worst he could excuse everything.

'The first time I stopped on my drive away from Star Palace,' said Rosandra, 'was at the Peugeot dealer in the city.'

There was a change, she was volunteering the story herself. But also her attitude was different, Jem thought, more determined, the way she sat forward, as though she had something urgent to tell, a message of great importance, and was eager to say it.

'It was fairly late by then, maybe eleven o'clock. I dropped the keys in the letterbox at the dealer's with Regina's note. Then I took a taxi to a twenty-four-hour car-hire service in the city centre, the only place I knew that would be open that late. I wanted to put more distance between myself and Star Palace. I thought Thony might track me down. I worried he might force Regina. I thought of a car chase along veld highways, red dust flying. But I was wrong thinking Thony would follow me. As far as I know that didn't happen. The pregnancy scare was my best safeguard.

'I bought what I needed at a late-night café. I hadn't had anything to eat since the water ices in Nieuw Israel. I got lots of things to celebrate my freedom – a Flake chocolate that I ate then and there, straight down, a heaven all of my own, and then also apples and chips and peanuts, new mascara, new deodorant, I remember it all exactly, new soap, a litre of Coke, and because I wanted to be prepared, a pack of two condoms, they were liquorice-flavoured. And in the fast-food section I got fried sheep's brains and onions on a roll, because after seeing them in the butcher's at Nieuw Israel I kept wondering how they'd taste.'

'Yes,' said Jem, making a wry face.

'They tasted of detergent,' she said. 'But I was hungry so I ate the lot.'

She leaned even further forwards, elbows on the table. Her freckles, though darkened by sunlight, lost the impact of contrast from this angle, Jem thought. He saw the freckles had the same texture as the rest of her skin. They were no extra sheath, the borrowed skin of a faun, but part of her, almost schoolgirlish, were they not so becoming.

185

2

At midnight, Rosandra told Jem, she left the city, taking one of its arterial avenues lined with sulphur lights, the southern branch of the highway she once travelled with Bass. She drove past the back yards of the suburbs that supplied the centre each day with white office workers, hairdressers, alternative pottery, Cornish pasties; she skirted road works and the green incandescence of a power plant, heading south and east.

After sunrise, several hours later, the veld began to lose its evenness. Its pits and hollows were sprouting bush, stripling trees. The sun now shone full in her face, the road and horizon were alight. It gave her an uneasy familiar feeling, not being able to see in the brightness, the burning light. She pulled over and rested till seven.

The next town she passed was just off the highway. She stopped in for petrol. Beside the petrol station was a Kentucky Fried Chicken where the pump attendants and other town workers were ordering party packs for breakfast. Standing in the cool concrete shadows next to the bowsers she drank two styrofoam cups of Kentucky Fried Chicken tea, the one after the other, hungrily. It was just past eight o'clock. Across the way a hairdresser put out a blackboard asking ladies to offer themselves as guinea pigs for today's trainees' examination. At ten o'clock Rosandra drove out of town without most of her hair.

'But now your hair's long again,' said Jem.

'I cut my hair short once in my life, and it was then,' said Rosandra. 'It was some time ago.'

'Your hair is beautiful long. I couldn't imagine you without it.'

'I think Thony felt that way too. That's why I cut it. Some girls say cutting their hair short takes courage. I had my hair cut because I was

186

nervous. Thony knew about fancy-dress parties and disguises, but maybe he wouldn't think I could cut my hair to hide from him. The hairstyle was very short, shaved at the back.'

'And at the front?' Jem asked.

He wanted to see it exactly. He wanted to exceed Thony's interest and picture her hair exactly. But Rosandra ignored him.

Though in the strong light of noon the tar and the road signs glittered cruelly, she told him, she drove for miles without sunglasses, worried that their comfort would lull her to sleep. She kept on without protection till afternoon.

At another petrol station she bought more chocolate, but it melted in the heat, the sticky liquid settling in the criss-cross patterns of the passenger seat. Then she began to descend into dark green valleys. It must have rained recently. High up, along the edges of the hills, the sunlight reflected off the waterfalls in the forest made sudden bursts of brilliance, interrupting the green.

In the first valley a driver who seemed to want to overtake instead kept drawing level, once on a bend, and fixed his eyes on her. He gaped his mouth invitingly as though suggesting she offer a thumb to be sucked. The silent, hungry action looked ridiculous, but keeping her eyes straight ahead, accelerating, she sensed danger. Despite his expressions of disgust Thony could have her followed. Regina, she trusted, would not say anything, but Thony had his ways and means. He would choose a fast driver, not unsophisticated like this man. She would be identified, flagged down, and then, if she didn't stop, pressed into the mountainside. Who knew? Dead or alive, Thony might have ordered. There was the strength of his body against hers, the hard bone, the crush. And his hands reddened by mud, he cleaned them on the stones. She lowered the sun-shields and put on her glasses. Some miles further on the man in the car turned off into a valley town.

Behind her, in the west, the sun blazed on the brink of a hill, the edge of yet another valley. In the car, firmly closed to the outside, heat mounted and the smell of chocolate grew rancid. The smell made her thirsty. She grew more uncomfortable. She did not know how the air-conditioning worked and did not want to stop to find out. Her hairstyle above the glasses made a good show in the rear-view mirror, but when another driver overtook twice, leering down at her from his driving perch, she began to sweat again. From the places where she usually sprayed perfume her skin exuded a strong odour.

187

She scrubbed at these places with tissues, then tucked the paper into pads under her armpits. The tissues, which were pink, became stained with yellow. Her spirits were slowly sinking with the altitude of the car. The freedom of last night, that sense that she could take on anything, drive anywhere, evaporated.

As the valleys unfolded the vegetation changing from grassland to bush grew lush. By the side of the road were farm stalls of black creosoted wood, brightly lit with bags of oranges, grapefruit and lemons, suspended like lanterns. At each stall city cars were drawn up, so Rosandra drove on. Though the heat was as intense, the sky took on the colours of dusk. A green-blueness washed over the eastern horizon, as though the air were drawing off the colour of the bush.

Then Rosandra saw a sign that told her she was twenty-five kilometres from a border checkpoint and accelerated again, with ease. The sign defined a need and told her what to do. She was given a border and a way out. She tried to imagine where exactly on the map she was, probably somewhere close to the white spaces on school wall charts where national colour ended and there were no more diagrams of wild animals and swamp land. The towns she passed were familiar as names of orange-growing estates, name-tags on bags of litchis. But how far south this was, or east, she had no clear idea. Maps disappeared from her experience along with Bass. On diagrams in television news, this area, an area somewhere up or down this border, was shown as shaded, marked with stripes. Terrorists moved here, was what the shading indicated.

Crossing the border, Rosandra thought, a new beginning. She'd imagined she could drive on and on, until she reached the sea, or Bass's ancient African cities and kingdoms of treasure, or until her petrol ran out. But a ten-kilometre sign confirmed it: a definite reality. The border cut across her path. Unexpectedly it worked to lift her tiredness and to free her again. The land was as green and tropical as Eden Island. Ten kilometres away was the white space where known ground ended, where another country began, with different laws and rules.

Feeling less hurried she stopped for a whisky soda, Regina's drink, at a hotel a stone's throw from the border. She sat out on the verandah. Her drink was warm. While no one was around she slipped out her pocket mirror to have a thorough look at herself. She'd spent twenty-four hours without properly tending to her face. The hair style was looking very good, smart and unrecognisable, but her skin had seen no water or make-up since yesterday. Eye pencil was caked in her eye corners, the pores along the sides of her nose were more distended than normal, an effect of the heat. She put the mirror away and then caught sight of her legs, badly in need of waxing. How quickly disintegration set in. One day without a shower, and already her body was sprouting and growing ugly. Since the weeks her belly swelled without reason unpredictable growths possessed a preternatural, upsetting life of their own. Without looking in the mirror again she padded powder over her face and neck.

On her way back from the bar, this time with a whisky on the rocks, she bought two postcards and two stamps. Postcards were like address cards, she thought, to be dropped off after a change of location: Eden Island, Nice, now this place, somewhere on the border.

The postcards carried pictures of the hotel taken in another season. Both cards she used as announcements of a holiday, the messages were identical. She began without names: first, 'just to say . . . alone for a little holiday', then, 'having a peaceful time at this hotel . . . x marks the spot where I am sitting.'

She sent one card to Thony at Star Palace, one to the Whites and Jem.

And that card too I have, Jem thought.

'It was the best thing I could have done,' Rosandra said. 'In the case of Thony, that is. I made things clear. I said I wanted to be alone. He could read between the lines. He could see that it was a goodbye.'

And the card to Cradock was unimportant, a replica, no doubt copied from the other.

'It's hard to believe though. Wouldn't he have wanted to track you down for security reasons, if nothing else? Because of what you knew? It was in his power to find you anywhere, over the border or not. He could have made Regina speak.'

'He could have made Regina speak but I don't think Thony cared enough. Not any more,' said Rosandra. 'He didn't want me. What I knew may have been important in a way, but only in a small way. He might have wanted to bring me back because of pride, but probably he didn't feel like making the effort. I saw the change in his face the day I showed him my strange shape and then again in London. In the beginning I was an important interest because of how I looked, and then I lost that look. By leaving I was out of his hair and he let me go. I buried myself. It shows how little I'd been told, how little I knew. I wasn't much of a danger.'

189

'But the security,' Jem persisted. Again she was evading the point. 'Thony was defence-conscious. You were a breach of security.'

'From his point of view, what did I know? Something about his art collection, and that looked above-board, didn't it? And something about guns for personal protection. He didn't know about me overhearing Michaelis. Michaelis didn't either I suppose. Maybe Thony didn't know that much about the Michaelis business himself. But that's difficult to believe. Michaelis couldn't have been creaming off a proportion of arms intended for the government without Thony's knowledge. They were probably running the deal together. There was also the fact that I hid the Bass connection from Thony, that damaged me too. No, when I left I'm sure it was useful to him. He didn't want me any more.'

But Jem couldn't believe it. Interest in Rosandra didn't wane in a day. Thony worshipped her, she was the symbol he desired – she had said so herself.

'You said a minute ago that when you were on the road you worried he would give chase.'

'I was imagining things,' said Rosandra. 'Thony had power he could use if he wanted to follow me. But he didn't. He didn't care.'

'And you? Did you care?'

That was the real question, Jem thought. Last night on the stoep he prepared his lips to ask it. But be easy on her, he warned himself. Now the words were uttered before he had time to weigh them. Would she give a straight response?

'Did I care? I don't know. How can I say? Sometimes when I think of Thony I see Michaelis's face, dark and preoccupied, photogenic. Other times I see Thony's own face, always talking, the skin on his face moving, his eyes. I think of not being able to understand what was going on. When I think of Star Palace I remember the Dome, how big it was, those beautiful glossy aloes delivered to my doorstep. I think of Thony's paintings and not being able to understand them. When I was with Thony I liked it, to hear him speak. His dreams came alive, they were real, all around us. I was charmed. I believed in the way he saw me. And I liked his touch, as I already told you once or twice. Maybe I cared for that.'

She didn't want to answer, Jem thought. Her answers were inventions. She was beautifully inconsequential, she said the first thing that came into her head.

*   *   *

Out on the hotel verandah, Rosandra said, she felt eyes on her, the waiter. She pulled her hemline down tight over her thighs. She ended the second postcard, the one to Cradock. The waiter, standing in front of her holding his tray against his chest, said the border post kept office hours. If she wanted to cross tonight she must hurry. She paid him to mail her postcards in the nearest town, on the Republic side.

The border post was to the side of the next hill. All around the valley sides looked exactly the same, densely covered with forest, Thony's paintings. There were two prefabricated huts, one on either side of the border. The hut on this side had its window cracked across and mended with masking tape. Across the road was a boom barrier looking flimsy as cardboard. Chickens pecked around it. On the far side an official slept in a wooden chair under a patchy thorn tree. Another official was standing on the steps leading up to the customs hut, squinting into the setting sun.

Rosandra's passport caused no difficulty, but on the far side in the new country the apples she had bought in the city were confiscated. The official pointed to a sun-crisp proclamation pinned to his office wall and the apples were divided between him and his colleague. Under his khaki shirt, which hung open, the official wore a T-shirt advertising the Star Palace logo, two circlets of stars.

'The purpose of my visit is to take a holiday,' Rosandra explained.

He nodded in a genial way, encouraging further information.

'A holiday, like visiting casinos,' said Rosandra.

She pointed at the man's belly and he covered up.

'Visiting places like that,' she said.

'You like Star Palace casino?' said the man.

But she had made a blunder. She shouldn't mention what she must leave behind. The evidence was there before them: the leather passport holder, the one Thony gave her, bore the Star Palace logo too. The man looked at it.

'People like Swazi casinos too,' said the man. 'They tell us when they drive back after the weekend. They make a killing. I'll go one day. When I make the jackpot.'

So there was no danger in what he was saying. He was being pleasant, making conversation. He idly turned her passport in his hands.

'How do I get to the capital from here?' asked Rosandra.

'There are signs to the casino,' said the man. 'Near the casino is the capital. Follow the signs.'

She should have known. At a radius of fifty kilometres from Star

191

Palace, signs directed travellers to its many wonders, the international Dome, the three different hotels, the second biggest aquapark in the Southern Hemisphere.

The official's colleague was walking round her car, inspecting it.

'Fast car, fast woman,' he murmured as Rosandra walked past.

The car cut out twice before she managed to manoeuvre it back on to the road. Chickens scattered. When she looked back the two officials outlined in dusty pink light were kicking an apple between them, bouncing it off the sides of their feet. The glitter of the Star Palace logo reflected off the chief official's shirt.

After passing five illuminated billboards directing her to the three major, world-standard casinos in the capital, Rosandra concluded the town could be little more than a cluster of casino hotels, like Star Palace. The side road she took instead was narrower, deserted, and in bad condition. After a while there were no more signs. A man driving a donkey cart was illuminated by the car headlights. He was a visitation, suddenly brilliant, immediately blotted by the dark. The drive was growing dreamlike; bright images, a red-and-white painted fence-post, a pyramid of silver milk cans, road signs, were outlined against a dark ground, half remembered even as they passed. Beyond the noise of the car she became aware of an encompassing silence. She stopped the car a moment to listen. She heard only frogs. There was a swamp close by, or a river. The air was fresh and damp. On either side of the road were low banks of grey clay pebbles. Beyond there was night sky. She was far across the border now, released into this boundless darkness, but her tiredness drew limits where last night, close to Star Palace, she felt none. She wanted a bed.

She was almost through the village before she became aware of it, a billboard for washing powder, then houses, a grassy verge. The road was moist with dew, its smooth mud surface indicating habitation. It was not much later than nine but the settlement lay in darkness.

A murky light veiled by a net of insects marked the entrance to a hotel. No cars stood in the car park. Out in the dark a generator throbbed weakly, hydrangea bushes crowded the concrete path to the light and the door.

The hotel foyer held dark, imposing pieces of furniture, looking as though they were once built to support significant figures. Long red polished corridors led away into shadows, past the shapes of dark wood doors. There was no one at the reception desk. The last guest in the visitors' book had registered a week before. Another dull light, a patch

192

of yellow without glow, showed in the bar at the end of a corridor. There were three people in the bar, a barman with his arm draped statuesquely across the shoulders of a very small woman looking half asleep, and a white drinker, a man with thin shoulders hitched up just under his ears as though from time spent leaning on bars. Along the top shelf of the bar was a string of fairy lights. Two lights only were shining, a dull red, a very dim blue.

The drinker's face was a surface of dark hollows. On both sides he had a condition that looked like pink-eye and when he drank he sighed loudly like a child drinking milk. He was not a guest, Rosandra thought. He was young, his clothes muddy, gardening clothes. He probably lived somewhere in the dark town, he came here to drink.

But whatever he was he represented opportunity. He was alone, anonymous, in a town across the border without a name. There was a chance that what she had planned could now happen quickly. The doctor's warm, wet fingers in London, she could move on from that; that impression could now be smoothed away.

Not only because of her plan but because of her tiredness the rest of the evening felt mechanical, as though both of them had arranged it in advance. She put the first word, which was hello. She bought him several whiskies and said she was called Rosandra – Rose. His name was Dave or Sam or Damian. His speech was indistinct. He held his glass in front of his mouth even when he was not drinking. After a while the barman went to lie on a camp bed in the shadows of the next room. His girlfriend turned off the fairy light switch and leaned her body against the bar door, more than half asleep. Once, his one distinct sentence, the drinker asked Rosandra what she was doing in this old colonial hole.

'This hotel?'

She said she was on holiday; she spoke about wanting to be out of the country, across the border. These things were safe to say. He pointed with a bent finger, cat's paw hand, at a wooden sign. Its faded lettering said that the hotel was the former mountain resort of sugar-cane barons. This bar was their hang-out. He said something about Swazi dances on the lawns at lunch-times. Bowls and then drinks all night. Gossiping about servants in the bedrooms.

He went round behind the bar and fetched a bottle of cane spirit. His movements were uncertain but habit-formed, he must be a local. His legs were very bony. Sex would be blunt and clumsy, she imagined, very short, unmemorable, unremembered by him. She thought: this is luck.

Once he had perched the bottle on the bar he seemed to forget about it. The barman snored softly, a small sound for a large man. Her companion stared silently at the darkened fairy lights. Then she made to leave and he followed her without a word. She walked him down the corridor, the hotel steps, the smooth road, paths where his feet took him. He told her, in broken sentences, he hated it 'back there' too, that hateful country, that ugly place, those mean, fat, scheming people. She agreed with him, squeezing his arm like a friend. His skin smelt of dry grass and sun. She liked the contrast of the smell in the damp night. When he put his hand on her breast at his house door, which was unlocked, his touch was gentle in its neutrality. She remembered Thony's touch – it seemed to have happened long ago. They moved to his bed in darkness, walking hand in hand, formally side by side, processing. On the bed were loose papers, books, empty bowls and dry spilled food, rice, oats, muesli. He did not clear these away.

But his love held firm, Jem reassured himself. These things she was saying didn't make a difference. His love cleared her of blame. His hope made him confident. Very soon she would come to the end of her story. There was finality in her expression, that way she was sitting forward, more determined. This was the aftermath of the time with Thony, episodes explaining how she came to be here at this table. She was talking her way towards him. Their true reunion would follow. Once she was done he would speak. Then at last he would embrace her.

3

The next morning, Rosandra said, she was introduced to her new hosts by way of their conversation. They were sitting in a group outside and she was still in bed, lying by open windows. The subject of their conversation was herself.

The man – his name was after all Damian – kept silence and when he spoke sounded sullen, no doubt hung-over. The questions put to him were abrupt and comprehensive. How did the woman get here? Was her car hired? What did she want from Damian? Did she have luggage? In between questions toast was being made, knives and plates passed round. There was clattering, people interrupted questions to chew.

Damian kept doggedly to a single line of defence. He said that most men, yes even those present, confronted with a blonde woman who wanted sex, would have done exactly as he did. By taking the sex.

'And with what consequences?' asked the main questioner.

He spoke with a quick confidence. Damian was pressed by him and his voice grew more sullen. He scraped a knife on a plate.

'You would have done better?' he asked sarcastically.

'Yes,' said two people, two men.

'You two, you have nothing to say about this,' said a woman's voice, the only one. 'Go back to your necking.'

The two men seemed to oblige. They joined Damian in silence.

'He has a point,' said the same voice. They called her Lee. She brought in a new tone. 'You guys pretend you're above all that and ideologically OK and then you go for the first blonde white girl that comes along. Look at me. That's why I got here, isn't it?'

The confident voice conceded a quick laugh and asked for cigarettes. There was a long search for matches, mingled in with a gathering of knives.

'But she can't go now,' said the woman. 'Now that she's here.'

'Damian, think carefully one last time,' said another person, carefully, weighing words. 'Are you sure she gave no indications why she came to this place?'

'I've told you what I know,' said Damian.

'Lee's right. The woman can't leave now,' said the first questioner. 'It would be too dangerous. So the first thing to do is take back the car. If we get her to drive it down to Mbabane, Sipho can take the bakkie, follow her and bring her back.'

Sipho was the careful voice.

'About four o'clock,' Sipho said, as Rosandra stepped outside into the middle of the group.

Damian looked at her sideways in greeting, his pink-eye more angry than last night. The sharp morning sun lit each face as it lifted up to hers, a row of sun-lighted noses. The group was sitting on the lawn in a semi-circle like a tribunal. The grass was still covered in dew. The man who stepped up to shake her hand was the main questioner. His grip was quick and firm like his voice but he was younger than he sounded, he could be no more than twenty-five, as were his friends. He introduced himself by a name that did not seem to sit easily in his mouth and Rosandra wondered if it was his own.

To follow suit, Rosandra said to Jem – and maybe there is still reason to protect him – she too would change his name. Let him be Ahmed, she said.

'I didn't mean to listen but I couldn't help hearing some of what you were saying there,' she told them.

She wished again she'd shaved her legs. All of them, including Lee whose hair was short like hers, very blonde, and the two embracing lovers, ran their eyes over her body. She spoke up to attract their attention in a different way.

'I just want to say I'm here sort of by accident. I've left my boyfriend. I've never been to this country before. I hired a car in the city and drove and drove and eventually crossed the border. I didn't want to go to the casinos so I came here. I don't have a map so I don't know where I am.'

They stared at her as though taken by surprise.

'I don't mind staying on here because I don't have any plans.'

'According to Damian you were saying last night that you hated life in that country across the border as much as he does. Would you say

196

'that is true?' said Ahmed, standing close beside her so that to speak she had still to face the whole group.

'That's true, but it wasn't my main reason for leaving and driving here.'

Ahmed stepped closer and blew on her neck. Rosandra felt her body freeze. This was too close. His breath smelt strong, of cigarettes and buttered toast.

'Your hair was cut yesterday,' he said. 'Why? Did you want to change your appearance? Were you trying to hide from someone?'

'Yes,' said Rosandra. 'My boyfriend.'

'Give her a break, Ahmed,' said Lee. 'It's probably true. Ex-boyfriends often beat the shit out of women.'

Ahmed frowned at Lee but retreated. He squatted down beside a man who had been lying on a blanket all this time. He was staring up at the sky. That person must be Sipho, Rosandra calculated.

'We're going to ask you to take your car back to the nearest hire office and to spend time with us for a while,' Ahmed said. 'The community we have here is involved in a few important assignments. It's a bit unfortunate that you came at this time. Outsiders are interfering and we like our privacy. We're going to ask you to be careful with any information you may receive. Even when you leave we are going to demand that you don't say a word to anyone. If you do there could be trouble. In particular for you.'

It was a threat. He spoke it as casually as if he were exchanging telephone numbers.

'I guessed from what you were saying earlier that secrecy was important,' said Rosandra. 'I heard you from the bed.'

'And how does that make you feel?'

'If I must stay, I must stay. I can keep a secret.'

Suspicion sharpened Ahmed's features again. His mouth was severe and his face seemed to lengthen. But the others were losing interest. One of the lovers was twisting his partner's hair into plaits.

'Don't you have people who will be out looking for you? What about the boyfriend? What about family sending out search parties?' Ahmed asked.

'I work as a model in the city,' said Rosandra. She tried to adopt Ahmed's kind of speech, rapid, efficient. 'I often go away on long assignments. I am a free agent. I drove here to have a holiday. My boyfriend could try to follow me but I think he probably won't.'

'If he does,' said Ahmed, more softly, 'it will take him a long time to find us. We have no phone, no postal service. This property is registered as a holiday cottage. It belongs to Damian's grandfather. We keep the place going. We mow the lawn, look after the house. We expect you to help with things while you're here. We all pull our weight.'

Ahmed poked Sipho in the ribs with his foot, a nudge of friendship, and he grunted lazily and rolled away. The interview was over. Rosandra looked down the long slope of the garden. Beyond the flat grassy place the lawn led down to a dense thicket of pampas grass. Beyond that the land fell away into a deep forested valley, and then a yet deeper valley, full of mist. The house faced the valley. It was roughly built and whitewashed. There were many windows, unevenly spaced and of uneven sizes.

'Here, have some toast,' said Lee, holding out a plate of buttered slices and a blunt knife and a jar of bright red jam.

'Pulling weight' in the community in the white house, Rosandra found out within the first few days, meant exhibiting what Ahmed called skills. Sipho's skill involved long hours spent working in the toolshed on tasks that were not named. Ahmed sometimes went in to help him, and to speak fast-flowing monologues to which Sipho replied with short murmurs. Ahmed's time was often taken up holding private conversations. These mostly took place amongst the pampas grasses, usually in the early morning with strangers who came in by night, drank many mugs of Ricoffy, and left again before breakfast.

On alternate weeks Ahmed went further afield on his business and then Lee took over as group leader. Her chief skill was talk of a different nature, long evening discussions out on the verandah on themes called historical necessity and production and communal structure, which, as it grew late, she turned gradually and without a shift in seriousness to talk about personal anxieties and old love affairs. In these discussions she held the floor and asked the questions. The others spoke, describing long heartaches and brief encounters. Ahmed was not often present at these talks.

Rosandra liked Lee. She was straightforward; her movements were deft and quick. Only at night when she stopped and talked was her body still. Rosandra followed Lee around the house as she tidied, straightened, cleaned. After a while she began to help her in this task, a duty which was not rated by Ahmed as a skill.

Lee told Rosandra that she grew up in a North Coast beach resort where, closely watching her brothers, she learned to surf. At fifteen she bleached her hair and left school to work in a sports shop. Then one day, as she told the tale, she woke up and saw the light. She wanted no more of injustice. She grew friendly with radical students at the university – it was here in this city, Rosandra said to Jem. Getting friendly involved sleeping with key student leaders, one of whom was Ahmed. She joined Ahmed in exile. She said she kept him on his toes. He was very fond of leadership, she made sure he didn't grow infatuated with it. Sipho was a friend Ahmed made in exile. Damian was a fellow engineering student.

The skill of the two lovers was to cook the evening meal. Their speciality was lentils spiced with asafoetida. The lovers told Rosandra they came from Port Elizabeth via Mosselbaai and Cape Town. Everywhere they seemed to have fallen foul of the country's segregation, sex and drug laws. They said their names were Max and Joshua, though again Rosandra thought the names were too carefully pronounced, like special labels. She was not wrong. Lee told Rosandra that Max and Joshua renamed each other when they came to this country, to symbolise the start of their new life.

In exchange for the use of his grandfather's house Damian was relieved of important duties, the need to demonstrate distinct skills. Sometimes he tended the garden, he tinkered with the two Datsun trucks and the lawnmower. Other times he daydreamed and stared at the view. Having Damian around meant there was always someone to run errands down to the store at the other end of the village, next to the hotel, to buy necessaries, tea, matches, razor blades. However, if he met a distraction on the way Damian often got his errands wrong or forgot them altogether. Distractions came in a number of forms. The sight of an expensive car or the sound of Afrikaans spoken by visitors to the town developed into intense feelings about fairness and rights. The force of his outrage drove Damian to return to the house immediately to talk to anyone who was available, mostly Lee, sometimes the lovers. Both Max and Joshua spoke Afrikaans but on account of their skin colour did not upset Damian.

On their second night together Damian lost concentration while stroking Rosandra's thigh. His hand fell away from her body. He sat on the edge of the bed smoking a cigarette and then, muttering something indistinct about prickly heat, went to sleep in the living room where there was an extra bed. It was not a warm night.

Rosandra suspected Damian was feeling troubled about having brought her to the house. Then another thought struck her. She looked down and saw in the light of the candle the shadow of her stomach mark showing through her white shirt. It was very noticeable, dark on white skin. Maybe he'd caught sight of it. To an untrained eye it might seem a shadow only, a trick of the light, but to Rosandra it looked suspicious, like a hidden guilt, and it was also ugly, as always.

On the third night Rosandra moved into the living room and left Damian his bed. No one commented on the change. In the days that followed Damian spoke to her as though she were a casual visitor, Lee's friend. For much of the time he kept to himself. It was the habit of most people in the house.

Ahmed wanted Rosandra to develop some or other skill, he said, so that she would find her place in the group and have something to contribute. At the same time she would learn to get over her boyfriend. But there was no problem with that, Rosandra knew. She was trying anyway to suppress memories of Star Palace. And with each day that passed it seemed to fade further away.

On her second day at the house Ahmed suggested photography as a skill, but Rosandra pointed out that her job entailed standing in front of cameras not behind them. The fourth morning he asked about secretarial skills. Rosandra was in the kitchen making breakfast for everyone. Lee said that models did not usually type. Rosandra, coming in with Ahmed's buttered toast, confirmed that this was true. She could not type. Then Sipho mentioned her driving skills.

'You should have seen that woman the other day taking the bends down to Mbabane and back,' he said. 'First in the hired car, then in our bakkie. She's a born driver, a natural. The vehicle made no difference. She drives like Niki Lauda and at the same time like a lorry driver, fast but steady. Very steady.'

When Sipho spoke people usually fell silent whatever they were doing to listen. It had something to do with his skills in the toolshed. They respected his opinion. Now they looked at Rosandra with new interest. She felt pleased and shy. Unexpectedly she had something to offer in exchange for her board, something that wasn't her figure or face.

So Rosandra became a driver. At first this meant little, other than that she help Lee clean and tidy and make toast while bearing a designation that sounded official and was approved by Ahmed. She was of course not yet trusted. Even if they did plan to send her on reasonably important errands, Ahmed said, they couldn't tell her exactly what would be involved. The group didn't forget she was an outsider. Damian still didn't meet her eyes, Sipho generally ignored her. On the way back from Mbabane he might have been inspecting her driving but he had not made conversation. When she'd glanced at him he turned to look out of the car window. Ahmed too stayed wary. Sometimes he stood at his office door – it opened on to the living room – and watched her helping Lee clean.

But she could wait. By now it was a role she had perfected, sitting around waiting for a job, being watched. It was her hidden skill. This was an in-between time, a pause before deciding what to do next. It suited her to stand outside of things, waiting, watching.

People who wait see interesting things. At night, as she lay in the living-room bed, she heard, long after the time that most of the others were asleep, visitors move through the house, often in a hurry, panting, to rest an hour or so, sometimes on the couch, sometimes under her bed, their breathing like the fluttering of moths. At such times she was grateful she had her distance, a freedom, that she was not involved. Action entailed plots and mysteries. Under a blue sheet was the dead squashed face of a shot man; Michaelis drew coup plans on his serviette. Up here in the house in the hills, if she sat out her time, it was safe, and some day Ahmed would see fit to let her go. The figures in the night could never be Thony. If Thony came for her – though he would not – he would drive up in a fast car, carrying expensive weapons. The people who came through the house by night were armed, but not expensively. She saw the shine of metal – knives, she thought, maybe a rifle or two – when they lit cigarettes in the dark.

But she had forgotten that her record of indifference and standing outside things wasn't perfect. It was difficult to remain completely neutral, ignoring the action around her. There was also another thing. In Ahmed's group waiting in fact meant involvement, preparation, lying low. Waiting wasn't neutral.

The day came when, uncharacteristically flustered, also panting, Ahmed asked her to drive a load of what he called manure across several valleys to a certain village. He said he had organised a companion for her but the person had for some reason not arrived and the manure must be delivered without delay. When Thony asked her to help carry a piece of black gun tubing across London she did it without question. And she hung the icon with poised hands. There, at Star Palace, she moved along with events, she didn't resist. So by the same token, when Ahmed asked her this favour, she couldn't think how to refuse. She owed it to him in exchange for hospitality.

It helped that she was as used to unexpected developments as she was to waiting. Here again the time spent with Bass and Thony stood her in good stead. She drove the truck's heavy load across the valleys, left the vehicle beside a deserted hut as instructed, walked away from the truck, losing sight of it, again as instructed, and spent half an hour resting under a thorn tree, chewing grass, smelling the bush, facing away from the direction of the hut – take the whole thing really casually, Ahmed said. Then she drove the truck back up into the hills to the house. The vehicle was now empty. When she arrived back after her walk the load of manure had been removed.

On the way home, obeying Ahmed's directives, she destroyed the map he had drawn for her. It was the first map she had ever followed. As the pieces fluttered out of the window she remembered telling Thony and then also Michaelis about her father David losing his faith on the road. The faith flying in the air like bits of tissue. Passing several donkey carts also carrying manure, remembering back to the night she drove here, she realised that she had left the white house for the first time since her arrival. She'd stuck her head out, an animal emerging from a hide-out. The thought unsettled her peace, the sense of patient waiting. After this drive, she felt, she was no longer as safe as before.

4

The heat on the esplanade was mounting. It must be far hotter than the first day. Rosandra fell into silences and spoke a sentence and was silent again. Jem stared out to sea. The heat worked like a drug, transfixing, deadening. White lights winked across Rosandra's field of vision. Sun on the water, sun on car steel. Jem was holding his head in his hands. She was sure her story was falling into disconnected pieces. She was telling only some of it. Other parts she was remembering, not speaking. She saw them pass in a loose chain, separate, separated from her. Like events that happened to another person, elsewhere. The gong that was rung at the hotel up the road and woke them in the morning, the quarrel that always took place, each evening like a ritual, between Joshua and Max before they started cooking, Lee's disastrous weekly experiments with her sewing machine. These were everyday impressions not worth talking about, photographs without captions, glances between people forgotten as soon as exchanged, the look of a face. Lee, her swollen eyes when she woke in the morning. There wasn't any need to describe these things. Here, at this beach café, under the force of this heat, they had no point.

And the sense of what she was saying, these consecutive episodes, one thing after another in a beadlike row, was blurring. The white heat was settling over them and Jem was waiting for a final statement. She could see it by his pose, leaning forward, elbows on his knees, a picture of patience, listening faithfully like a true friend. What should she say, what leave out? There was the night they saw the comet. Shall I tell you about the comet? she asked him. But that was a sad time to remember, a nostalgic time.

'Go on,' said Jem.

The night they saw the comet, Rosandra told Jem, would be the last night they were all together. They went up to a high mountain, quite far from the village. They let Rosandra drive to show off her skill. Sipho cooed softly when she took the corners. That night she felt she was among friends.

The comet was the one everyone was expecting. As they walked to the cliff edge Lee said some people were speaking about apocalyptic beginnings, historical shifts. Ahmed sniffed, disbelieving, but Sipho said you never can tell. The comet might not cause historical change but seeing the comet might inspire people to make change for themselves. From this night on a new order might emerge. They could be creating it even as they spoke.

'OK, Sipho,' Max said, clapping him on the shoulder. 'Tell our sceptic. Make him see sense.'

Though weather reports indicated it would be clear, a strong wind blowing straight up over the lip of the cliff brought mist. The evening grew hazy. They sat on blankets and waited hours. Max and Damian had plotted the exact place on the horizon where the comet would appear. But they had no luck. There were no stars visible and no comet. Once Max pretended he saw something. He fell back into the dew in mock awe. They played along with him a while. Then they made up rhymes about comets to the tune of freedom songs, which meant mumbling to resonant Xhosa vocals that only Sipho could pronounce.

They so much wanted to see a comet their eyes played tricks on them. Rosandra took off her glasses and saw silver shapes in the low sky, wheeling like the lights at Star Palace. The memory made her feel guilty. She felt her thoughts were visible to everyone. She put the glasses back on, looking round quickly to see who might have been watching. It was beginning to seem a breach of trust, not telling the group about Star Palace. But she felt the danger. How would they take it? What must she say to prove herself? That she'd suspected things but wasn't involved, had played along, chosen to stay, then left when it got bad? But she knew too few details – about guns, paintings, aquapark equipment, how guns were matched to paintings – to be convincing. She didn't know how to begin. To say the boyfriend she'd told them about was an arms magnate, international entrepreneur, casino king.

When Lee began to shiver with the cold Rosandra decided to tell a story. She told a tale of a man who, travelling in a far wasteland in search of beautiful dreams, met children wearing strange filmy glad-rags like the wings of dragonflies. They pursued him and cried out to him to be their king. But because he had a mission he refused.

204

He went on with his journey to cooler southern lands. In the south, he had heard, dreams of immortal beauty visited travellers on the road in broad daylight. Rosandra saw her friends' eyes shine, watching her, listening. So, decorating and expanding as she went, she told another story, about a man, perhaps the same man, who was searching for a lost African city. He searched everywhere, in the savannah and in dense forests and rift valleys, and in the end, when he realised the city might be forever out of reach, lost in deep caves or across impassable deserts, he built one for himself, a grand palace with towers and colonnades rising out of a lake like a vast moat, dangerous with whirlpools and tidal waves.

Sipho took up the story-telling thread from Rosandra. It was a good thread, he said, but maybe he could bring it down to earth. He told a story of his grandmother, an upstanding fierce old woman who was a devout Catholic and yet went about with the amulets of her ancestors' faith sewn into the hems of her church dresses. This woman, Lindiswe Frances Nyembe, lived in a township close to the place where the old Indian prophet, the man who believed in justice and peace, what was his name, Gandhi, once set up a communal centre. She used to tell the children in that area – there were many children, many houses in all directions – about this old prophet. She would tell them that his spirit still lived there in that place and they should honour it. But as the years went by the pressure on that land grew very great. There were so many people, so little land, and so much anger in the people that it became more and more difficult to tell them to show respect for that special piece of earth and the spirit of the man who once lived there.

And so the day came, Sipho said, that the people were so severely pressed against the walls of their shacks and – even though their bellies looked like balloons – so hungry, that they moved and built their tin-can homes and cardboard-box shacks even where the prophet's house had been. And so they forgot about him. And then the grandmother, feeling the anger and distress of the people but also the distress and sadness of the spirit of the place, asked why in this land must everything that was good and strong and long-lasting be trampled into the earth? Why could the prophet's place not be preserved while at the same time giving room to the people? She asked her children and her grandchildren this question, over and over again, and she went also to the city authorities and asked it there. People could not completely ignore her because she was an old woman and demanded respect. Every so often – to this day, Sipho imagined – she went into town to visit the municipal offices and to ask these difficult questions, and every day she prayed, and so she tried to keep a piece of history surviving on the land.

'And so, Sipho, she was the person who first politicised you?' said Ahmed.

Sipho paused before replying.

'No, it was only a few years ago, that incident with the Gandhi land,' he said.

The mist was growing steadily thicker and colder and the audience became restless. Lee scolded Joshua for not bringing a thermos of tea. Ahmed leaned closer to Rosandra and squeezed her hand warmly. Again Rosandra felt guilty about Thony, Star Palace, her silence. The group offered friendship. She must give confidences not stories in return. They trusted her, so she must prove her good faith and come clean with her past. Something had to be said, soon. An interview with Ahmed in the pampas grasses.

So in the end the comet passed them by. They rolled up the blankets and walked back to the car in a high wind and had to content themselves with having seen the sunset.

'We live on a hill and we never bother about the sunset,' said Lee.

'We're too busy,' said Ahmed. 'There's work to do.'

'You know, I think I saw a comet shape in the mist just after sunset,' said Joshua.

'O ja?' said Ahmed, scoffing.

'Yes. I think I did too,' said Rosandra.

Eyes again turned to her, listening, glowing red in the car lights, animal-like. It was a discovery – this power in speech, this surprising power. People paused, they wanted to hear her. During her stories they stretched, getting comfortable, they absent-mindedly plaited their fingers, bit their lips. They were imagining what she was describing. They saw children with wings like dragonflies; they saw the sunset once again.

The late after-sunset light had briefly ignited the haze. A transparent patch showed through the clouds, greenish, and orange at the centre, as large as a hand, where the comet should have happened.

'I'm sure I saw it too,' said Lee.

She squeezed Rosandra's hand, a sudden pressure on the fingers like Ahmed's.

Then Rosandra drove them home through a muddy mist.

Two nights later, because there was another dense mist, Sipho chose his moment to leave the house. He had stayed three months. Rosandra drove him to a railway siding in the middle of nowhere and left him there. He was to follow the railway line till morning and then try to catch a ride at the sugar plantations at the other end. After that Rosandra didn't know what he would do. He slipped out of the truck without saying goodbye. The mist immediately covered him.

On the way home she took a wrong turning. When she arrived back at the house the thick cloud cover was lifting and the sky lightening behind it.

Ahmed was waiting up for her.

'I had to make sure you weren't about to leave us,' he said, partly in jest.

'I'm still here,' said Rosandra.

She took off her glasses the better to see him. They had smudged over with condensation in Ahmed's warm office.

'I haven't seen you without your glasses before, Rosandra,' said Ahmed. 'You're a very beautiful woman.'

Rosandra said nothing. She was dead tired and eye-sore. Cleaning didn't seem to help the cloudy effect in the lenses. She wondered about getting hold of a new prescription out here in this remote town. Probably it would take weeks. Before glasses could be ordered it might be time to leave. And with Sipho going that possibility seemed more real.

Sipho's departure unbalanced the group. One night the pre-supper scrap between Max and Joshua developed into a more serious argument. The two of them exchanged whispered accusations for the duration of a night and then Max moved outside to sleep amongst the pampas grasses in a tent. Out of respect for their skills in the kitchen, and maybe because no one other than Joshua had the trick of managing the temperamental gas stove, cooking came to an end. People ate cold food, rice crispies, gherkins, fruit in cans, alone in their bedrooms, and this soured tempers. Lee's evening discussions lapsed.

Ahmed began to persuade Rosandra to try reading some of the books in his office. He possessed many rows of them, Penguins arranged on pine shelves in blocks of orange and blue. Rosandra, dusting in the office, thought the rectangles of colour made a fine wall display, a good decoration instead of pictures.

'Why should she have to read your books?' asked Lee.

'So she can participate in discussion,' said Ahmed. 'So she can become a fully fledged member of the group.'

'She is,' said Lee.

'Maybe she wants to give further expression to that hate for the state across the border that she told Damian about on her first night here. She hasn't told us much about that yet.'

'Maybe she can do it in her own words,' said Lee, 'and in her own time.'

Rosandra heard them from the kitchen where she was making a salad for the evening meal. She was slicing cucumber and red-orange tomatoes. The salad was a way of getting everyone to sit around a table together. But the discussion between Lee and Ahmed continued through the evening, and in the end only she and Damian ate the food, Damian with his head down, his eyelids pale pink patches, strictly observing the new rule of silence in the house. In this silence Lee and Ahmed were clearly audible in their bedroom, accusing each other of a variety of vices, of jealousy and hegemony, and then stupidity and possessiveness, and finally a lack of love.

Two nights later, a Saturday, Ahmed called Rosandra into his office. The others were up at the hotel. If there were guests, old films were shown in the bar on Saturday nights. No one knew what was on tonight, Hollywood classics maybe, said Lee, flicks from the forties, but they went along anyway. Rosandra guessed that her important talk with Ahmed might take place here in the office and not in the pampas thicket after all.

'I've been wanting to speak to you alone for a while,' said Ahmed, friendly but dispassionate, neutral. 'To see how you're getting on. It's time we got to know each other better.'

He boiled water on the primus stove in the corner and made Ricoffy. There was no milk.

They sat cross-legged on the carpet in the office, facing each other.

'I hope you don't mind me saying this, Rosandra. I feel, I don't know, an affinity with you. From the day you first came. Like a trust. I respect your silence. You know how to keep information to yourself. You seem to me very strong. Like I say, I respect that. You made us very vulnerable when you came. But I know you won't betray us.'

'I won't betray you,' said Rosandra. 'You took me in and fed me.'

'Your charm is these cute, irrelevant comments,' said Ahmed, 'but behind that silence there's endurance and strength and a lot of thinking going on.'

Rosandra gave a half-smile. He seemed to be offering compliments. However, his gaze was thoughtful.

'You could easily have betrayed us the night you gave Sipho the ride,' he said. 'If you were a spy. Or even if not. People do things like that.'

'Yes, I could have betrayed you,' said Rosandra.

'Do you know what Sipho was carrying with him?'

'No,' said Rosandra, 'but I can guess. Ammunition, a rifle. Maybe an AK 47.'

'Sharp,' said Ahmed. 'You know the name.'

'You learn from watching television,' said Rosandra.

But she did not watch television. She overheard Michaelis. The day in the park was very distant, another world, a far country. She couldn't tell Ahmed about Michaelis before she told him about Thony. Tonight, maybe, she could work up to that point.

'You lost your way the night you took Sipho to the railway line,' said Ahmed.

He was prompting her, wanting her to say something, confess about herself.

'Yes, you didn't give me a map that time,' said Rosandra. 'Maybe some time during the night I could've got in touch with my contacts and told them about Sipho and betrayed all of you.'

'You didn't though. You didn't have time to get to Mbabane and back. I worked it out. And you didn't have enough information to tell anyone anything useful. You still don't.'

Ahmed shifted his position on the carpet so that he was sitting beside her.

'Anyway, I trusted you,' he said.

Rosandra tested possible openings. There were so many ways of beginning. Remember that story I told you about the man who built the lost city of Africa, she could say. Well, the thing is, he was the boyfriend I was trying to escape. Or not so round-about and chatty. Rather straight to the point. I should tell you about the time I lived, no, worked at, was photographed at, the big casino over on the other side, yes, Star Palace. Well, something you may not know – it could be important that you know, because of what I think you and Sipho do – the casino may be a centre, partly out in the open, partly underground, for trading in arms with all kinds of people. Yes, at Star Palace. But it was difficult to find the right words. The minute she began it would look suspicious. I was the friend or if you like trial agent of the man in charge of the operation. No, it couldn't be done, not now, in the middle of their first proper conversation, not when he was talking about trust, and getting closer.

'There are so many possible weak links in the business we're involved in,' Ahmed said. 'You just have to trust your luck. You believe in what you're doing anyway. And you take risks. A situation can look a fair deal and you accept it and go with it, and then it goes wrong and the person who made the decisions, like me, can come out looking bad. All you have to rely on is your own judgement.'

'Your intuition?' said Rosandra, thinking of leaving Star Palace, leaving Eden Island, flying out, driving away. Intuition grew sharper with practice.

'I don't like to call it that,' said Ahmed. 'It's not very scientific. I like to say judgement. You make calculated guesses based on evidence. Like recently we've been put on to a very interesting contact in the city, someone who seems sympathetic, a brother. He may be very useful. In fact he has already given us help. If you stick around you might have a chance to meet him. But this is the kind of thing you have to take on trust. There's no way of knowing it'll work out.'

He paused, looking at her, trying to make her out. She felt his eyes on her body, hairline, mouth arms legs. She was aware of him breathing very close beside her, like on the first morning.

'In fact, I mention this man for a reason,' Ahmed said. 'You may have heard of him. He's in your line of work. His cover is that he runs a model agency in the city.'

'Yes?' said Rosandra.

The name couldn't be familiar. She wasn't a city model. Once she'd been the flame of the Star Palace king.

'So he works as the head of this agency but really he sets up caches for us inside the country. He has contacts on the régime's side, but he's our man, a comrade.'

'How do you know?'

'That's what I mean by judgement. He has built up trust gradually, over several meetings. He has met with several different people. We think he's OK. He's a black guy like me. He passes himself off as one of these new black entrepreneurs, which is very clever. I was thinking you might know the name of his agency. It's called the Mike T. Shepherd Modelling Agency. He works out of offices in Bok Street.'

There was something in what he said, like a passing memory. Was it the name of the street? It again reminded her of Emmie. She couldn't think why. She was getting as bad as Damian, reacting to the sound of a language, the tone of speech. Then Ahmed put his hand on her inner thigh.

'I don't know the name,' said Rosandra.

'Don't worry for now,' said Ahmed. 'You'll get a chance to meet him some day soon anyway. If things work out with him. And if you stay with us.'

'If I can stay, I will,' said Rosandra.

'Let's go to bed together,' said Ahmed.

He changed topics smoothly, without hesitation. He knew how to manage a conversation.

'I don't think so,' she said.

'I want to be honest with you,' said Ahmed. 'You were honest when you came here. You first came into this house to find sex. You slept with Damian.'

'Yes, that's what I decided,' said Rosandra.

'As I've already told you, you're a very beautiful woman, Rosandra. I'm very attracted to you.'

His eyes were close, big pupils. There was no expression in eyes this close, only small light reflections. She remembered Bass's eyes as he stuck shells on to her skin, concentrating. Thony's wet eyes as he came close to explain his dreams, took her throat in his mud-red hands to make the oysters slip down.

'I'm sorry,' Rosandra said, moving away.

He released his hold on her leg. He went over to his bookshelves and brought down a book, one next to the golden spine that bore the name *Siddhartha*.

'I want to read this to you,' said Ahmed. 'I'm not good at expressing my feelings, you see. I can talk politics, but emotions are difficult to describe. I let this do it for me. I found this passage the other day. You see, I think I could spend time with you, Rosandra. I think we can make good comrades. This expresses what I feel. It goes: "It is not our task to come together, as little as it would be the task of sun and moon, of sea and land. We two, my friend, are sun and moon; sea and land. Our destiny is not to become one. It is to behold each other for what we are." Now, that's good, don't you think? It expresses how I see you. How we could be, you and me. Together. I respect you, Rosandra. You fascinate me.'

'What you read sounds good,' said Rosandra, 'though I don't understand it. I don't read much, not politics or poetry.'

She was squinting down at the text, trying to read sideways, trying to make out the meaning without touching him. She thought about Lee, what she would say about this, whether she knew.

'You don't think that's good?'

211

'I said it was good, but I don't understand how it fits.'

'Don't worry,' he said. 'Maybe it'll become clearer.'

He put his arm around her shoulders.

'Was your argument with Lee serious?' said Rosandra.

'Lee and I have a very open relationship.'

'She didn't tell me that.'

'Maybe the context wasn't right. We all take our own time trusting each other.'

He stroked her hair. His touch was not as light as Thony's.

'Show me the mark you have on your belly button, Rosandra,' he said.

'Sorry?'

She hadn't heard him right, surely, but she held her hands to her stomach, pressing inwards. She wanted to move further away.

'Damian said you had a fascinating mark on your stomach, like a birthmark. It has a beautiful shape. It's the colour of brinjals. That's not his description, it's mine. It's my fantasy. I've been wondering about it. Your little hidden blackness.'

Rosandra laid hold of her shirt with both hands, hard, pulling it down. There was this thought only – he mustn't see.

'I don't think I want to show it,' she said.

'Come on,' he said, teasing, beginning to tickle her a little under the arms.

She wrenched back and stood upright.

'Please, Ahmed,' she said, 'not *yet*. Not now.'

He cocked his head, as though listening for something, thinking sharply about what she just said. He dusted his hands.

'OK, as you like. Not *yet*, not now,' he said, mimicking her emphasis and laughing in his brisk, confident way.

It took a moment, but the promise in what she said seemed to persuade him.

'We'll leave it at that then. Not yet but soon. I'll wait and want.'

He got up to make more Ricoffy. The primus roared and smoked. Rosandra stood at the door, holding the handle, confused, also relieved, in part. His mind had moved to other things; he had his answers. However, she was still thinking about Thony, about saying it now, now that they were further apart, more formal. I was the friend no playmate accomplice-in-training of – But the interview was definitely over, the closeness was lost. She could tell by Ahmed's movements. He put away the book, on the wrong side of the golden spine, she noticed, then he went over to his desk, very brusque, and placed a pile of papers squarely on the blotting paper in front of him.

'If you feel like it,' he said, 'choose a book and stay to read. I've got plenty to do but I don't mind guests. The carpet is a comfortable reading mat.'

Above their white table, Jem saw, a mirage had formed. The air seemed mobile, a spirit thing. The sun drained her skin of colour. His own face burned, it hurt to move his cheeks. In the moving air her freckles swam, dancing crazily before his eyes. Her loose shirt, ill-cut, hung awry on her shoulders. He did not like her to look untidy. He should offer to lift and straighten it, as a friend. He could run his hand down her back, down her hair, still in the guise of a friend, bending over to look, to wonder. And she would sit passively. Her beauty manifested itself carelessly, uninterested, without effort. She was a model, she let people look. She stood under the magnolia tree with Jem sitting goggle-eyed in the hedge.

'I want to tell you something,' Rosandra said. 'That time with Ahmed brings it back.'

Now it comes, Jem thought, at last, a mite of a confession, a sign of trust.

'It's a silly thing, maybe vain, but I know it's all right to tell you. One of the reasons I came down here on this holiday was to be examined by a world-famous dermatologist in this city. His rooms are in a high-rise further down the esplanade, looking out over the sea. I went to see him two days ago, after the shoot at the elephant reserve. I had some time.'

'Not about your mark?' said Jem.

'Yes. About the mark. I think it's spreading. It's definitely growing darker. I still wonder about malignancy. But mainly I wanted to find out if he could reduce it or cut it out. He's an expert. There might be tricks he could do, skin grafts, those kind of things. I'm sick of this mark. It's unsightly. It exposes me.'

She could show it to him without fear, Jem thought, and he would bring back a sense of proportion. It was something he could do for her. It is not as large as you think it is, he would say, not a growth, or a fist, a hand or Antarctica, or however you've described it. But what she'd just told him about Ahmed held him back. He was shy. Ahmed's eyes travelled over her body. He couldn't ask to see, not now. She'd feel him examine, coming up too close.

'I'm sure it's not as bad as you say,' he said.

'I may have to tell myself that many times in my life,' Rosandra said. 'The dermatologist said the mark is too large to be removed. It's permanent. I'll carry it with me always. I asked if little pieces could be removed, like shaved off the sides. He said no. Skin like this must be treated with respect. Thony was right. I shouldn't expose it to the sun.'

'It's part of you, Rosandra.'

'I'm afraid so,' she said.

The sweat was pouring off him. Gratified, Jem saw that Rosandra too was soaked through. Loose bits of hair were sticking to her forehead and cheeks. The two of them were the only ones at the café still braving the open air. The mirage over the table shimmered more brightly than the white light coming off the sea.

'We're being silly about this heat,' said Jem. 'Let's go into the café. They have air-conditioning. We could have iced water. And I have a surprise for you.'

The heat was kind because it dulled anxiety. From now on the conversation would be a matter of course. He would have to say certain obvious words, but he could weather that. Many people had said them in the past. And the time was right, it was his last chance. The main thing was to make the meanings clear. The worst would be to bumble, to have to repeat the clumsy phrases all over again. But after their two long conversations, and the two weeks that had passed since their first meeting, at least they were used to the idea of each other. It made things easier. They knew about each other. She'd told some secrets. He loved her the more in spite of them.

He winked at a waiter who waited unhappily under the café awning, his face in shadows.

'I don't think I want to go in yet, Jem,' said Rosandra. 'Now that the worst damage has been done and our clothes are sweated through and we're boiling, let's stay outside. We did it the first time, two weeks ago.'

Just in time Jem gave the waiter another sign. He saw the waiter's legs disappear into the café.

'When hot, why not get hotter?' said Rosandra, and pulled up her shirt and tucked it into her bra. 'I love to feel the sun on my skin.'

And the mark was shocking. Jem saw. She was right about it, the ugliness. And Susan White was right to make her hide it. The mark covered all of her stomach, disappearing under her tucked shirt and into the band of her skirt. And it was dark purple. Its edges – like tentacles, yes – reached back around her ribs. The skin looked smooth, thick and glossy, unnaturally healthy and alive. It was embarrassing to see.

'You don't really like the look of it, do you, Jem?'

She was watching his eyes. Her stare. He couldn't return it.

'Do you blame me for wanting it removed?'

'I don't blame you for anything, Rosandra. But I'm thinking of the doctor's advice. Maybe you don't want to expose that skin to the harsh sunlight.'

'It feels good, Jem.'

'I'm sure it's not healthy.'

And so despite the planning and the hoping the timing was wrong after all. The waiter arrived with a large smoking ice bucket holding the champagne, and white roses in an iced vase, and iced glasses, exactly as he'd planned it yesterday, exactly as he'd ordered early this morning when, his throat tight with nervousness, he telephoned the café.

Rosandra was absorbed by the display. She watched the waiter's hands spread a pink tablecloth, smooth it and place the glasses. Possessed by some madness, the heat maybe, she tucked her shirt up higher, showing even more dark flesh. Jem saw the waiter trying to concentrate on what he was doing, setting down the bucket between them, trying not to look. But the mark drew eyes, Jem couldn't stop staring. The scene was an embarrassment, it was the most unfortunate way to begin.

'A little surprise for you, Rosandra,' Jem said.

The waiter withdrew, staring now, frankly agape.

'No, Jem,' said Rosandra. 'Please don't.'

'White roses to match your name,' said Jem.

She pushed back her wet fringe and showed him her pale white eye sockets, her pale eyes. She unfolded her shirt and pulled it down.

'Jem, I think I know what you want to say. I don't think you should. I think we should stop here. We met to reminisce. Tonight I fly back home. You know that. We have different lives. It was nice seeing you. I've enjoyed catching up with things, putting things in order, bringing things back, I liked that. Let's leave it at that.'

'This is a gesture, Rosandra,' said Jem, lamely putting his arms around the ice bucket, the roses, as though to spirit them away, start all over again. 'The last thing I want is to put you in a difficult position. I'll be honest with you. Over the years I've had hopes. I wanted badly to see you again. Often the hopes looked like impossible dreams. But over these last two weeks we seemed to find something – like an understanding. What you told me made things more clear. I saw I could have a purpose in your life. I can give you a home. I want to create conditions so that you won't be in danger again. That's all. It's very simple. I want to make sure you'll be OK. I won't touch you if you don't want it, I won't tell you what to do. I just want to see you. I feel a lot for you.'

So it wasn't as difficult as he'd feared. The emotion made it easy, also the look of the white trembling skin round her eyes, unprotected.

'Jem, I have a home, I have a job. I have a place to stay. You haven't heard the end of my story yet.'

'I can't see you go, Rosandra. Anything could happen to you. You're not safe alone. This has become a violent country. Thony might still be looking for you. I have big important feelings for you, a great deal of love and friendship. I'll do anything to make you secure.'

'You know, it's a funny thing,' said Rosandra, 'in the time that has passed I haven't found out much about love.'

'I won't say, let me teach you about love. I'm not saying that.' Was he stuttering, he wondered. He wanted to say everything at once, so she'd believe. 'I don't like to press you. I just want you to know what I feel. Rely on me.'

'I wonder,' said Rosandra. 'People fight for the things they love, don't they? Love has to do with defence.'

'I don't know about that. I just want to give you a home, to protect you. I saw it all a couple of nights ago, after everything you told me. And after today it's even clearer. I want you to be safe from people like Thony, like Ahmed. If you're alone, men like that will never leave you be.'

'I didn't ever mean to suggest Ahmed was a bad man,' said Rosandra. 'That wasn't the point of what I told you. Ahmed had strong beliefs. He was prepared to fight for them.'

The roses were bruising and crumpling in the heat. Jem felt a depression heavy as the heat, as impenetrable. The plan was not working and it made no sense, this farcical marriage proposal in an urban beach resort, this absurd attempt to make a secure future, to win Rosandra after three meetings, a childhood of staring through a hedge.

'Rosandra,' Jem said slowly, wearily, and once again he felt like a geography instructor, 'the fighting must stop some time, or this nation and all of us will perish.'

'That brings me to telling you about my other mission in this city, what I did yesterday,' Rosandra said. 'It was the third task after the shoot and visiting the dermatologist.'

She spoke as though the proposal was already a thing of the past and they could begin moving on to lighter topics. Jem didn't know where to look.

'It links up with what happened after Ahmed and I had our talk,' Rosandra said. 'So maybe you'll be interested.'

5

'That abrupt end to the conversation with Ahmed didn't improve the tension in the house,' said Rosandra, pressing and crushing fallen rose petals with a little finger. 'I began to avoid him. I didn't know what I would say if he spoke to me again. I didn't know if I should speak to Lee. Who would I be betraying? As the days went by the people in the house who hadn't quarrelled with one another also stopped talking. There was no news from Sipho and no word about his movements. The group was waiting, we grew nervous. People talked in their sleep.

'One day Damian set off on a hike by himself and the next day I asked to go to Mbabane for a while. I needed a break. No one was driving anywhere at that time. My skill was useless, I felt like a spare part. By that stage, I thought, they could let me go. It was safe. But it took all of Lee's persuasion to convince Ahmed of the fact. In the end she fixed me up to stay with friends of hers, old surfing connections who lived on the outskirts of Mbabane. Only then did he let me go. But the night before I left he went so far as to lend me one of the bakkies to drive down. He didn't want me to have to hitch a ride. I suppose it was a guarantee that I'd return.

'The outskirts of Mbabane where Lee's friends lived turned out to be the staff housing of one of the big casino resorts. So I might have felt at home if I hadn't been hoping for a holiday. On the other hand a casino resort meant entertainment. For the first time I watched gambling at close quarters, and the strip routines and the big ox roasts on a Sunday.

'One of Lee's friends was a real bunny girl. She had varicose veins in her legs from doing too much work on high-heels. This girl had several boyfriends she saw on separate weekends. One was a travel agent's assistant, and one was a croupier, and another, the serious one, was from a North Coast town, somewhere close to here. He'd come into politics via doing drugs. On LSD one day he saw a vision of brotherhood and peace. He saw women standing on a plain ululating, holding hands. He gave up drugs to teach literacy in rural areas. One night when we were all sitting around talking he told me that the Indian nationalist leader, Gandhi, whom we probably knew from the film or the video, had lived once in this city where you and I are now. He set up a community to teach its members self-help and the values of freedom and peace. People grew their own food, prayed. The community, said this man, was called an ashram. I thought to myself, that's a good idea, to teach people these things, self-help, freedom. And then I remembered the story Sipho told on the night of the comet. His severe old grandmother must live close to that place, I thought. The ashram must be where she tried to keep peace with the prophet's forgotten ghost.

'After that it was like this modelling trip had to happen. This city was where I was sent on the shoot, this was where the well-known dermatologist lived, and here was also Sipho's place, the ashram. There was a sequence in it. What that man told me was a sign telling me to come and meet the old woman. I'd always wanted to visit this city, and now I had this sign. I would come to find out about the mark on my skin and then I'd try to find Sipho's grandmother. I had no information other than what Sipho's story told me. She lived in a slum, she was likely to be a strong presence in her community. But I thought people would know about the prophet's place.

'Yesterday morning I took a taxi to the township the bunny girl's boyfriend named. When I gave directions the taxi driver looked at me oddly, like I was strange in the head. He said the squatter area of this township was far, far larger than the part with brick houses. It extended across a valley and over the next hill. So how I was going to find a single old woman, no matter how much of a presence in the community, in the middle of all that?

'The taxi driver smoked clove cigarettes. As we drove we listened to the request programme on the radio. Things were pleasant. I knew the words to some of the songs, I felt I was doing the right thing. But then, when the road petered into a track leading between shacks, the taxi driver said he was going no further. We were on the slope of a hill. The shacks extended further up the hill. The smell of open sewers in the heat was strong. The driver poured rose water on his handkerchief and gave it to me. There were people everywhere going about their business. How did it feel? As though I was naked, too white.

My shorts were too short, I was showing too much skin. I felt I was insulting people.

'No one knew about Sipho's grandmother or about the ashram. I asked many passers-by. The word wasn't familiar, and the name of its founder wasn't familiar. I couldn't blame them for not knowing. Struggling for space amongst those shacks couldn't leave time to think about prophets. But I thought it might also be that we weren't yet in the right place. I decided that maybe Sipho's grandmother's influence still had to reach that spot.

'To find the whereabouts of the ashram I next went to the city museum. The building looks a bit like the government buildings on Eden Island, a big stone dome, steps that make your knees ache when you go down them, a forest of pillars in the front. The chief curator, a fiftyish man from Edinburgh, had the answer. The taxi driver wasn't far wrong. We'd been close to the location of the former ashram, but because it had been left deserted many years the shanty town grew over it. Like dandelions, said the curator. Now even the foundations of what had existed were blotted out. From the point of view of the shanty town the area had probably looked wastefully empty, the curator said. But he also said I'd be a fool to go back to try to find the place. "To court their anger" were his words. Living in pondoks – he pronounced the Afrikaans as though it was English – didn't encourage people to be calm.

'But I went anyway, after buying a new dress, dark blue, ankle-length, like a church uniform. I was determined to find Sipho's grandmother. I had a reason for this, Jem. I had to make my peace. The taxi driver who drove me this second time was even less eager to take on the hillside. He said I should walk. He would wait half an hour for me provided I paid. I said I would pay him the price of two hours if he would stay for one.

'It came to nothing. By now it was close to five o'clock. People were moving quickly along the road. They didn't want to stop and listen. My pronunciation of the grandmother's name was incorrect. On top of that I was mumbling. I was embarrassed. My clothes were again wrong. The fresh cotton showed its newness in the setting sun.

'The hour was almost up when I ran into a middle-aged woman wearing a maid's uniform. She seemed in a hurry but when I approached her she stopped and came up close, concerned, like a mother. I thought of Maria at home, how she cared. In a whispering, urgent voice this woman told me I was a fool to be here. I would be robbed, stoned, worse than stoned. But no one had laid a finger on me, I said. In fact few people were interested in looking my way. Then when I spoke what I thought was the name of Sipho's grandmother her face changed completely, the worry lifted, she was suddenly genuinely interested. She repeated the name, getting the sounds right, it rang a bell for her.

'She hailed another woman passing by. They talked, and the first woman grew downcast. She told me the news was bad. Sipho's grandmother was no longer around. Dead? I asked. No, maybe not dead. The story was confused. The grandmother had been taken once by the police, beaten. After that she became very sad. For a woman who always had things to say she grew quiet. Then she disappeared again. Maybe the police took her. She hadn't been heard of in weeks.

'By then it was time to return to the taxi. The driver was on the point of leaving. All the way back I was faced with his stony silence, disapproving. When he saw where my hotel was, here on the esplanade, in the executive part of town, he kissed his teeth.

'So I returned to the hotel room having failed in both my tasks. I was tempted to call you at the last minute to cancel our meeting today. For a few hours last night I wanted to go straight home, I wanted to be out of the country. I felt useless. Apart from doing my job and the pleasure of seeing you my errands in this city ended in nothing. In a way, you see, everything depended on this visit. I had to see Sipho's grandmother. As I sat there in the hotel room on the king-size bed – it was just like Eden, with the padded button pattern in the headboard – as I sat there I felt my little pilgrimage had led nowhere. Yes, the shoot's been OK, I can do that stuff now, stand like so, holding my legs shoulders hair this way, that way, I've been trained. But this other disappointment towered over me. Beside that the dermatologist's opinion didn't feel important. I can, I suppose, live with wearing one-piece swimsuits for the rest of my life.'

'I don't understand,' said Jem. 'I can see it meant something seeing this old lady. I don't see why it was as important as all that.'

'Like I said, I had to make my peace,' Rosandra said. 'Everything depended on it. It was a way of repairing things. I wanted it to succeed.'

'But you didn't know this woman. You briefly knew her grandson. I don't see why it mattered so much seeing her.'

'It matters,' said Rosandra in a tired voice.

Her expression suggested the reason was obvious. She shouldn't have to pass it on.

'It matters because of what happened to her grandson. I had to tell her he is dead. In case she hadn't heard yet. I wanted to explain.'

Sipho's death, Rosandra told Jem, must have happened while she was staying with Lee's dancing and surfing friends. There wasn't much she could say about how he died. No one knew anything definite. That's the way these things went, something like that Cradock leader Jem mentioned. They suspected he was killed. The evidence suggested he must have been killed.

She arrived back at the house up in the hills to find no one at home but Lee. The others were at unknown destinations. Joshua, Lee thought, had taken money his mother loaned him to fly to a rock concert in Harare.

For those few days alone together Lee and Rosandra had something like a holiday. They didn't cook or clean and they used house petty cash to buy treats at the store, ice-cream, liquorice all-sorts, biltong. They grew closer. Rosandra thought she had found a friend. Lee took the opportunity, which usually wasn't possible, of speaking about her own troubles and old love affairs. Her lovers were difficult to tell apart. They were either teenage surfers who she said had plenty of technique on their boards but none in bed, or they were student leaders who liked the sound of their own voices and skinny blonde women who had read Marx.

To confide something in return Rosandra told Lee about the time she was invited on a tropical island trip by a friend of her father's, a man who was interested in art photography. To take interesting shots he made her look like a mermaid by sticking shells on to her skin. She also told Lee about her so-called ex-boyfriend, the one she'd just left when she came to the house. He was a businessman, she said, who reclaimed the desert and provided land and work for displaced people. He gave her gold chains to express his passion. Rosandra wanted to tell Lee more but she hadn't yet found a way of telling the truth. She didn't know how to say it, the words wouldn't come.

The news about Sipho was brought by one of their night-time

sojourners. What with Ahmed and Sipho away it was the first such visit to the house in some weeks. The visitor stayed one hour, he woke only Lee. Two days later Damian came home and confirmed the news. He read it in a week-old Republic newspaper he found somewhere on his hike, in a café on the road, he said. It appeared that Sipho was ambushed, trapped and driven to ground, about two hundred kilometres away from the Swazi border. He was alone, travelling on foot. He was probably shot on sight. Damian's report listed what he was carrying. It said he was laden with arms. RPG-6 hand grenades, an RPG-2 portable rocket launcher, several assault rifles, much more, they guessed, than he needed for his own protection.

After that the three of them didn't know what to say to each other. Sipho's death meant a serious loss. It meant his mission, whatever it was exactly, was unaccomplished. He was a quiet man. It was wrong for him to go out in a blaze of gunfire. And his death had a special meaning for all of them. The group knew about his going. Ahmed worked with him, everyone saw him off. It was possible that a person in the house had betrayed him.

The person who betrayed Sipho, Rosandra said, needn't have been someone who knew what he was carrying. It was someone who knew that he was going into the Republic, and when he went in.

For the first few days Damian, Lee and Rosandra tried looking at each other bravely, openly, as though with expressions of trust, but their thoughts and dreams were suspicious. Damian woke them in the night shouting. His pink-eye flared up savagely. They grew uncomfortable about leaving the house. They pretended to read, pretended not to listen for cars passing along the main road through town. It was as if they wanted to be prepared for another visit, a night-time call. All three of them, not only Damian, invented excuses not to go to the store. Lee began avoiding the living room where Rosandra still slept and their confidences about old boyfriends abruptly ended. One day Lee took Rosandra down into the pampas thicket, out of Damian's earshot, to ask if it was true – as he reported before he left, though at the time Lee didn't want to believe it – that Rosandra had wanted to go to bed with Ahmed. In other words, Lee asked, after everything she had done to make her feel welcome, had Rosandra tried to take her man behind her back?

It was in this way then that she was accused. She should have seen it from the beginning, but it was only at that moment that it struck her what a clear suspect she was. The suspicion was there even in Lee's position, in the way she stood side-on, and the uncharacteristic stillness of her body. Rosandra was the outsider. Her origins were unknown, and if known murky. She had no convictions, no politics, no anger to speak of. And, most important of all, she herself felt guilty. She felt as though Damian's inflamed gaze was always on her. She couldn't meet Lee's eyes. Yes, she hadn't minded Ahmed touching her, she hadn't spoken to Lee about their conversation. And she drove Sipho to the railway siding. She was involved, implicated. By being in that house she had become guilty. Somehow, she was convinced, she had helped betray Sipho.

'By being there I had made things go wrong,' Rosandra said. 'Feeling guilty was a proof to me. I felt I influenced events in the wrong sorts of ways.'

'But how can you be guilty without doing wrong?' said Jem. 'Or without knowing you have done wrong? How did your being there change things?'

Jem spoke in confidence. He still embraced the roses, leaning forward on the table to bring his face closer to hers. He wanted to dispel her delusion by this closeness. Maybe he could be of help to her after all. Maybe, in spite of her rejection, he could fulfil some function in her life.

'It's simple,' said Rosandra. 'During that conversation with Ahmed about betrayal I should have spoken. I should've told him the things I knew. About Thony and Star Palace. When I saw Lee's hurt face out there in the garden this was clear. This was why I was guilty. It was dangerous that I kept quiet.'

'But it was as dangerous for you to speak.'

Before, two weeks ago, even at their last meeting, her lack of concern distressed him. Now it was different. He'd wanted her to show knowledge of wrong, a burden of experience, he wanted her to come clean. But now that wasn't important any more. Because she didn't manage guilt well, she made it up like she invented stories. In this case with Sipho she had nothing to worry about. She should use that lightness of hers to advantage.

'You were adopted by the community,' Jem said. 'You couldn't do much about that. But you owed them nothing. How could you begin to take responsibility for them? If you'd told them about yourself would that have saved them?'

Rosandra was not interested, so she shouldn't take things to heart in this way, Jem thought. A person who is not interested doesn't wilfully betray. She entertains no plots, no hidden intentions. Rosandra erred only by accident, by unfortunate proximity. Her guilt could be lifted, it could be brushed away like dust.

'This is the way I see it,' Rosandra said. 'When I arrived in the community I was already guilty. I brought danger with me to that house.'

Like a body brings the smell of its bed, its home, its hotel room, Rosandra thought, she carried her past with Bass and with Thony along to the house on the hill. She carried the smell of the casino, the warm, handled-metal smell. Jem said the word fortune – her fortune followed her. Generally she'd been lucky, she'd taken chances, taken things as they came, been open to luck. But after a while her fortune developed a kind of theme and the theme stuck. Her fortune was false appearances, men carrying and hiding arms. Sipho was tied up in that fortune. She'd not thought of it exactly in this way before, but telling Jem about these past few years made the sequences clear. The one event unfolding into the next, Bass's training preparing her for Star Palace, the favours for Thony and the favours for Ahmed running into one another like mingling dye. Carrying hidden arms. There was the dead man with the blue sheet over his face. She told no one about him. The day she buried that image she must have become guilty. She acquired a hidden past.

'I always thought I was free to slip away,' Rosandra said. 'When I left Star Palace I took a car and drove across a border and thought I was safe. I even thought I was free. I thought I was getting away from everything. And maybe I did for a while. I escaped Bass, I thought I could escape Thony. I think I'm free now. But that time I wasn't successful. Slipping away can be like lying. You blank things out. You avoid mentioning them.'

Escaping was a kind of forgetting, Rosandra thought. Going with the motion of experience, not thinking back. But her fortune caught up with her. Maybe she got it wrong, that once, the correct style of waiting, watching, being sufficiently vague, sufficiently unconcerned, distracted in the right kind of way. That one time she got it wrong. It was like there was a special destination reserved for her in that house in the hills.

'You never wronged people,' said Jem. 'Not with intention.'

Rosandra counted off the links of the heaviest gold chain on her arm.

'Damian could have betrayed Sipho,' she said, 'but probably didn't know enough to do so. He didn't know where Sipho was going, he wasn't trusted with information. If they had wanted to Joshua and Max could have tried to betray Sipho but it seems unlikely. It wasn't in their interest. They represented a different cause. Lee was a suspect but, as she told me, she hadn't had Ahmed's trust for a while.

'On the night of our conversation Ahmed took me into his confidence. What did that mean? Maybe he was trying to tempt me into betraying Sipho. Maybe he was working for Sipho's death. On the other hand, maybe he genuinely wanted to trust me, he wanted me to be his comrade. Whatever it was I think I should have said what I knew. When he was speaking I had that flashback feeling I told you about. It was like I knew something about the information he was giving me. But I kept silent. That silence was part of my guilt.'

This heat is growing severe, Rosandra thought. In the humidity it was difficult to focus. Outlines were diffused by the haze. A few more sentences and she could go back to the hotel, to the king-size bed, the jacuzzi, and then, tomorrow, the airport and home. Jem was a good friend but this speaking was becoming a punishment. She was getting upset and he looked unhappy. It did them no good, going over things like this, Sipho, Thony's schemes, the ashram, tying them together, spelling them out.

'You weren't guilty, Rosandra,' said Jem. 'You had no idea what sort of hornets' nest you were stepping into.'

'But I should have realised, I should have seen.'

It seemed so obvious, she thought, the missing piece, the missing word, so obvious it almost felt not worth saying.

'Ahmed mentioned a new contact in the city, a black entrepreneur in my line of business. He said this man set up arms caches for people like Sipho and himself though pretending to be on the side of the régime. This man ran a model agency, the Mike T. Shepherd Agency. The clue was obvious. I should have seen it.'

'I don't understand.'

'If I hadn't been hiding things and worrying about guarding my own skin I maybe would have seen it. Michaelis's surname was Herder, that's the Afrikaans for shepherd,' said Rosandra.

'Is that all? That says nothing,' said Jem.

He was disappointed, almost, but also reassured. Her guilt was an embroidery, a fantasy like her stories.

'I think it says a lot,' said Rosandra. 'It could be the clue to unravelling a whole network. I think the man in the city was Michaelis. Which means that the agency was, I'm sure, an underground office of Star Palace Limited.'

'But it could also be a coincidence. If that's all you know there's no reason for blaming yourself as you do.'

'One thing leads to another,' said Rosandra. 'Coincidences can have a shape. The name might have meant nothing, but it was a sign to speak. I should have told Ahmed that I knew of a double-dealer. It might have been a warning.'

'And it might not. You must forgive yourself, Rosandra. This is not something to go on carrying around with you.'

'I forgive myself but it's worth saying what could have happened if we'd had better luck and taken other chances. If Ahmed was involved with the wrong side, say was a brother in arms with Michaelis, and if I'd seen the clue, I could maybe have helped Sipho. I could have discovered things. I could have passed on what I knew. I was in a position to help.'

But she was taking it too far. She was offering a fantasy as reparation when her feeling of responsibility was enough. She was deluded by guilt, Jem thought. Guilt set her imagination dancing. She created new plots, a different past. Guilt told her she betrayed Sipho. Guilt invented a hundred phantom ways to save him. And she needed only a little guilt. With that he would be satisfied. A little guilt was an absolution. It worked like love. Love was strong enough to help her. To love someone is to wear the cloak of their guilt.

He took her hand. Though she kept her face behind the roses he attempted to look into her eyes.

'Look, Rosandra,' he said, 'you've tried to find a solution. You feel the responsibility. It's enough. You tried to see Sipho's grandmother to explain things.'

For the first time the mask of her face lost its calm. Her cheeks were drawn, her nose was pinched, whitened. Ropes of strain showed in her neck, the pulse in her throat beat heavily.

'No, nothing has been resolved,' she said. 'I can't do much about it but I can't deny it either. Ahmed is I don't know where. Sipho's grandmother has disappeared, Sipho is dead. Somewhere, maybe, Michaelis is calmly dealing with people. Thony too. Who can I tell about this? Who will believe me, after what has happened, where I've been? Who will it help?'

It was past noon and the rickshaw had drawn up on the pavement close by, the green plumage damp. When Jem caught his eye he waved in quest of his last ride of the morning.

'You've told me the whole story, Rosandra. That must help. Maybe you want to tell me more, to make it clearer. Maybe you want to tell me some other time. Just remember I don't blame you. I want to help you.'

She sat back abruptly and the movement jerked her hand out of his. She looked around her and her hair lifted. A curve of gold. She caught sight of the champagne bottle, its foil top glistening, its sides dry. She held her hand against it, testing.

No, she thought – and the thought was sharp as an outline – no more of this, it gets us nowhere at all, talking, brooding, we have other things to do.

'Come,' she said, in a different voice, alert, suddenly brighter, 'let's have some champagne, Jem. Warm champagne tastes like lemonade. It's OK.'

She wanted to change the subject, he saw, give things a new mood, a new look. He could oblige. He uncorked the champagne, the foam drenched the roses. He could oblige with whatever she wanted. She wiped the champagne flecks off the rose petals with a finger and licked the finger like a child.

'It's possible you're right,' she said, licking, looking around her, at the hot-dog kiosks, at the blooming of umbrellas on the beach. 'Maybe it's not as serious as it sounds. Maybe I've had too much sun, I'm feeling high. That's why I'm exaggerating things. What I've been through has made me feel special. I felt I had, you know, special knowledge. But that could mean nothing, couldn't it? I mean, maybe I talked myself into it.'

She reached out and touched his hand again. It was a tender gesture but held no promise, no firmness. It was a punctuation mark, a final stroke. She was shedding her guilt like a delusion, a bad dream, it was one of her inconsequentialities. He let his hand lie beneath hers. Then, as though she was placing something in storage, putting it down, leaving it, she patted his fingers and withdrew her hand.

'This is the problem with reunions,' she said. 'You tell each other stories. Memories return. I think stories probably create guilt feelings. One thing leads to another and you see, in a way, patterns of fate.

Like destiny. It seems as though there should be a way of linking things up, this person with that person, this secret with something else you know.'

Jem slipped the champagne cork into his shirt pocket. Tonight he would place it in the cardboard shoebox. He looked at the ships lined up on the horizon. The air this afternoon was blue-white, gauzy, not brown like the last time.

'And there's also been a lot of good luck in my life,' she said, her voice still bright, trying to divert him. 'Like this job, Jem. Things have worked out quite well for me in Mbabane. It was Lee's friends in the casino who fixed me up with the contacts. My work's not big-time, though the last few months have looked more promising. But I'm a fashion model at last. Bass must've seen it written in the stars.'

'Your mother told me all about your job,' Jem said.

'Don't you think it lucky? I went down to Mbabane a second time almost immediately after that conversation with Lee. I was given the job within a few days. I've now had it for nearly a year. My boss does fashion displays for local shops, mainly group shots. Coming down here was the first big venture. He likes to work with African motifs but his favourite theme he calls international or cross-communal. I am the white representative, the blonde white. My boss says he thought up the theme long before Benetton came up with its Colors idea. He says he's been international for years. Benetton stole the idea from him.'

She was hugging herself, rubbing her hands up and down her upper arms. Yes, she had luck, Jem thought. Luck meant running with the consequences. And she was preparing to say last things. He could tell from that quick-fire brightness in her voice, the way she picked up her handbag, fiddled with the clasp.

'I rubbed total sun-bloc all over me this morning but it doesn't seem to have made a difference,' she said. 'I feel there is sunburn under my skin.'

But her arms were white as alabaster.

'It was wonderful seeing you, Jem,' she said. 'This trip was a good break. It has made me look forward to next week, to ordinary work again. You shouldn't worry about me. I'm in another country. I still feel Thony can't reach me, though no doubt he could find where I lived if he wanted to. I'm happy. My flat is five doors away from where I work. I like my work. I give my extra cash to development agencies. That's part of the debt I think I must pay Sipho. Lee I don't see, though I know she is in Mbabane. No one knows where Ahmed is.'

She put on lipstick, a violent scarlet, using a pocket mirror, not his glasses. The scarlet didn't suit her freckles. The freckles were dark blemishes on her face.

'It's nice to have made proper friends with you, Jem. You were always just the boy next door.' She laughed. 'Now I know we can call each other up sometimes and have expensive international phone conversations.'

Rosandra was making fun. But Jem could not. His lips felt leaden, he could not smile.

'We must write postcards to each other. Regina and I write postcards often, about once a month. Regina is still a receptionist. She works at a different casino, one on the coast. She still jokes about having a ready-made tan. Things grew too hot for her at Star Palace. The night manager's fiancée ended up accusing her of having an affair with her guy. I've thought about going down to visit her, but I suspect maybe Thony has shares in the place where she works. The postcards are fun to exchange. Regina never addresses me by my real name. She simply calls me Rose. That's my modelling name. Rose. It's safer.'

They both looked out to sea. An aeroplane passed overhead, very loud, a desperate roaring. Tomorrow she would be in an aeroplane, airborne, Jem thought, leaving, sitting with her back straight and her long-boned legs tightly folded. For a few last moments she still sat in front of him, a shape outlined against the steel-white sea, pale, stark, everybody's goddess, not Desdemona – Desdemona didn't survive.

'This is so African, isn't it?' said Rosandra.

She wished he'd join her talking about something else. His expression was so glum, so silent. It would be nice to forget what was unpleasant. They had talked, they had learned about each other, they were friends.

'Even with the funfair in the background, and the ice-cream and the champagne, it just feels African,' she said. 'It must be the smell of the heat. That's why I like Mbabane. You can appreciate Africa for what it is, big and hot and intense, without all that crowding I saw yesterday.'

'In the townships AK 47s are selling for cheaper than stolen TV sets, or a flight to Mbabane,' said Jem.

He wanted her to flinch. He wanted her to need his advice. She must turn to him. Her shoulders moved beneath her shirt, an expression of poised and gentle exasperation. She'd told her story, but she said only the right things. She made an unscathed picture, a perfect figure. Her skin, as always, shone with a pale lustre. Not once during their conversation did she blush.

Jem downed his third glass of warm champagne. It tasted poisonous. He felt violent and driven. He thought his hand would crush the glass.

'Like I said, the city is growing too fast for its own good,' he said. 'Gangs increase in size. They get their money from unknown sources. They have huge arms caches. They mean business, most likely war. There are people behind it all bent on disruption. There'll be much more betrayal and bloodshed in this country before there is peace.'

But she did not want to hear him. She continued looking out to sea. On the horizon she imagined a thin blue cloud. It was like one stroke of a brush on a bluer space of sky. The cloud was disconnected from everything. Staring at it long enough she could begin to feel its lightness. She wanted to feel its lightness. To drift. The cloud drifted upwards, it almost dissolved. It uplifted. It was very blue, Maria's colour.

'One day,' said Rosandra dreamily, 'I want to go on holiday again on Eden Island and get away from it all.'